# ENFORCING HOME

## A. AMERICAN

# PROLOGUE

TRIALS AND TRIBULATIONS OVERCOME, I was looking forward to some quiet time. Life was starting to take on the comfort of routine, tending to the tasks of daily life in this new world. With some familiar faces moving into our little community, there were more hands available, more could be done each day. I looked forward to the quiet days I foresaw ahead; we all did.

The addition of Miss Kay to our group was profound. For Jess, Fred and Mary it was a homecoming of sorts; for the rest of us she would become the grandmother we no longer had. For Sarge, she would become much more. Ian, Jamie and Perez were also a welcomed addition. They were solid and reliable when the chips were down. With them on board we certainly were a formidable force.

But life, especially life as we now knew it, was never predictable, and becoming complacent was dangerous. Gone was 24/7 news cycles and seven-day weather forecasts. We lived in the present; and the present provides very little warning. We had to guard against becoming complacent, for there would be no second chances.

# CHAPTER 1

I looked over at Sarge as he drove, "I noticed you and Miss Kay were kind of friendly at the lake."

Without taking his eyes from the road, he replied, "She's a sweet lady."

"She didn't seem to have much to say yesterday."

Sarge wrinkled his nose, "This is a lot for her, everything that's going on."

Pausing for a moment, I looked back out through the windshield, "Hopefully she'll be better here, with the girls. Where was she all day? I only saw her a couple of times."

He nodded, "I think she'll be fine here. She said she wanted some alone time, so I let her be. She'll be alright."

He turned off on the dirt road and stopped in front of Gena and Dylan's house. Gena was on the porch by the time I got out of the truck.

"Hi Morgan, hi Sarge!" She called out as I opened the back door.

"Hey Gena," I said as I hefted a large kettle from the backseat.

"Hi Miss Gena," Sarge waved as he walked up to the gate. His hands were shoved into his pockets; and with that goofy smile, he looked for all the world to me like Andy Griffith.

"What'cha got there Morgan?" Dylan asked stepping out onto the porch, wiping his hands with a cloth.

"Some of the most tender pork that'll ever cross your tongue," Sarge said.

"That sounds wonderful!" Gena shouted, "Some fresh meat sounds great."

"I figured since you guys couldn't make it, we'd bring you some," I said as I handed the kettle to Dylan.

Looking a little embarrassed, Gena said, "I really wish we could have come, but I wasn't feeling well. The medicine doesn't always work."

"No problem, let us know if we can help," I said, giving Gena a smile. Looking at Dylan, I added, "you guys enjoy that pot-o-pig,"

"I appreciate that, thanks a lot." He took a deep whiff across the top of the kettle, "damn that smells good!"

"Hope you two enjoy it. You can thank Thad for the smell; he cooked it," I replied.

"Oh we will," Gena said as she took the kettle from Dylan and headed into the house, "I'm starving."

Sarge smiled, "We'll leave you two to eat, let us know if you need anything."

Dylan nodded, "Will do," then looked at me, "thanks Morgan."

I waved him off, "Don't mention it."

"Say, what's with the star?" Dylan asked.

"Oh, you don't know do you?" Sarge crowed. Stabbing his thumb at me, he replied, "ole Morgan here's the new Sherriff!"

Dylan looked confused, "Sheriff? Sheriff of what?"

"That's what I asked, the north end of Lake County; or so they tell me," I replied.

Dylan scoffed, "Better you than me!"

I smiled, "Thanks for the support."

"No problem; you've got my vote. Let me know if I can help."

"Don't worry, we will," Sarge replied.

"We?" Dylan asked, "You his deputy?"

Now I laughed and pointed at Sarge, "You actually think his ole ass would listen to me?"

Dylan smiled, "No, probably not."

"Definitely *not*." Sarge replied.

"See what I'm dealing with?" I said to Sarge, holding my hands up.

Dylan shook his head, "Y'all are crazy as shithouse rats; you know that don't you?"

I shook my head and waved, "We'll see you later Dylan," and started back for the truck.

"Thanks for the pork!" Dylan called out.

As Sarge pulled out onto Highway 19, I said, "They seemed pretty happy about the pig meat."

"I imagine anyone would be these days."

I stared out the window for a minute, "What the hell am I supposed to do with this whole sheriff thing? I mean, are we supposed to be riding on patrol, or what?"

"I figure you'll sort it out when the time comes. I have a feeling what you need to be doing will make itself pretty clear to you when the time comes."

I let out a long sigh, "That doesn't make me feel any better; really it doesn't."

Sarge laughed and slapped me on the shoulder, "Don't worry, I got yer back."

"Hmmf, yeah, with both hands on my shoulders."

Now Sarge really laughed, "No greater joy than a fat butt boy!"

As he turned towards the barricade, I said, "You truly are twisted."

Mike and Ted were manning the barricade. Mike sitting on the top log, stretched out like a cat on top of the TV, the old style of course. Ted was leaned over the same log resting on his elbows. Sarge pulled up and stopped, neither of them moved.

"You guys going to keep watch tonight?" I asked.

Mike's head rocked back and forth, "Yeah, we got it."

"We reworked the board with Danny and Thad. It's all taken care of tonight, Morg," Ted added.

"Good, I'm ready to get some sleep," Sarge replied.

"You sleeping alone tonight?" Mike asked.

Without saying a word, Sarge gave Mike a quick hard shove, rolling him off the log. Mike let out a yelp and hit the ground with a thump and a clank as he and all his gear followed the law of gravity.

"Hey, what the hell!" He shouted as he sat up.

"Learn to respect your elders, son," Sarge shot back, getting a chuckle from both Ted and me.

"Elders my ass," Mike replied as he dusted himself off.

"That was some good eats today Morgan," Ted said.

"Don't thank me, Thad did all the cooking."

"And he did it a fine job of it," Sarge replied. "Come on Morgan, let's get you home."

"Thanks guys, I appreciate you being down here and keeping an eye on things," I said.

Ted waved me off, "De nada."

Sarge dropped me off at the house. Mel was sitting in the living room, a kerosene lantern casting its yellow glow across her old antique dresser. I fell into the couch beside her and grabbed her hand, "Hey babe." She smiled and squeezed my hand. She had a large coffee mug resting on her thigh, one I got on a road trip to Texas. "What'cha drinking?"

"I found a pack of MRE apple cider; want some?" She handed me the cup.

I took a sip and smiled. Handing the cup back, I said, "That's good; I mean it's awful, but it's good."

"Awfully good," she said as she took another sip.

"That's one way of putting it. What's with the lantern, why are you using that?"

"I like the light, it's nice," she replied.

Mel reached over and clanked her cup against the star, "So, what's with this, what's it about?"

I plucked the badge from my vest; and I stared at the gold star lying in the palm of my hand, "It wasn't my idea."

Mel took the star and held it up, "I would hope not." She turned it around, "Why'd you say yes?"

"It wasn't really a request, they just showed up and told me."

She handed the badge back to me, "So what are you going to be doing?"

Running a hand through my hair, I said, "I just asked Sarge that same question."

"And what'd he say?"

"He said I'd know when the time came."

Mel stared into her cup, "That doesn't make me feel any better." My head rocked back on the sofa as I let out a short laugh. A little annoyed, she asked, "What's so funny?"

"That's the same thing I said to Sarge."

Setting her cup on the table, Mel said, "I just want things to calm down, to be kind of normal." She laid her head on my shoulder, "I want to know when I go to bed at night that I'm going to wake up to a day where there isn't going to be some tragedy, shooting, fires or whatever else is coming that we don't even know about yet."

Leaning back on the couch, I pulled her over and wrapped my arms around her. After a moment I said, "It isn't that bad. We're all still here; and we've beat everything that's come at us."

I rubbed her arm, "I don't know, I kind of like it, things are a lot slower now, I'm always home."

I felt her move, "Really? You seem gone a lot to me."

"Oh come on; I'm home every night."

"I'll give you that."

"It's kind of like Little House on the Prairie, sitting here in this light."

Mel snorted, "More like Little House of the Apocalypse."

I started laughing, "Now that is funny!"

She pinched my arm, "Shhh, you'll wake the girls."

"Ok, ok, quit pinching me. Where's Little Bit; she in her bed or ours?"

"She's in hers."

"Good, she's getting way too big to pick up and carry to bed."

Mel stood up, "Well I'm ready for bed, you coming?"

"Yes I am."

———— ⊁ ⊁ ⊁ ⊁ ⊁ ————

Thad sat with his back against a fence post. His long legs stretched out towards the fire burning near his feet. Smoke slowly rose into the clear evening sky nearly masking the odor of pig shit and urine. He could hear the hogs bumping the side of the barn as they jostled for sleeping positions in the thin layer of hay that still covered the floor. He pushed the end of a log into the fire with the toe of his boot, and leaned back with his hands behind his head. Hearing footsteps, he looked over to see Jess's smiling face.

"Hey Thad, mind some company?"

He returned her question with a broad smile, "Shore thing; pull up a bucket and have a seat."

Jess picked up one of the buckets that universally seemed to be around barns. Turning it up, she thumped the bottom, knocking off some dirt. Planting her bucket, she sat down, "Ain't you had enough smoke for one day?"

Thad stared into the fire, "No such thing as too much hardwood smoke; I really enjoy it."

Jess closed her eyes and took a deep breath, "I guess you're right, it smells really good."

They sat in silence for a moment, both staring into the flames that licked around the logs. Jess finally stirred; stretching out a leg, she reached into her pocket. She retrieved something as she leaned forward on her knees, fumbling with the object.

"What'cha got there?" Thad asked.

Jess held the silver star out. Thad smiled, "Got me one of them too."

"You really think they want us to be the police?"

"We ain't police; we're sheriff deputies."

Jess looked at him, her face twisted into a humorous smirk, "An Morgan is the Sheriff?"

The breeze shifted, blowing smoke into Jess's face. She fanned at it with her hand, "It always follows me," she said turning her head.

"Say rabbit." Thad said.

"Say what?"

"Rabbit; the smoke will move away."

She stood and picked up her bucket, "No it won't, that's just silly."

"Suit yourself. Back to your question; it does look like he's the Sheriff."

Jess planted her bucket and took a seat, "But what makes him Sheriff; I mean, who gets to decide that now? Isn't the Sheriff supposed to be elected?"

"Normally the Sheriff is elected; but these ain't normal times. From what Morgan told me, Captain Sheffield made him the Sheriff."

"You really think we're going to be doing anything?" Jess asked.

Before Thad could answer, the breeze shifted again, pushing the smoke towards him. He waved a hand at the smoke, "Rabbit. I have a feeling we'll be doing a lot. It all depends on what Morgan wants to do really." The smoke slowly moved away from Thad.

Jess was looking at him, "Hey! That actually worked!"

Thad smiled, "Told you."

"It feels kinda funny," Jess said as she held the star up. "I would never have dreamed I'd be a cop."

"Deputy," Thad corrected her.

"Deputy," Jess replied with a smile as the smoke shifted once again, pushing it towards her. Waving the smoke away, she cried out, "Rabbit!" The smoke persisted to wrap around her head, seeming to get worse. "It didn't work!" She shouted as she rose to her feet.

Thad laughed, "You wasn't holding your mouth right."

Wiping a tear from her eyes, she asked, "What?" Thad let out a deep laugh. "I think your rabbit is full of it, I'm going inside."

Still laughing, he called out to her, "Just wasn't holding your mouth right!"

"Whatever, rabbit!"

Shaking his head and laughing to himself, Thad turned his attention back to the fire. He was still smiling when a voice called out, "Mind if I have a seat?"

Thad jumped, looking up to see Sarge walk out from the trees as the darkness deepened. "Yeah, have a seat; you scared the shit out of me."

Sarge plopped down on the bucket Jess had abandoned, leaning his carbine against the barn. "Well I didn't mean to do that, just saw yer fire and thought I'd visit."

"You're always welcome to visit." Looking back the direction he'd come from, Thad asked, "what are you doing out wandering around?"

Sarge spit in the fire, "Just out for a walk; what was Jess fussin' about?"

"Aw, the smoke was bothering her. Told her to say rabbit; she tried, but it didn't work for her."

Sarge snorted, "Wasn't holding her mouth right."

Thad's head rocked back as he laughed, "That's what I said!" Sarge looked up and smiled. "She was talking about the whole sheriff thing; she wondered who made Morgan Sheriff, and what gave them the right."

Sarge listened and nodded, "Well he surely is the high Sheriff now; ole Sheffield set him up. I gotta say I didn't see it coming; surprised the hell out of me."

Thad chuckled, "Yeah, me too; just a bit to say the least."

"You'll be alright Thad, you guys will do a great job," Sarge replied.

Thad stared into the fire for a moment, "What do you think it will mean; what do you think we'll be doing?"

Sarge sat up and stretched his arms high over his head, "Shit Thad, what's the speed of dark?"

With surprise and raised eyebrows, Thad relied, "Huh?"

"Who knows? Last time I asked my magic eight ball a question, it replied, ask again later. You guys are in the perfect situation though; you're on the pointy end of the road back to a normal life. You'll get to help shape the future. You'll just have to take things as they come, but you'll do alright." Sarge waved his arm out over the fire, "all of you will do alright."

Thad smiled, "What's the speed of dark; that's funny." His smile faded as he stared into the fire; then he slowly started to nod his head, "I think you're right." He looked back up at Sarge, "I think we'll be alright."

Sarge slapped his knees and stood up, "I know you will, Thad; I know you will."

"So long as you're around, I think we'll be just fine," Thad replied.

Sarge wagged a finger at him, "No, no, no, I'm not the boss, Morgan is the high Sheriff. He's the boss now."

Thad smiled, "Yeah, like you're really going to listen to him."

Sarge started to walk off, "I will." Then he stopped and looked back over his shoulder, "to a point," he added with a smile before continuing on.

A big smile spread over Thad's face, "Yeah, that's what I thought, good night Linus."

Sarge waved over his shoulder, "Night Thad."

# CHAPTER 2

THE NEXT FEW DAYS SEEMED to drift by as our routine really came together. Pulling duty at the barricade, hunting and gathering and tending the garden filled everyone's time. Though everyone stayed busy, no one was ever rushed. There was plenty of time for all of us to do what we wanted as well. For me, that usually meant thinking of ways to improve our situation. When I had real down time I would monitor the radio, listening to the increasing traffic drifting through the ether. I never talked to anyone; just listened. I wanted to know what the rest of the country was like, how others were making it; and more importantly, *what* they were doing to make it.

Thad and I were on the barricade; it was early morning and the air was damp. Leaning over the barricade, I said, "I been thinking about chickens."

Thad quickly replied, "KFC or Popeye's?"

It gave me a chuckle, "Don't even start that! Man, I loved Popeye's."

"I like, liked, KFC; that was good chicken," Thad replied.

"Ok, before this gets out of hand and drives me crazy, I'm talking about our chickens."

"What about 'em?"

"We let them out every day to fend for themselves; but I've been thinking of a way to supplement their feed."

"It sure wouldn't hurt 'em none; what you got in mind?"

"I don't know what it's really called; but for lack of a better name, I'll call it a maggot bucket," I said.

Thad snarled his lip, "Mmm, sounds delicious."

"The chickens will think so. Take a five-gallon bucket and drill some holes in the bottom; then throw some carcasses or parts of some critter in and hang it up."

Thad thought about it for a minute, "Just let the flies land in it and lay eggs huh?"

"Yeah; the maggots will fall out the bottom, free feed."

"I wouldn't put it too close to the house."

"You think Mel would complain?" I asked.

Thad laughed, "I think Mel and Miss Bobbie would slap the taste out of your mouth."

Now I was laughing just thinking about it, "Yeah, they'd take turns."

"One on either side!" Thad said, as he laughed harder.

Getting over the humor of the moment, I said, "I think today when our shift is over I'll make it and put it up."

"I'll help, so long as you hang it far away from the house."

I nodded, "Sounds like a plan."

We spent the next couple of hours talking and enjoying the early morning; it was so quiet. With no man-made noise, the world seemed so calm and peaceful. Nature is not very noisy, at least not around here. I was listening intently to the world around me when I heard Thad. "Morg." When I peered over, he was looking down the road, to the north. I followed his gaze to see a small group of figures walking towards us.

"Looks like they got kids," I said.

Thad stepped out towards the road, "Looks like it; I see at least two adults."

I stepped out as I put the binoculars to my eyes. "Let's see," I said as I glassed the approaching group. There were definitely two adults, and what looked like a teenager and two smaller kids. Even with the ten-power glass, I couldn't make out much about them.

"See any guns?" Thad asked.

"I can't really tell yet; maybe in a couple of minutes. Here, take a look," I said as I handed him the binoculars.

Thad put them to his face and watched the group for several seconds. "I don't see any long guns; they sure look rough though."

"I noticed that as well. Couldn't see much, but they seemed kind of raggedy. Let's step back behind the barricade and see what they look like when they get here."

While we waited, Tyler showed up with Jase and Edy Thad leaned back on the logs, "Hey Tyler, out for a walk?"

Tyler tussled his son's hair, "Yeah, just wanted to get the kids out of the house ya know."

Thad knelt down to be on the kids' level, "You two taking your dad for a walk?"

"Yeah, we're hunting!" Jase shouted.

Clearing my throat to get Thad's attention, I nodded towards the road; we could see the group now. Thad's impression was right; they were a sorry looking bunch. They all wore dirty clothes; and the two kids of seven or so both had dirty faces. It was disturbing to see the rings of dirt around their mouths. You couldn't help but wonder what they were eating to cause such a buildup of filth. The man, distinguishable from the woman only as a result of his nappy beard, was as grimy as the two little kids. His hair was long, past his shoulders; and his clothes were so dirty that they appeared to have a sheen of grime, particularly on the front of his pants. A tattered cloth dangled from one hand; and periodically he would raise it to his face, to wipe at his mouth.

The woman looked no better, wearing clothes that hung from her, obviously too big for her small frame. They were closer now, and the most striking thing about her was the hollow look in her eyes, barely visible through the tattered strands of hair hanging in her face. She didn't so much walk as she shambled, her arms seemingly disconnected from her body as they wobbled back and forth at her side.

"Damn they look sad," Thad said.

"No shit, they look rough."

"Man, am I glad I'm here," Tyler said dismissively.

As they came abreast of our road, the man began to make his way towards us; and the rest of the band followed without question or notice. Thad and I both gripped our weapons a little tighter as they approached. The man stopped several feet away, "Got any food?"

"Sorry, we don't," I replied.

He didn't react to the answer. He coughed and wiped at his mouth; and with a ragged voice, he asked, "Got any water?"

We were still in the habit of keeping the five-gallon water jug at the barricade full, "We can help you there," I replied.

He stretched an arm out behind him and waved his hand in a *gimme* gesture. One of the two that appeared to be teens, though their sex was indiscernible, produced a couple of old plastic bottles from a pack and handed them over. He shambled towards the water jug and began coughing, again wiping his mouth with the tatter of cloth. He held the greasy-looking bottles up. I pointed at the jug and said, "Help yourself."

The two younger ones of the group noticed Jase and Edy,

and came over, as kids will always do. And soon the four were running around in an impromptu game of tag. The little boy from the group wasn't very fast, and the smaller Jase was able to catch him with ease. The child would cough and hack, wiping at his mouth.

Nudging Tyler, I whispered, "Call the kids back."

Tyler looked at me, "They're just kids; let 'em play."

"They're sick; look at 'em, coughing all over the place like that. Call them back."

Tyler called the kids; it took a minute to get them to come back as they were wrestling on the ground. The kids returned to their dad, Tyler collecting them around him. He looked down at his children then back to me, "You think they're going to be OK?"

"Oh yeah, I'm sure. We just don't need to take any chances." I reached down and tickled little Edy, she squealed and squirmed, "especially with these little guys."

"Alright guys, let's go find Mommy," Tyler said as he shepherded the kids towards home.

"Wash their hands when you get home," Thad said.

"Good," I added.

Tyler nodded and waved as he made his way back towards home.

The bearded stranger started to fill his bottles from the jug, occasionally coughing, and not bothering to turn his head. The cough was ragged and sounded angry. Beads of sweat built up on his forehead, which he mopped away with the same cloth. After filling his bottles, he turned and walked back out to the road. His group fell in with him as one of the bottles was passed around for all to have a drink. They walked away without saying another word, just continuing their trek to the south. I was watching them walk away when I heard a splash. Looking over,

I saw Thad standing over the water keg which was lying on its side on the road.

He looked at me, "I don't think anyone needs to drink from this before we clean it."

I looked at the jug, "You're probably right; that cough didn't sound so good."

"He had a fever too, I think the others were sick as well, I saw at least one of the others coughing."

"And they didn't even say thank you; ungrateful shits."

Thad grunted, "I think manners are waning these days."

Doc and Jeff showed up to relieve us. I was glad to see them, as I was getting hungry. "I appreciate you boys taking time out of your busy schedules to come give us a break," I said.

"Make sure my relief is on time; I've got a tee time this afternoon," Doc fired back.

Jeff pointed to the water keg, "What happened to that thing?"

Thad looked back at it, "Oh, we had some folks come by; they needed water. They was sick; so I dumped it. No one can drink from it till I can clean it."

"What kind of sick?" Doc asked as he hung his pack on the end of the barricade.

"Coughing, hacking; and the man looked like he had a fever. I know a couple of the others with him were coughing too."

"Yeah, he kept hacking and wiping his mouth with a nasty ass little rag; wiped the sweat from his head with it too. Whatever he's got, he's spreading it all over," I added.

"Where'd they come from?" Doc asked.

"We didn't really talk to them. He just asked if we had food and water. After filling their little bottles, they walked off without so much as a thank you," I answered.

"Which way were they going?"

I pointed to the south, "Towards town."

Doc looked up the road, and then back at the keg, "You guys didn't get near them did you?"

"Oh hell no. He would have had to spit that stuff at us; we was plenty far from him," Thad answered.

"Good, make sure you guys wash that thing really well; your hands too."

"We will. I'll mix up some bleach for it," I said.

Doc nodded his head and Thad and I headed for the ATV. He drove with me, riding bitch and holding the keg. As we drove home, the Hummer was headed the opposite direction. Ian was driving with Jamie riding shotgun, and Perez up in the turret. Thad rolled to a stop as they came up.

"Where you guys headed?" I asked as Ian pulled up.

"Into town to get a couple of things from the armory," Ian replied.

I nodded, "Let Sheffield know there may be some sick folks headed his way, they didn't look good."

"You'll probably pass 'em on your way in," Thad added.

"Will do; we're going to go so we can get back before dark," Ian replied.

I waved, "Be careful." Thad goosed the ATV; and we went back to Danny's place where we hopped off and set the keg out by the well.

"Get me that bleach powder and I'll clean this thing up," Thad said as he stepped off.

"Sure thing; be right back."

I went over to the house and found some of the calcium hypochlorite in the shop, and grabbed a bag. Coming in the backdoor, I found the house empty; and I headed back to Danny's. My girls were out front when I got there, and I smiled when they saw me. "Hey girls, what are you guys doing?"

Little Bit was holding her .22; and Taylor had her H&K slung across her back. And Lee Ann had her H&K slung over her shoulder. "We're going hunting!" Little Bit shouted.

"Good deal, I need some guts!"

"Eww, for what?" Lee Ann asked.

"Need it for a chicken feeder I'm going to make."

"I don't even want to know," Taylor replied.

I waved them off, "You guys just go shoot some rats."

"I will!" Little Bit shouted as she ran off with her sisters in tow.

Danny came out of the house with Tyler, "What up?" He called out from the porch.

"Hey man; the women folk inside?" I asked.

"Yeah, they're in there; what are you guys up to?" He asked.

"I'm gonna make a chicken feeder; you got an empty bucket lying around?"

Danny smiled, "How many you want?"

"Give me that powder," Thad said. I tossed him the little bag of chlorine. "I'll clean this thing while you make yer gut bucket."

Danny looked at me, "Thought you wanted a chicken feeder."

I smiled, "I do. Come on; I'll show you."

Danny and I went over to his sheds; yes, sheds, plural. He has several. He's one of those guys that doesn't throw anything away and brings home all manner of stuff he thinks is useful. I used to tease him about his hoarder starter kit; now I'm very thankful for it. Danny retrieved a bucket from one of the buildings and set it down on the splitting stump.

"Here's your bucket; what now?"

"We just need to drill some holes in it," I said. Then I explained the concept to him. When I was done, he was nodding his head.

"That's a hell of an idea; where'd you come up with that one?"

"I don't remember; read it or heard it somewhere. It was stuck in my head till last night; just popped out," I replied.

Danny laughed, "I think we need to shake your head and see what else comes out."

"Like a snow globe?" I asked.

"I was thinking more like a cup of Yatzee dice."

I laughed at the comment.

Thad cleaned the water keg while Danny and I worked on the feeder, what little work there was. It didn't take long to drill the holes, small ones, a quarter of an inch, in the bottom. That's all there was to it, just a bunch of holes drilled in the bottom. Tyler milled around the shed; there wasn't enough work for one, let alone three.

"Now what?" Danny asked.

"Now we need something to put in it," I replied.

Aric, Jess and Fred walked up as we stared at the perforated bucket, "I don't think that's going to hold much," Aric said.

"I hope not; the maggots need a way to get out," I replied with a smile.

"The maggots?" Jess asked, "I don't even want to know."

"Arm feeling better, Aric; no sling?" Danny asked.

Aric held the injured arm up, "Yeah, it's getting better. Doc said I need to start exercising it some; so I'm starting out slow."

"That's good; is the wound closed now?" I asked.

"Pretty much, I mean it's not like healed completely, but I don't have to bandage it now."

Fred patted Aric's shoulder, "It's a lot better now. Doc said it's healing really well. I'm glad we don't have to bandage it anymore."

"You dodged the infection bullet; lucky," Danny added.

Aric nodded his head, "Way lucky. I'm lucky to be alive; an infection would have killed me."

I laughed, "You're lucky the old man didn't kill you out of spite for shooting him."

"No shit, I'm really glad he's better too; not even using that cane anymore," Aric replied.

"He still uses it from time to time; but I think it's because he wants to, not because he needs to. And I wouldn't call it a cane either," I said with a chuckle.

Aric smiled, "Oh yeah, walking stick; it's a walking stick."

Off in the distance the sharp crack of a .22 barked. I looked off in the direction of the sound, "Looks like the girls are getting me something for my feeder."

Jess looked at the bucket again, "I still don't want to know." She was shaking her head as she walked away; I couldn't help but laugh.

A sudden clanging caught everyone's attention. I looked over at the house and saw Bobbie on the porch working a short piece of rebar inside a triangle made from the same. "Lunch is ready!" she shouted.

"Where'd that come from?" I asked.

"I made it," Danny said. "Had some half inch rebar lying around, and used a propane torch to heat it and bend it."

Thad had finished his cleaning and joined us. "That's pretty neat; like old times," he said with a smile.

Everyone slowly filtered into Danny's, taking seats at the tables on the back porch. Lunch was a stew of sorts, as were most meals these days, along with some Kudzu chips. Danny hurried through his lunch, as he and Sarge were scheduled to relieve the guys at the barricade after lunch. Everyone had some sort of chore for the day, and talk focused around those tasks.

Sarge was sitting with Miss Kay at the end of one of the tables; they were spending more and more time together.

"I'll give you guys a ride up to the barricade if you want after dinner; I'm going up into Altoona," I said.

"What are you going down there for?" Tyler asked.

"Just going to check in on Gena and Dylan, then go to the Kangaroo and see what's going on up there."

"I'll go with you; I don't have anything on the schedule for a few hours." Tyler said.

"Sure man; I need someone to go with me."

"Daddy, can I come?" Little Jase asked. He was sitting beside Tyler at the table, with stew dripping from his chin.

Tyler looked at me; and I shrugged, not seeing anything wrong with it. Tyler looked down at his son and smiled, rubbing his head; and he replied, "Sure thing little buddy." Jase smiled and kicked his legs, making him bounce in his seat. "Just finish your lunch." The little boy began to shovel the stew into his mouth.

"You sure about that?" Brandy asked.

Tyler looked at me, "We're not doing anything dangerous; just riding up the road. I don't see why not."

I nodded, "Yeah; it's just a short ride."

Not looking totally thrilled with the idea, Brandy nodded, "Ok."

The air was suddenly split by the sound of automatic weapons fire. My head snapped around. The weapon paused after about ten rounds, then started again; and this time it was joined by another. Without saying a word, everyone began moving. Danny and I both ran towards the ATVs parked under the pole barn. Danny was a little faster and got there first; so I hopped on behind him, shouting, "Go, go, go!"

The two weapons were stuttering in alternating spurts of

fire as we sped out the gate and down the road. I glanced over my shoulder to see Thad and Tyler following right behind us. As we bounced down the road, I pulled the charging handle on my carbine back to check the chamber. Seeing the brass, I released it, and thumped the forward assist knob with the palm of my hand, and then verified the safety with my thumb. By the time that was done, we were almost to the barricade. The guys there were pointing to the south; so Danny swung into the driveway of my old place.

Racing through the property, I saw men rushing through the trees along the rear fence; and tapped Danny on the shoulder, pointing. He nodded and raced towards them. They paid no attention to us, and I quickly realized why; it was Sarge and Ted. I looked in the direction they were running and saw another man in front of them. Mike was running like his ass was on fire. Danny quickly realized who they were and was already changing course. It's amazing how much you can perceive in such a short amount of time; this all happened in seconds.

As I looked over Danny's shoulder, I saw Little Bit running towards us. She looked scared, but not in a terrified kind of way; it was kind of odd. As we skidded to a stop, I jumped off and ran towards her.

"What is it?" I shouted as I scanned the area behind her.

She slammed into me and looked back, "There's men; they were after us!"

"Where are your sisters?" I asked as I started to move in the direction she pointed.

"They're over there. They told me to run!" She said as Danny, Thad and Tyler sprinted past me.

I looked back quickly and asked, "Are you okay?"

Clutching her rifle tight to her chest, she nodded; so I turned and ran on. I found everyone standing around a body on the ground. Danny had his arm around Lee Ann; and Taylor was squatted down in front of a large oak. Smoke was rising from the muzzle of her H&K that was lying across her lap. She was crying, her face red as she rocked back and forth. Seeing she was ok, I looked back at the body with Ted kneeling beside it.

I went over to Taylor and asked, "Are you alright?" She nodded; and I asked, "What happened?" She just stared at the body on the ground.

I walked over to Lee Ann and Danny. "What happened?" I asked her.

Unlike her sister, she wasn't crying. Lee Ann was staring down at the man on the ground, seemingly indifferent. "We were sitting down for a minute, waiting to see if the squirrels would come out; and all of a sudden, there they were, running right at us."

I looked down at the man on the ground. He was thirty-ish; and, unlike most people today, had shaved in the last couple of days. His hair was kind of raggedy, in a bad haircut kind of way; someone who had no idea how to cut hair had apparently had a go at it. He was still alive, though bleeding profusely, the source of which I couldn't determine; and Ted was questioning him.

"If you want help, answer my questions. What were you doing?" Ted asked calmly.

He didn't answer; just looked at Lee Ann and raised a finger to point at her, then looked at Taylor. While he didn't say it, I for one knew what it was about.

"Women, you're looking for women?" I asked.

He nodded slightly in reply, "Yes, now help me." He raised a blood-covered hand and looked at it.

"Where are you guys from?" Ted asked.

"You're not going to help me are you?" The man asked, watching blood run down his fingers.

Ted pulled a battle dressing out of his vest. "I told you I would, if you answer all my questions."

Sarge kicked the man's foot, "You from around here; you guys holed up around here?"

Before he answered, Mike trotted up, "Found a blood trail; if we move fast we can follow it."

"Go ahead, we got this," Sarge said.

"Thad you come with us," Ted said.

"I'll come too," Tyler said.

The four of them quickly ran towards the ATVs, and soon were speeding towards the road, leaving Sarge, Danny and me with the girls and a dying man. Sarge squatted down beside the man and smiled, "So, you were telling us where you're holed up."

I turned and went over to Taylor and squatted down. She wasn't crying now, but was still rocking back and forth. "You ok?" I asked.

She nodded again, then said, "I peed my pants." It was then I noticed the wet stain on her jeans.

"That's alright kiddo; we'll get you home and you can clean up. You were scared; and it's alright."

"I wasn't scared, really. I mean, not in a normal way. It wasn't until after I shot him." She looked at me and said; "I shot him." Tears began to run down her cheeks again.

I looked back at the man who was obviously in even more pain, if that were even possible. Sarge was applying his unique brand of persuasion; so it was more than possible. Looking back at Taylor, I said, "You did what you had to. Remember, we talked about this before; I said it would be hard."

"I can't believe I peed my pants. I wasn't scared when I started shooting. I saw them running towards us;" she paused and looked at the man, and her eyes narrowed. "He had this really creepy smile on his face." She looked back at me, "it went away when I picked up my gun." Looking back again, she said, "it went away quick."

I patted her knee, the dampness reminding me of her embarrassment. "It's ok; you did good. You protected your sisters."

She looked right into my eyes, "I don't ever want to do it again."

"Neither do I," I said with a smile. "And that's a good thing; if you liked it, it would be a problem. You're fine."

She looked at Lee Ann, "She shot one too I think."

"How many were there?" I asked.

"There were three of them; I think Ashley even shot at them."

"Did they have guns?"

"Yeah; someone shot at us as they were running away, I think. It's hard to be sure; the guns were so loud. I know it's weird; but when I was shooting, it felt kind of good," Lee Ann replied.

"It felt good because you didn't just have to be a victim. You had a choice; you had your own power."

The man let out a yelp and Taylor jumped. I looked back to see Sarge pushing a rather large piece of hickory into the guy's torso; it was hard to tell exactly where. I looked back at Taylor, "You and Lee Ann go back over towards the house and stay with Little Bit." I pointed, "she's just over there behind the juniper trees."

Danny had already ushered Lee Ann away from what was taking place, thankfully. As Taylor walked over to her sisters, I waved Danny over. "Hey man; can you take them home?" I asked as the poor bastard dying in the dirt continued to cry out. Sarge could be heard from time to time adding emphasis to his questions.

He nodded, "Yeah, they don't need to be around this."

"No, they don't. Do me a favor; check Little Bit's rifle."

His head cocked to the side, "For what?"

"See if she fired it."

He looked back at her, "Did she shoot too?"

"Taylor thinks she might have; just check it and see."

Danny nodded, "Alright, I'll see you back at the house."

"Thanks," I said as I turned to head back to the task Sarge was currently engaged in.

As I walked up, Sarge was squatted by the man's side, wiping blood from his hands on the man's jeans. Looking down, it was obvious the questioning had come to an end.

"He tell you where they were?" I asked.

"I've got a pretty good idea; you'll probably know where it is from the description."

I shook my head, "How do you convince a dying man to tell you anything?"

Sarge looked at me and with a straight face and said, "By not letting him die as fast as he'd like. There are worse things than death, my friend." He slapped me on my shoulder, "come on; let's go to the barricade and wait on the guys to get back."

"What the hell's going on?" Doc asked as we walked up.

"Some guys tried to grab the girls," I replied.

"No shit; did you guys get them?" Jeff asked.

"We didn't; but the girls did," Sarge said.

Jeff and Doc both looked at me. "Taylor shot one of them; and Lee Ann may have hit another one," I said.

With a look of concern, Doc asked, "How are the girls dealing with it?"

"Taylor took it pretty hard. She pissed her pants, and was pretty shaken up," I replied.

Doc nodded, "I bet; I'll talk to her later. The first time

you're engaged in that, it can really affect people. She needs to talk about it, and air her feelings."

I nodded, "I'd appreciate that. I will talk with her too; but it would be good if you did first."

Sarge had walked out to the road and called out, "Here they come; looks like they got one of them."

We walked out to the road and could see a man walking down it towards us. Ted was right behind him sitting on the front rack of the ATV as Tyler slowly drove behind the man. Thad was following on the Polaris. We waited as they approached.

"He ain't bleeding," Sarge observed. I looked closely at the man. "There was a blood trail. This guy ain't bleeding; so there was at least one more," he added.

When they were within shouting range, Sarge called out, "Where's the other one?"

Ted was just behind the guy with his weapon at low ready. He jerked his head and replied, "Lying on the side of the road back there; dead."

"You sure he's dead?" Doc asked.

"Oh yeah, he's dead," Thad called out.

In a moment they were before us. The prisoner stopped and took us all in, obviously unsure of what was about to happen to him. I was looking him up and down; and he was surprisingly calm considering what he'd just attempted.

"What do you notice about him, Morg?" Sarge asked.

I looked back at the guy, and some things began to really stand out. "He's clean, recently shaved; and his hair's been cut by someone, like the other guy."

Sarge nodded and looked over at me grinning, "Good eye Sheriff." He looked back to the guy and started questioning him, "What were you guys up to?" He didn't answer. Sarge stepped towards him, "Let's just cut the bullshit now; you can play all macho, but I assure you I've broke harder men that you. Just answer the questions, or we'll move on to the hard way."

Mike and Tyler walked up. "And he likes it the hard way," Mike said as he passed the guy. Then he looked at Sarge and said, "I think I know where more of his people are."

"Do tell," Sarge replied.

"There are some guys up at the old store on the corner; they gave us the stink eye as we rode by."

"How many were there?" Ted asked.

"We should know soon!" Tyler shouted. We all looked to where he was standing in the road. "Looks like they're on their way here."

The prisoner looked at Sarge, "Now you'll see who's the hard man."

Sarge replied by swinging the muzzle of his carbine and hitting him in the mouth. He yelped and grabbed his face. It had to hurt like hell. Ted, Mike and Thad walked out into the road, all three were shading their eyes against the sun's glare. "Two, no three ATVs headed this way," Ted said.

"You two get out of sight; let's see what these shit birds want," Sarge said. Then he looked at the guy we had, "on your knees."

Instead of doing as he was told, he looked at Sarge, "What?"

"I ain't got time to explain," Sarge said as he smashed the butt of his carbine into the guy's gut. The prisoner immediately doubled over and fell to his knees, supporting himself with his hands. Sarge kicked one of his hands out from under him, and he crashed onto the rough pavement. Quickly producing a pair of handcuffs, Sarge secured his hands behind his back.

"Here they come." Thad said, as he walked back behind one of the gabions filled with sand.

I knelt down beside the guy on the ground, and pulled one

of the bandannas from my pocket. Grabbing a fist full of hair, I lifted his head; and when he opened his mouth to complain, I stuffed it in to his muffled complaints. Sarge grinned that evil grin of his, "Nice touch."

As I rose to my feet, the three machines rolled to a stop in the road. Each had two men on board, all armed with ARs or AKs. The men quickly dismounted and spread out in the road. They looked much like us, all wearing one form or another of military fatigues, and some kind of load-bearing gear, sporting pistols, knives and magazines. A tall man with a very neatly trimmed beard and jet-black hair stepped in front of the others. Sarge, always the socialite, broke the ice, "What can we do for you fellers?"

"We're looking for a couple of our guys; was wondering if you've seen anyone." He spoke confidently, standing in the road with his weapon gripped across his chest. I took a moment to look at each of the men. They all had their weapons at the ready, fingers outside the trigger guards, and no doubt thumbs on the safety.

"I don't think we've seen anyone you'd be associated with," Sarge replied.

The man looked at the trussed up form on the ground, "Who's that?"

Sarge looked back, "Oh that; that's just some scumbag we caught trying to snatch a couple of young girls here."

"Can I see him?"

I knelt down and once again grabbed a handful of hair. Raising his head, I asked, "This one of yours?"

He didn't answer; just stared at the guy. After a moment, I turned his head towards me and then pulled the bandanna from his mouth. Then, nodding my head towards the road, I asked, "You know him?"

He rolled his eyes towards the road, "I'm sorry Billy!" Before he could say more, I stuffed the cloth back into his mouth.

As I rose to my feet, Sarge Said, "I suppose that other one on the side of the road down there is yours too."

You could clearly see Billy's jaw muscles tighten, "He is; where's the other one?"

"You mean was; and the other one is in the same condition," Sarge replied.

"So you've killed two of my men," Billy replied, the agitation clear in his voice.

"We didn't; but I don't guess it much matters who did it. They needed killin'. Tried to snatch the wrong girls; our girls know how to shoot," Sarge replied.

"So you say," Billy replied.

Sarge laughed, "I don't say; the evidence is pretty damn clear. Two of 'em are dead."

"Not what I mean; you say they were trying to grab some girls," Billy replied. Before Sarge could say anything, one of Billy's men spoke, "Billy this is bullshit!" Billy raised a hand in reply, and nothing more was said by his minion.

"No, he doesn't say; my daughters do. They're the ones that shot the sacks of shit," I replied.

Billy looked at me for the first time, "Nice broach."

I looked down at the star pinned to the center of my vest and grabbed it. Turning it up, I replied, "It is; isn't it."

"What about him; what are you going to do with him?" Billy asked.

Sarge looked at me, "I don't know, Sheriff; what do you want to do with him?"

I hadn't even thought about it. I looked down at the form lying in the leaves and dirt on the road, *what to do?* Looking back up at Billy, I said, "He's guilty of attempted kidnapping, of minors no less." I looked back at him, "Looks like he'll be executed."

That last word stirred Billy's men. "Like hell!" One of them shouted, as they all seemed to start moving.

"If you don't want to lose more of your men today, I suggest you put a leash on your dogs!" Sarge shouted.

"We've got 'em outnumbered!" Another of them shouted.

Billy raised a hand again, "That we can see," his eyes darted around. "Why don't you just punish him some way; whip him or something."

Sarge smiled, "Shit. That's like eating pussy through panties; just ain't good for anyone involved."

Billy nodded at his trussed toady, "It'd be good for him."

Sarge glanced back, "Somehow I don't think the lesson would stick the same."

Billy looked up and sniffed loudly, "You want me to just let you kill another one of my men?"

"I don't remember asking your permission," I shot back.

"You willing to start a fight over some trash that's guilty of trying to grab kids?" Sarge asked.

Billy rolled his head, his neck giving an audible pop. "They're young; you know how it is. It's not exactly easy to get a date these days."

Hearing the words, I felt my blood rise. My ears got hot; and I could feel the rage building in me. "So they try and snatch an eight-year-old girl! You think that's right? You sick fucks rape kids?" I shouted.

Without skipping a beat, Billy asked, "How old was the other girl?"

The statement slapped me in the side of the head; I was speechless. Sarge, however, was not.

"What's the age limit for your rape victims. I mean; what's too young?"

I didn't wait to hear the answer. "It doesn't matter; you fuckers need to kick rocks." I pointed to the prisoner, "this one stays here. And if I catch any more of your sick fucks trying to grab anyone, anywhere, I'll put a bullet in their head too!"

Billy rolled his shoulders and stiffened, "If you're going to do it, then do it." He looked at the man on the road, "Execute him."

Again, I wasn't ready for the response. It wasn't until Sarge looked at me that I realized it really was going to happen, right now, right here. I pulled the guy to his feet and snatched the bandanna from his mouth. He immediately began begging Billy to help him, to take him home, as if this were all up to him to decide.

I looked back at Billy, "You want to watch? Fine by me." I quickly drew my pistol and raised it; as the muzzle swept past the man's head, I squeezed the trigger. The blast cut his pleas in midsentence as the body fell to the ground, issuing a geyser of blood in an arc. The world slowed; time seemed to blur, like putty being pulled. The sound of the casing hitting the road and bouncing echoed in my head.

Billy's men all jumped, Billy didn't even blink. Instead, the corners of his mouth pulled down slightly as his head slowly nodded, the movement barely perceptible. Without saying a word, he turned and climbed onto one of the ATVs; and his band of miscreants followed his lead. In a flurry of sound and dust they were gone. It was surprising really; they simply mounted up and left, without a word said.

Ted came out of the woods; he was shaking his head. "We should have ended this here while we could."

"And some of us would have died," Sarge said.

Mike came jogging up, "Why didn't we kill those fuckers?"

"They're just going to come back," Ted added.

"I was waiting for the shooting to start," Thad said.

"I'm with Sarge. There were too many of them; someone would have been killed," I said.

Ted spit into the dirt, "You know they're coming back,"

Sarge was looking out towards the road, "I figure as much; we need to get them a really nice reception ready."

"How are we going to know when, or where for that matter, they're going to come?" Tyler asked, wiping beads of sweat from his forehead. It was still mild out; so it wasn't the heat causing his head to leak.

Sarge looked at Mike, "You said you think you know where they're laying their head at night?"

Mike nodded, "I do." Then pointing to the body on the ground, "if Chief Loan here hadn't popped that guy's grape, we could have asked him." The reference to the street execution by the Police Chief of Saigon in 1968 wasn't lost on me.

"No sense cryin' over spilled brains at this point. Teddy, you two go see if you can find them. Get an eyeball on them and see what we're up against," Sarge said as he rolled the dead man's head over with the toe of his boot. "Damn, that forty-five makes a hell of a hole."

"We'll go after dark. Let's get some comms set up," Ted said. Then he slapped Mike on the shoulder, "come on; let's get our shit together."

"You want some help?" Jeff asked.

"You can help provide security if you want. We're going to ride in close, and then proceed from there on foot. You can hang back and cover the ATVs," Ted replied.

Jeff nodded, "Sounds good; I'm in."

"Get your marbles together and let Teddy shake you down before you head out," Sarge said.

"I'll help you guys get ready; but I'll stay here to assist with security," Doc said, following behind the guys.

"What's your plan; you going to try and hit them where they live," I asked.

"No; I figure they'll be coming soon enough," Sarge answered.

"I think we need to increase our firepower up here. We need to bring one of the buggies up here with one of the machineguns on it; maybe keep it out of sight, but have it here just in case. We can park it in the woods there," I said, pointing into the trees at the north side of the road.

"That sure would make me feel better," Thad added.

"We can do that. Thad, why don't you come back with me and we'll set it up. You can bring it back up here," Sarge said.

I stayed at the barricade with Tyler while everyone else went to prepare for the night's activities. I was thinking of what could have been done differently, if we should have just punched the clock and gone all OK Corral right there. I know someone would have been shot; those guys were far too well armed. Even if it weren't an immediately fatal shot, it may as well be. Infection, or the need for advanced care, would only result in a lingering and miserable death.

Tyler couldn't stop looking at the body; the pool of blood the head was lying in had turned really dark and started to gel. I could see him look at the body, then at me; but it didn't matter… it was done. Maybe I shouldn't have shot the bastard; but what do you do with miscreants like that? They were trying to take my girls, *my girls*. On second thought, it's exactly what they needed. Back in the day, they would have been arrested, maybe put in jail, maybe. Some shit-bag lawyer would claim they were sick, and that therapy was the proper remedy for them, not prison. They would do it again, though. I looked down at the body, *but not this one.*

I could tell it was eating Tyler; so I finally asked the obvious question, "Is that first one you've seen?"

Tyler looked down at the body again, "It's the first time I've seen someone shot like that, right in front of me."

I leaned over the barricade and rested my head on my forearms, letting out a long breath I said, "It gets easier."

I could feel him looking at me. His confusion, fear and uncertainty were palpable. Finally, I asked, "What is it?" He hesitated for a moment; so I straightened up and looked him. "Go on, spit it out."

"I don't know if I could do that. I mean, one minute the guy's on the ground, and you're talking about him like he isn't here; and in the blink of an eye you're blasting his brains out. It was that fast, I blinked and didn't even see it."

"You saw it, but your brain is still conditioned to the way things used to be. That's a horrible thing to see; so your brain is doing you a favor and blocking it out."

He stared at the body for a long time; then asked, "How many?"

I shook my head, "I try not to think about it."

Thankfully, Thad and Sarge pulled up on the smaller of the two buggies. A SAW was mounted to the top of it. Their arrival ended Tyler's questions. Thad backed the buggy into the woods, making it nearly impossible for it to be seen from the road. Sarge wandered over as Thad was laying some brush over the front end.

"You alright there, Morg?" He asked.

I nodded, "Yeah. What else could be done about it; damn sure couldn't let him go."

Sarge snorted, "Don't make it none easier."

I grunted, "No shit."

"You go on home; check on them girls. I'll stay down here for a while; just get a relief set up for us later."

I nodded, "Thanks, I'll probably come back with Danny; just don't feel comfortable having any of the girls down here after dark considering what's going on."

"Good call; don't forget Doc is around to help out."

"You got any spare night vision; yours is way better than what I've got." I asked.

"Yeah, we brought a set down here." Sarge pointed to the buggy, "there's a radio in there too; if the guys call in, you'll hear it up here as well."

"Don't worry Morg; we got it," Thad added.

"I appreciate it; I'm headed home," I said as I started to walk off.

I didn't feel well, an exhausted nauseous feeling settled over me. Looking at the ground as I made my way home, I could smell rain, that earthy odor that often announced an advancing storm on a warm day. It wasn't long before the first drop hit me on the back of my neck. Soon, the tan oak leaves that littered the road were glistening with moisture as my clothes started to soak up the water. It was fitting really; the rain was the perfect addition to my mood.

Hearing tires grinding on the road and the rumble of a diesel, I looked back. Ian was waving from the turret of the Hummer, soaked from the rain. Perez pulled up and stopped beside me, "Hey sailor; want a ride?" He asked.

"Thanks; but I'm good," I replied. As I looked up, I added, "I'll walk; the rain's helping to clear my head."

"I can dig it; been a rough day huh?" Ian asked.

Squinting against the rain, I looked up at him. "Yeah; you guys get everything from the armory?"

"We did; Sheffield wants to see you, tomorrow," he replied.

"For what?"

He shrugged, "Hell if I know; I'm just the messenger."

"Alright; dinner should be ready soon."

"We're good; we ate at the armory. We're going to get some shut-eye so we can relieve you later. Sarge said you were coming back down for a watch; we'll come take over after some sleep," Perez said.

I looked in at Jamie, "You sure? You've had a long day too."

Jamie nodded, "We're sure."

I offered a weak smile, "Thanks, I'll see you guys later then."

Ian slapped the top of the Hummer and Perez pulled away. I stood in the rain for a moment and watched them as they made the turn and headed home; then continued my walk in the rain.

# CHAPTER 3

**M**IKE CAME INTO THE LIVING room of the house. Doc was sitting on the sofa with his feet on the coffee table. His head was laid back on the cushion and his hat pulled down over his eyes. "Hey Doc, you got a stethoscope I can borrow?"

Without moving, Doc replied, "You and Ted playing doctor again?"

Mike didn't miss a beat. "No, ever since the time I played proctologist, Teddy won't play with me."

Doc's head rocked back and forth on the sofa as he reached into his pack lying beside him on the couch. He fished around, pulling the apparatus out and tossing it in Mike's direction. "Don't break it; and bring it back."

Mike snagged it in the air. "No worries; I won't hurt it."

Now properly equipped, Mike went back to the bedroom and opened the closet door. Looking at the huge safe, he smiled. "Hello gorgeous," he said as he slipped the ends of the scope into his ears. Pulling a Sharpie out of his pocket, he uncapped it and held it in his mouth as he placed the chest piece against the safe just above the dial.

After giving it several spins to the right, he began turning it very slowly, listening intently as the dial moved. After rotating the dial about one third of a full revolution, he heard a faint click through the earpieces. He released the dial and smiled, noting that it was set on 36, which he wrote down on the safe. He capped his marker, "That's enough for today;" and laying the stethoscope around his neck, he headed out to the living room. Tossing it back to Doc, he said, "Thanks, I'll need to borrow it again later."

"Didn't get in huh?" Doc asked from under his hat.

Ted was in the kitchen, and asked, "Get into what?"

Doc wiggled his feet, "Houdini here is trying to get into that safe."

Mike looked at Doc with mock surprise, "Why; whatever gave you that idea?"

"You want in that can? I can get you in," Ted said.

Mike stared at him for a moment. He knew better than to ask; but curiosity got the better of him, "Oh yeah, how?"

Ted reached into his pack lying on the counter and pulled out a small block and tossed it to Mike. He caught it and smirked, "I want whatever is in there in one piece," and tossed the block of C4 back to Ted.

Ted caught it and shrugged, "Whatever; it'll get you in though."

"I'll try my way first."

Ted held the block up, "You'll want it later. I'll hold onto it for you," he smiled, winked and shoved the block back into his pack.

Mike gave him the finger in reply. "I'm going to get some sleep before our fun tonight."

"Good idea; now shut up so I can too," Doc replied from under his hat.

I was in the bathroom changing into some dry clothes; the rain had soaked me to the bone. The house was quiet. I assumed Mel and the girls were at Danny's house, which was fine by me for the moment. Dropping my wet clothes in the tub, I toweled off and put on a dry set. After changing, I went out to the living room and sat on the couch, listening to the rain as it pelted the roof. I laid my head back on the sofa and closed my eyes. As soon as they closed, the image of the bullet crashing into the man's head I had just executed flashed into my mind. It was as if I had been jolted. I quickly sat up and slipped a holster onto my belt. Picking up the Springfield, I looked at it for a moment, turning it over slowly.

The gun was wet, rain thankfully; and I used the towel to dry it. Dropping the mag, I replaced it with a full one from the vest and pushed it into the holster. I picked up the carbine as I went out the door for the short walk to Danny's.

Mel was sitting on the porch with Little Bit in her lap. Lee Ann was in front of her with her legs hanging off the porch, her H&K laid across her lap. Bobbie, Jess, Fred and Mary were there as well. I tried to look upbeat as I approached, doing my best to smile, "Hey guys."

Mel looked up; it was obvious she could see through my attempt at hiding my mood. "Where's Taylor?" I asked.

"She's inside lying down," Jess replied.

I looked at Lee Ann, "You alright kiddo?"

She shrugged, "Yeah, did you find them?"

All eyes were on me, waiting for my response. I surveyed the faces of those before me, "We did; and they won't be bothering anyone any time soon."

Lee Ann cocked her head to the side, "Did you kill them?"

"I hope so," Little Bit replied.

"You better have," Mel added.

Danny walked out on the porch, "What's the word?"

"The word is the three that were after the girls are no more," I replied.

"And?" Mel asked.

"And there are more of them."

"We're going after them aren't we?" Jess asked.

"Yeah; we can't let them come back," Fred added.

"Mike and Ted are going to go find them later tonight. We don't know how many there are, or where they are. We have an idea, but we've got to get some more info," I said.

"You think they'll come back?" Danny asked.

I looked up at him, "You know they are; three of theirs are dead."

The statement caused a flurry of comments. I told everyone we needed to keep our eyes open, especially at night. Jess and Fred were convinced they would be back tonight, but I thought it unlikely. Their leader, Billy, seemed like the kind of guy that would surely want his revenge; but he would probably plan it and pick the time and place to act on it. While we were discussing this, Miss Kay walked out on the porch. She was perpetually smiling it seemed; she announced, "Dinner's ready."

"I'll run get Brandy," Jess said as she hopped up. I was pleased to see the .45 I gave her jutting out of a back pocket of her jeans; *she needs a holster,* I thought. We went in and had a quiet dinner; no one talked much. Taylor wouldn't come down; she stayed upstairs in the bed. I for one was happy there was no conversation; what I'd just done was weighing heavy on my mind. Miss Kay tried to lighten the mood with cheerful conversation, but it didn't go far. I was brought around by Danny talking about the chicken feeder.

"We got your chicken feeder running," He said.

I was caught off guard by the comment; and it took Little Bit chiming in to bring me around. "Danny put the guts of the squirrels we killed today in a bucket. He said it was a chicken feeder." She screwed her little face up, "chickens eat guts?"

I smiled, "Actually they will; but the guts aren't for them. The guts are for the flies."

"Eww, they're going to eat the flies?" She asked.

Laughing, I replied, "No." I leaned across the table towards her, "they're going to eat the maggots!"

"That's disgusting," Lee Ann offered.

"You have a bucket of guts to grow maggots in?" Miss Kay asked.

I relayed the concept to everyone, with Little Bit adding colorful details on the design. Once the description was done, I sat in silence with all eyes on me. Little Bit was beaming, smiling from ear to ear. Finally, Miss Kay spoke up, "That is amazing; I would never have thought of that."

"Yeah, how'd you come up with that?" Fred asked.

"I read a lot."

"Yeah; too much," Mel added.

I smiled, "not anymore." Looking at Kay, I said, "thanks for dinner; it was good." Then I got Danny's attention, "we have to go to the barricade."

"What? Why you? You need to come home with us," Mel shot back.

"I'm sorry babe; we have to go. The guys are going out to find the rest of the group that came after the girls; and someone has to watch the barricade."

"Why can't Thad do it?" She asked.

"He's already down there."

"Why not Tyler and Aric?"

"Tyler is already down there too," I replied.

"I can go." Aric offered.

"Me too; I'll go," Fred added.

"I know you would," I replied with a halfhearted smile. "But we've already discussed it, and we don't want any women down there right now."

Jess jumped to her feet, "What! We're just as capable as you are!"

I did my best to explain the situation as delicately as possible. "I know you are. It's not that I think you are not up to the challenge. These guys aren't looking to take food or weapons."

Jess crossed her arms indignantly, "We can still do our part!"

I walked slowly to her. "I know; but these guys are looking for women. They were trying to take the girls; do you understand that?" She stared back at me for a moment, "what do you think they wanted them for? Think about it for a minute; what do you think they would do with you." I pointed at Fred, "or her," then at Mel and Bobbie, "or them?" Lastly, I pointed at Little Bit, "or her and her sisters?"

I watched their faces and could see the realization slowly come over them collectively. Jess relaxed; she had her demons already to deal with. She knew the horrors I was trying so hard not to say. She slowly sat down beside Mel and looked at Little Bit, "Let him go." She looked back at me, "he's only trying to take care of everyone."

Mel let out a loud sigh, "I know he is; but why is it always him?"

"It's not just him; I'm going too," Danny said.

I looked at Mel, "And it's not my ass on the line really. Ted and Mike are going out tonight to find these guys."

Jeff's voice came from the kitchen, scaring the shit out of everyone in the room. "Me too; I'm going with them." All eyes were now on Jeff. He smoothed his beard that was now down past his collar, "I know you think Morgan is always hanging his ass out in the breeze, that he takes a lot of risks; but the reality of the situation is just the opposite." Jeff nodded at me, "We're all here because of him in one way or another. It's like he's got some weird gravitational pull that holds all this together. We all owe him. I know I do; he saved my life, took me in here." He looked at Jess, "He looked out for you, got you to your family; shit went south and now here you are. Brandy, I know you haven't said anything, but he's saved your family as well." Brandy nodded slowly. "We all take risks today; it's just the way of it." He finished what he had to say and shrugged, "jus' sayin'."

Jeff's statement shocked everyone. He'd never said so much at one time before. Once again the room fell silent until yet another voice surprised everyone.

"I agree; I know he saved me." It was Mary. She was sitting on a chair against the wall; and until that moment, I had no idea she was even in the room. She was dealing with her own demons.

The sudden realization that Mary was there caused me to jump once again. I looked around the room, "Is there anyone else here I don't know about?"

"I think this is everyone," Jess said.

"You gals think you're not being allowed to participate; but it's quite the opposite. We have no idea where these guys are going to come from. I seriously doubt they are going to come through the front door. They'll probably watch us for a few days and find a soft spot to come through, probably through the woods somewhere." I scanned the room, "it will be up to you gals to stop them if that happens."

"They're going to sneak in here?" Little Bit asked as she shrank back against Mel.

"They're going to try kiddo; but we're going to stop them," I replied with a smile.

"Yes we will," Jess added.

"Until this is over, everyone needs to be extra careful. Stay close to home, and never go anywhere alone. We have to stay together; if anyone is alone, he or she runs a risk of disappearing."

The room was full of solemn faces, the weight of the situation settling over them. Danny and I needed to get to the barricade, and Jeff needed to hook up with the guys. Mel decided to stay at Bobbie's. Brandy would wait there until Tyler returned from the barricade, then they would go home. Jess, Fred and Aric would all go home; Thad would be there as well. It would be better to have everyone together in groups.

I kissed Mel and Little Bit. Lee Ann never was much of one for a kiss on the cheek; but she did stand up and give me a hug. I smiled and razzed her, "Awe, I feel so special." She smiled and rolled her eyes. "Whatever," she replied as she twirled and walked away. I knew then she was going to be alright.

It was still raining, so I ran home quickly and put on my rain gear. A poncho serves its purpose well and has many uses aside from wearing, but I hate the damn things. You're always wet from the knees down, and they seem to be a perfect gutter for directing water into your boot. I put on my rain gear. It was expensive when I bought it, but Blackhawk makes some awesome gear. Once dressed, I wandered back across the fence. Danny and I loaded onto one of the ATVs, headed for the barricade; and Jeff took another and headed over to meet the guys.

"Miss Kay has dinner waiting on you guys," I said when we stopped.

"Good; I'm starving," Tyler replied.

"You think we should go warn Miss Gena and Dylan about these guys?" Thad asked.

I shook my head, "I wouldn't. They could be watching us;

and we don't want those guys to know they have anything to do with us. That could make them a target."

"I agree," Sarge replied.

"You guys take off; we've got this," I said.

"Sounds good; I'm hungry," Thad replied.

"And I'm wet," Tyler replied.

They loaded up and quickly left, leaving Danny and me in the dark as the rain continued to pelt us. Once they were gone, I went over to the war wagon and pulled the NVGs out. These things were amazing. I once heard someone say that having them made it *unfair* for those that didn't have them. The device I held in my hand certainly proved that statement true. Third generation Mil-Spec equipment is light years beyond most of the commercial equipment available, though I was truly thankful for mine when I needed it. Had I known then what I know now about the quality of the equipment, I would have bought my own PVS-14.

I took the NVGs out to the road, turned them on and scanned the road north and south, and then the field across the road. Seeing nothing, I turned it off and walked back to the barricade. Danny was tying a poncho up in the trees near the buggy, his headlamp illuminating the paracord he was knotting.

"Good idea," I said.

"I thought it would be nice to have someplace out of the rain," he replied. He finished the knot he was tying and let the limb go. It popped up, and the poncho snapped tight.

Stepping under the poncho, I stuffed the NVGs into the pocket on my rain coat. Danny pulled his poncho over his head and hung it on a limb. "That's better," he said.

I reached into the back of the wagon and grabbed a couple of buckets; they had lids on them and held an assortment of gear. Setting out our new stools, Danny and I took a seat.

"I like the smell of the rain; washes things clean," Danny said.

I looked out towards the barricade where the body of the man I'd shot earlier still lay, "Yeah, it does."

"There was an empty round in Little Bit's rifle."

I looked over at Danny; all I could see was his silhouette, "I was afraid of that."

"Doesn't really mean anything. She was out hunting; could have been from a shot at a limb rat."

"Could be. I'll never know though; not going to ask."

Headlights suddenly illuminated us. I looked down the road and could see the other wagon coming towards us in the Hyena. The guys were headed out for some sneakin' and peekin'. They pulled up and stopped. I got a chuckle looking at the three of them. They were all camo'd out, faces blackened with grease.

"You know, with those beards you guys look like the cast of Duck Dynasty," I said, getting a laugh out of Danny.

Mike, who was standing up in the turret, stiffened. He ran his hand through his beard, "I guess I do strike quite a manly image; not as old as Phil, but I'll take it as a compliment."

Ted's head rocked back as he looked up at Mike. "You're no Phil; Si maybe."

Mike kicked the back of Ted's seat, "I'm not Si!"

Now Jeff's head rocked back, "Dude, you're Si, hands down."

Mike looked at Danny and me. I shrugged, "Sorry dude, Si all day long."

"I think he's more of a Godwin," Danny said. We all immediately started laughing.

"No shit," I nearly shouted, pointing at Mike. "He's a skinny Godwin."

Mike shrugged. "Whatever Jack," he said, getting us all to laughing even harder.

"What's your plan for the night?" Danny asked.

"We're going to move closer to them, then get out on foot and see if we can find a place to keep an eye on 'em," Ted said.

"Be careful," I offered.

"Keep your radio close, we'll check in every couple of hours," Mike said.

"What's your call sign?" I asked.

"Godwin," Ted replied, starting to laugh again. Then he asked, "What's yours?"

"Boomhauer," I replied before Mike could hang "Si" on us.

Ted slapped the steering wheel, "I like it! Keep that radio close," he said.

As they started to pull away Jeff began to mumble like the character, straight faced; and I couldn't even begin to understand him. I smiled as they turned out onto the road. The headlights cut out at the same time, leaving only the sound of the big wagon as they headed off into the darkness.

Danny and I sat under the poncho for most of the night. From time to time I would wander out and take a look with the NVGs; each time there was nothing to see. The rain certainly was keeping everyone under cover for the night; though anyone that may be out would surely be up to no good. The guys checked in once, saying they were leaving the wagon and moving out on foot, while Jeff would stay to keep an eye on their ride.

Returning from a survey of our surrounding area, I fell onto the bucket. Danny held his hand out, catching rain cascading off the poncho. "This is going to be good for the garden."

"Yeah; I just hope it doesn't turn into a daily thing. Every three days would be good."

"Yeah, but you know what the summers can be like."

"Yeah, hotter'n the hinges of hell," I replied. The mere thought of it made me start to sweat.

Danny grunted, "Yeah, but the rain helps cool it off."

"Unless the sun comes out, then it just steams you in your hide."

"We'll soon see," Danny said. I rose to take another look.

I walked out to the road with the NVG and scanned both directions again, just as I had several times before. Not seeing anything on the road, I scanned the field across the road. Off in the distance I saw a light. When looking through one of these you cannot mistake seeing light; it is literally blindingly obvious. I quickly lowered the device and closed the eye I was looking through it with. Using the other eye that still had decent natural night vision, no light. Taking another quick look, I could see it again. It was moving back and forth like someone using a flashlight. I turned and called Danny out; and he quickly trotted up.

"What's up?"

I pointed in the direction I saw it, "You see anything out there?"

Danny stared off into the darkness, "No," I handed him the NVG. He took a look, then lowered them, still looking off into the distance, then raised them and looked again. "Why can't we see it, too far?"

"I don't think so. I think it's an IR light. I think someone out there is using night vision equipment and it's an IR source."

"Why would anyone be out in this shit?" Danny asked aloud.

"And why would they be out there?" I replied. The area the light was coming from was part of a large cattle ranch, empty open pasture land broken occasionally by bay heads full of palms and cypress.

Danny lowered the optic again, "Yeah, there isn't shit out there."

"I'm thinking tomorrow we'll go out there and take a look around; I'd like to know who's out there."

"Me too. There may not be anything to worry about, but the fact they have that kind of equipment makes me curious."

"That's what I was thinking," I replied as I headed back for the cover of the poncho. "Let's get out of the rain," I called over my shoulder.

Ted drove south, heading towards Altoona. The buggy was blacked out and he was using the NVG to see. Considering the danger of the mission at hand, they were all wearing radios with an earpiece and mic; stealth was a paramount concern.

Keying the mic, Ted asked, "Where we headed there Pocahontas?"

"Up ahead is a road called Demco; make a right on it. It will cut through an area of planted pines, They are somewhere west of a clear-cut," Mike replied through the radio.

"You don't know where they are past that?" Ted asked.

"No; we caught up to them near the intersection. We'll just have to look for them."

Ted keyed his mic, "Jeff, we're going to find a hide for the buggy; and you're going to stay with it. Mike and I will move out from there."

Jeff fumbled for the PTT, or push-to-talk button, on a cord attached to the radio. Not used to the equipment, it took a minute to find it. "Whatever you boys need."

Ted rounded the corner at Demco and drove slowly down the narrow road. The right side of the road was open pasture. Large oaks broke up the fields and offered some character to what would otherwise be a very mundane landscape. It also offered points of concealment. The left side was just the opposite. Thick planted pines; even at only a few years old, they defeated any attempts at observation. The right offered an escape; the left, nothing but potential threats.

After half a mile or so, the landscape changed. At a small bend, the road cut through an oak hammock, with trees no more than ten feet from the side of the road. *Ambush alley,* Ted thought.

"Eye's up Mikey," Ted said into the radio.

"Got it," Mike replied.

There was no ambush though, and the road slowly began to rise. At the crest of the small hill sat a house not yet completed. Ted drove up to the house and stopped out front. It was a large place, obviously someone's dream home, or at least it *was*.

"Jeff, you come with me. Mikey; cover us," Ted said as he shut the buggy off.

Jeff got out and joined Ted at the front of the vehicle. "We're going to clear this house quickly; just follow my lead and keep your eyes open," Ted said. Jeff nodded and Ted added, "you ready?"

Jeff nodded; Ted looked at him, then at his weapon, "You sure?" He asked.

Jeff looked down at his weapon and shrugged, "Yeah."

Ted reached over and flipped the large safety off on the AK Jeff cradled. "Now you're ready. There's no time for that shit if someone starts shooting in there." Ted held his trigger finger up. "This is your safety; keep it off the bang switch unless you're going to pull it."

Jeff nodded, "Ok, got it."

Ted started towards the house with Jeff right behind him. The house had a large three-car garage, and they entered through large opening where the doors would have been if things were different. Inside, the house was empty. The floors were bare concrete; and the walls were unpainted drywall. Using simple hand signals, Ted led Jeff through the house, and it was quickly cleared.

"It's clear; pull the buggy into the garage," Ted called into his radio.

"On my way," Mike replied.

They were standing in the garage when Mike pulled around. "Back it in," Ted said into the radio. Taking a small light from his pocket, he used it to light the way for Mike, guiding him into the garage.

Once Mike was out of the ride, the three gathered up. "Let's take some time to look and listen. We don't know where these guys are; so let's see if they'll give us some idea," Ted said.

The three men walked outside into the clear night. The moon was waning but provided plenty of light for the NVG devices to clearly see the land around the house. The area behind the house faded from open pasture to thick woods. Across the road and far off of it, was another house that ran east to west in front of them. Ted and Mike walked out away from the house a short distance and slowly scanned the whole of the area around them.

In this new world the nights were so quiet that sound traveled a long way. Off in the distance behind the house the yipping of coyotes drifted through the night; a large pack from the sound, possibly carrying on over a successful kill. Ted scanned the area where the tree line met the sky, a trick very handy when using night vision equipment as any light on the ground would illuminate the canopy of trees above the source, as well as emit a glow into the sky.

Seeing nothing in any direction, Ted walked out to the road and looked back to the east, taking several minutes to observe the area they'd just traversed. Turning a hundred and eighty degrees, he looked to the west. He was standing in the middle of the road, staring down the centerline when a sudden flash of light caught his eye. The usual method of wearing a PVS-14 NVG is mounted to a helmet or other headgear over one eye. The other eye is saved for unaided night vision. Both eyes are used, kept open while operating.

When Ted saw the light through the device he immediately recognized the fact he had not seen it with the unaided eye. He'd also instinctively crouched when seeing the light, and had begun moving towards the side of the road. He called Mike and told him to join him at the end of the driveway. When Mike arrived, Ted told him what he'd seen. They observed the area for several minutes.

"Does it look like there's a glow down there to you?" Mike asked.

"It's really faint if it is."

"You think it was an IR source you saw?" Mike asked.

"I didn't see it with the naked eye. Someone down there has some sort of device."

"Probably some commercial stuff."

"Yeah, but it could still be passive. I think at least we need to go that way and check it out. If these guys have that kind of gear in their kit, we need to be careful," Ted replied.

"For sure. I'm going to get the SAW; if we need to break contact it'll help."

"Throw some extra ammo in my pack and bring it too," Ted replied.

Mike ran back to the garage and told Jeff what they were going to do. He cautioned Jeff to keep his eyes and ears open, and to call them if he so much as thought he heard anything. Gathering the gear, Mike ran back out to the road where Ted was waiting.

"Alright; let's do this," Ted said.

They moved across the road. Using a ditch there for cover, they headed in the direction of the light. This sort of movement is tediously slow. Take a step and listen; take a step and listen. All the while your head is on a swivel. After a few hundred yards they came to another area of planted pines. *Should be the state tree,* Ted thought. They left the ditch and entered the trees, the needles providing soft footing and canopy keeping the underbrush to a minimum.

They moved along through the sparse pines for a short distance before Ted held up a fist and slowly dropped to one knee. Mike silently mimicked Ted, turning slightly so he could keep an eye on their back-trail. After taking a quick look to the rear, he focused on Ted. Ted pointed to his eyes with two fingers in a V, the signal for *I see.* He then held up two fingers, telling Mike he saw two people. Ted motioned to a short bushy chokecherry, and the two moved under it.

"Let's watch these guys for a minute," Ted said.

They watched the two figures, which stood close together, keeping very quiet and very still. It wasn't too long before one of them raised something to his face. Suddenly a bright light came on, emitting from the device he held to his eye while scanning the area. Mike and Ted watched, comfortable in their hide location. When the operator was satisfied with his check, the light went out, and the man lowered the device.

"Interesting," Ted whispered.

"At least it's passive," Mike replied.

"I think we found them. Let's back out, move across the road and try to get around them."

Mike replied by giving Ted a slight squeeze on his shoulder, and then fell back. Ted followed him, and they slowly made their way back through the trees before crossing the road after a brief security pause. As they came abreast of the two men, they paused once again. Ted paid attention to their behavior. They stayed quiet and still for the most part.

"They have a little discipline," Ted said.

"Yeah; but they think they're safe in the dark though. They squirm around a little," Mike added.

"Not as safe as they think they are."

"Want me to take 'em out?" Mike asked with a grin.

Ted looked at him, his face glowing green in the NVG, shaking his head he replied, "Not yet Dexter. Come on; let's move out and see what's behind them."

This section of Demco road was dirt, the pavement giving way to the ever-present sugar sand of north central Florida. Mike and Ted were moving down the north side of the road when Mike grabbed Ted's shoulder again. Ted immediately stopped and glanced back. Mike gave him the *I see* signal, and pointed down to the road surface. Ted looked down to see numerous footprints in the sand, coming from a trail on the opposite side of the road. The tracks turned down the road heading east, the way they'd just come. Ted nodded and moved out, going about thirty yards before taking a knee on the side of the road.

"Let's parallel it and see where it goes," Ted said. Mike nodded, and they quickly crossed the road, one at a time.

It didn't take long for them to come to a compound with considerable activity. In the center of the property was a large home with a screened-in pool. And there was another home beside it, obviously part of the same group. Scattered around these two structures were a number of RVs and travel trailers, as well as tents of all sorts. Fires, small and large, burned throughout the property. Around each of these were varying numbers of people.

"Can you imagine what that pool looks like?" Mike wondered aloud.

"Pay attention shit head," Ted popped back.

"Don't worry, I'm getting a head count."

Along with the houses, trailers and tents were a couple of large outbuildings. Ted was looking intently at a large barn behind the larger of the two houses. It was well lit, the low rumble of a generator coming from it.

"That barn is full of ATVs and shit," Ted said.

"Yeah, see that fuel tank?" Mike replied.

Ted nodded and made a mark on the sketchpad resting on his knee. They continued to map the compound as well as count the people there, combatants, potential combatants and non-combatants. Everything they saw was marked out, livestock, potential fuel and water stores, everything. After about an hour, Ted twirled his finger in the air. Mike nodded, and the two moved out. Ted checked his watch as they moved; *almost midnight* he thought.

As they approached the sentry post, Ted moved off into a hide where they could both see the people on sentry and the trail they used to move to it. They had been in the hide for nearly an hour when two people appeared from the trail, walking down the road towards the sentries. The guys watched as the relief took place. Little was said between them, the relief taking place quickly. Once the relieved pair was on the trail to the compound, Mike and Ted slipped out of the hide and made their way back to the house where Jeff was waiting. As the house came into sight, Ted keyed the mic on his radio, "Coming in."

After a short pause, Jeff replied, "Come on in."

Ted looked at Mike. "Shit," Mike said.

"Switch to the bravo channel," Ted said as he pulled his radio from his vest. Once they'd changed the frequencies on their radios Ted said, "They're going to be expecting us to come from this side; let's move around to the rear of the house."

"Why can't anything ever be easy?" Mike moaned as they moved out.

They watched the house carefully as they moved, seeing no signs of life. Once at the rear of the house they took a knee. "Alright, you stay here; I'm going to move around to the other side. I'll let you know when I'm in place; then we'll move on them."

Mike nodded and Ted moved out. As Ted made his way around the far side of the house, Mike watched closely for any movement in the house. Just as before, there was no sign anyone was there. Ted moved quickly; and in no time Mike heard Ted whispering in his ear. "Two in the garage; I can see Jeff sitting on the floor."

"Roger that; I'll hit the back door," Mike replied.

"I'll take these two; when you hear my shots, go in."

Mike started to move towards the house in a low crouch. He wasn't very thrilled with the idea of entering the house alone. Someone to open doors to make the entries faster and more dynamic would be much better; but they had to do this, now. As Mike came up to the rear of the house, he heard the muffled report of Ted's suppressed rifle, two shots in rapid succession. Mike quickly jerked the door open and moved through it. As he came into the kitchen, a figure rounded the corner.

The muzzle of Mike's weapon hit the person in the chest; and at the same instant, Mike pulled the trigger. With the muzzle in contact with the man, all the gas from the shot followed behind the bullet, entering his chest and causing a massive wound.

"Shit!" Mike muttered; and then he proceeded around the corner.

He moved through the house, finding no one else. Keying his radio, he said, "Clear."

"Police the body," Ted replied.

Mike moved back to the lifeless form lying on the kitchen floor. The wall was splattered with blood and tissue. He didn't bother checking the upper body, as it was a disgusting mess. Giving the pockets a quick pat, he removed a pistol from a holster on right hip, and magazine from the left front pocket. Rolling the body over, he removed an AK mag from one of the back pockets. Picking up the rifle that the corpse still gripped, he moved to the garage.

"What'd he have on him?" Ted asked.

"Couple of weapons," Mike replied.

"No radio?" Mike shook his head, "Good, I was afraid he had one; these two didn't," Ted said. Motioning to the two bodies on the floor with the muzzle of his weapon, "let's get the hell out of here."

"Where's Jeff?"

"In the buggy; they roughed him up, but he'll be alright."

"I'm sorry, guys. I never heard them coming," Jeff said from the buggy, holding his battered head.

"Don't sweat it man; at least you let us know something was up," Ted replied.

"I never would have thought about it." Jeff nodded his head, "you guys are good."

"That's why we went over the challenge/reply with you." Mike kicked one of the bodies on the floor. "This is the reason."

Before leaving, Jeff and the guys had gone over the procedure for their return. They would call him on the radio and let him know they were coming in. If there were a problem, and he wasn't alone, he was to reply with *come on in*. On the other hand, if it were clear, he would reply with, *all clear*. It was a simple system that would sound innocuous to anyone hearing it.

They quickly headed home. Ted was still worried those guys

might have somehow managed to get a message out. Jeff sat in the passenger seat, not saying anything. He held his bloody face in his hands, letting his head bob against the rail. Ted looked over at him. It was obvious he was hurt; but it looked like he was mostly ashamed about what had happened.

# CHAPTER 4

I woke up feeling hot and sticky, a slight sweat covering me. Kicking off the blanket, I got up and looked at Mel. She was covered only in a sheet. *Good idea* I thought; time to go with only the sheet now. Scratching my head, I stumbled into the bathroom and turned on the shower before leaving a foamy piss in the bowl and my drawers in front of it. Finding my way back to the shower, I stepped in and let out a yelp. The water was cold as shit, but refreshing. Washing quickly, I grabbed fresh clothes and dressed. In the new world I wore my clothes for several days. Clean clothes were a luxury.

Wandering out to the kitchen, I opened the small fridge and grabbed the half gallon Mason pitcher that held the elixir that made life worth living, sweet tea. And my life was quickly coming to an end. We had plenty of sugar still, but the tea bags were running low. I limited myself to one glass a day, first thing in the morning; and I loved it. Tipping the Mason jar up, I let the magical liquid fall into the back of my mouth, and closed my eyes. I savored it for a moment, holding it there. *Wine ain't got shit on this,* I thought as I finally swallowed it.

I sipped the tea as I got my gear together. Since I was the only one up, I took the opportunity to clean my weapons. They'd gotten pretty wet the night before, and now was a good a time as any. Mel came out half way through the cleaning of my carbine. Seeing it disemboweled on her dining table wasn't the best good morning I could have offered.

"Hey babe," I said with a smile.

She folded her arms, leaning against the door to our room, "What do you think you're doing on my table?"

I held the bolt carrier of my AR up, "Looks like I'm cleaning my rifle."

"You have a workbench for that out in your shop," she replied with no sense of humor.

"Sorry babe. I was up early, and it was quiet." Looking down at the disassembled weapon, I added, "it's kind of like therapy."

She passed me going into the kitchen; "You need to keep the therapy to your shop."

I quickly reassembled the carbine and packed my kit as Mel lit the kerosene stove. "You going to be here for breakfast?" Mel asked.

Wiping the table with the handkerchief I kept in my cleaning kit, I smiled and replied, "That would be great."

"The girls would appreciate it."

Leaning the rifle against the wall, I asked, "Would you?"

Mel set a pan over the flame and looked up, "I know you're busy."

Walking over, I wrapped my arms around her, "I'm never too busy for you."

In reply, she reached back and rubbed my face. Her lack of words spoke more to me in that moment than anything she could have said. I fussed around the kitchen with her, grinding coffee for her in the small hand grinder; she preferred coffee in the morning. It was a secret I'd kept from everyone. I'd found a small bag of some froo froo artisanal coffee in the house with the guy that shot himself and brought it home to Mel. After mixing some of the last flour and water, I set the tortilla skillet on a burner and lit it. As the skillet heated, I headed for the girls' rooms.

Opening Taylor's door, I looked at her for a moment. It was always funny to me to see her sleeping; she always appeared to have been blasted into whatever position she was in. I sat on her bed and gave her a nudge, "Hey kiddo, wake up." She rolled over and looked up at me through squinted eyes. "You coming out for breakfast?"

She sat up, "Sure, I'm hungry."

"Get dressed; I'll get your sisters."

Going into Lee Ann and Little Bit's room, I grabbed the blanket covering Little Bit and jerked it off. "Rise and shine sleepy head!" She immediately curled into a ball. I did the same thing to Lee Ann, and she performed the same roly-poly routine as her sister. It brought back memories of my dad waking me up as a kid, or when he would come into the bathroom when I was taking a shower and toss ice water over the top of shower curtain. I grinned; these girls have it easy. I grabbed Lee Ann by the big toe and started to pull her out of bed. She kicked my hand with her other foot, and then looked up.

"Quit!" Seeing me, she apologized.

I smiled, "It's OK, come on; we're going to have breakfast."

Little Bit got up, rubbing her eyes and wandered out to the kitchen. Taylor was out there when I got to the kitchen; and Lee Ann came out right behind me. The girls helped, rolling the balls for the tortillas; and I pressed them out. A minute on the grill and they were ready. Our breakfast was simple, scrambled eggs wrapped in tortillas. It was nice sitting at the table with the girls and Mel, talking, laughing, just being together.

Taylor looked better today, actually smiling and laughing a little. It was good to see her bouncing back from it. Lee Ann was her normal self. It appeared to have had little effect on her, which was good, but could also be bad. Maybe it was because she didn't know for certain, unlike her sister, that she'd actually killed someone. Taylor knew. She'd looked the man in his eyes as she shot him, hard for anyone to deal with.

When breakfast was done I gave everyone a hug and strapped on my gear. Kind of a surreal version of the old days, getting ready for work; except now I put on a pistol and sling a carbine over my shoulder. Saying bye, I went out the door.

"Mornin'," Sarge said as I stepped out on the porch. I jumped at the sound of his voice and spun around.

"You scared the shit outta me! How long have you been out here?"

"A while, I saw you having breakfast with the girls and figured I'd let you be." He looked up at me and smiled, "you needed it." The dogs were at his feet and he was scratching Drake on the head.

"You hungry? I think there's a little left," I said.

He waved me off, "Nah, leave it for them girls."

"So, to what do I owe the pleasure of your smiling face this morning?"

"The boys found them guys last night," Sarge replied, a more serious tone in his voice.

"And?"

"And it's going to be a tough nut to crack. These guys found Jeff while Ted and Mikey were out sneaking around the woods."

I stopped and looked at him. Fearing the worst, I asked, "And?"

"They roughed him up pretty good, but they got dealt with; three more ole Billy Boy can add to the tally."

Relieved, I let out the breath I didn't realize I was holding. "That's gonna piss him off even more."

"That's what I figure."

"I guess we need to come up with a plan today."

"We'll work on it later. Right now we've got to go to town; the Captain wants to see us," Sarge said as he stood up. The dogs followed us out to the Hummer. Sarge opened the door to the Hummer, "hop in." Meathead immediately jumped in, taking up the passenger seat.

"What the hell does he want? We've got enough shit going on," I replied. Then I looked at the dog, "get your ass out of there." I opened the door and waited, Meathead just stared back at me.

"Let him be; he wants to go for a ride to."

Sarge started the truck and headed towards the gate. "Guess we're about to find out what ole Sheffield wants. Let's go get Thad and Danny; I want the guys to stay here. Between them and Ian's crew they should be able to keep this place secure while we're gone."

I shrugged, "Guess it won't hurt much to get out; I wanted to go to the store on the corner anyway today."

At Danny's house Thad and Danny hopped in with us, and I climbed up into the turret, thinking it would be a nicer ride. Danny offered to take the position, but I told him I wanted to. He could ride with Meathead.

"How are the girls?" Thad shouted.

I ducked my head down inside the truck. "Good; better than I would have thought really."

Thad smiled, "That's good news; I was worried about Taylor."

When I stood back up I saw Doc walking down the road, his ever-present backpack slung over his shoulder, and his weapon hanging from its sling. Sarge stopped beside him.

"Hop in with us Doc; we're going to town," Sarge said.

"Sounds good to me; got nothing else to do right now," Doc said as he climbed in beside Thad.

Doc looked at Meathead, "Damn that mutt stinks. Don't you ever give him a bath?"

Poking my head back inside I smiled, "Nope. Even if I did he'd still smell like death."

At the barricade Sarge stopped again; Ian and Jamie were there. "Mornin' Gyrene," Sarge said to Ian.

"Semper Fi," Ian replied with a smile.

"Keep your eyes open; that bunch of shit heads will probably be sniffin' around," Sarge said.

"We got this," Jamie replied.

Sarge smiled at her, "I know you do." Looking back at Ian, he said, "the guys are going to be doing roving patrols around the back door and a few other places."

Ian nodded. "Yeah, we're in contact with them; they're staying in touch on the radio."

Sarge nodded, "Good enough."

Ian looked up at me with one eye squinted. "You know how to run that thing?"

I patted the SAW; "I'm sure I'll figure it out."

Pointing at the muzzle, Jamie said, "Keep that pointed at the bad guys."

"I tried." I swiveled the weapon over the roof of the truck, "but it won't go down far enough to get to Sarge."

Jamie laughed. I thought I was out of his reach, until that the ball on the top of that damn walking stick hit me in the thigh. Luckily for me, it just off the mark the old man was aiming for. "You point a gun at me in a dream, and you better wake up and apologize," Sarge barked.

I ducked down. "I'm sorry," then acted like I was thinking, "sorry, sorry, sorry."

Thad erupted in laughter, then added, "Me too, I'm sorry."

Everyone caught on and before long it was one continuous chorus of *sorry* bombarding the old man between the laughter from all directions. Sarge looked around, "Keep it up you bunch of smart asses; keep it up." He paused for a moment, then added, "you can kiss my ass!" Stomping on the gas, the truck lurched forward. I was laughing so hard I had to catch myself. Thad slapped my leg, and I could hear him still chuckling.

We rode down to the little store and Sarge wheeled into the parking lot. Business was picking up and there were a number of people set up offering an assortment of things for trade. When Sarge stopped, I climbed out and slung my carbine, heading straight to one of the tables. It was filled with jars of honey and candles of assorted diameters.

"Hey Mario, Shelly; good to see you guys," I said, extending my hand. Mario gripped it and smiled.

"Good to see you too," he replied with a firm shake.

Shelly came around the table and gave me a hug. "It's good to see you too."

The rest of the guys came up, and I introduced everyone. Thad picked up one of the jars on the table, "That's some fine looking honey."

"Yeah, Mario runs D&J Apiary, a pretty big operation back in the day," I said.

"Still is," Shelly replied with a smile.

"I guess so; your staff wasn't much affected by all this," Sarge said.

"We lost a bunch, only because we couldn't get to them; but we've still got quite a bit," Mario answered.

"How's business?" Danny asked.

"Good, we've got plenty to trade," Mario replied.

"We'll take some," Sarge said, sliding four jars across the table.

"You guys can have them; it's good to see Morgan, and to meet you fellas," Mario said.

Sarge reached into his pocket; "I appreciate it, but we'll pay." He held out a silver eagle, "this be enough?"

Mario smiled, "If you insist," he said as he took the coin.

Sarge smiled, "I do. Thank you for the trade; this'll be a real nice treat for everyone."

Mario pocketed the coin, then reached out and tapped the star on my chest. "What's that all about; I see you guys are all wearing them."

"Eh, I was kind of made a Sheriff," I replied.

"Made?" Mario asked.

I waved him off, "It's a long story."

"Why aren't you guys wearing one?" Shelly asked Sarge.

"Cause we're not part of it. We're still in the Army, so we can't be civilian law enforcement," He stabbed a thumb in my direction, "I work for him."

Thad laughed and I snorted, "Yeah, fat chance."

"Are you really a Sheriff?" Shelly asked.

"As real as they get now-a-days; why you need something?" I asked.

Shelly looked at Mario, "Well, maybe. I was going to handle it; but if you're the law," he trailed off, "I don't like having anyone deal with my problems."

"You know me; I'll help you in any way I can. What's up?"

Mario nodded his head, "You'll see here in a minute, 'cause here it comes."

We all turned to see two men walking down the row of tables. At each they'd stop and talk to who was there; and at a couple, take something from the table before moving on to the next.

"What's that about?" Danny asked.

"They say it's to pay for their protection, that they protect the traders here; so they should be paid for their service," Shelly replied.

Looking at Mario, I asked, "Have you seen any trouble around here?"

"The only trouble we have is them; they want honey." He turned and looked at the Kawasaki Mule sitting behind him; "and of course they want that."

"They want candles too; actually, they want everything. They take from everyone around here," Shelly added.

"Fuck them," Sarge snorted.

"That's what I said," Mario replied. "They haven't tried too hard yet, only because I've got just as many guns as they do."

I looked at Mario wide-eyed, "They got that many?" And smiled.

Mario smiled in return, "Here anyway."

The two men approached the table, looking us over as they did. We all moved to make room for them just so we could hear what they had to say.

"Mario, you have ours ready for us?" The taller of the two asked.

"I'll tell you the same thing I told you last time, fuck off."

"And we told you last time that wasn't going to work for long," the man replied. He waved his arm out behind him, "everyone else here pays; you have to too."

"And why is that?" I asked.

He looked at me, "This don't concern you none; mind your own business."

When Thad was serious his voice took an even deeper baritone, "It is our business."

"Unless you plan to pay for your honey, do like the man said; fuck off," Sarge said.

The man looked back at Mario, "Billy's not going to be

happy about this; he wanted those candles. He said to tell you if you gave us any trouble that you'd have to deal with him next time."

"Billy?" Sarge shouted, "Tall fucker with a beard, black hair?"

The two men stiffened a bit, "Yeah." He looked at me, then the badge. "You the ones that killed our three men the other day?"

"No; my daughters killed two of them," I said.

Mario interrupted the conversation, "Look, I'll give you a peace offering."

The man looked at Mario, "I knew you'd come around to your senses."

I looked at Mario, trying to let him know that we had his back. He winked at me in reply. Looking back to the two men, he said, "It's over here," and headed towards the Mule.

The two men followed him, and I started to, but Shelly grabbed my arm. I looked at her curiously. She shook her head, so I stopped and watched Mario lead the men to collect their tax. At the Mule Mario reached into the bed and pulled out a box and handed it to one of the men, then a second to the other man.

"That's honey," Mario said as he picked up another box. "This one has candles; who wants it?" Mario asked with a smile.

"I'll take it," one of them replied.

Mario lifted the two top flaps of the box, quickly gripping the sides, and pitched it at them. The bees had been in the box all morning and weren't real happy about it. They exploded from the box, covering both of their faces. Mario casually walked away as the men screamed and dropped their boxes, the jars breaking as they hit the ground.

"Oh hell no," Thad said. "I don't do bees," and started to walk away.

Danny was hot on his heels, "Me neither."

Sarge started to laugh as the two men slapped at the mass of bees on their faces and arms, only encouraging them to sting even more. As soon as the first bee was struck it released the *sting here* pheromone. Both men screamed and thrashed as they tried to get the stinging insects off them.

Doc and I responded the same, "Holy shit!"

Mario stood back and watched as one of the guys broke out into a run, what I call a blind lateral panic. No clear destination, just a deep need to get the hell away from where he currently was. The other man fell to the ground, his face already beginning to swell.

"Damn Mario, I ain't never seen anyone use bees as a weapon!" Sarge shouted.

"Yeah, I picked the meanest damn hive I have. I got stung every time I worked the damn thing. It was hell getting them into the box." He looked at the man writhing on the ground, "but worth it."

"I guess so; that ole boy sure doesn't look good," Sarge said, looking at the man on the ground.

"That guy's going to be dead in a minute; I believe he's allergic to bees," Doc said.

"That was the craziest thing I've ever seen; I mean damn," I said, still shocked at what I was seeing.

"Shame that honey was wasted," Sarge said, pointing to the two boxes.

"Oh, that wasn't honey," Mario replied.

"What the hell was in them?" I asked.

"Pig shit," Mario replied with a smile. "I'm not going to waste honey."

Mario's reply set Sarge to laughing again; he slapped his knee and pointed at Mario, "Damn I like your style!"

Just as Doc predicted, the man on the ground slowly stopped struggling. Even after he was motionless the bees continued to sting him, dying in the hundreds. Eventually they began to form a ball in a small oak tree; they'd found their queen.

"You going to get them back, trap the swarm?" I asked.

"Hell no; like I said, they were mean to start with. They served their purpose," Mario replied.

"That one old boy will probably make it home; they're going to be really pissed off," Sarge said.

Now that the remaining bees were making their way to the tree, Thad and Danny walked up.

—※—※—※—※—※—

"We're going to have to deal with them soon; we can't leave something like that wandering around out here," Thad said.

Sarge was still staring at the man on the ground, "We will soon enough."

Danny and Doc walked down the tables and returned the items taken from folks sitting there. A couple of the people expressed fear, not wanting to take the items back, saying they didn't want any trouble. Danny would just leave it on their table and walk away if they wouldn't take it. Doc was looking the people over as he walked. Seeing a group, he stopped and watched them for a minute; turning back, he called Thad and waved him over.

Thad walked over, "What's up?"

"You said there was a group that came through that looked sick the other day." He pointed to a group of people sitting on the sidewalk in front of the store, "is that them?"

Thad studied them for a moment, "Yeah, I recognize the guy sitting beside the wagon. He's the one that came and got water."

Doc nodded in their direction, "Were those kids with them?"

"They had kids; I can't say it was those kids."

Doc walked towards the group; a woman sat wiping the chest of one of the children with a cloth. He stopped a short distance from them, "Hi there."

The woman looked up but didn't respond. Doc took a good look at the child. He was small and frail, seven, maybe eight years old, and dirty. The woman went back to mopping at the kid's chest; and Doc took a good look at the lesion she was wiping. As the woman tended to the open sore, the child coughed and hacked. Doc took a couple of steps back. Everyone in the group had a cough, raspy and angry sounding. Having seen enough, he made way back to the group.

"That's a problem over there," he said, pointing at the sad cluster.

"What's that?" Sarge asked.

Still staring at them, Doc replied, "I can't be certain, but I think they have a pretty nasty case of TB running through all of them."

Shocked, I replied, "TB?"

"Can't be certain without a test, but I've seen it before; and it sure as hell looks like it."

"What can we do for them?" Danny asked.

"Nothing. It takes some serious antibiotics to clear that shit up, especially as advanced as they are. The kid has an open lesion on his chest, probably goes in pretty deep too."

"Only thing we could do is quarantine 'em," Sarge added.

I looked over at him, "How the hell are we going to do that? We'd have to feed them and everything; we can't do that. Not to mention that taking people against their will is screwed up."

"They're going to spread that shit wherever they go; they're a walking time bomb," Doc added. Then he looked back at them, "it would be more merciful to just kill them."

"What?" Danny asked.

Very seriously, Doc looked at him, then at all of us, "Have you ever seen anyone die from this shit?" He looked around again. "Of course not. Here in the US we could handle it when it popped up; but in the rest of the world it's a killer, and it's a miserable lingering death."

"We'll worry about them later; we got to get to town," Sarge replied.

Loading up, we headed into Umatilla. It had been a while since I'd come through town, and the profound change was really starting to show. The streets were littered with leaves and limbs. We had to drive around a large limb near the old Ocala National Forest building; it was blocking the road. In town the parking lot of the Save-A-Lot was littered with trash; it made me wonder where it all came from. The Pizza Hut had been looted to no end; all the windows were busted out, the blinds hanging out and swaying in the breeze. I'm sure the Save-A-Lot was in the same condition; we just couldn't see inside from the road.

At the intersection of Central Ave and Bulldog Lane is another convenience store; and a McDonald's sits caddy-corner across the street. This was the new hub of life in Umatilla. This store, just like the one in Altoona was used as a market of sorts. A number of crude stalls filled the area under the canopy, mingling with the gas pumps. The traders there were offering anything they thought someone might want, and a load of crap no one would.

As we passed by, we drew the attention of everyone there. As always, the kids that seemed to be everywhere these days came running out towards the road. From my perch in the turret I got a bird's-eye view of them as they waved and whistled. For better or worse, the change had returned kids to a time maybe sixty years in the past. Boys ran in groups, many mounted on bikes. Spears, bows and BB guns were nearly universal. The natural state of things was returning.

The adults all stood to watch as we passed, one woman waving. I waved back as we rolled through. Leaving Umatilla, we entered an open stretch of highway, and Sarge sped up. The wind in my face felt nice. I stood up and closed my eyes, enjoying the sense of speed as the wind rushed past. We passed the two grocery stores, their parking lots now empty, those that had been camped there having moved on. They had left their trash strewn about, mountains of it. At this point I dropped back into the turret and shouldered the SAW; this area just didn't feel very friendly.

Sarge slowed as we approached the barricade of cars just outside Eustis; this time though, it was manned by Guardsmen. The car serving as a gate was pushed aside, and we rolled through without having to come to a stop. The guys and gals at the barricade waved as we passed through; it was nice to see friendly faces. I observed the lakefront as we passed it on the way to the armory. It was crowded with people, each of the little pavilions on the boardwalk along the lake packed with people fishing. It almost looked as though they were each claimed by a family or group of one sort or another. A couple of these small shelters had blankets or tarps hung to block the sun; and I saw smoke coming from more than one of them. Nothing like cooking up a fresh catch.

Rolling into the armory, we were met by Sheffield and Livingston. "Well, well, look what the cat dragged in," Livingston said with a smile.

I popped my head out of the turret, "Dr. Livingston I presume?" Livingston smiled as I dropped down in the truck.

"Morning Captain," Sarge said as he got out of the truck.

Sheffield stuck his hand out, "Morning Linus." Sarge shook his hand as the two headed for the building.

Livingston was talking with Thad and Danny when I finally extracted myself from the truck. Livingston looked at me. "Morning Sheriff," he said with a big smile. In reply I gave him the finger.

"So what's up?" I asked.

"Let's go inside," Livingston replied.

Following him into the armory, I noticed an older black man sitting in a chair against the wall. What struck me about him was the crease in the jeans he wore, like they'd just been pressed. He had a hat pulled down over his eyes and his arms crossed over his chest, like he was asleep. A tooth pick was hanging limply from his lips.

"Who's that?" I asked Livingston.

"You'll meet him later; we've got bigger issues at the moment."

In the conference room it felt stuffy; the lighting was dim as well, giving an overall depressing feeling to the place. As we sat down, the lights in the room finally flickered to life.

Sheffield looked up, "About damn time."

"Alright, we're here; what's up?" Sarge asked.

"Where's your crew?" Livingston asked.

"They were up all night, so we left them behind," Sarge replied.

Sheffield raised his eyebrows, "Trouble?"

"Nothing we can't handle."

Sheffield looked at Livingston, "You want to lead off?"

Livingston opened a folder in front of him. "First the bad news; those buses of DHS prisoners never made it to Frostproof."

"What?" I asked.

"We received a radio call from Frostproof, wondering if we had any information about that. We sent out a heavy patrol from our end; and they sent one from theirs. In an effort to prevent the convoy from having to drive through heavily populated areas, they were taking a longer route, using highway 33 out of Groveland.

"We found the buses on Fussell Road just north of Polk City. The buses were shot to shit and burned. One of the gun trucks was still on scene. We were able to account for eleven troops KIA on scene with six MIA." Livingston closed the folder, "this was a very well coordinated complex ambush."

Sarge sat listening, rolling a pencil on the table, "Do we have any idea who pulled it off?"

"We found several fighting positions with mountains of brass, and wire for command-detonated devices. It had to be other DHS assets."

"Were there any DHS casualties?"

"There were several corpses on the buses, but they were burned so badly we couldn't tell much about them."

Sarge rolled the pencil across the table, "So these assholes are on the loose again."

"It looks that way," Sheffield added.

"You think they're headed back here?" Danny asked.

Sarge looked across the table, "I can guarantee they are; those assholes are wanting some payback."

"We don't know where they are or what they're up to. We've discussed this with Frostproof; and we think that it would be unlikely that they would try to return here. We believe they are linking up with additional DHS units," Sheffield said.

"Of course they linked up; we assume that. Whoever ambushed the convoy had their shit together; and you can bet your ass we'll see them again," Sarge said.

"Great; just what we need with the trouble we're having now," I said.

"What's up?" Livingston asked.

"They're just a local group throwing their weight around; nothing we can't handle," Sarge said.

"Sure you don't need some help?"

Sarge waved him off. "Nah; we can handle these dipshits. Hell, we've already killed six of them."

"Seven," I corrected him. Sarge looked at me, "The bees killed number seven."

"Oh yeah, forgot about that; damndest thing I ever saw," Sarge replied with a smile.

"Bees killed him?" Livingston asked, a nervous look on his face.

Sheffield waved a hand, "I don't want to know about this shit right now."

"While we're on the bad news train, there's something else we need to talk about," Doc said.

"We're all ears," Sheffield replied, thankful for the change in direction.

"I saw some people earlier today that I'm fairly certain were carrying TB."

"TB?" Sheffield nearly shouted.

"I'm not sure which form it is, but I'm reasonably certain it's TB. You need to spread the word to your people."

"What can we do about it?" Livingston asked.

"Right now the only treatment is not catching it. Washing hands is a big one of course. You should have your people in particulate masks if they're interacting with the public; you won't know who has it. Anyone coughing should be a concern; but that's the only thing you'll probably notice."

Livingston looked at Sheffield, "Should we quarantine people?"

Sarge laughed, "How do you propose to do that? Where you going to put them, how you going to feed them?"

"It would be the best course of action, but I don't think it's very practical in the current environment," Doc added.

"We'll have to find a solution to this situation; we can't simply allow infected people to move about freely," Sheffield added.

"We don't have the resources to confine anyone; if you choose to go that route it's totally on you," I said.

"We'll figure something out. But for now we'll spread the word here in town, and you should do the same as well."

"We will; but my biggest concern at the moment is the DHS issue. If these guys come back looking for revenge it's going to get pretty hairy," I replied.

"We've already got an issue we're dealing with; we don't need this right now," Danny said.

"Right now we don't know where these guys from the busses are going. If anyone sees them or thinks they do, we need to pass the word, immediately," Livingston said.

"We'll keep an eye out on our end; anything else?" Sarge asked.

Sheffield looked at Livingston, "Go get Cecil."

Livingston left the room and returned with the old man I saw sitting outside. "This is Cecil Montgomery," Livingston said; then he introduced all of us to him. "Cecil is going to oversee the planting of crops. He's got a tractor, and said he'll lend his tractor if we supply the fuel."

"That's great news; we've got some plants going as well," Thad added.

"We have a lot to get going if we want to try and feed these folks," Cecil said.

"How are you going to protect the crops once they're planted?" Sarge asked.

"We'll handle that," Livingston said.

"What do you need from us then? You wouldn't be telling us about this if you didn't need something," Sarge said.

Sheffield shifted in his seat, "We do need something from you. We need Morgan to handle the civilian law enforcement issues here in town."

My head snapped around, "What? What's wrong with your Sheriff? You've got one here in town."

"He's missing," Livingston said.

"Missing?" Sarge asked.

"We don't know where he is. He disappeared a couple of days ago; we're looking for him, but no one has seen him."

"No one's admitting to it," Sarge shot back.

"Right now we have no reason to believe anything underhanded has happened to him; he's simply missing. What we need from you is to come to town every couple of days to deal with any issues that come up. We'll handle detaining anyone if the need arises; but you'll have to come to town to deal with them," Sheffield said.

I listened to what he had to say, growing more and more irritated. "This is bullshit; I don't have time for this crap. You guys hung this deal on me, giving me an enormous area to oversee; and I reluctantly accepted it. Now you want me to have to come down here every other day; we have enough to do without this crap."

"Look, we need to keep things separated; we as the military can't get into civilian law enforcement. That's where you come in," Sheffield replied.

"Name a new Sheriff, pick out a new one."

"We thought about that; but for now, you're it."

I thought about it for a minute, "Then just call us on the radio when you have something that needs attention. I don't have time to ride down here just to see *if* you have something that needs my attention." Thinking about it a little more, I added, "you need a judge; that's what you need. I shouldn't be the one making decisions on what to do with people caught messing up."

"We're working on that as well," Livingston replied.

"Anything else?" I asked.

"Cecil here will need some help; was hoping you guys could assist," Livingston replied.

Sarge looked over, "What can we do for you Cecil?"

"We might need some fertilizer; and I could use a bigger disc. I have a forty-eight incher, but a sixty would be better."

"We'll look around and see what we can find," Sarge replied.

"I think I know where one is," Danny offered.

Sarge slapped the table, "There you go; we'll round it up and get it down here. Gentlemen, if we're done here we've got plenty of work to tend to."

"That's all for now," Sheffield replied.

We filed out of the room, and could hear the generator powering the lights inside humming out in the maintenance building. Livingston came out and said something to one of his NCOs, and soon it was silenced. Cecil came out and Sarge waved him over.

"You're going to try and plant enough to feed these folks?" He asked.

"We'll do our best; someone needs to do something."

"If there is anything we can do, just let us know."

Cecil removed his hat. "I have another idea." Looking back, he said, "but these boys don't want to hear it."

"What's that?" I asked.

"You boys is from up Umatilla way, right?" I nodded. "You know the old orange juice plant?" Again I nodded. "You know about the power plant there, right?"

"Yeah, they have a small gas turbine there don't they?" I asked.

Cecil nodded, "Sure do; and it was off line when everything went to hell. I bet it would run."

"So you want to try and restart the plant?" Sarge asked. Cecil nodded.

"That would be a lot of work. Morgan might know a little about it, but the rest of us damn sure don't," Danny said.

Cecil looked at me, "You an electrician?"

"I was for a long time; worked on gas turbines around the country for several years."

"And you worked for the power company," Danny added.

"For a little while," I replied to Danny. Then I looked back at Cecil, "but I don't know anything about that plant."

Cecil smiled, "I do; maintained it for years before it was shut down."

"Really?" Sarge said, rubbing his chin. "You know it inside and out then?"

"Like my wife's ass in the dark," Cecil said with a smile.

Sarge smiled, "I think we're going to get along just fine."

"What you guys are talking about would take a lot of work. We'd have to do a shitload of line work, opening switches and whatnot to regulate where the power goes. It would take a small army," I said.

"It wouldn't be that hard; open a few switches, maybe replace a few transformers, and we could have some power," Cecil said.

"What about the gas? You said it was a gas turbine; I assume you mean natural gas," Thad asked.

Cecil nodded, "Indeed it is." He leaned in a little closer, looking around, "did you know there's still gas flowing?"

"What? How could there still be gas?" Danny asked.

"It isn't everywhere, but it is still flowing in places. I've seen it," Cecil replied.

"Alright, before we get too far ahead of ourselves on this, we'll get you a disc and bring it up here in a few days. I'd like you to go with us to the plant so we could look at it and see if it's even possible. You can show us the gas too," Sarge said.

Cecil smiled, "Sounds good to me. You fellers get me a disc, and I'll get some crops planted."

We headed for the truck; it was time to get back home. Thad came up beside me as I walked. "I been thinking Morgan; remember the day we saw them sick folks at the barricade? Tyler was there with the kids; they were playing with those kids. If it is TB, they could be sick."

I looked around, "Where's Doc? We need to talk to him about this, and see what he thinks."

Doc was waiting for us at the truck. Thad told him the same thing he'd said to me, and Doc thought about it for a minute. "You're not going to like it, but we need to quarantine them, keep them away from everyone for a couple of weeks."

"Is that really necessary?" I asked.

"At the moment it's all we can do; if they are carrying TB, they're still in the incubation period. They would not be symptomatic yet, and making others sick."

I sighed, "Alright. When we get back I'll give them the news; they should be fine, but it is better safe than sorry."

All I could think about on the ride back was having to tell Tyler and Brandy that we were locking them into their house. The thought of taking someone's freedom like that was hard. I know if I were the one receiving the news, it damn sure wouldn't go down easy. I surely hoped they would understand. I was sitting behind the SAW, scanning the sides of the road; so I never really saw any of it.

Rolling through the gate, I waved at Jamie as we passed. She was smiling, but the smile slowly faded; guess I wasn't smiling back. Sarge went to Danny's house, Brandy was probably there. After climbing out of the truck, Sarge asked, "You want me to do it?"

"No, I need to do it. Let's go see if they're here."

Walking up to the house, Jeff was sitting on the porch looking rough. Both eyes were black, and his lip was swollen. I stopped on the step, "How you feeling man?"

He stared straight ahead, "Like shit."

"Don't sweat it brother, it all worked out," Danny said.

Jeff looked down at the ground. "I didn't even see them; they snuck right up on me."

"It's alright; we'll deal with them soon enough," I replied.

He looked at me with a look I'd never seen before, hate maybe. I wasn't sure, but it was intense. "I want to be there."

I nodded and went into the house. I could hear Brandy out on the back porch talking to Bobbie. I went out there with the guys in tow. As I stepped out the back door I looked for Doc. He was behind Sarge, and I motioned for him to come up.

Looking at Bobbie, I asked, "Where's Mel?"

"She's at your house doing something with the girls."

Looking at Brandy, I let out a long breath. "Brandy, where's Tyler?"

She pointed down to the pond; he was there fishing with the kids. I called out to him and waved for him to come over.

"What's wrong?" She asked.

"I'll explain it when Tyler gets here."

Tyler came bounding up the stairs. "What's up?" He asked, looking at those assembled.

I paused for a moment, not knowing exactly what to say, how to say it. "Remember the other day at the barricade, the people that were there?" He nodded, but seemed unable to speak. "Doc thinks they have TB; your little ones ran out and played with them, remember?" He nodded again.

"Is there something wrong?" Brandy asked.

"I don't know exactly how to say this, but we're going to need you guys to stay in your house for two weeks. If they are infected, we need to make sure the kids didn't contract it. We can't have that spreading here."

Tyler stood motionless, taking it in. Brandy seemed to panic.

"Why?" She asked, looking at Doc. "Do you think they're sick?"

"We don't know; and it's just a precaution. It's only for two weeks," Doc replied.

"We'll bring you food and anything else you need. It's just best for everyone here," I said.

"Tyler, you OK with this?" Sarge asked.

Tyler looked at him and nodded. "Yeah. I, I understand why." He extended his hand to Brandy. "Come on; let's go home."

Brandy rose to her feet, taking the kids by the hand, and started towards the door. She stopped and looked back; tears were already staining her cheeks.

"It'll be OK, Miss Brandy; we'll take care of you. If you need anything at all, just let me know," Thad said with a smile.

"I'll be over later to check the kids and explain some things to you," Doc said.

Tyler nodded, and they left the house.

"What's this all about?" Bobbie asked.

"Just what they said; they could be sick, and we can't take any chances," Danny replied.

"And you think it's TB?" Bobbie asked.

"We're not certain. Some people came through that may have it, so it's better safe than sorry."

"I'm going home; I'll see you guys later," I said. I was tired and wanted to just get away for a minute. Crossing the fence, I could hear Little Bit yelling in the house. Opening the door, I was greeted with chaos. Mel was trying to hold Little Bit down on the sofa. She in turn wasn't having any of it, and was kicking and screaming.

"What the hell's going on?"

Mel looked up exasperated, "She's got a tick, and I'm trying to get it off her."

"Just wait a minute, wait a minute!" Little Bit shouted.

"Chill out kiddo; it's just a tick. Let Mom get it off," I said.

"Let me see it, I want to see it," Little Bit said.

"Look; it's right here," Mel said.

Little Bit looked at the parasite, "Eww, it's so big, get it off!"

I laughed out loud. It was too funny; first she didn't want Mel to mess with it, and now she wants it off. "Just sit still then," I said.

Using tweezers, Mel gripped the tick and quickly snatched it out. Mel held it up, "There, that wasn't so bad was it?"

"Let me see it," Little Bit said, taking the tweezers. She took it outside and placed the tick on the handrail. She then mashed it. The door was open and I was watching her, "Ewww, that's so gross!"

She made me laugh again; the kid was so funny.

Mel sat back on the sofa, "What are you doing home?"

Sitting beside her and laying my head back on the cushion, I said, "Just needed a break."

"What's going on?"

Closing my eyes, I told her about the people we suspected of having TB, and how dangerous it was. And then I told her about having to quarantine Tyler and Brandy for two weeks.

"That's so sad; I hope they are alright."

Sitting up, I said, "I'm sure they are; it's just a precaution." Looking around, I asked, "where are the girls?"

"Where do you think? Sleeping."

Looking back towards their rooms, I asked, "How are they doing?"

"Better now. I think they'll be fine," Mel said as she stood up. "Want some chips?"

"Wow, you make some?"

"Yeah; made them today with Bobbie."

"That'd be good."

Mel went to the kitchen and returned with a bowl of kudzu chips and a glass of tea. I smiled at her, "I knew there was a reason I kept you around."

Handing me the glass and bowl, she slid onto the sofa beside me. "That's the only reason you keep me around?"

Sticking a chip in my mouth, I glanced sideways at her. "You do have other worthy assets."

"Hmm, is that so?"

Smiling, I replied, "Oh yeah."

We spent the afternoon lounging on the sofa, snoozing, not asleep, but almost there. Little Bit even piled in as well, lying on the opposite end with her legs draped over me. It was pleasant, just hanging out. As the light coming through the windows began to dim, I patted Mel's ass, "I need to get up."

She sat up. "Me too; I need to go help with dinner."

# CHAPTER 5

MIKE STOOD IN FRONT OF the safe again, Sharpie in hand. He'd been working on it for about an hour and determined there were three wheels on the lock, so he only had to figure out three numbers, a simple group two lock. By turning the spindle he'd listened for the faint tick of the flywheel, picking up the first wheel in the wheel pack. As the rotation continued, he heard the faint click of the additional two wheels, known as picking-up the wheels.

He'd already determined the contact area on the drive cam. This wheel isn't associated with the combination directly; but once Mike knew where on the dial the drive cam made contact, he was able to begin his graph of possible combos. Knowing the contact area for the drive cam, between seventy and eighty, Mike spun the dial to twenty-five, known as parking the wheels.

From this point he slowly rotated the dial again, as the dial passed twenty-five he listed for the faint click of the drive cam, that click he ignored and the rest he counted, confirming there were only three wheels. Now for the hard part.

Mike spun the dial to the right and set the dial on zero. From there he spun the dial, listening for the faint click of the contact area. Each time he heard it, he marked the numbers on the safe with the marker. Each time, he reset the dial three digits off from the previous search, doing this around the entire dial. When he was done, he had a series of numbers marked on the door of the safe. With the numbers he needed, Mike left the safe and went to a small room that served as an office. Rummaging around in the desk, he found a pad of graph paper and pencil and headed back to the bedroom.

Sitting on the foot of the bed, he laid out his graph. For the short axis on the left side, he wrote down the contact points for the drive cam, and then one set for the right side. The long axis of the graph, he laid out with the three-digit offset of the dial, starting at one, then four, seven and so on. Just as he was about to get to the good part, Ted came into the room.

"Hey, ruck up, time for a walkabout."

"Aw man, come on, I've almost got this thing whipped," Mike moaned.

"It ain't going anywhere, let's go."

Shaking his head, Mike tossed the pad on the bed and followed Ted out of the room. After getting his gear on, he found Ted in the kitchen.

"Alright, let's do this."

"You carrying that thing?" Ted asked, pointing to Sarge's Minimi.

Mike looked at the short weapon and shrugged, "Yeah, if we bump into anyone it'll get their attention."

Ted picked up his M203, "Yeah, I know what you mean."

The light outside was fading, and when they stepped out, Doc was standing in the front yard. He looked back over his shoulder, "You guys going on a prowl?"

"Yeah; when did you get back?" Mike asked.

"Few minutes ago."

Mike reached into his cargo pocket and tossed Doc the

stethoscope. Doc caught it and inquired, "When did you take this?"

"Early this morning," Mike replied with a smile.

Doc stuck the instrument into his pocket, "Don't take my shit without asking dickhead."

"You got it back; besides, it was for some important shit."

"That safe? It's probably full of dildos," Doc fired back.

Ted started laughing, "Now that would be funny!"

"Hey, where's the old man?" Mike asked.

"He's still at Danny's. Tyler and his family may have been exposed to TB, so we quarantined them."

Mike screwed his face up, "Damn, TB; that's going to suck."

"Yeah, well, hopefully it's nothing," Doc replied as they made their way down the street.

The guys went to the south, towards the tree line at the end of the street. They were being careful to be sporadic in their patrols, never going the same way twice. There wasn't a real plan to these foot patrols, just to be moving and keeping an eye out. After going into the woods about thirty yards, they turned east and increased the interval between them. The pace also slowed, stopping often to look and listen. There was no conversation, no cutting up. While this was more than likely to be as uneventful as the previous patrols, all three took it seriously.

The area was thickly covered with palmettos and scrub pines. The brush made everything invisible from their waists down. All three were wearing NVGs flipped up on their helmets. It wasn't totally dark yet, but the light was fading fast. They'd made their way along the southern border of the neighborhood and were just turning to the north to walk the eastern side when Doc saw movement. His head snapped around as his weapon came up, and he flipped the NVG down to get a better look.

Through the green murk of the device he could clearly see the side of a head, an ear and part of a black clad shoulder.

"Contact right!" Doc shouted as he squeezed the trigger on his weapon, at the same moment he was dropping to the ground. The world closing in around them as they dropped into the palmettos, Ted and Mike both swiveled, taking one step forward to pivot while dropping down as well. Mike opened up with the short machinegun; soon all three men were firing.

Ted rose up to his knees, "Moving!" He shouted.

Almost in unison, Doc and Mike screamed, "Move!"

Ted jumped up and ran forward thirty or so feet, firing as he did, before dropping down. Once on the ground, he called out, "Check!", letting the other two know he was changing mags.

"Okay!" Doc replied, then turned towards Mike, "Moving!"

Mike paused on the trigger for an instant, "Move!" At the same Ted's rifle re-entered the fight.

Mike could see Doc, and waited for him to reach his new position. As Doc dropped out of sight, he called out, "Check!" He was answered with an "Okay!" from Ted and Mike.

Mike continued to work the brush with the machinegun in short bursts. As soon as he heard Doc's weapon begin firing, he rose to his knees, "Moving!" Ted and Doc acknowledged the call, and soon Mike was up and rushing forward as well.

Ted's radio crackled in his ear, "*What the hell's going on out there?*" Sarge asked.

"Wait one," Ted replied.

During the encounter none of the men noticed the sporadic, ineffectual return fire. As Mike was moving forward, two men broke cover, trying to run. Mike shouldered the weapon and let out a long burst cutting down both men. Seeing the two men fall, Mike scanned the area and noted that Doc and Ted were still firing slowly into the bush. Mike didn't see any other movement or hear any return fire, so he called out, "Cease fire, cease fire!"

Doc's head appeared above the palmettos, like a prairie dog coming out of its hole. He looked around, then at Mike, "Clear?"

"I don't see anyone else; there are two down up there," Mike jutted the muzzle of the weapon forwards.

"Change the belt on that weapon before we move up to check them out," Ted said.

Mike dropped to his knee and pulled out a green plastic container with a belt of ammo for the weapon. He pulled the leading end out and connected it to what was left of the other one. With the weapon now ready, he rose to his feet, "Ready."

The three men moved up, Mike staying a little behind them to provide cover should it be needed. Ted found the two men, lying face down. As he approached them he put a round into the head of each of the bodies, he wasn't taking any chances. When in doubt, gray matter out. Doc came up and flipped the first body over, "Oh shit; this isn't good."

"Nope; if they're already sniffing around, we're behind the eight ball," Ted replied.

"What is it?" Mike asked.

"They're DHS goons," Ted replied. He then knelt down and gripped a subdued DHS patch on the shoulder of the corpse and ripped it off.

Doc quickly searched the two bodies. As he was doing so, Ted called Sarge, "Hey Swamp Rat."

"*What's up?*"

"We made contact on the southeast corner, two DHS goons."

There was a pause, then Sarge replied, "*You sure about that?*"

"Yeah, bringing you back a souvenir."

"*Take it to Danny's place.*"

"Ten roger,"

The weapons were stripped from the bodies, as well as the packs and any other gear. They distributed the load amongst themselves and headed for Danny's place.

———— ✻ —— ✻ —— ✻ —— ✻ ——

Fred and Aric were sitting on the couch together; she was napping in his arms. Thad, as always, was outside. If he wasn't tending to the hogs, he was working in the garden at Danny's. He was one of those people that always needed to be outdoors. This time Jess and Miss Kay were with him. He'd cut a palm down earlier, and they were slicing it up and feeding it to the hogs, well, most of it.

"This is pretty tasty," Miss Kay said, holding a small piece of swamp cabbage up to inspect.

"Told you; we eat it too," Thad replied as he chucked a piece into the pen where the hogs immediately set on it.

"I like it raw. It's ok cooked, but I like how it crunches when it's fresh," Jess added.

Kay took another bite, "I think you're right, Jess. I like the crunch too; this would be wonderful in a salad. How did you guys find this?"

Thad tossed another handful of cabbage into the pen. "Morgan; he comes up with all kinds of stuff."

"He seems a little strange to me," Kay replied, wrinkling her nose.

Jess wiped her forehead with the back of her hand, "He's a good guy though; he'll do anything in the world for you."

Almost in a whisper, Kay replied, "But did you hear what he did to that man?" She looked around as though someone could be listening. "He just shot him in the head."

"Some people just need shootin', Miss Kay. Morgan just comes to the realization a little faster than most," Thad said.

"And does it," Jess added.

Kay shook her head, "That just doesn't seem normal to me."

Thad stopped for a moment. "Miss Kay, those men were trying to take his daughters, all three of them at once. Any man would do the same. We just live in a world now where justice can come immediately. No long drawn-out trials, no bunch of lawyers trying to find some loophole you get you off on. If you did it, you did it."

"But what if he's wrong? You can't undo that sort of thing," Kay replied.

"When you're caught in the act, there's no question."

The conversation was interrupted by a sudden burst of gunfire. Everyone immediately looked in the direction of the cacophony of sound. Thad reached for his shotgun, never far from him, then looked at Jess. She already had her pistol out.

"Get Miss Kay inside."

"Come on Miss Kay; let's go," Jess said, taking her by the arm.

As they were going into the back door, Aric and Fred were coming out. Aric had his rifle, and Fred had a pistol.

"What was that?" Aric asked.

"We don't know," Jess replied as she ushered Miss Kay into the house.

The gunfire intensified, and the sound of fully automatic fire filled the air. Fred and Aric ran out to Thad; they stood together and listened.

"I wonder who it is?" Fred asked no one in particular.

"From the sound of the guns, I'd say it was Mike and Ted," Thad replied as he stared off into the distance.

After a few moments the fire died down, then stopped completely. Thad looked at Aric, "I'm going to find out what's going on. You guys stay here so Jess and Miss Kay aren't alone."

Aric nodded, and they started back towards the house. Jess appeared in the door as they got close, "It stopped?"

"Sounds like it, Thad's going to go see what's up," Fred replied.

Jess looked at Thad, "This is BS Thad; all I have is this pistol. I want a rifle. What the hell am I going to do with this if someone shows up with that kind of firepower?"

"Yeah, me too; I want a rifle," Fred added.

"Let me go see what's going on. We've got plenty of rifles; I'm sure we can get you guys one."

"Good," Jess replied sternly.

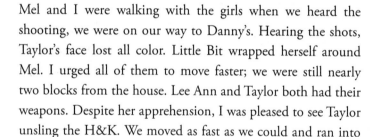

Mel and I were walking with the girls when we heard the shooting, we were on our way to Danny's. Hearing the shots, Taylor's face lost all color. Little Bit wrapped herself around Mel. I urged all of them to move faster; we were still nearly two blocks from the house. Lee Ann and Taylor both had their weapons. Despite her apprehension, I was pleased to see Taylor unsling the H&K. We moved as fast as we could and ran into Thad as he rounded the corner.

"What the hell's going on?" I asked.

"I don't know; you heading to Danny's?"

I nodded, and together we made our way to his house. Sarge, Danny and Jeff were on the front porch when we got there. Sarge filled us in on what he knew so far.

"The DHS, again?" Thad asked.

"They sure as hell got here faster than I thought they would," I added.

"What's this mean? We had to run from them before. Are we going to have to again?" Mel asked.

"I don't want to go back to the river," Little Bit cried.

"I'm not going!" Lee Ann stated.

"Ain't nobody going anywhere. We're going to finish this once and for all, right here," Sarge said.

"I agree," Danny added.

It wasn't long before the guys arrived. They piled the weapons and gear from the two men on the front porch. Mike started to go through the packs as Ted filled the old man in on what went down.

"Find any radios on 'em?" Sarge asked.

Ted shook his head, "No, I expected them to have comms, but we didn't find any."

"Hmm, that seems a little odd," Sarge said, rubbing his chin. "You sure they are DHS?"

Ted tossed the patch to him, "They both had these on."

Sarge looked at the patch. "Guess we'll have to assume they are. If they are starting to do recon of the area, we need to get ready for them."

"What are you thinking?" Danny asked.

"We need some defensive positions."

"Bunkers?" Ted asked.

The old man sat down on the edge of the porch. "It wouldn't hurt to have a couple. I also think we need to pull back from the road down there, and beef up the barricade so you can't just drive through it. And we need to create a fallback position at the first intersection; put a bunker there."

"How are we going to do that? We don't have any sandbags," Danny said.

Sarge looked up and smiled, "There's other ways to build bunkers. Right, Teddy?"

"Oh yeah; I've got an idea or two."

As we were talking, Fred and Aric walked up. "What's going on?" Aric asked.

Sarge filled them in on what we knew, and that he wanted to build some bunkers. I could tell Fred had something on her mind. She was chewing on her fingernails; and I'd known her long enough now to know that was her signal that she wanted to say something.

"What's on your mind, Fred?" I asked.

The question surprised her, and she looked around. "Oh, well; Jess and I were talking."

"And?" Sarge prodded with a smile.

"And, well; we want rifles." She said it in the way a teenager would first try to ask for a car.

"That's a good idea; should have been done a long time ago," Sarge replied.

His reply seemed even more of a shock to her. She looked around again and smiled, "Good."

"We're also going to run you gals through some training. Mike and Ted will handle that; teach you how to use those rifles effectively."

Slightly annoyed, Fred looked at Sarge. "We know how to use guns."

"That's not what I meant. Knowing how to pull a trigger, and knowing how to employ a weapon in a firefight are two different things. We're going to make sure you can do the latter. Turn you girls into a regular fighting force."

"I want to learn too."

Everyone looked up to see Taylor standing in the door of the house. She stepped outside and Lee Ann followed her, "Me too."

"Now wait a minute, I don't like the idea of you girls doing this sort of thing," Mel countered.

Before I could reply, Sarge stood up and put his arm around Mel's shoulder. "I know what you mean. They're your little girls. But think about what happened the other day; they were lucky. We're about to be up against some folks with a real chip on their shoulder; they're going to be playing for keeps. I think it would do you good to carry a weapon as well." Sarge looked at Bobbie, "you too."

Mel let out a long breath, "Why does it always have to be this? Why is it always *something* else to have to deal with?"

"Shoot, for the most of the world this is how it's always been. We see it on the news, Darfur, Iraq, Syria; it was always other places. Now it's here; it's just the way the world works. We were lucky in that we always had clean water, reliable power and advanced society. But it was a thin façade, as you now see. Soon as that screen dropped, the natural order began to take hold, survival of the fittest." Sarge looked at the women assembled, "and we're going to make sure you're the fittest bunch of fightin' females in these parts!"

"I don't particularly want to be running around the woods with you guys," Mel replied.

"Then don't. But if someone comes in here and tries to stir up some shit, I want you to be able to settle it."

"Hey, I'm in," Fred said.

"So are we," Lee Ann added.

Mel looked up at her daughters, "I guess I am too then."

Sarge clapped his hands, "Good, that's settled then."

"When are we going to start on those bunkers?" Thad asked.

"We need to round up some sand wrenches and get that tractor," Sarge said. Then he looked at me, "you guys have some chainsaws, right?"

I nodded. Before I could reply, Aric asked, "What's a sand wrench?"

I laughed. "It's the primary tool of the subterranean installation technician." Aric stared at me, obviously even more confused.

"It's a damn shovel, numbnuts!" Sarge barked.

Aric smiled, "Oh, I get it now."

I shook my head, then asked Sarge what the plan was.

Sarge jutted a thumb at Ted, "He'll fill you in; just go round up your equipment."

"We have to get that disc for Cecil loaded onto a trailer and take it to town."

"I'll help you load it; then I can get with Ted and start on what he needs," Thad said.

"Good, let's get to it. Come on Teddy, I'll show you what I was thinking," Sarge said as he started to walk away.

"Fred, you and Jess come over when you're ready and we'll get you fitted out with a rifle," Danny said.

She smiled and nodded; then she and Aric headed out.

I headed back towards the house to get the truck and trailer. Danny had found the disc in one of the barns in the neighborhood; it was like new and should serve Cecil well. Mel walked with me.

"I think it's a good idea for you and the girls to get some training," I said.

"I don't want to, but he's right. If someone comes in here, I want to be able to deal with it; and it would make the girls safer." Mel looked at me, "anything that does that, I'm all for."

I put my arm around her shoulders, "That's what it's all about, keeping all of us safer."

She reached up and grabbed my hand, "Are you going to town?"

"Yeah, I have to drop off the disc. Why, you want to come?"

She shrugged, "Maybe next time. Let me spend some time with those guys so I'll have some idea what I'm doing."

"You're welcome to come along any time babe," I replied and kissed her head.

# CHAPTER 6

ONCE THE DISC WAS CHAINED to the trailer, Thad headed towards Danny's place with the tractor. Danny would ride with me into town, I wanted someone else to go as well. We were heading towards the barricade when I saw Aric and Fred, and I called Aric over.

"Hey man, feel like a ride into town?"

He looked at Fred, "Sure I guess."

"We just need an extra set of eyes. It won't take long; we're just dropping this off and coming right back."

"You don't mind do you?" Aric asked Fred.

She smiled and shook her head, "No, go."

"We won't keep him long," I added with a smile.

Aric jumped in and we headed for the barricade. Jeff and Perez were manning it; I waved as we passed them. I was surprised to see both of them smoking.

"Where the hell did they find cigarettes?" I asked.

Danny was looking back, "No idea; wish they would find some Cope."

I laughed, "Yeah, me too."

"What's this thing for?" Aric asked, stabbing a thumb over his shoulder.

"They're trying to get some ground ready to plant in

town and needed a bigger disc. We're just going to drop it and head back."

Aric leaned back, "Fine by me; it's nice to get out."

In Altoona I pulled into the Kangaroo and parked near Mario, who was there trading honey and related products.

"Hey Mario, Shelly; how you guys today?" I asked as I got out.

"Good, how about you?" Mario replied.

"We're good. How's business?" Danny asked.

"Getting better," Shelly replied.

I looked around the parking lot and noticed there were more people out looking to trade. There were more tables set up, and one guy was even building a small booth out of scrap plywood.

"See those tax collectors lately?" I asked.

Mario laughed, "Nope, not since our last encounter."

"That's good; looks like it's having an effect on the people here," Danny said.

"It sure is. Once word got out, more people started coming. Plus, they're trading things they wouldn't before because they were worried that those guys would take it," Shelly said.

"I'm going to go look around," Aric said.

"I'll go with you," Danny said as the two walked off.

As I watched them walk away, I said, "It's good those troublemakers aren't around; but it makes me nervous, you know. I'd rather know where they are."

Mario leaned back against his table, "I know what you mean. I've been keeping an eye out for trouble."

"Do that," I replied, then looked around. "Also keep an eye out for anyone you don't recognize; we had a run-in with a couple of guys that we're pretty certain were DHS."

Mario looked surprised, "Really? I thought those guys were gone; thought the Army ran them off."

I filled him and Shelly in on what I knew about the ambush, and that no one knew where they were. We talked about the possibility that they could return looking for some revenge, and what that would mean to folks around here.

"We'll keep an eye out for them. If we see anything, we'll let you know," Shelly said.

"You guys have working radios?" I asked.

Mario smiled, "You know it; got my repeater up and running right before everything went to shit."

That piece of news surprised me, "Really, no kidding?" I took a pad and pen from my pocket; handing them to Mario, I asked him to write the settings down. "I'll program my handheld with it so we can stay in touch. If you don't mind, I'll give it to the Guard as well so we can all communicate."

Mario wrote all the settings down and handed the pad back. "Fine by me; that's why I set it up."

"How's the solar system holding up?" I asked. Mario had invested heavily in solar back in the day. His entire bee operation was powered by independent systems at each building.

"Best money I ever spent, my friend."

Our conversation moved on to livestock. Mario had a nice flock of chickens, and kept some hogs as well. We agreed to trade some hens and sows with one another, to introduce new blood into the lines. It was always a good idea to do so, though contrary to popular belief, inbreeding in meat production isn't a bad thing. But there comes a point where it's necessary to bring in new stock. After chatting a little longer, I went off to find Danny and Aric.

I caught up with the guys as they were looking at jewelry laid out on a plastic folding table. The woman behind the table was clean, something that really stood out today. Not only her clothes, but her hair was done. It wasn't up to the old standards; but by today's yardstick, it looked really good. Aric was examining a ring.

"It's a real diamond," the woman said as I walked up.

Looking at the stone, I let out a low whistle, "What's that, two carats?"

The woman smiled, "Two and a half."

"It's really nice," Aric said as he set it back on the table.

I picked it up and looked at it, "I bet Fred would really like it."

Aric was still looking at it, "Yeah she would."

A small blue bag on the table caught my eye. I knew the color; it was Tiffany's blue. I picked it up and shook out a sterling silver cuff with the Tiffany and Company logo on it. Mel loved Tiffany's back in the day, and her collection of their jewelry grew accordingly with my gun collection. I observed Aric still looking at the ring.

"How much for the ring?" I asked the woman.

"What are you trading?"

"I don't have anything to trade," Aric replied.

Reaching into a pocket on my vest, I took out several Morgan silver dollars, "How about silver?"

The woman studied the coins for a moment, then looked at me, "You the Sheriff?"

I glanced down at the badge, "I guess so."

She looked at Aric, "You a deputy?" Aric nodded in reply. "You the ones that ran off those ruffians that was taking from everyone?"

I nodded, "We helped anyway."

She studied me for a minute then said, "Twenty dollars."

I winced; it was a high price, "Ten."

The old gal's eyes narrowed. I could tell she loved the bartering, "Fifteen and not a cent less."

"Morgan, I don't have any way to pay for it," Aric said.

I held up the cuff, "Fifteen if you throw in the cuff, and not a penny more."

The woman stared at me for a long moment, her eyes barely visible as she squinted. "You drive a hard bargain, Sheriff." She held her hand out, "deal."

I shook her hand and put the cuff back in the bag and dropped it into my pocket. Counting out fifteen Morgan's, I handed them over. She smiled as the heavy coins clinked into the palm of her hand. I picked the ring up and admired it.

"This sure will make Fred happy," I said as I held it out to Aric.

With uncertainty, he took the ring. "I don't know what to say; I can't ever repay you."

I slapped him on the back, "You don't owe me anything. You're part of the family here man. As far as I'm concerned, you bought that ring. And if you tell Fred I did, I'll deny it and call you a liar," I said with a smile.

Aric finally smiled, "Thanks Morgan; thanks a lot."

We made one more stop by the booth that was under construction. A skinny little man was hammering an old wood sign to the side of the booth that had come from a Baptist church. The rest of his building materials were in a wagon hitched to a mule. The wagon, much like the booth, was an amalgamation of different materials. The axle was from some sort of car; and the bed planks were of various dimensions. The mule was harnessed using webbed straps that were probably ratchet straps in their previous life. The old fella was ingenious, if nothing else.

"You setting up church?" Danny asked.

The man looked at the sign, "Naw; it was just a nice big piece of wood. I'm in the tool business, sharpening, fixing, trading."

It was then I saw the large sharpening wheel. It was mounted to a stand and was probably motor-powered when it was new. But the motor and parts of the frame were removed to allow room for the treadle that now powered it.

"How's that thing work," Danny asked.

The man smiled, "Like a dream." He stepped behind the wheel and gripped the top of the stone wheel. Rocking it a couple of times, he gave a mighty shove and the wheel began to turn. He put his foot on the pedal and pumped it, keeping the stone going. "I can sharpen anything on this."

"That's pretty cool," Danny said, nodding his head.

"Yeah, I think we'll be giving you a little business," I added.

"I trade for about anything, I should be up and running tomorrow."

"Good to know. We'll be seeing you," Danny replied.

We left the old fella to his task and headed back to the truck. As we drove towards Eustis, we talked about the wheel and the ingenuity it took to make something like that. Work was coming back.

"A couple of years ago no one would have ever thought about taking an electric motor off of something like that, let alone butchering it up the way he did to make that pedal work," Danny said.

"That kind of problem solving is worth its weight in gold now. We lived in a disposable society; when something broke, you threw it away. There was never a thought given to fixing something. *Throw it away; we'll buy another one*, was how people lived," I replied.

I was just as guilty. We all were. I loved the modern world we'd created; it was so easy. Life was easy. Everyone was disconnected from where everything came from to such a degree that no one cared. Our food came from the corner store; and if you didn't like that one you simply drove across the street to the competitor. Clothes and electronics came from one of a few big box stores. Or, even better, you could order it online and it would be delivered to your door with no more effort on you part than a tap of your finger. Was it any wonder there was an entitlement mentality with the generations that only knew that way of life?

My generation was the last one to grow up before the internet and cell phone. We played outside all day without a care in the world from our parents about our safety. We rode bikes without helmets, cars without seatbelts, and even rode in the bed of pick-ups. But as the world *advanced,* all that went away. It was suddenly unsafe to do any of these things, and crimes against children increased.

But now, kids play outside all day, and gone are the bike helmets for those kids fortunate enough to have a working bike with two good tires. Whereas it had become socially unacceptable to own firearms among a large portion of society, it is now understood that they are a must-have tool. Not only for self-defense but to provide food for the table. Once again we were intimately connected to where our food came from. Whether it was pulled from the ground or hunted and killed, feeding oneself and family was a very personal thing.

As I drove past the orange juice plant, I looked over at the top of the exhaust stack of the power plant, the only thing visible from the road. Cecil seemed to think we could get it up and running; but I simply couldn't imagine the work that would be involved. The small plant wouldn't be able to service a very large area based off how things used to be; but with so little surviving, it could provide power to a lot more now. But to do that we'd have to open a lot of switches to isolate the area we wanted to power. Not to mention we'd have to hope the transformers were good.

But before any of that could become an issue, there was the plant itself and its fuel, natural gas. Cecil said gas was still flowing in places; this was a huge surprise to me, as I thought it was all out. But then I didn't have any gas at my place, so I wouldn't really know if it were out or not. Cecil said he could show us; and I was certainly curious to see that.

At the barricade of cars, we rolled through without stopping, the old Suburban now recognized by all the troops. Eustis seemed to be hustling and bustling. Along the shore of the lake, Cecil had already begun the tilling, and several people were out in the broken soil with hand tools. I saw Cecil standing with Livingston and several Guardsmen. He had a large paper in his hand and was motioning to different points along the lakefront. I parked the truck on the road, and we walked over.

"Somebody order a disc?" I called out as we approached.

Cecil turned and smiled, "I sure did; you're just in time."

We made pleasantries for a few minutes, talking about the work on the lakefront and the state of things in general. When Cecil excused himself to go get the tractor, Livingston said he needed me at the HQ. Aric and Danny said they'd handle unloading the disc, and I followed Livingston towards the armory.

"What's up?" I asked as we crossed Bay Street.

"Got some civilian law enforcement issues for you to deal with."

I rolled my eyes. "What is it?" I asked, the irritation clear in my voice.

Livingston kind of laughed, "We've got a couple of guys that were caught stealing chickens."

"You gotta be shittin' me. Why is it always chickens? Everyone steals chickens."

"The owner caught them in his coop and brought them to us. They fessed up; said they were hungry."

"Yeah, no shit, who isn't?"

"Well Sheriff, they're your problem now," Livingston said with a smile.

Inside the armory, I found the two men being guarded by a couple of soldiers. They looked like what you'd expect a chicken thief to look like, dirty threadbare clothes, long hair and unkempt beards. One of them was a character straight out of a Mark Twain book. Wearing overalls and no shirt, he sat barefoot on the floor. When I walked up, they looked up at me.

"You the Sheriff?" The one in overalls asked.

"Sadly, I am. Why'd you steal the chickens?"

"We didn't steal anything," the other replied.

The one in overalls looked sideways at his partner, "Cause we got caught before we could get gone."

I laughed, "At least you're honest."

Sheffield walked up, "Well, what's it going to be?"

"Yeah Sheriff, you sending us off to the big house?" The one in overalls asked.

Taking off my hat, I scratched my head. "Hell, I don't know. They tried to steal and admitted it; but it was only chickens, so I don't know what to do with them."

"Well, according to other people around here, it isn't their first time," Sheffield replied.

"First time gettin' caught," the barefoot chicken thief added.

Here was a true conundrum, these two were guilty for certain; they admitted it. But what to do with them? It surely wasn't a capital crime; but at the same time, some sort of punishment was merited. Then I had an idea.

"Shaming."

Sheffield looked at me, "Say what?"

"Public shaming; it was used a couple hundred years ago for just this sort of thing. Take them to the flag pole in front of the concert shell in the park. Cuff 'em up to it and hang a sign around their necks with their names and the fact they're chicken thieves. They can spend two days there."

The man in the overalls didn't like what he was hearing, "Do what? You can't do that to us!"

I laughed, "What'd you expect? You know there's no jail; it's not like we're going to hang you for chicken thieving. This will do; but if you get caught again you probably won't like what I come up with next."

"Works for me," Sheffield said. He ordered the two soldiers guarding them to see to it.

As the two men were being led away, I asked Sheffield if there were anything else.

"No, that's it for now."

"Good, I got shit to do. I'll see you guys later." I replied as I headed for the door.

By the time I got back to the truck, the disc was already hooked up to Cecil's tractor. Cecil was in the seat steering the machine along the edge of the lake. After covering only a short piece, he stopped. Danny ran out to him with a cinder block and placed it on the disc. Once again Cecil drove along the lake, and he looked up at Danny and nodded. They'd found the appropriate weight needed to get the disc down deep enough to break the ground.

"That one big enough for you?" I asked.

Cecil smiled, "It's fine, just fine." I looked at Cecil, "You said the gas was still on in places?"

Cecil nodded, "It is; there's a gas line just outside of town.

I was out there not long ago and smelled gas. I thought that was kinda odd; you know things having been down so long. So I went over to the pipe and put my hand on it; I could feel the flow of the gas."

"Can you show us?" Danny asked.

Cecil nodded, "Sure."

"Hop in; let's go have a look," I said as I started around the truck.

Cecil got up front and Danny and Aric hopped in the back. Cecil said the line was over near David Walker Road, so I headed south on 19. I hadn't been through this part of town since the trip to the Sheriff's office. It looked much like it did then. There were few people around, and weeds were choking the sidewalks and parking lots. They were even forcing their way up through cracks in the road where the concrete gutter met the pavement. With no traffic to pound them down, they were reclaiming every place they could.

I turned onto Orange Ave and drove around behind the high school. There were several houses in the area, and a few of them had small gardens planted in their yards. One house in particular I remembered as always having collard greens planted in the old days. The stalks of those plants were nearly six feet tall then. They were still there, still being tended. I don't know who lived there, but they were taking care of their garden. At David Walker, I swung right. Cecil told me to pull up to a gate on the right not far from the intersection.

I stopped at the gate and we got out, following Cecil through the fence. A large pipe came out of the ground at an angle, and traveled several feet before it dove into the earth again. There were several devices mounted to the pipe, pressure regulators I would assume. Cecil walked up to the pipe and put his hand on it.

"Still flowing."

I put my hand on it and could feel the vibration of gas moving through the pipe. "Wonder what's using all the gas, where it's going?"

Cecil shook his head. "No idea, but it is moving."

Danny laid his head on the pipe, pressing his ear against it. "I can hear; it's like a rumble."

"I thought the gas was out," Aric said.

"We all did; but something is using it," Cecil replied.

I looked at him, "Do you know anyone with gas service in town?"

He nodded and smiled, "I know where you're going. I thought the same thing. But I have gas at my house. The range and water heater are gas, and I don't have any."

"So the main line is flowing but there's no service in town?" I shook my head, "doesn't make any sense to me."

"Me neither. Someone turned a valve someplace." Cecil replied.

"Who would turn the gas off and why?" Danny asked.

"I want to know where this gas is going. Someone's using it," I said.

"I've looked for valves that could have been shut off, but haven't found any. Wish I knew someone that worked for the gas company," Cecil said.

"You got time to take a ride over to the plant, see if there's gas there?" I asked.

Cecil nodded, "Sure, I was hoping you'd want to."

"Let's go."

We drove back through town, getting a strange look from Livingston as we passed the armory without stopping. As we passed the intersection of Highway 44, Cecil was looking out the window. "I haven't been this far from home in a while."

"Hard to get around now-a-days isn't it?" Danny asked.

Cecil chuckled "You could say that."

We pulled up to the gate of the plant. A large chain with a heavy padlock held the gate closed. Cecil hopped out and took a set of keys from his pocket and removed the lock. Pushing the gate open, he waved me through and secured the gate behind us. Getting back in, Cecil directed me around the back of the plant towards the generator. Parking the truck, we got out and looked at the old machine.

Cecil looked up at the exhaust stacks of the old power plant, "I used to maintain this thing; spent a lot of time out here. It was cheaper for them to make their own than it was to buy it."

"I did for several years too. The ones I worked on were a lot bigger though," I replied.

"Where's the gas come in?" Danny asked.

Cecil pointed, "Back here."

We followed him back around the structure to find a yellow pipe about six inches in diameter sloping up out of the ground.

"Here it is," Cecil said as he laid a hand on it. He looked up and smiled, "See what you think."

I put my hand on the pipe and felt the same vibration, "Feels like it."

Once again Danny laid his ear on the pipe, "oh yeah, I can hear it."

"So, can we start it up? We could have power," Aric said.

"Not yet. We need to check it out first, not to mention we need power just to get it running," Cecil said.

"Yeah, we'll have to find a big ass generator," I replied.

Danny shook his head, "Why does a power plant need power to get it running; that doesn't make a lot of sense."

"It seems counterintuitive, but something has to provide the power for the all the stuff that makes this thing run. There are all kinds of motors, valves, thermocouples and other instruments that need power," I replied.

"I'm glad you guys know what you're talking about, because I damn sure don't," Aric added, shaking his head.

"Well, now we know there's gas here. But we've got a lot to do before we try it," I said.

Cecil looked up at the power lines overhead, "Yeah, we'll have to go around and do some line work too."

I laughed, "We'll make sure this thing is going to run before we start climbing poles."

Cecil smiled, "That's for you young bucks. I ain't climbing any poles."

"Me neither, I'm not climbing any of those. I don't like heights or electricity. Combine the two and it's not just no; it's *hell* no!" Danny said.

We all laughed and headed back for the truck. After dropping Cecil off, we headed for the old concert shell at the park. I wanted to check on the two chicken thieves and see if Livingston actually did what I said. As we pulled up I could see he had indeed. The two men were tied back to back with the flag pole between then. I could see a large piece of cardboard hanging from one of them, but couldn't yet read it.

We walked across the park, or maybe market was a better term for it now. There were tables scattered throughout the park. Those that didn't have a table had spread their offerings on blankets; and a couple of the more industrious vendors had cobbled together small stalls. As we walked through, I suddenly noticed all the smells. There was the smell of fire, cooking meat, raw fish and some less desirable odors mixed in.

I nodded to the two Guardsmen standing watch over the two men, "They giving you any trouble?"

One of them smiled, "Nah, not now anyway. They finally figured out this was for real."

The sign read: *My name's Tommy Lowell, and I'm a chicken thief.*

The other man had a sign around his neck as well. His name was David Morris. Tommy looked up at me as I read the sign. He wasn't as cocky as he had been at the armory.

"Gonna steal anymore chickens?" I asked.

He looked around the park, "Naw, I reckon not. Everyone thinks I'm a thief now."

"You are a thief, dumbass," one of the guardsmen replied.

"You're not just a thief, you're a chicken thief!" The other guardsmen added with a laugh.

Tommy lowered his head. Maybe it was shame; maybe it was disgust. I told the guards they could let them go tomorrow. They said they'd pass it along to the relief. As we walked back to the truck, Danny snickered.

"Who thought that up?"

"I did; didn't know what else to do with them."

Aric shook his head, "That would suck, everyone looking at you like that."

"That's the whole point," I replied.

With the business in town taken care of we headed back home.

---

Thad cut the saw off and stepped back to watch the tree fall. The long leaf pine landed on the ground with a thunderous crash. Sarge started to laugh, "I'll be damned Thad, you hit it perfect."

Thad smiled, "Told you I could."

"Damn, Thad; didn't know you were a lumberjack," Mike added.

"I've dropped a few trees in my day," Thad replied.

"Let's get to it," Sarge said; then started the small saw he was holding.

They went to work cutting the limbs out and bucking the trunk. Sarge wanted logs seven feet long. This one would give them three sections. They were going around the neighborhood cutting select pine trees. As the logs were bucked, Thad would throw a chain around several of them and drag them to the construction site with the tractor.

"Back the tractor up over here!" Sarge shouted.

Thad climbed on the machine and backed it up to the logs. Ted was dragging the chain under one of them as Mike hooked the other end to the draw bar on the back of the tractor. The logs were pulled one at a time so they could be chained together. Once all three were out on the road, the chain was wrapped around them, and Thad headed out. Thankfully, this tree was rather close to the site. Last time the logs slipped out and Thad had to re-hook them by himself.

As Thad pulled up, Jeff waved to him and ran out to unhook the logs. He gathered the chain up and handed it to Thad.

"Before you go, can you scoop some more out?" Jeff asked.

Thad nodded, "Sure thing."

Jeff called down to the girls that were digging in a hole. They gladly got out of the way so the tractor could get in again. Jeff pointed out what he wanted Thad to move. It didn't take long for the tractor to move what it could get to.

Thad waved, "I'll be back!"

As the tractor pulled away, Jess let out a loud sigh and hopped back into the hole. "It ain't gonna dig itself."

"How big does this thing have to be?" Taylor asked as she dragged her shovel back into the pit.

"You can see the marks the old man put on the ground," Jeff said as he jumped back in beside Jess.

"Uhhgg," Lee Ann moaned as she joined everyone in the pit.

"Why are we doing this again?" Fred asked as she heaved a load of dirt over the side of the pit.

"I guess they're worried about someone attacking us, and want some defensive positions," Jeff said as he slung a spade of dirt out.

"How many of these do we have to build?" Taylor asked.

"At least two, I think," Jess said.

As they were talking, Mel, Little Bit and Miss Kay walked up, pulling a green wagon.

"Anyone thirsty?" Kay called out as they got close.

There was a unanimous *yes!* from the pit as everyone started to come out, thankful for any reason for a break.

"How's it going?" Mel asked.

"Slow," Jess replied as she took a cup from her.

On the wagon was a five-gallon water jug. Mel handed out cups. Jess was first in line. As she was filling her cup, she looked back, "It's cold!"

"We put some ice in it," Kay said with a smile. "I thought you guys would like that."

Jess turned the cup up and took a long drink as Lee Ann filled her cup, "Oh that is so good!" Jess shouted.

"Yeah, those Berkey filters are the best thing we ever bought," Mel said.

"I'm glad you did," Jeff said, taking a drink.

"It's so hot out, this is great. Thanks for bringing it down here," Fred said.

"Looks like you've got a lot done," Kay said.

"But we still have a lot to do," Taylor replied.

Mel took the shovel Taylor was leaning on. "I'll help," she said, and walked down into the pit.

"I wanna help!" Little Bit shouted. Lee Ann quickly gave up her shovel to her little sister.

Jeff walked back into the pit and showed Mel what they needed to dig out. They went to work with Little Bit's help, such as it was. Everyone got back to work, taking turns as they were one shovel short. They would alternate taking a break, giving each person a chance to rest. Miss Kay made sure everyone had water, bringing cups down and making them drink.

"Why is the back of the hole sloped like this?" Kay asked.

Jeff straightened up and leaned on his shovel, "Thad dug it out with the tractor. He can drive it down in here on the backside. The front side is the side we're worried about."

"Where are those big logs going to go?"

"I think we're going to be standing them up," Jeff pointed to the front side of the hole, "over here and on the sides. Then they'll lay longer ones across the top like beams and more across those, then it will all be covered up."

"In the movies, bunkers are always made of sandbags," Taylor said, shading her eyes with her hand.

Jeff shrugged, "You got a pile of bags somewhere?"

"If we had them, not only would we be digging a hole, we'd be filling all those bags," Fred added.

Taylor looked at the pile of logs, "I like this idea better."

Mel laughed, "I just hope we don't have to use this thing, whatever it's made of."

"You and me both," Kay said with a laugh.

Little Bit passed her shovel off to Jess and looked at the logs, "So this is going to be like a fort?"

Jeff smiled, "That's exactly what it's going to be, a fort."

"Cool! We're going to have a fort!"

Jeff looked up and smiled at her, "That's right kiddo, we're doing this so you can have a playhouse."

She hopped up and down clapping her hands, "Yeah!"

Jeff shook his head and went back to digging.

Taylor stood up, a look of disbelief on her face, "You mean we're doing all this so she can have a playhouse?"

"No, that's not why. He's just messing around," Mel replied as she tossed a scoop of dirt out of the hole.

"I can play in it though, can't I?" Little Bit asked.

Mel rubbed her head, "You'll probably be able to."

Little Bit smiled, "Good," and tried to push the shovel back into the earth.

As they were working, Thad pulled back up on the tractor with another load of logs. Jeff started out of the hole and saw Sarge's Hummer bringing up the rear, so he stepped back down to continue digging.

Mike and Ted unhooked the logs as Sarge inspected the work. Little Bit ran up to Sarge and wrapped her arms around his leg.

"Mr. Sarge, we're going to have a fort!"

He smiled at her, "We sure are sweetie." Sarge looked at the growing pit, "looking good; we can start putting some timbers in this thing."

"I was wondering what the plan was," Jess said.

Kay walked up to Sarge with a cup of water, "You look like you need a drink."

He smiled, "Why thank you, Miss Kay." He took the cup and downed the water. "Man that's good, nice and cold!"

Kay smiled, "We put some ice in, thought you guys would like it today. It's hot out."

Jeff stomped his shovel into the dirt, "Well, what's the plan?"

# CHAPTER 7

WE STOPPED AT THE BARRICADE to shoot the shit with Perez and Jamie. Perez lit a cigarette as I stopped.

"Where in the hell did you find those?" I asked.

He smiled and took a long drag, "Got my ways."

"He stole 'em from the camp when we were pulling out," Jamie added.

"They had smokes there?" Danny asked.

"They did; I got them now," Perez replied with a grin.

"Wish they had some Cope."

I looked at Danny. "If they did, it's burned up now."

"How are things in town?" Jamie asked.

"Same ole same ole. We dropped off the disc and got out as fast as we could. You guys see anything down here?"

Jamie shook her head, "No, it's been quiet."

"We're going to go check on the bunker," I said as I dropped the truck in gear.

Jamie and Perez waved as we pulled away.

We found everyone gathered at the crossroad where the bunker was being dug. Sarge had everyone gathered together, going over the next part of the plan. They all looked up, hearing us approach. Little Bit ran up as I got out.

"Daddy, we're going to have a fort!"

I smiled at her, "I know, kinda cool isn't it?"

She clapped her hands again, "I can't wait!"

Sarge walked around the pit. "Well, the easy part's done."

"The easy part!" Lee Ann shouted.

"Yeah, what do you mean the easy part?" Fred asked.

"Now we have to get these timbers in place," Sarge replied.

"I gotta take a piss," Mike said as he headed towards the bushes.

"Shake a bush," Sarge said as Mike disappeared.

"How are we going to move those, they're huge!" Jess said.

"Aww, we'll get it done. Ain't as hard as you think," Sarge replied.

There was a sudden rusting in the bushes, we looked over to see a small tree swaying back and forth, "Shakin' a bush boss, shakin' a bush!" Mike shouted.

Sarge shook his head, "You're retarded!"

Mike came out of the bushes and looked at him with a slack-jawed expression, and in his best Forest Gump voice said, "I'm not wetawded, I'm bwain daaamaged. It's diffwent, mamma said so." He paused for a moment, then made a slurping sound and wiped his chin with the back of his hand.

It set most of us to laughing, "I couldn't help it," Mike said. Mel looked at him, "That's not very nice."

"Ignore him Mel, he's an idjit," Sarge said.

Mike rubbed his chin and looked up. After a moment his head snapped around, "Guilty!"

Sarge looked up to the sky and implored, "Why me? What'd I do, what'd I do?"

Ted was laughing, "I told you in the Philippines not to feed him."

"Hey!" Mike shouted, "We're not talking about the Philippines!" Now Sarge was laughing.

"What happened in the Philippines?" Mel asked.

Ted looked at Mike and crossed his arms, "Oh, Mikey here found himself a lovely lady…boy."

"Dammit!" Mike shouted as he started to walk away.

In a sing song voice Ted called out, "I love you long time!"

"Hey Mikey," Sarge called out, then looked at Ted, "What was that girl's name?"

"Maria."

"Mikey, Mario, er uh, Maria wants to know if you're taking her to the big PX!" Sarge called out, then doubled over laughing.

Mike replied by giving Sarge the finger over his shoulder.

"What's the big PX?" Miss Kay asked.

"Over in places like the Philippines young ladies who wanted to come to the US would try and hook up with anyone in the service. The US was often referred to as the big PX."

"In his defense, she did look like a girl," Ted said.

Sarge smiled, "Yeah she did, except where it mattered most."

"What are they talking about Mommy?" Little Bit asked.

"Nothing honey," Mel replied and looked at Sarge. "They're done talking about it anyway."

Sarge smiled, "Ten roger, mom; we got work to do."

"I think you guys were mean to Mike; look at him," Kay said.

Sarge waved the comment off. "He's a big boy; he'll be fine."

With that out of the way, Sarge got back to business laying out the bunker construction. It took everyone and several tools to get those logs into position. We had to use come-a-longs to move some of them. The smaller ones were rolled into the hole and stood up, a small trench being dug around the edge of the pit for the bases. They were dropped into the trench and set side by side. A second row was placed behind these, covering the joints where the front logs met. This way a bullet couldn't pass through the joints into the bunker.

Additional holes were dug in the center of the pit and logs stood up in these to offer load-bearing support. The tops were cut off to the same height as those on the front and sides. We were tamping the dirt in around these when Doc showed up.

"Edy is sick," he announced as he walked up.

"What's that mean?" I asked.

"Without testing, I can't confirm that it's TB; but I also can't rule it out."

"Keep an eye on her Doc, there isn't much we can do though," Sarge said.

Little Bit looked up at Mel, "My friend's sick?"

Mel smiled. "She'll be alright; Doc is taking care of here." She looked up at Doc, "right?"

Doc walked up to Little Bit and knelt down. "Don't worry; I'm the best doctor around here. I'll take care of her."

She studied him for a moment, then asked, "Aren't you the only doctor around here?"

Doc laughed and looked at Mel, "Smart kid."

"She'll surprise you."

Doc pinched Little Bit's stomach and said, "Which is why I'm the best!" She smiled.

"It's time to relieve the watch. Who's coming?" Doc asked.

Aric stepped up, "I think it's me and you."

Doc stood up and shouldered his bag, "Let's go."

As he started to walk off, Sarge grabbed his shoulder and leaned in close, "Let me know if anything changes with the little girl."

For all his hard-assed outward appearance, Doc knew he was rather soft inside, especially for kids. He looked at Sarge for a moment, nodded and walked off.

Fred grabbed Aric's hand and gave him a kiss, "Be careful."
He smiled. "I will; we're good."

As they headed to relieve the crew at the barricade, Sarge said, "I think this is enough for one day. It's getting late and we have security to pull tonight, so some of you need to get some rest."

"Oh thank God," Taylor said as she dropped her shovel.

"I need to check on the garden," Thad said.

"Bobbie and Mary should have dinner ready when we get there," Mel said.

"Good, I'm starving." Lee Ann shouted.

I called Doc and Aric and told them I'd give them a ride up to the barricade. Sarge said he wanted to go as well.

"You going to be there for dinner?" Mel asked.

I nodded, "Yeah; just going to drop these guys off."

I was turning the truck around when Ted ran up and rolled in through the open window on the back gate. I looked at him in the mirror shaking my head. "If there's a hard way to do it, these guys know it." Rolling up to the barricade, we all got out.

"About damn time. I thought you forgot about us," Ian said.

"Quit yer belly aching Gyrene," Sarge said.

"I'm glad to see you," Jamie said.

"Anything happening up here?" Ted asked.

"Nope, we haven't seen a soul," Perez replied.

"You guys go get some chow," Sarge said.

"Hey Morgan, can you give us a ride?" Perez asked.

"Go ahead, we'll hang out here for a while," Sarge said.

We loaded up and headed towards the house the three of them were sharing. Jamie said she wanted to change her clothes and rest for a while. Pulling up in the yard, Perez hopped out and said "Wait here for a minute," and ran towards the house.

"What's he up to?" I asked.

Ian shrugged as he pulled his gear out of the truck, "Hell if I know."

Jamie said goodbye, and headed for the house. Perez came back out carrying a plastic bag and handed it to me through the window. "Here, this is for Danny; I don't like the stuff."

The bag was heavy, I opened it and looked. "Holy shit, where'd you get all this?" I asked, taking a log of Cope out of the bag.

"It was in the camp; found it when we were pulling out."

Looking at the cans, I asked, "What in the hell were they doing with this stuff?"

Perez shrugged, "Hell if I know. They had all kinds of crazy shit. I think they went out to scavenge early on, and took whatever they found."

I looked in the bag. There appeared to be eight or nine logs of five cans each. "I'll give him half of it." Smiling, I looked back up at Perez, "I like it too. Thanks."

He waved as he walked off. "Don't worry about it; you're just lucky you don't smoke."

As I pulled out onto the road, I ripped a can from the plastic and ran my fingernail around the lid. Opening it, I took a pinch and put it in my lip. It was a little dry, not too bad, but it was good! I thought how excited Danny would be on the way to his house, then I had an idea. When I got to his house I stuffed the bag under my seat and dropped the can in my pocket as I walked up to the porch.

I could hear people out back. A quick look in the window verified that no one was inside, so I walked around the porch. A large pot sat on one of the picnic tables with bowls and silverware laid out. Danny was sitting on a large chase lounge with Bobbie.

"Dinner's on the table over there," Bobbie said.

"Thanks, I'll get some in a minute," I replied as I stepped over to the screen door and spit.

Danny looked at me quizzically. I returned his look with a smile and sat down. He didn't say anything, just looked at me. After a minute I went back to the door again. This time he sat up, "What are you doing?"

"We both know Bobbie would have slapped me sideways if I had spit on the porch."

"You're damn right I would have," she quickly replied.

Danny looked at her, then at me, "What are you spitting?"

"Oh," I reached in my pocket and removed the can. Holding it up, "Just this."

Instantly, he was on his feet, moving towards me with his hand out. "Where'd you get that?"

"A little bird gave it to me," I said as I tossed him the can.

Danny quickly opened the can and took a pinch, "It's a little dry."

Holding my hand out I replied, "Well, then give it back if you don't like it."

Danny looked at the can, "Oh I like it!"

I smiled, "You can keep it then."

"But where'd you get it?"

"Perez had it."

"Got anymore?" Danny asked.

I smiled, "Maybe. If you're nice to me, I'll give you a log."

"A log! Sweet."

Bobbie moaned, "I thought the spit bottles were gone!"

"Me too!" Mel added.

"Don't worry, there isn't that much; it won't last long," I replied.

I got rid of the mouthful of worm dirt and sat down to eat. I was hungry.

———*——*——*——*——*——

Sarge and Ted hung out at the barricade for a while, then headed back to their house. As they walked, they talked about the group Ted and Mike had watched a couple of nights before.

"What do you think of them?" Sarge asked.

"They've got someone with some tactical skills. They had watches out, but they're sloppy."

Sarge thought for a moment, "What I can't figure out is why we've only just now come across them."

"I thought about that too, how a group that big could be here and us not see them. But they had several travel trailers, campers and trucks to pull them. They rode up that day on ATVs, so they've got some fuel. Maybe they were on the move and just landed here."

"Maybe they don't have enough fuel for the trucks and got stuck here," Sarge replied, still thinking.

"Might be part of their MO, move into an area, take what they can and move on."

"That's what I'm worried about, that they're just traveling scavengers."

Ted kicked a rock down the road, "Maybe they'll move on now that they hit some resistance."

Sarge shook his head. "No, I have a feeling that ole Billy Boy will want him some get-even. He didn't strike me as the type to run from a fight."

"Maybe we should go take another look then. We haven't seen or heard anything out of them since our last trip."

Sarge looked at Ted, "And that really worries me. I think we'll do that, go take another look. I'll go with you this time; take that sea-goin' bellhop too."

"I'll come up with a new route; don't want to go the same way again."

"Yeah, they could be expecting us," Sarge smiled. "Let's not make it easy on 'em."

As they came to the door, they heard Mike inside shout, "What the fuck!"

They quickly went in. Not seeing him, they went through the house. "Mikey!" Sarge shouted.

"Back here!"

They found him in the bedroom with the safe, the door standing open and him in front of it.

"Holy shit, you actually got it open!" Ted shouted.

Mike turned around holding a couple of large pictures in his hand. "Look at this shit!" He said, handing one of the pictures to Ted. "This is what some asshole had in his safe."

"I remember this cartoon, Calvin and Hobbes. But why is it in a safe?" Ted asked.

"Let me see it." Sarge said, taking the picture from Ted. He studied it for a minute, "It's a signed and numbered lithograph; that's why it's in the safe."

Ted looked at it again, "So?"

"Are you two really that ignorant?" Sarge asked. Both just stared back at him. "In '92 Bill Watterson took a sabbatical for a year from writing the comic. He gave these out to newspapers that kept running the series. They're very rare." Sarge looked past Mike. "What else is in there?"

"Just a bunch of junk."

Sarge stepped forward, "Get out of the way dipshit. Let someone with some sense look at it."

Sarge stepped in front of the safe and looked around, having to take out his flashlight to get a better view. He took a bottle of wine from the bottom of the safe and held it up. Reading the label, he whistled.

"What's that?" Ted asked.

"It's a 1945 Chateau Mounton-Rothschild, *l'ann*ée *de la victoire,*" Sarge said in nearly perfect French.

"It's wine, let's drink it," Mike said reaching for the bottle.

Sarge slapped his hand, "Get your booger pickers off it! This isn't just *any* wine. This was bottled at the end of World War Two. This is a very special wine."

Mike sneered at the bottle, "Still say we should drink it."

Sarge put the bottle back in the safe and continued to poke around. Finding a black leather case, he removed it. Once out, he realized it was a holster. Unsnapping it, he removed a German Luger pistol.

"Now we're talking!" Ted said.

"It's a '41 SS Luger," Sarge said, inspecting the markings.

"Cool, let me have it," Mike said.

"The last thing we need is for one of us running around with a damn Nazi Luger. I think we'll leave it here," Sarge said as he put it back in the safe. Looking back at Mike, he asked, "You know the combination to this thing now?"

"Yeah," he replied, handing Sarge the piece of paper with the combination.

Sarge shut the safe and locked it. "Good; whoever owned this thing had some interesting tastes."

"And collected some weird shit," Ted added.

Mike snorted, "Tell me about it; I was hoping it was full of cool shit, not this crap."

"You inbred Neanderthals; this **is** cool shit. There are some really expensive and rare things in there. This guy was a collector of some sort. There are coins, watches and all sorts of stuff in there," Sarge shot back.

"It may have been valuable at one time, but it ain't worth shit now," Mike replied.

"Dinner's ready down the road. Let's go get something to eat," Sarge said as he headed for the door.

——— ✳ ——— ✳ ——— ✳ ——— ✳ ———

After dinner, Thad went to the garden to tend to the plants. He was often there, it relaxed him. He was adjusting the stakes on the tomato plants when Mary walked up, "Can I help?"

"Sure; hand me that twine?" Thad replied.

Mary handed him the roll and knelt down, "They're getting big, the plants."

Thad smiled. He was proud of the garden. "They sure are; I tend them every day."

Mary held the top of one of the plants so Thad could tie it, "They're so green."

"Yeah, just takes the right fertilizer, some water and plenty of sun. Lord knows we've got plenty of that lately."

"What are you fertilizing them with?"

"Pig shit." Thad caught himself, "I mean, manure."

Mary laughed, "Pig shit is good fertilizer."

Thad laughed, and then took a more serious tone. "You ok? You don't talk much."

Mary nodded, "I'm getting better. I was shaken up when I got here, but I'm doing better little by little."

Thad cut a piece of twine. "You had a rough time, huh?"

She picked up a stake, "Not as bad as Jess." She looked up at Thad, "but she's really strong. I wish I were as strong as her."

Thad patted her shoulder, "You'll be alright. You're stronger than you think."

Mary smiled and they continued to work in the garden,

pulling weeds and propping up plants that needed additional support. Thad tended the plants gently; they were important. A food source like this was more valuable than gold at the moment.

"I can't wait for this okra to grow out," Thad said.

"I like okra. Look, this one has a fruit on it already," Mary replied.

"Fried okra is my favorite."

"How are we going to fry it? We don't have any shortening."

Thad smiled, "I got something better, hog fat. We butchered a hog and I rendered the fat, we got lots of it. Morgan showed us how to make a flour from Kudzu roots, and we can dust 'em in that and fry 'em up."

Mary smiled, "I can't wait."

Thad looked at the little bud at the base of a flower, "Looks like you're going to have to."

"That's alright; it'll be worth it."

Thad stood up, "I think we're done here. Let's head in before the skeeters come out."

They walked back to the house together. As they walked up on the porch, Mel let out a sigh and fell onto one of the picnic tables. Bobbie looked over and asked how it went.

---

"Brandy looks fine. I set the food on the porch and backed up into the yard. When she came out to get it, we talked. She said Edy is sick, but not bad. She thinks it's just a cold. Tyler came out and said she was already getting better."

"I hope so. I hope everything is ok," Bobbie replied.

"Me too; but who around here's had a cold?" Danny asked.

Mel looked at him, "That's what I was thinking."

Thad let out a loud sigh, "There's nothing in this world I hate more than little ones being sick."

Bobbie looked at me, "I guess now I understand why you quarantined them."

I felt horrible. I didn't think it would happen. I shook my head, "Let's hope it's just a cold, and that they'll get better."

Jess came out on the porch carrying an oil lantern. She set it on one of the tables and sat down. Fred came out and joined her. The two sat there uncomfortably as we talked about the situation across the road. After a moment I noticed that they seemed out of sorts.

"What's eating you two?" I asked.

Fred looked at Jess, like she was nervous to speak. Before she could say anything, Sarge, Ted and Mike came around the porch. "Evnin' everyone," Sarge announced.

Mel stood up and walked over to the picnic table where a large pot sat with the night's dinner, "You guys hungry?" She asked as she picked up a bowl.

Mike smiled, "Miss Mel, that's not a question you ever need to ask me. If you got food, just hand it to me."

Mel loaded his bowl with some of the venison stew that was the night's dinner, "Here Mike."

Sarge stepped up and intercepted the bowl, "Mind yer elders, snot nose."

Mel slapped his hand. I thought I would faint. "Mind your manners, Linus." I'd never heard her use his Christian name. Hell, I didn't realize she knew it.

Sarge stopped, stunned like a deer in the headlights. Mike smiled broadly and gently took the bowl, "Thank you, Mel."

Sarge stood there for a moment, uncertainly. "Now, Linus, would you like a bowl?" Mel asked.

Sarge nodded, "Yes ma'am."

I started to laugh. It was funny. Here was the hardest, crustiest old bastard amongst us being rattled by my wife. It's amazing how a woman can affect a man, as I was about to learn. Mel looked at me, pointing the ladle she was scooping the stew with. "If you know what's good for you, you'll shut up."

I was caught completely off guard. This was the woman I'd known since high school. The one that I snuck around with, riding on the back of my motorcycle. I'd known her for nearly thirty years; and yet, at this moment, I didn't know if she were serious or not. So I did what any intelligent man would do; I shut up. Mel filled a bowl for the old man and handed it to him. He looked at her, "Thank you, Miss Mel."

"You're welcome, Linus. There's enough for seconds if you want it." She replied. Mel then looked at Ted. "Ted, would you like some?"

Ted, probably the smartest man amongst us, smiling and dripping with politeness replied, "Yes ma'am, please."

As Sarge walked past me, he winked. I was still confused. Then he took a seat across from Mike. Glancing at Mel as he lowered himself into his seat, he whacked Mike on the knuckles with his spoon. Mike let out a yelp. Sarge quickly jabbed his spoon into his bowl and took a bite. And with pure innocence in his voice, asked, "What's the matter, Mikey?"

Mike shook his hand and grinned at the old man, "Oh nuthin'." He held his hand up as if to inspect it, "I think I got a splinter."

Sarge, smiling as he chewed, replied, "Gotta watch them splinters."

Mel didn't see it. I couldn't imagine how she didn't; I saw it all. Maybe that was it, the difference between men and women. She'd called him out when he was there in front of her, but now that moment was gone. All I knew was that she'd just put the old man in check; I was still amazed. But one thing was certain, these guys never ceased to crack me up.

I noticed Jess fidgeting again, and asked what was up. She looked at Fred, and Fred said, "You guys said you were going to get us a rifle."

I stood up, "Indeed we did. Let's go see what we have."

Sarge and the guys followed me into the bedroom where the weapons from the camp were kept. There was a pile of them. I deferred to Sarge to decide what would be best for the ladies. Sarge picked through the weapons, pulling two ARs from the assortment. They were the ones from the DHS goons killed earlier, and in great condition.

"I think this would be good for you two." Sarge said, inspecting the rifles. "Nearly new, hardly fired and only dropped once."

"Are they French?" I asked.

Sarge laughed, "Tomorrow we'll spend some time at the range to get you up to speed."

Jess took the weapon and looked it over. Mike reached in and grabbed the muzzle of the weapon once when she swept him with it. "Never put anything in front of this you don't want to destroy."

Jess blushed, "Sorry."

"It's ok; you'll learn," Sarge said.

Mike and Ted spent some time going over the controls of the weapons for the girls. They needed some familiarization now since the weapons were going with them tonight. Since they didn't have any training yet, Sarge gave them each one loaded magazine, telling them to not put them in the weapons tonight.

"I'm giving you these because the rifles are useless without them. But I don't want you to put them in your weapon until you've had training. You'll have plenty of opportunity to run and gun."

The girls nodded and promised not to load them. Fred said Aric knew how it worked, and if anything came up, he would take care of them. That was a bit of a relief, knowing he would be there to ensure there were no *accidents*. Now that arming them was taken care of, everyone started to head to their respective houses. Danny and I were scheduled to relieve the barricade shortly, so I walked Mel and the girls home.

"I want to go fishing tomorrow," Little Bit said as she followed behind us.

I looked back, "We don't fish for fun anymore kiddo; those fish in the pond are a resource we can't mess with."

"Maybe we could have a fish fry; it would be nice. I think everyone would like the change in menu," Mel said.

"Yeah! A fish fry!" Little Bit shouted.

"Can we help catch them?" Taylor asked.

I wrapped my arm around her. "Sure, I think it's a good idea, fish fry tomorrow!"

After getting the girls settled, I kissed Mel and told her I'd be back in a few hours. This time she didn't resist. She just gave me a hug and told me she'd see me later. It felt good that she was coming to accept the way things were. I found Danny sitting on one of the four wheelers, and hopped on the back.

Pulling up to the barricade, I hopped off. "You guys head back and get some supper."

"Sounds good to me," Jeff said as he climbed on the ATV.

As Doc was about to get on, I stopped him. "Little Edy is sick."

He paused for a moment, "Mmm, let's hope it's nothing serious."

"What do you really think?" Danny asked.

"We'll just have to wait and see; too early to know yet," Doc replied. "In the morning, I'll go over and check on her. But there isn't much I can do for her."

"Well, let me know what you think after you see her," I said.

He nodded and mounted the machine. Jeff started it up and they headed down the road.

"Well, here we are again," Danny said as he rested on the barricade.

I joined him, "Yeah, kinda like groundhog day, huh?"

Danny nodded. After a moment, he said, "But it isn't bad; I kind of like it."

We hung out for a couple of hours, talking a little and walking out to the road to scan it in both directions. As usual it was quiet, nothing happening. I was out in the road looking up at the sky with the NVGs, looking for satellites. It was something I used to do with the girls, a game of sorts. It always amazed me how fast you could find one. One time we spotted the International Space Station. It's the only thing up there that big. It was so bright and moving incredibly fast, so we couldn't see it for long. But the girls got a kick out of it nonetheless.

I lowered the device and scanned the field across the road, and once again saw the small light. I took a look without the aid of the device and couldn't see it. Lowering the device, I looked again and saw it. This time though it appeared it was coming across the field, towards us.

"Hey man, come out here," I called to Danny. Danny came out and I handed him the tube, "Take a look out there, see the light?"

Danny looked across the field, "Yeah, looks like he's out in the middle of the field this time."

"That's what I thought; almost like he's coming straight at us."

Danny watched the light for a moment, "Sure does. He isn't very stealthy about it; he's right out in the open."

"Maybe he's not hiding."

Danny handed me the device back, "Maybe he doesn't know we have NVGs."

"Let's keep an eye on him and see what he does."

We walked back to the barricade and settled in to wait. From time to time we would check on the progress of whoever was out there. Each time, he was closer. It didn't take long for him to close the distance to us; and he was standing in the field just on the other side of the fence from us.

"He's just across the fence," I said.

"What's he doing?"

I handed Danny the tube, "He just squatted down, just sitting there."

Danny took a look, "Well this should be interesting."

He was less than a hundred yards from us. He'd done nothing to this point to give any indications of hostility. However, it was a little unsettling to have him just sitting there watching us.

"He has to know we can see him," Danny said.

Looking through the tube at him, I replied, "I would think so." Just as I said that, the man across the road rose to his feet and started towards the fence. "Here he comes."

I watched as he slipped through the strands of wire, rather quietly I noted. As he approached the pavement, I leaned over to Danny, "He's getting closer now. When I give the signal, let's light him up. It'll wash out his NVGs. Let's see what he does."

We rose to our feet, and just as he was walking onto the road, I said *now!* We both turned on the lights mounted on our carbines. The intense LED lights caused the man to stop and raise his hand to shield his eyes. Reaching up, he removed the NVGs from his head, still shielding his eyes with the other hand. In the light, we could see his weapon was slung over his shoulder and his hands empty, except for the goggle.

"Damn, that's bright!" The stranger called out.

"What do you want?" I asked.

"Those lights out of my eyes for starters. That'd be great."

We lowered the lights from his eyes a bit, but kept him lit up. "Thanks, those things are bright as hell."

"Now, what do you want?"

"I've been watching you guys, and just wanted to drop in and let you know I wasn't a threat. I've been in the area for some time."

"We've seen your lights a few times; but what makes you think coming up here in the middle of the night is such a good idea?" Danny asked.

He shrugged, "I don't move during the day if I can avoid it. I prefer to lay low and try and stay out of sight."

"Why, who you hiding from?" I asked.

The man laughed, "Hell, everyone! You been out lately?"

"Yeah, we get around."

The man nodded, "Yeah, you guys have four wheelers and trucks. I've seen them." He paused for a moment and pointed to the water jug, "is there water in that?" I nodded. "Would you mind?"

"Sure, come on up, just keep that rifle slung."

He raised his hands, "I'm not looking for trouble. I knew you guys have night vision equipment. That's why I walked straight in like I did, so you could see me."

He came up and filled a stainless water bottle from the jug, and quickly drained it. I was looking him over, trying to get a sense of him. The bottle he held was blackened from countless fires from the looks of it. He carried an AK and wore a chest rig full of magazines high on his chest. He was tall, and struck a rather intimidating appearance. Strapped to his hip was what looked like a Glock of some variation; and the handle of a large knife jutted out in front of him. On his back hung a small pack. From the way it sagged, it was obviously heavy. He refilled his bottle and took a seat on the barricade.

"So what made you come here tonight? Why now if you've been around for so long?" Danny asked.

He looked back over his shoulder, "I got pushed out; there's a large group moving around out there. I bumped into a couple of them last night, and they weren't particularly friendly."

"We didn't hear any shooting; what happened?" Danny asked.

He shook his head, "There was no shooting, I handled it quietly."

"With that?" I asked, pointing to the knife.

He quickly drew what turned out to be a Kukri and held it up. "No. I was actually taking a shit when they showed up. I had my etool out to dig a cat hole, so I cleaved his head in half with it."

"With an etool?" I asked.

He dropped his pack and pulled a short shovel out. It had a wooden handle and a small spade head. I recognized it as a Spetsnaz shovel. "Yeah, they have a lot more uses than digging." He twirled the tool in his hand, "I dig with it, chop and cut; hell, I've even cooked on it." He looked up, "makes a hell of a frying pan in a pinch."

"What's your name?" Danny asked.

He rose to his feet, and with a powerful swing, slammed the etool into the top log of the barricade, where it sank a full two inches into the pine.

"Name's Dalton. What's yours?"

"I'm Danny; this is Morgan."

"Ah, Captain Morgan. I've sailed with him in the past. He took me to places I don't remember on adventures I can't recall."

He paused for a moment in deep thought. "Come to think of it, those weren't very good times." He looked up and smiled, "And that's why I don't drink anymore."

Danny and I both glanced at one another. I, for one, had no idea what the hell he was talking about. Danny just shrugged.

"I guess none of us drinks much anymore," I replied.

"I quit long ago. Wasn't good for me, or anyone around me for that matter."

"What's your plan?" I asked.

Dalton looked around. "You guys keep a constant guard up here, right?"

I nodded, "Yeah."

"Would you mind if I crashed up here for the night? I really need some good sleep."

I certainly wasn't expecting that; I figured he might ask for food or something, not to sleep. I looked to Danny, and he was obviously just as perplexed as I was.

"As I'm sure you can relate, that seems a little strange," I replied.

He nodded. "I know, but I think I can close my eyes here. There are two of you, and you haven't tried anything yet." He looked me over for a minute, then pointed. "What's with the stars?"

"it's a long story, but I'm kind of the Sheriff around here."

Dalton smiled, "That's even better then. If you're the law, then I know I can trust you."

"The question is; can we trust you?" Danny said.

Dalton cocked his head to the side. "I'm going to be asleep. If anyone is vulnerable, it's me."

"Or you could be part of a group we're having issues with," I fired back.

It had suddenly come to me that he could be one of Billy's

boys sent to gather some Intel. Or maybe to try and get on the inside and cause some trouble.

"You mean that group that was back over there?" Dalton asked, pointing to the southwest.

"What do you mean, was?" I asked.

"Just that, was. They moved."

"Is that who you bumped into?" Danny asked.

Dalton nodded, "Yeah, they moved out into pasture land over there. They're holed up back in a little swamp. They got a lot of people, vehicles and dogs. Dogs are a problem, see. They can smell and see you before you do them. Hard to deal with dogs, but there are ways."

"I'm going to lay it out for you; we have no way of knowing who you are. You could be part of that group, and that would be a problem."

Dalton removed his Boonie hat and scratched at his head, "I can see your conundrum. How about I give you guys my weapons? I want to sleep right here; not looking to go into your neighborhood."

I thought about it for a minute and looked at Danny, "What do you think?"

"If he's unarmed, I don't see an issue with it."

Looking back at Dalton, I said, "Alright. If you're willing to do that, you can crash here."

"Smashing!" Dalton shouted. "Where do you want me to put my gear? I just need to get my sleeping gear out."

"Go ahead and get that; then we'll secure your stuff."

Dalton removed a bivy bag and a poncho liner from his pack, and tucked his water bottle under his arm. "This is all I need."

"Just leave your stuff right there. You can sack out over here," I said, pointing to a spot under the brush on the side of the road.

Dalton laid his sleeping gear out and quickly got in the bag. Without saying anything else, he disappeared into the bag, pulling the poncho liner up to cover his face. Danny and I moved up to the barricade and set Dalton's gear off to the side. He'd laid his pistol on the top log, so I dropped it into his pack and zipped it up. Danny picked up the AK and removed the magazine, then ejected the chambered round. Once the weapon was secure, he placed it on the pack. In quiet voices we talked about our guest.

"What do you make of him?" I asked.

Danny half shook his head, "Hard to tell; seems a little weird to me."

Glancing back at the sack, I said, "He's definitely different."

About an hour later, Thad and Mike showed up to relieve us. We shared the story of our visitor, pointing out his sleeping form. Danny showed them where his gear was stashed.

"Well you certainly don't see that every day," Mike said.

Thad was looking at the bag, "You trust him?"

I shrugged, "He hasn't done anything, and he gave up his weapons."

Mike wrinkled his nose, "He been snoring like that long?"

I chuckled, "Yeah, almost as soon as the sound of the zipper stopped that racket started."

"He shore sounds like he needed some sleep," Thad added.

Looking at Mike, I said, "He also said Billy's group has moved, at least I assume it's Billy's."

"Really? We were just talking about taking another look at them. I was worried they would bug out."

"We'll talk to him tomorrow. I think he knows where they are."

Danny stretched, "You ready to go? I'm tired."

"Yeah man, let's go."

Mike looked back at Dalton, "Don't worry, we'll keep an eye on him."

"It's all good. See you guys later," Danny said as he climbed up behind me on the ATV.

Danny dropped me off at my place then headed home. Meat Head came running out of the darkness barking, until he realized it was me. He came up and nuzzled my hand, so I patted him on the head. I didn't see Drake; a black dog at night is kinda hard to see. I realized he was there when I tripped over him. Turning on the light on my weapon, I saw him raise his head; he didn't even bother getting up.

"Sorry Drake," I said as he laid his head down.

Little Girl was lying on the porch; she never bothered to get up either. I looked down at her, "Lot of good you are." Her tail thumped the porch in reply.

Going in, I took my gear off and headed for bed. I was tired.

# CHAPTER 8

I WOKE UP BEFORE MEL OR the girls. The house was quiet; I was still getting used to the silence. It actually bothered me. As a product of the modern age, I wasn't accustomed to it. It had taken months for me to be able to go to sleep without the white noise of a fan in the room. Not to mention having tinnitus didn't help; my ears rang constantly. Trying to keep quiet, I dressed and slipped out to the kitchen in bare feet. I poured myself a glass of tea and sat on the couch to put my socks on.

Outside, a heavy dew settled on everything, driving the dogs to the porch. I found them there sprawled out when I went out to put my boots on. They seemed even lazier, if that were possible. Drake lifted his head to look at me, while Meat Head and Little Girl just raised their eyes a bit at the sound of the door.

"Look at you lazy asses," I said, pulling the leg of my pants over the boots. "You guys are worthless."

They replied by drumming their tails on the porch, and it brought a smile to my face. *If only my life were so easy.* Crossing the fence to Danny's, the light breeze that had picked up, brought the undeniable odor of decomposition to my nose. I walked over to the chicken feeder and checked it out. I had not done that since it was installed. The ground below it was alive with maggots, and checking inside revealed many more.

More for fun than anything else, I went to the coop and released the birds. There were many eggs in the laying boxes, but I left them for Little Bit to gather. It was one of her chores to check for eggs. The birds ran in the direction of the feeder. I guess they knew where their breakfast was. I watched and laughed to myself as they made short work of the grubs on the ground. The chickens had no idea where the grubs came from, that the source was hanging just over their heads.

I was about to climb onto one of the four wheelers to go to the barricade, but decided to walk. It was still cool out, and we really needed to be conserving our gas. Passing Tyler's house, I stopped and waited for Doc, who was coming down their drive.

"What's the verdict on Edy?" I asked.

"She's definitely sick."

"Damn."

Doc stopped, "But it gets worse; so are Tyler and Brandy."

I was stunned, "What? Mel didn't say anything about them."

"They're trying to hide it, but both of them have fevers. Sweat was beading up on their foreheads and both were coughing. They said it was allergies, but I know better."

This wasn't good. The last thing I wanted was for anyone here to come down with a cold, let alone TB.

"There isn't much we can do for them, is there?" I asked.

Doc shook his head. "No, some people beat it." He paused and looked me in the eye, "but most don't."

I nodded, "Kinda what I figured."

Doc looked around, "Where are you headed?"

"Up to the barricade; we've got a guest up there."

Doc raised his eyebrows, "Really, who?"

I shrugged, "Don't really know much about him, except his

name's Dalton. He showed up last night and asked if he could sleep up at the barricade; said he was tired."

"Sounds a little shady to me."

"That's what we thought. But he gave up his weapons and crawled into his sleeping bag and went to sleep."

"Well, let's go check him out," Doc said as he headed up the road.

I looked at the bunker project as we passed it. We'd be back to work on that today once everyone was up and going. Sarge was of the opinion that it was really needed, or would be. We stopped for a moment and talked about it. Doc said they were trained on constructing such emplacements since sandbags weren't always available. I asked if they would be sufficient, "As long as they don't have rocket launchers."

I looked down at the earth and log structure, "Great."

Doc slapped me on the back, "Don't worry, they don't have that kind of shit."

"I sure as hell hope not."

When we got to the barricade, Sarge was there with Ian and Jamie. Thad and Mike were still there as well. I could see Dalton was still in his bag, and Sarge was eyeing him with suspicion. As I walked up, he pointed to Dalton's prone form. "What the hell's the idea of this?"

I shrugged, "He didn't seem like he was a threat." I looked over, "Hell; he's still asleep."

"No I'm not," Dalton said as he sat up, pulling the poncho liner from his face.

"Well, good mornin' Sunshine," Sarge said with a smile.

Dalton took in the group as he scratched his head, "Damn, did it rain last night? You guys multiply faster than Gremlins." He extracted himself from the bag and stood up, stretching and groaning. "That's the best damn sleep I've had in forever, thanks."

"Not a problem," I replied.

I did a round of introductions, Sarge shook his hand and gave a quick nod. Once everyone knew who everyone was, I told Sarge what Dalton had said about Billy's group. Sarge listened then asked, "You know where they are now?"

Dalton was filling his water bottle and replied, "Yeah, they're out there in ranch land, holed up in a big swamp." He took a long drink from the bottle, "It's like they're expecting a fight."

"They should be, sooner or later," Sarge snorted.

"You had a run-in with them?" Mike asked.

"Yeah, part of the reason I came up here. I've been living out there for weeks. It was good for a while, plenty to eat, plenty of water and no one around. Then they moved in and started sending out patrols. I ran into one of the patrols. Actually, they ran into me."

"What happened?" Sarge asked.

Dalton shrugged, "I split one of 'ems head open and got away. I'm not much for the whole group dynamic. I prefer to work alone."

"Hard way to live; man's gotta sleep at some point," Sarge replied.

"Which is why I'm here. I didn't say it was the best way to be, just the way it is."

"Could you show us where they are?" Mike asked.

Dalton nodded, "Sure, I don't think they're going anywhere."

"Alright, we'll discuss this later. Let's go get some breakfast," Sarge said.

Dalton perked up, "Breakfast?"

"Yeah, come on; we'll feed you too," I said.

He clapped his hands, "Alright!"

"But you'll have to work for it. We have a little project we're working on that you can help with," Sarge added.

"Fine by me; I'm not scared of hard work."

Mike chuckled. "Neither is the old man; he'll lie down and go sound asleep right beside it."

Sarge looked at Dalton. "Ignore him; he was kicked in the head by a mule when he was young."

"Yeah, he was trying to milk it!" Ian shouted.

Dalton laughed. "I like you guys; you're my kind of people."

I picked up his pack and rifle and handed them to him. "Here, take these with you." Dalton nodded and slung one over each shoulder. I wasn't worried about him at this point. Besides, there were more of us than him.

Ian and Jamie were there to relieve Mike and Thad, so they walked with us. As we passed the bunker, Dalton asked if it was the project Sarge mentioned. We stopped for a moment to show him what we were doing, and told him why.

"Can't say I blame you. Looks pretty sturdy. I only had one run-in with them; but I watched them for quite some time," Dalton said.

"What was your impression?" Mike asked.

Dalton thought about the question for a minute, "They're a pretty big group with a lot of shit. They've got dogs that, from what I can see, are there for no purpose other than as an alarm system. But they move like a hoard with little discipline. They seem to think they're safe simply because of their numbers."

"Would you take 'em on?" Sarge asked.

Dalton smiled. It was a sadistic look. "I could take them all on if I were so inclined and wanted to devote some time to it. I like to hunt men. One at a time they would fall, quietly and when they didn't suspect it."

Mike laughed a movie-bad-guy laugh, "I like this guy!"

ANGERY AMERICAN

Dalton smiled and contorted his face into a hilarious bad-guy display, "I like you too." He wagged his eyebrows up and down to emphasize it.

Mike laughed uproariously. Sarge shook his head, "Just what I fuckin' need." And he started down the road towards Danny's house.

I turned into my driveway to check on Mel and the girls, letting the rest of the group continue to Danny's. The dogs came trotting up and followed me to the house. Opening the front door, I called out, "Hello!"

Taylor came around the corner rubbing her head with a towel, "Mom's at Bobbie's house."

I stepped in, "What are you doing here?"

"I wanted to take a shower. The water's cold," she said with a smile.

"But it feels good doesn't it?" I smiled back.

She smiled, "Yeah."

"You coming over for breakfast?"

She nodded, "Yeah; soon as I get dressed, I'll be over."

I nodded and started to leave but turned back, "How are you feeling? I know a lot has happened lately, how are you doing?"

She looked at me. "I'm good, Dad. Doc talked to me; he's really nice. I did what I had to do, and I'm good with that now. It's not what I wanted to do, and I don't want to have to do it again; but I will if I have to." She paused for a moment, and I could see she was looking for the right words. "It's just so different now. I was thinking about college before, or maybe about getting a job. Now I have to think about hunting, taking care of my sisters and defending them." She leaned against the wall, "But I actually like it.

"We're all together now; you don't have to go to work anymore. Now we concentrate on the things that matter. I mean, I wish this hadn't happened, but I'm good with it now. I'm happy."

I smiled and walked over and wrapped my arms around her, "You have no idea how happy I am to hear you say that."

She hugged me tightly, "I love you Dad."

I kissed the top of her head, "I love you too. Hurry up and get you some breakfast."

I left her to get dressed, and headed outside. The dogs once again followed me as I walked towards Danny's. I was uplifted though; that little talk with Taylor really affected me. To know she was going to be alright, that her head was in the right place; it lifted a weight from me.

Rounding the corner at Danny's, I heard laughter, a lot of laughter. Everyone was on the back porch, and I could hear Dalton's voice. From the sound of things, he was entertaining the group. Coming up on the porch, I saw Dalton sitting at one of the picnic tables with everyone sitting around talking. Finding Mel and the girls, I sat down with them.

Bobbie and Miss Kay came out of the house with a large skillet of scrambled eggs and set them out. Dalton looked at the pan, "Are those real eggs?"

"Yes sir, fresh from the chickens," Kay said as she scooped some onto a plate and handed it to Jess.

Each time she loaded a plate, Dalton's eyes were glued to it as it passed before him. Kay naturally served the women and girls first, as it should be. But Dalton did get the first plate after them. Closing his eyes, he held it up to his nose and inhaled deeply.

"Man that smells good. The last time I had eggs was in the spring when I found a Sandhill Crane nest." He scooped a bite into his mouth. His body went limp as he chewed, "Oh man that's good." Getting a chuckle out of everyone.

Kay smiled, "I'll take that as a compliment."

"It is. From the bottom of my heart, it is." Dalton replied as he took another bite.

Mel leaned over as we ate and whispered, "Who is he?"

"He came up last night, seems like a decent guy."

"Is he going to stay here?"

I shrugged, "Dunno; we'll see."

As we ate, we discussed the day's activities. There was a lot of work to be done; fortunately, we had enough bodies to tackle it. Sarge wanted a patrol to go out. It would be him, Mike and Ted. The rest of us were going to work on the bunker. The design was well understood at this point, and we hoped to finish it today. The addition of Dalton would certainly help. Once everyone was fed, we got things ready for the day.

Thad brought in one of the water jugs and put what ice we had in it. The hand tools were being gathered and loaded into the Suburban. Danny was out checking the chains on the saws and I was dragging out a wheelbarrow when Kay came up.

"Morgan, we have a bunch of eggs, too many. Do you think you could go trade some with those people down the road for some vegetables?"

"Yeah, I'm sure they'd like them."

"I'll go get them for you. It would be nice to have some fresh veggies."

After shoving the wheelbarrow in the back of the truck, I went inside. Kay had a basket full of eggs; I had no idea the chickens were so productive.

"Wow, how many do we have left?" I asked.

"Several dozen. I'm just worried they're going to spoil."

Picking one up, I noted, "We could always preserve them."

"How are we going to do that?" Bobbie asked from the sink.

"I know there's some mineral oil around here somewhere.

All you have to do is wipe them with oil. Covering the shell completely prevents them from spoiling. They'll last a long time."

Kay leaned against the bar and crossed her arms, "I've never heard that. You sure it works?"

Nodding, I replied, "Oh sure, the other way is to use this stuff called sodium silicate, commonly called waterglass; but we don't have any of that. The mineral oil will work just fine."

Kay looked at the basket, "In that case I'll take some of these out. There will still be plenty to trade; but if we can store them, we can certainly use them."

Kay took a couple dozen out of the basket. Bobbie said she had some mineral oil, and they would coat the eggs with it. I took the basket out to the truck and set it in the front seat. Everyone was already walking down to the bunker. Mel and the girls waited for me. As I got in the truck, Little Bit asked if she could drive.

"I think you'll still fit. Climb up here," I said, patting my lap.

She quickly stomped her way into my lap. Amazing how kids always manage to step in the one place you don't want them to. I steered us out the gate and let her take over. As we passed those walking, she was sure to honk and wave, making sure everyone saw her *driving*. Once everyone arrived, we got to work. I was hoping we could finish this project today. All we had to do was roof the structure.

With the center loadbearing poles in place, we laid logs across them that spanned the width of the bunker. With the ends resting on the outer walls and center supported, the basic structural foundation was complete. We then started covering the top with more logs.

"We're going to need more," Thad said as he rolled the end of a log into place.

Danny, Thad and Dalton volunteered to go with him to cut more, and they headed off with the tractor. While they were gone, the rest of us put the last logs we had in place and took a break.

I'd just sat back against the wall of the bunker when Jess asked, "Are we going to get some weapons training in today?"

"I'm sure you will. We're almost done with this. When they get the next load here, that should do it." I looked up at the logs over my head, "I've been thinking about the roof. I want to spread some plastic out on it and cover it with dirt to keep the rain out."

"Good idea, I was thinking the same thing," Jeff said.

Lee Ann and Taylor were sitting in opposite corners of the bunker asleep. I envied them; teenagers could fall asleep anywhere. I remember those days of falling asleep in class. Man I miss that.

I decided to try and speed the process up. "Hey Jeff, want to help me spread the plastic on what we've already got down? We could even start piling the dirt on."

Jeff jumped up. "Yeah, let's do it."

Everyone except the two sleeping princesses pitched in as well. Fred, Jess and Aric spread the plastic while I started shoveling dirt into the barrow. Jeff moved some dirt to create a ramp on one side of the bunker so we could get it to the top. It took a couple of loads dumped there as well, but we finally had a ramp to the top. After several back and forth rolls to compact the loose dirt, we were able to roll it up to the roof and start dumping.

We set up a pretty good system. With Mel helping me fill the barrow, Jeff would roll it up and dump, and Jess's crew would spread it out. It didn't take long to cover the portion of roof that was ready. Once we'd done all we could there, we started working on the sides. I wanted to pile as much dirt as we could against the walls. It would help hide it in a way, and increase the ballistic protection some. We were working on the front, packing dirt and pieces of wood around the viewports when Thad showed up with more logs.

"You guys got a lot done!" He shouted.

"We're working on it," I replied as I unchained the logs.

"I think one more trip will do it," Thad said as I handed him the chain.

Looking back at the logs he'd just delivered, I agreed. "We'll have these in place by the time you get back."

As he rode out of sight, we got back to work. By the time the cutting crew returned, we had the last load of logs in place and were shoveling dirt onto them. The guys took a minute to grab a drink of water and cool off. Dalton filled a cup and took a long drink.

"Man, that's like some sort of magic," Dalton held the cup out looking at it. "I haven't had ice water in forever." He refilled the cup and drained it again.

"Yeah, we're lucky. Makes it nice on a hot day," Danny replied.

We all pitched in to get the last logs in place. We completed the rest of the roof with that last load, and pulled the plastic over it. The girls were up from their nap, and I put them to work on the roof spreading the dirt dumped there. The job was almost complete, and we were winding down when Sarge and the guys showed up. They were a bit of an odd sight as each of them was carrying a rake.

Jess shielded her eyes from the sun, "You guys been gardening?"

"Kind of," Ted replied with a grin.

"We rake the trails we patrol. That way if anyone walks on them we can tell," Sarge said.

Dalton was nodding his head, "Good idea."

"Now that you guys are done raking, can we get to our training?" Fred asked.

Sarge smiled, "Yes ladies. Let's go have lunch and we'll get to it."

"Lunch?" Dalton shouted. "You people eat three times a day?"

"We try," I replied.

He slapped his stomach, "Damn, I'm going to get fat!"

"It isn't much, but it keeps us going," Mel said.

"I'm going to run over to Gena and Dylan's house really quick to trade these eggs. Miss Kay wants some veggies, and I'm sure they have some."

"Can I come?" Little Bit asked.

"Sure kiddo."

"I'll come with you too," Danny said.

As everyone got ready to head back to Danny's, Mel told me to hurry. I promised I would as we loaded into the truck. I stopped at the barricade and Ian came up to my window.

"Seen anything?" I asked.

Ian waved the question off, "Nope, nothing."

"Just the heat, man it's hot!" Jamie added.

"And only going to get worse," Danny replied.

Jamie wiped her forehead, "Great."

Pointing with my thumb over my shoulder, I said, "The first bunker is done. I guess we're going to be moving this position back there."

"Why? We won't be able to see the road from back there," Jamie asked.

I shrugged, "It is not mine to question why."

Ian laughed, "Whatever, I don't care either way."

Danny leaned forward, "You still have water?"

Ian nodded, "Yeah, we're good."

"We're going to run trade for some veggies; be right back," I said as I put the truck in gear.

"By Mister Ian!" Little Bit shouted.

Ian and Jamie waved as we turned out onto the road. Danny was looking out the window and commented that we needed some rain.

"It's dry; just be careful what you wish for," I replied.

Pulling up at Gena and Dillon's, I shut the truck off as Dylan came around the side of the house. He waved when he saw us.

"Hey Morgan, Danny. What brings you boys by?"

Taking the basket of eggs off the seat, I replied, "We were hoping to trade you guys some eggs for some veggies."

He smiled, "We can do that; I'd love some eggs."

As we were talking, Gena came out on the porch. We said our hellos, and Dylan told her we wanted to trade some eggs. She too smiled, "Oh that would be great! We have a lot of veggies; I've been canning for days."

"Bring 'em in the house," Dylan said. "You want canned or fresh?" Dylan asked.

"I think fresh, they won't last long," Danny replied.

Gena looked at Little Bit, "And who's this?"

I put my arm around her, "This is Little Bit."

Gena smiled, "Hi Little Bit."

She smiled, "Hi."

Gena, took her hand, "Come with me, I have something for you."

We followed Gena into the kitchen to find nearly every horizontal surface covered with fresh vegetables. Jars were sitting where the produce wasn't, both full and empty. It was an impressive amount of food.

"Damn, looks like you guys have been busy," I said.

Dylan looked around, "Yeah, and we're eating as much as we can stand too."

"I wish our garden was producing like this," Danny said.

Dylan smiled, "That greenhouse is the best thing I ever did. Had no idea at the time it would save our lives, but it sure is."

Gena took a jar down from a shelf and set a plate out on the table. She spooned a large piece of honey comb out onto the plate, "You like honeycomb, don't you?"

Little Bit licked her lips, "Oh yes ma'am."

Gena handed her a fork, "Here you go."

She quickly set about eating the comb, honey running down her chin as she tried to stuff pieces too large into her mouth. She smiled as she chewed, rocking in the chair. It made all of us smile.

I handed Gena the basket. "Here are the eggs, Gena."

She looked at the basket, "Oh they look wonderful. They'll be so good in omelets."

She set the basket on the counter and removed the eggs, placing them on a small towel in the sink. When the basket was empty, she started filling it with produce, asking all the while if we wanted this or that. We replied we'd be happy with whatever she gave us. She piled tomatoes and cucumbers, peppers, onions, squash and green peppers into the basket. Not done there, she gave us a big bag of okra, another full bag of green beans, and finally, a large bag of greens.

I looked into the bag of greens, "What are these?"

"That's New Zealand spinach. We've got so much of it, there's no way we can eat it all."

Dylan grunted. "Yeah, I've been poopin' green for a damn week."

I looked at what she was preparing for us, "Gena this is too much, really."

"No, no; you guys take it. We have more than we can use. It'll go to waste if you don't take it. That greenhouse really produces," Gena insisted.

Little Bit finished her honeycomb, and wandered around the kitchen sampling the other offerings. Gena was all too happy to give her anything she showed interest in, and nothing was refused.

"You're not hungry are you?" Gena asked.

Little Bit smiled, "I haven't had lunch yet."

"Looks to me like you just did," Danny said with a laugh.

"I think you've had some of everything we have now," Gena said looking around the kitchen.

I looked at the pile of food. "Gena, our trades are always lopsided. We always come out on top of the deals."

"Don't worry about it. We've got more than we can use. I'd rather give it to you than throw it away. You brought these eggs, and we really need them; so we're just as thankful."

"Well, if you need anything, don't hesitate to ask us," Danny added.

She waved us off, "Oh don't you worry about it."

We walked out on the porch carrying the produce. "Let me put this away," I said.

Little Bit looked at Gena, "Thank you for the honeycomb, Miss Gena."

Gena smiled, "Oh, you're welcome, sweetie."

A sudden burst of automatic fire sounded in the distance. We all looked in the direction of Altoona; it wasn't very far.

"What the hell was that?" Dylan asked. The firing continued in long bursts.

"That sounds like a machinegun; it just keeps going," Danny said.

I looked at Gena, "Hey, could she stay here for a minute?"

"What is it Daddy, I don't want to stay here; I want to go with you."

I patted her head, "It's probably nothing kiddo, but I need to go check it out."

Gena knelt down, "You can help me with my canning. You didn't see the stove out back. You want to help?"

"Thanks Gena," I said as I headed for the truck.

Danny hopped in and looked over, "What the hell are we going to do against a damn machinegun?"

"Let's just go see what it is," I replied. The gunfire was still sounding in the distance.

We pulled out onto the road and I stopped, looking towards Altoona. We didn't see anything in the road, but it was still a little far off. I slowly started to roll towards the store, both of us keeping our eyes peeled. As the Kangaroo came into view, I could see a number of people on the ground. There were a few others that appeared to be trying to offer them help.

"What the hell happened here?" Danny asked.

"I don't know. See any shooters?"

"No"

We rolled into the chaos in the parking lot. There were several people who were obviously dead. The shouting and crying of those injured and those trying to help them filled the air. We both hopped out, weapons at the ready. I grabbed the first person I came to and asked what happened.

"Some soldiers showed up and started shooting. They just rolled up and opened fire."

"Soldiers, are you sure?"

"They were driving a Hummer and were in uniform! Hard to miss the big damn machinegun they were shooting!"

I went back to the truck and grabbed the handheld radio. I called Sarge, "Swamp Rat, you there?"

*"Go for Swamp Rat."*

"Get Doc up to the Kangaroo, there are several wounded up here. We need some help."

*"We're on our way."*

"Don't bring the Hummer."

*"What?"*

"I'll explain when you get here; just don't bring the Hummer."

We tried to offer help to those we could, but we didn't have much to work with. I wrapped an old t-shirt around the leg of a man that was hemorrhaging. Blood was pumping from a wound just above his knee. I wrapped the shirt around his thigh above it. Pulling the ASP from my vest and extending it and using it as a handle, I torqued the shirt to make an expedient tourniquet. He screamed in pain as I applied more and more pressure. When the blood stopped spurting out, I stopped and told a woman that was with him to hold it in place, and then moved on to another person.

Danny was working on a woman; though from what I saw, it was a futile effort. She'd been shot in the chest and was gasping for air. A thick froth of blood filled her mouth every time she tried to get a breath. There wasn't much that could be done for her in our current situation. It was only a matter of time before she would die.

It wasn't long before I heard the sound of Sarge's war wagon, and looked up just as they pulled into the parking lot. Both buggies skidded to a stop and Doc immediately jumped out. Ted and Mike were with them, and they too went to work on some of the wounded. Sarge walked up and asked, "What the hell happened here?"

I shook my head, "I don't know. They said soldiers pulled up in a Hummer and opened fire."

"Soldiers?"

"That's what they said. Said they were in uniform and driving a Hummer."

"I'm going to go call Sheffield and see if any of their people were out here," Sarge said as he headed towards his buggy.

I found a woman picking up the stuff she was trying to sell and putting it back on a table. "Excuse me, where were the guys that were shooting located?"

She looked up with tears in her eyes and pointed out towards the road. "They were over there. They just started shooting; didn't say a word, just started shooting."

I walked out to the road where she pointed and found spent brass and links scattered in the road. Kneeling down, I picked one up. I found a 7.62 round with a Lake City head stamp. It surely looked like mil-spec ammo. I took the case over to Sarge so he could examine it too.

"Sheffield and men are on their way here. He said they didn't have anyone out this way," Sarge noted as I walked up.

"Then who the hell was it?"

"I have a theory; but let's wait for Sheffield."

Jess, Fed and Aric were in one of the buggies as well. They'd each paired up with one of the guys, and the teams of two were working on wounded, doing what they could. As I looked around, I noticed that we needed more supplies. We were woefully ill-prepared to deal with this situation, and people were going to die today as a result.

It wasn't long before a convoy of Hummers and trucks arrived from the direction of Eustis. I didn't expect the reception they received. Some people ran, and others threw things at them. Mike tackled one guy that took a shot at one of the trucks. It was obvious the people here thought the Guard was responsible for the shooting. The Guardsmen quickly jumped in to assist the wounded as well as controlling the angry crowd.

Sheffield and Livingston walked up to where Sarge and I were standing. Sheffield was taking the scene in.

"What the hell happened here?"

"From what I've been told, a Hummer pulled up and opened fire on the people here. They said they guys were in uniform. Without saying a word, they opened up on them, then drove away," I replied.

"That's insane, we wouldn't do that. We didn't have anyone out this morning," Livingston said.

"We know it wasn't you guys," Sarge said.

"Then who the hell was it?" Sheffield nearly shouted.

"DHS," Sarge said flatly.

"Why in the hell would they do this?" Livingston asked, looking around.

Sarge snorted, "Isn't it obvious? This is a basic unconventional warfare tactic. They're trying to get the population turned against you, against us. We know you guys didn't do this, but we're going to play hell convincing these people it wasn't you."

"You really think they would stoop that low? Killing people just so they can blame it on us?" Sheffield asked.

"You're damn right I do. I know it for a fact; who else could it be?" Sarge shot back.

Sheffield was looking at the bodies, "What can we do to counter this?"

"We need to do everything we can to help. We need to tend to these wounded and help bury the dead."

As this conversation was happening, Doc ran up. "Guys we don't have the shit we need to deal with this. We're doing what we can, but it just isn't enough."

Livingston sighed, "We brought everything we had."

Sarge looked around. Everyone there was doing the best they could with what they had. After a moment he said, "I'll get us some more supplies. They won't be here today; but by God, next time we'll be ready to deal with this."

"Next time?" Livingston asked.

Sarge looked him in the eye, "Next time; this is the opening salvo. You bet your ass there's more of this to come. I'd also start to expect bombings where people gather as well."

"We need to find these sons of bitches," Sheffield said with more than a little hate in his voice.

"I'll see what I can do about that too," Sarge said matter-of-factly.

We spent the rest of the afternoon moving some of the more severely wounded into town where they could receive additional care. Some of the dead were buried on site while others were taken to the homes of family members to be interred there. By the end of the day, the level of distrust between the civilians and the Guard had subsided a little, but it was still palpable.

I told Sarge I had to go get Little Bit. He told me he would see to things there; so I rounded up Danny and we headed back to Gena's.

"Man, that was frickin insane," Danny said.

"I know, hard to believe people can be so horrible. Shooting innocent civilians just to make them hate the Guard. That's fucked up."

At Gena's, we found them around back. They were still hard at work on the canning. Dylan carried a load of jars into the house. As he passed by, he asked what happened. When we told him, he couldn't believe it.

"That's just horrible," he replied.

"Tell me about it. You should have seen it," Danny said.

Dylan wiped the sweat from his face, "We'll keep an eye out for 'em. If we see anything, I'll let you know."

"Thanks man," I said. Then I called Little Bit; it was time to get home.

Perez, Ian and Jamie were at the barricade when we got back. I stopped long enough to tell them what happened. They had some choice words for the perpetrators of such a cowardly act. Ian was really bothered by it.

"Just like Iraq. They did the same kind of shit over there," he said, shaking his head.

"Hopefully we can get a handle on this before it gets out of hand," I said.

"Oh we will, one way or another," Ian replied.

I waved as we pulled off. I wanted to get home. What was supposed to be a short trip for some bartering turned into an all-day nightmare. We pulled into Danny's and carried the produce into the house. Little Bit, oblivious to what had gone on today, told Mel about canning with Gena. She grinned from ear to ear when she told her about the honeycomb.

"Sounds like you had a good day," Mel replied with a smile.

Kay took the produce into the kitchen and started going through it with Bobbie. There was considerable comment on the variety, quality and quantity of what we brought back.

"This looks wonderful, Morgan. Too late for tonight's dinner; but we'll have it tomorrow for sure," Kay said.

Thad and Mary came into the house. They'd been out at the garden, as was starting to become their evening custom. When Thad saw me, he asked what happened up the road. Danny and I relayed the afternoon's events for everyone. They were shocked, like the rest of us that had witnessed it.

"That's awful," Mary said.

"How many people died?" Kay asked.

"Seven," Danny replied.

"And the number will only get higher as some of those taken to town will die as well," I added.

Sarge and those with him came through the door. He had a look of determination on his face. Actually, he looked pissed. Fred and Jess looked spent. Both of them had blood on their hands and went immediately to wash up. Doc dropped his pack on the floor and fell onto the sofa, rubbing his face as he did.

"You guys look beat," Mel said.

Doc grunted, "It was a bad day."

"Dinner will be ready in a minute," Kay announced.

"We'll be back later," Sarge said as he headed for the door with Ted and Mike in tow.

"Where are you guys going?" I asked.

Sarge stopped at the door and looked back, "To get some help."

"From where?" Mel asked as he went out the door. She looked at me and I shrugged.

Dinner was a somber affair; there was no jovial conversation, no witty banter or joking. Once everyone had eaten, Thad announced he and Jeff were heading to the barricade to relieve the crew there. Jeff picked up an AK and followed him out the door.

I stood up from the table, "Well gang, I'm beat. I'm going home."

Taylor came up, "Dad, can we play a game or something tonight?"

"Baby, I'm just too tired tonight," I replied.

"Give Dad a break tonight, he's had a rough day," Mel said.

She frowned and Little Bit said, "I'll play with you."

"Me too," Lee Ann said.

Dalton was sitting quietly in the corner. He stood up and

walked over. "Morgan, I'm going to go up to the barricade. Thanks for dinner."

"We could find you a place to rack out if you want," I replied.

"Nah, I'm good. I prefer it in the field."

I stuck my hand out, "Thanks for your help."

He looked at it for a minute, then shook it. "Thank you for what you've done for me."

We said our goodbyes and headed home. I needed some sleep. The dogs greeted us at the break in the fence and jumped around the girls as we walked. They threw sticks and ran from the dogs, who gladly chased them. Mel and I went up on the porch and sat down. She held her hands out.

"I've got blisters from the shovel." I looked down and slapped her hand lightly. She quickly jerked it back, "Ow, that hurt."

I smiled, "Times are tough, times are hard; about time them pretty hands were scarred." I smiled like a Cheshire Cat.

Mel glared at me, "Not funny. And lame."

I raised my eyebrows, "Oh, you think you could do better?"

She looked over, "You're rude. You're crude. Guess who's not gettin' screwed." Now she smiled.

I jumped back, "Hey now, let's keep this friendly!"

She just glared at me, "That hurt."

I reached out for her hand, "Here, let me make it better."

She hesitated, obviously suspicious. "What are you going to do?"

Taking her hand, I replied, "You kind of massage it." I took her hand and opened her fingers. Trying not to laugh, I leaned over and spit in her palm. Before I could react, she slapped me in the side of the head with her wet palm.

"What the hell's wrong with you? Have you lost your mind?" She was shouting and I was only making it worse by laughing.

"Hey, you gotta admit it was funny." I tried to scoot closer to her on the bench. "Besides, I remember a time when".......... She cut me off, jumping to her feet.

Pointing a finger right my face, almost touching my nose, she shouted, "Shut up mister! If you know what's good for you; you shut up! I don't know what kind of crazy has got into your head, but you better fix it!" I raised my hands and tried to speak, but she cut me off. "Fix it!"

Mel stomped off the porch. As she rounded the corner of the house, I could hear her mumbling something about choking me. I still thought it was funny and laughed; *she'll get over it.* I went in and dropped my gear on the floor and fell into bed, fully clothed, for my safety.

---

Sarge went back to his place and fired up the Green Monster. Mike sat down at the table and asked what the plan was.

"We need some help; I'm going to call Fawcett and see what he can do for us."

"You think they'll help?" Ted asked.

"They're going to have to," Sarge replied as he tuned the radio. He picked up the mic and made the call.

"Clementine, Clementine, Swamp Rat." He repeated the call two times and waited. After what seemed like an eternal pause, there was a reply.

*"Go for Clementine Swamp Rat."*

"Clementine, we have a situation and need some assistance ASAP."

*"What's the SITREP Swamp Rat?"*

"We had a large civilian group attacked today. We need medical supplies and equipment. Additionally, we need some heavy weapons."

*"Who was the OPFOR?"*

"DHS posing as US Army, operating Army vehicles. It was an instability operation." There was another long pause.

*"Swamp Rat, get us the coordinates for an LZ. Clementine wants to bring you in as well as your civilian counterpart."*

"Wait one," Sarge replied. Looking at Ted, he asked, "What do we have?"

"We can use the field across the road; it's close." Ted pulled a map out of his pack and unfolded it on the table.

Sarge quickly identified the location on the map and relayed the coordinates over the radio.

*"Copy all Swamp Rat. Be at the LZ at 0330. Flight leader will be Dark Horse on this net."*

"Roger that, Swamp Rat out."

Sarge dropped the mic, "Mikey, you go get Morgan at 0300."

Mike nodded, "No prob, why do you think they want you to come in?"

Sarge shook his head, "I don't know; they must have some sort of Intel."

"I'm going to get some sleep then," Mike said.

"We all need to," Sarge said as he rose from his seat.

# CHAPTER 9

J EFF AND THAD HUNG OUT at the barricade, leaning over the top log. It was a quiet night and the sky was clear. The mosquitoes were bad when they first got there, but they'd finally let up. Jeff looked over to where Dalton was sleeping near the buggy. It'd been parked back there after the day's events.

"That dude sleeps like the dead."

"Yeah he does. I wish I could sleep like that."

Jeff walked around the barricade to the water jug. As he was filling a cup, he stopped and cocked his head. "Do you hear that?"

Thad stood up and walked out towards the road. Jeff followed him, sipping on the water.

"Someone's coming," Thad said.

"Looks like a truck."

"Sounds like a Hummer. I think it stopped."

They stood in the road watching the truck. It sat in the road a few hundred yards away. The diesel engine idled noisily.

"You think it's the guys from the armory? Maybe they're out doing patrols," Jeff said.

The truck suddenly started to move. It quickly picked up speed. Thad reached for Jeff's arm, "Let's get out of the road."

As Thad started to step away a burst of gunfire erupted from the truck. Thad ducked reflexively and ran towards the side of the road. Rounds whizzed past him and slapped into the asphalt around him. He dove into the shallow ditch at the edge of the road and looked for Jeff, but he wasn't there. The truck continued to fire on them as it closed at a high rate of speed. Thad crawled towards the barricade, looking desperately for some substantial cover.

As he crawled, he called out to Jeff.

"Jeff! Jeff, where are you?"

A spotlight came on; someone on the truck was searching for the side of the road as the gunner continued to rake the area around Thad. Suddenly another machinegun opened up. This one was right in front of Thad. He looked up to see Dalton standing in the road with a SAW to his shoulder firing long controlled bursts from the weapon. Thad glanced over his shoulder and saw a few sparks fly off the truck and the spotlight suddenly go black.

Dalton and the gunner in the truck traded rounds for a few moments. Dalton looked down at Thad and shouted, "Move!"

Thad jumped to his feet and ran. The truck shut off its lights and started to back up. Dalton was walking backwards towards the barricade as he continued to fire. He was forced to the ground when a second machinegun opened up from across the street.

"Fire! Shoot at the bastards!" Dalton shouted at Thad.

Thad took a position behind the barricade and started to fire at the new muzzle flash across the street. Dalton made his way to the buggy and shouted, "Reloading!" Thad kept firing across the street. The first truck came back into the fight. Rolling up closer, the gunner there opened up again.

"This crossfire is going to kill us; we've got to move!" Dalton shouted.

"What do we do?" Thad rolled on his back, trying to reload the AK in the dark.

"We can't sit here; we've got to go somewhere!"

Bullets tore through the brush around them. They slapped into the log barricade and chewed up the asphalt. They were crawling away from the barricade when there was a loud bang behind them. They stopped, straining to see the source of the sound, when the area was suddenly illuminated from above. Dalton took a quick look over his shoulder and saw an armored truck sitting in the field across the road firing at them.

From inside the neighborhood, another machinegun opened up, firing at the truck. Thad realized it was Sarge's other buggy.

"It's Sarge and the guys!" He shouted.

Dalton turned and began firing into the field, adding his weapon to the fight. Ted ran up and slid in beside them.

"What the fuck is going on?" He shouted.

"There's two of them. Another one is sitting down the road," Thad said.

Ted rolled over and looked at the truck as he fished a round out of his vest. He loaded the round into the M203 mounted under his M4. Propping himself up, he sighted in on the truck and fired. The round impacted just short of the truck, throwing dirt up over the truck. Sarge came crawling up beside them and rolled into Thad.

"What the hell is this bullshit?"

---

Mel shook me really hard, "Morgan, wake up!"

I was groggy. My head felt sloppy as I tried to wake up, "What?"

"Do you hear that?"

Sitting up, I asked, "Hear what?" Then I heard it.

"The shooting; do you hear it?"

I was suddenly completely awake, "Yeah, I hear it." I grabbed my gear and put it on. I was trying to remember where I had left my carbine when there was banging on the front door.

Mel let out a little yelp, "Who is that?"

Drawing my pistol, I said, "I don't know; get your gun."

Heading out to the living room, the banging grew in intensity. Taylor came out of her room holding her H&K, "What's going on?"

I pointed at her, "I don't know; go stay with your sisters." She disappeared into her sisters' bedroom.

Taking the flashlight from my vest, I lit up the door. I could see Mike on the porch, "Come on!" He shouted.

I quickly opened the door, "What the hell is going on?"

"Firefight at the barricade and there's a helicopter on its way to pick you and Sarge up."

"Helicopter? For what?"

"The Colonel wants to see you and the old man; but come on, we got to get to the barricade," Mike said in rapid fire. He could hardly stand still.

Mel came out wrapping a robe around herself. "What's going on; where are you going?"

"I don't know, just stay here and keep your guns handy."

"But—" Mel started to protest; but I grabbed my rifle from beside the door and ran out behind Mike.

We ran to Danny's and jumped on one of the ATVs. The sounds of the battle just up the road were echoing through the night. Danny came out of his house. "Come on!" I shouted as Mike took off.

We passed Fred, Aric and Jess as we raced down the road. They were running towards the barricade as well. Mike weaved all over the road as rounds snapped past us; the air seemed to be alive with incoming. He went off the road; cutting through yards in an attempt to get away from the incoming fire.

Mike slammed on the brakes without warning, nearly throwing me off. Jumping from the machine, he shouted, "Follow me!"

I ran behind him and we slid in beside Sarge as he was shouting to Ted, "Pop another flare!"

Ted was fumbling with his vest, trying to get a 20MM out of it. I looked around and could see Dalton and Ted both firing up the road. Thad was in the bushes off to our left shooting as well. I looked at Ted, "Where's Jeff?" He shook his head as he dropped a round into the tube, "I don't know!" He shouldered the weapon and fired it with a *thunk*. I felt the concussion of the weapon in my chest as much as I heard it. The round arched up into the night sky and popped, casting a brilliant white light. It was then I could see the armored truck sitting across the road spitting fire from a weapon mounted on top of it.

Sarge's radio crackled to life, "*Swamp Rat, Swamp Rat, Dark Horse is ten mics out.*"

Sarge fumbled for his mic, "Dark Horse the LZ is compromised, the LZ is hot! I repeat the LZ is hot!"

"*Copy that Swamp Rat, hot LZ.*"

Another voice came over the radio, "*Swamp Rat Bronco three.*"

"Go Bronco Three!" Sarge shouted back over the din of the fight.

Mike slapped me in the back. I looked back and he pointed, "Shoot!" I raised my rifle and started firing at the armored truck where I thought a gunner would be in the turret. The noise was hellish. Ted was still dropping 203 rounds on the truck, hitting it with one on the rear with no effect.

*"Swamp Rat, can you mark the friendlies? We'll engage the bad guys if you can mark your position."*

Sarge looked at Mike, "You got an IR strobe?"

Mike shook his head, "No. But I've got some IR chem lights."

"Get 'em out on the road in front of us," Sarge shouted. Then he keyed the radio; "Bronco Three, we're marking our position with two IR chem lights. Bad guys are west and southwest of there." Mike cracked the lights and threw them into the road, about ten feet apart.

*"Ah, roger that Swamp Rat, I've got your chem lights and see your bad guys. Put your heads down; we're coming in from the north."*

"Get down! Gunship inbound!" Sarge shouted.

We all tried to get flat; but I couldn't help myself, and looked in the direction of the truck. For an instant, I saw a flash. It was moving so fast; and suddenly the truck erupted in a huge explosion that lifted it from the ground. It landed in a flaming heap. Then I heard the gun on the helicopter open up. I couldn't see the other truck clearly; but I could see the sparks and fire flying from it and the ground around it as the rounds impacted. There was a thunderous explosion and the Hummer was destroyed.

We could hear the helos circling overhead. After a few moments, Sarge's radio crackled again.

*"Swamp Rat; it looks like the target is destroyed. Can you verify for Dark Horse?"*

"Roger that, Bronco Three; standby," Sarge replied. He stood up, "Mike, Ted; let's go check it out. Dalton, can you move up and cover us?" Dalton nodded and moved up to the barricade. "The rest of you keep your eyes open," Sarge said as they moved out.

I moved up beside Thad as Danny slid beside me. "What the hell happened?" I asked.

"They just rolled up and started shooting. We thought it was the guys from Eustis. I'd just told Jeff we needed to get out of the road when they started shooting."

"Where is he?"

Thad shrugged, "I don't know. I grabbed his arm just before they started shooting. We were in the middle of the road." He looked at me and shook his head. "I had to run."

"We'll find him," I said.

Sarge and the guys moved out across the field and looked around the burning truck. I could see them in the flames; the truck was a pyre. They moved towards the other truck, and after a few minutes I heard Sarge shout, "It's clear!"

As we were getting to our feet, Jess ran up. "What's happening?"

"I don't know; let's go see," I replied.

As a group, we walked out to the road. In the flickering light of the two fires, I could Sarge and the guys standing in the road in a half circle. My stomach sank, they were looking down at a form on the ground. Doc, who'd appeared from nowhere it seemed, knelt down and pulled something from his pack. He opened it and flapped out a Mylar blanket, covering the body. Jess ran ahead and Mike stopped her before she got to the body.

He wrapped his arms around her, "You don't want to see it."

"Who is it?" She asked, looking over his shoulder.

As I passed, I said, "It's Jeff."

Doc stood up, "There's nothing I could have done."

I nodded at him and looked down. We formed a circle around our fallen friend. We stood in silence as the light from the fires flickered around us. Thick black smoke billowing from the destruction hung low to the ground because of the dew beginning to descend. As we stood quietly, Sarge's radio once again crackled to life.

*"Swamp Rat, Dark Horse is inbound."*

Wearily, Sarge keyed the mic, "Roger." He looked at me. "Morgan; you need to come with me."

As he spoke, the Blackhawk thundered in low over the field where the truck was burning. We all looked up as the rotor wash caused the smoke to swirl.

"What's going on; where are you going?" Jess asked.

"We're going to meet some folks." Sarge replied. He looked back at Mike, "You guys stay here. You need to keep a lid on things today. Keep everyone close. Pull this position back to the bunker. If anything happens, call us on the Monster."

"We'll take care of this. Go get us some support," Ted replied.

"We got this, boss," Mike said.

Sarge jerked his head, "Come on Morgan; we got a bird to catch."

I looked at Danny, "Keep an eye on Mel and the girls for me."

He nodded, "Don't worry; we'll take care of them."

I followed Sarge as he ran out to the now-waiting bird. I copied his movement, ducking as we approached the open door where the crew chief waited. As we got to him, I heard the crew chief ask Sarge in a shout, "Sir, is that weapon secure?" He had on a flight helmet and his face was shrouded in a mask; he was an intimidating figure.

Sarge turned to me, "Drop your mag and clear the chamber; then put the mag back in."

I nodded and did as he said. I picked up the ejected round and put it back in the mag before slapping the mag back into the weapon. The crew chief gave me a thumbs up, and we climbed in.

The big helicopter suddenly surged with power and we were drifting up from the ground. In no time we were up above the trees, moving quickly away and still climbing. Looking out the open door, I could now see the coming dawn peaking over the horizon, somewhere over the Atlantic. We were only about fifty miles from the coast; and had it been full daylight, I would probably have been able to see the beach.

Sarge tapped me on the shoulder and handed me a headset that I put on, "You okay?" He asked once I had it in place.

I nodded, "Where the hell are we going?"

"Camp Riley up near Eglin."

"What the hell is going on?"

"Colonel wants to see us; told me to bring your ass too."

I shook my head, "Bring me for what? What the hell do they want me for?"

Sarge shrugged, "Hell if I know. He told me to bring my civilian counterpart."

"Your what? I'm not your civilian counterpart. I'm not in any leadership position around here!"

Sarge replied curtly, "You are now." He leaned back against the firewall of the helicopter, folded his arms, and closed his eyes.

I sat there for a moment staring at him, but it was apparent as far as he was concerned the conversation was over, so I turned my attention back to the view. Up as high as we were, the dawn came a lot faster than I would have expected. I watched the world below drift by, making note of the many small wisps of smoke I saw rising lazily into the sky. Nearly everyone cooked with fire now; and as their day began, the ritual of sparking a flame was once again the norm. A skill nearly lost to the incessant march of technology. It made me wonder how many people around the country died for want of fire.

Standing in stark contrast to those small wisps of smoke,

were the billowing columns of smoke from several very large forest fires. I counted three, and they reminded me of what we'd just experienced. It made me start to think of the rest of the country. Out west, California in particular, suffered from severe fires in the summer. It was a safe bet that millions upon millions of acres were burning at the moment. Without man interfering to stop them, the natural cycle would take over once again. Fire was a necessity for nature and an inconvenience for man. This time, nature would win.

It was also very cool as high up as we were, which was nice. I looked the crew over; there was a gunner on either side of the ship. Both of them constantly scanned the landscape below. The machine appeared to be in very good repair. It was clean, and seemed unaffected by current events, unlike most complicated machines. Even the crew's weapons were spotless. The feed chutes were filled with gleaming brass. It was like being in a different world, as if the recent past events had never happened. I settled in for the flight, having no idea how long it would last.

We flew for quite some time. I had no way of knowing how long because I didn't have my watch on. But after what certainly felt like hours, a large complex came into view. As we turned to make our approach I saw two Apache gunships above and behind us. I'm sure they must have been there the whole time, and were responsible for ending the fight earlier. The Blackhawk continued its turn, eventually lining up on a runway. The pilot, in demonstration of sheer skill, set the bird down without even a bump. The pitch in the turbine changed and the crew started to exit.

A Hummer pulled up and I followed Sarge, climbing into the backseat. The driver didn't say anything as he made his way through the base. It was kind of funny to stop at stop signs and traffic lights. Actual working traffic lights! I leaned forward and asked the driver, "You guys have power?"

He nodded, "Yeah, we got it back on about a week ago."

"How?"

"Our engineers got it back up somehow. I don't know what they did; I'm just glad to be able to take a hot shower now."

"Is there a power plant here on the base?" I wanted to know how they did it, what fuel it used, and where they were getting it from. I had questions, and wanted answers.

"Like I said, the engineers did it. I'm not an engineer." I wasn't going to get my answers from him.

The Hummer pulled up in front of a brick building and stopped. Sarge got out and I followed him inside. Here too, it was like a different world. A young man in a crisp uniform sat at a desk shuffling through papers. As we came in, he looked up, "You First Sargent Mitchell?" Sarge nodded. The young soldier pointed to a door, "The General is expecting you."

Sarge didn't say a word and headed through the door. Once I came in and closed the door, Sarge boomed, "General! They just giving stars away now?"

The man behind the desk stood up, "The selection pool is shallow now." He stepped around the desk and shook Sarge's hand. "Good to see you again, Linus. Looks like you guys have been stirring the shit with a big stick."

Sarge crossed his arms and rocked on his heels. "We're doing what we can, but we need a bigger stick." He looked back at me. "Colonel," catching himself he looked back, "General, this is Morgan Carter, the local Sheriff."

The man stepped up to me. "Sheriff, I'm General Fawcett; pleased to meet you."

"Good to meet you, General. But if I may ask, what in the hell am I doing here? I'm not really even a Sheriff."

"Yeah he is," Sarge quickly retorted.

Fawcett smiled and gripped my shoulder, "Have a seat Sheriff."

Sarge and I both took a seat, and Fawcett sat down on his side. Sarge looked around the room, "Nothing good ever comes from me sitting across one of these."

Fawcett smiled, "Let this be a first then. You guys probably aren't aware of the current situation, so let me fill you in. We've made considerable strides in securing the country. Assets that were outside CONUS were recalled, despite a lot of maneuvering from Washington. They'd hoped to keep those assets tied up and thus out of our reach. They seemed to forget we take care of our own.

"With the additional men and material, we've got the DHS on the ropes. I don't know what they were thinking to begin with, trying to stand toe to toe. It's been wholesale slaughter in places. As a result, they've moved into an insurgent posture. There are still a lot of them out there, and they are causing considerable trouble. Attacks on soft targets is on the rise."

"We just had our first," Sarge replied. "They hit a local market and killed a bunch of folks."

Fawcett picked a paper up from his desk and put on a pair of glasses. "The joys of growing old," he said, looking over the top of them. "You guys managed to take the camp down in Pine Castle and shipped the prisoners to Frostproof. But they never made it there." Taking off the glasses, he dropped the paper back on his desk.

Sarge nodded, "Correct; and it looks like they've got some new friends now because they brought some heavy hardware in. Had it not been for your Apache this morning, I don't know what we would have done."

"What do you need?"

Sarge rubbed the stubble on his chin, "I need something that can take out the MRAPs when they show up. Ammo, lots more ammo. I have a small shopping list." Sarge pulled a piece of paper from his pocket and handed it across the desk. Fawcett looked it over. I can do most of this for you; maybe not the quantities you want for everything, but I think we can square you away.

Sarge smiled, "I appreciate anything you can do."

Fawcett looked at me, "How's the civilian situation?"

"We need medical supplies, lots of them. We have nothing left in the area. We also have a suspected TB outbreak and could use antibiotics."

Fawcett's brow furrowed, "TB? How many?"

I shrugged, "I've got one family quarantined right now, but I know others that are infected have passed through. The source was actually a group passing through. We were pretty sure they were sick, but had no way to quarantine them."

The general noted, "We're seeing major outbreaks of TB, Cholera and other diseases we haven't seen in years, decades. Cholera is burning up the east coast and most major cities. California is a cesspool of disease. I can get you some antibiotics and some other equipment."

"We need more than that," I said shaking my head.

Fawcett picked up some papers from his desk, "You and everyone else. You're not the only ones in a world of shit these days."

"I know; I'm not blaming you. But I've got a bunch of people that were shot to shit by guys dressed up like your people." I pointed at Sarge, "When the Guard showed up after the massacre, the crowd assumed they were the bad guys returning, and started throwing things at them. We had to take one guy to the ground that was about to shoot one of the

Guard. If you can do something to show them you're on our side, I think it would make a huge difference."

Fawcett drummed his fingers on the desk. Picking up a clipboard, he flipped through the papers. "I can get you a field hospital with surgical capability."

I was stunned, "That would be great!"

He held a finger up, "Don't be so quick to agree; it comes with conditions."

I held my hands up, "Let's hear it. I'm game."

"It will make you guys a regional clinic. People will be showing up for treatment, lots of people. It could also make you an even bigger target for the Feds. They'll want to eliminate the resource. It's part of what they're doing all over the country."

"I thought you guys had the Feds on the ropes."

"We do in places, but it's a big country. There are plenty of places we can't deal with yet. We're leaving the cities alone for now, concentrating our efforts on more rural areas. We're making a big push right now in the Dakotas, Wyoming and Montana."

That confused me. "Why? There isn't shit out there."

"There's plenty there," Fawcett replied.

"Oil," Sarge said.

Fawcett nodded, "Exactly; we've got an operational refinery in New Castle. It's keeping us in fuel and other distillates."

"Why not concentrate on the gulf? There are way more refineries there." I noted.

"We own most of the Gulf already, but it's taking a lot of time getting those larger facilities up and running. New Castle was in shutdown mode and wasn't damaged nearly as badly, so we were able to get it up and running a lot faster. Plus, there are a lot of trains out that way we can use to move the product. Of course there's still a lot of work to be done to get them running."

I was surprised, "Wow, I had no idea. Back to your original

point; we're good with it. The DHS is already causing trouble. At least now we'd have a reason for it."

Fawcett nodded, "Okay then; just remember this is a DOD asset. If the time comes that I need it, I'll have to take it back. Just so we're clear."

Nodding, I replied, "I understand."

Fawcett picked up Sarge's note and looked at it, "Give me some time to get this together. I'll also get to work on the field unit. Why don't you guys go to the chow hall and get something to eat. I'll send for you when we're ready."

Sarge jumped to his feet, "Sounds good to me, General."

Fawcett looked at me. "Sheriff, would you mind giving me a minute with the First Sergeant?"

"Sure," I said as I headed for the door.

I went out and milled around. The place was buzzing with people. It looked like your typical office; it could have just as easily been a mortgage company. The one thing missing though was the ringing of phones. Instead, there were a number of large green consoles stacked around. They looked a lot like Sarge's Green Monster. It was from these the communications were handled.

After a bit, Sarge came out of the office and waved for me to follow him. I waited until I was outside to ask him what Fawcett wanted.

Sarge grinned. "Just to let me know the gloves were off, he said if we catch 'em in military uniforms, we can execute 'em."

I laughed, "If you've had the gloves on this whole time, I don't want to see what it looks like without them."

Sarge winked at me, "You have no idea." *Well that's disturbing,* I thought. "Come on; we're going to take a little detour."

"Where to?" I asked.

Sarge smiled, "Want to check on an old friend of mine."

I followed Sarge to a large fenced structure. A sign with an arrow read MOTOR POOL. "What the hell are we doing here?"

"I need a couple of things and want to visit an old friend."

Sarge walked in like he owned the place and made his way out to a large shop. Stepping through the door, he looked around and shouted, "Hey Faggione! You in here?"

A barrel chested man rolled out from under a Hummer. He was on his back on a creeper looking up at Sarge. Taking a cigar from his teeth, he smiled. "You better not be here to tell me you've wrecked my buggies."

Sarge smiled, "I told you I'd take care of them."

Faggione got to his feet. The cigar seemed to be in perpetual motion, moving from one side of his mouth to the other. "Then you just dropped by to say hi?"

"I need some oil filters and oil. Couple tubes of grease and a few other things," Sarge replied and handed him a slip of paper.

Faggione took the cigar from his lips, pinching it. Using it as a pointer, he gestured at Sarge, "I knew you wanted something."

Sarge looked at the stogie in Faggione's fingers. Pointing at he asked, "That's not the same ones I gave you is it?"

Faggione smiled and looked at it, "No. Yours were good, but this, this is straight from Havana."

"Cuba?" I blurted out.

Faggione nodded and Sarge implored, "Where the hell did you get those?"

"You wouldn't believe me if I told you."

Sarge crossed his arms, "Try me."

"We're making flights down there, doing a little trading if you will. One of our loadmasters has gotten real friendly with a Cuban Colonel named Felix. We bring him some whiskey and he gives us cigars."

"No shit! What kind of whiskey are you trading and where the hell are you getting that?" Sarge demanded.

Faggione smiled, "Come on Top, I can't give you all my secrets. It's business." Faggione reached into his blouse pocket and pulled out a cigar, handing it to Sarge.

Sarge took the finely rolled tobacco and ran it under his nose, inhaling deeply. "Damn that smells good."

Faggione motioned with his stogie, "Cuba's finest." He looked at the paper and then back at Sarge. "I can get this for you." Smiling, he added, "And since I like you and you hooked me up in my time of need, I'll add a little something to your order. On the house."

Sarge cocked his head to the side, "On the house?" Faggione nodded. "Bullshit!" Sarge bellowed. "There ain't no such thing as free!"

Faggione nodded his head slightly, "You're a smart man Top; let's just say you'll owe me one."

Sarge threw his hands up, "Oh for fuck sake! Last thing I want is to be in your pocket!" As he spoke, he dug around his vest and produced several silver dollars.

"Your money's no good here." Faggione replied with a wave.

Sarge squinted, "Oh yeah?" And went back into his pocket. This time coming out with a gold Krugerrand. "This any good?"

Faggione's eyes lit up, "Well now, I wouldn't want to be inhospitable and refuse you." He reached for the coin.

Sarge tightened his grip on it and looked Faggione in the eye, "You know how much this is worth. You better not come up short."

"Let's just say you have an open line of credit. I promise you'll be happy with what you get." Sarge released the coin and Faggione held it up to inspect it. Looking back at Sarge, he said, "It sure is a pleasure doing business with you."

"Just get my shit out to the Blackhawk that's taking us home," Sarge replied.

Faggione nodded and they shook hands. "Good to see you again, Top."

"Good to see you too," Sarge replied and spun on his heels and headed for the door.

We made our way to the mess hall. Inside, I stood and marveled at the place. The lights all worked, the floor was shined, and it was full of people talking and eating. Sarge led the way to the serving line. I picked up a tray and made my way down the line, stunned by the offerings. There were hamburgers, with buns....... buns! French fries, hotdogs, mac-n-cheese. All sorts of stuff I hadn't seen in a long time. Near the end of the line were several trays of cookies. I grabbed a double handful and stuffed them into my pockets.

Sarge glanced at me, "For the girls?" I nodded, and he grabbed a bunch and stuffed them into his pockets as well.

At the end of the serving line, a man in cook whites was dumping a large pail of brown liquid into a beverage dispenser. I waited until he finished and picked a cup from the stack.

"What is that?" I asked.

"Tea," he replied as he put the top back on.

Looking at the container, I said, "No shit?" The surprise must have been obvious.

He nodded, "Yeah, use that one. It's cold," he said, pointing to an identical container sitting beside it.

I quickly filled my cup and took a long drink. It was perfect. Not too sweet, just enough. I looked at the man that filled the container and asked, "You guys have tea?" He nodded, looking at me like I was an idiot. "Can I get some?"

He cocked his head to the side, "Tea?"

"Yeah, can I get some from you guys?" I asked.

He shrugged, "Sure. How much do you want?"

"How much do you have?"

He smiled, "A lot."

"Good; that's exactly how much I want," I said with a smile.

The guy laughed and told me to wait there for a minute. He left and returned a short time later with a large box the size of a small cooler. Setting it on a table, he said, "Here."

"Holy shit; that's a lot of tea bags!" I shouted.

He laughed again. Pointing at the label on the box, he said, "This ain't bags. It's lose tea."

"Lose tea? Shit, that's even more!" Then I thought about it, "How the hell am I going to make that?"

He shrugged and reached for the box, "If you don't want it".........

I slammed my hand on the box, "No, no; I didn't say that. I want it. I really want it. I'll take it. Thanks, you have no idea how much, but thanks."

He smiled, "No problem man. Especially if it makes you that happy."

I set my tray on top of the box and picked it up, "You have no idea friend." We carried our heavily loaded trays out to the dining hall to find a place to sit. Sarge looked around and nodded towards a couple of guys in flight suits. I followed him over and we sat down. I set the box beside my chair so I could keep an eye on it. The two guys looked over at our plates.

One of them gawked wide-eyed, "Damn; why didn't you get more? I can still see the edge of the tray."

Sarge held his hands over the tray like a teepee. Smiling he said, "Maximum angle of repose."

The reply confused him until his friend tapped him on the shoulder, "He means you can only stack shit so high before it rolls downhill."

Sarge pointed to the other man with his fork, "Exactly."

I wasn't much interested in the talk; I was busy piling pickles on my burger. Once properly dressed, I doused it with enough mustard to coat a chicken. Raising it, I took a bite, mustard and pickles squirting out the backside as if being uncontrollably purged. But it was awesome! I sat with my eyes closed, chewing until I heard Sarge.

"Good God, Morgan! Buzzards eating a dead possum make less of a mess."

I looked down at the tray, mustard and pickles covered everything on it. I didn't care though; it would still be good. Looking at Sarge, I said, "Leave me alone; I'm savoring the moment."

One of the guys looked at his tray. "If this shit impresses you, I feel sorry for you."

I grunted, "You should come hang with us for a while then. You'd be begging for this."

Sarge stuffed a fry in his mouth, "What's your call sign?"

One of them smiled, "Bronco three, Swamp Rat."

Sarge smiled back, "I had a feeling. Thanks for the help." Sarge leaned over and nudged my shoulder, "These are the boys that saved our ass this morning."

Sarge stretched his hand across the table, "Linus Mitchell."

One of them grabbed it, "Mark Phillips, this is Dennis McQuillen." Sarge shook his hand as well.

Dennis pointed his fork at Sarge, "First Sergeant Mitchell, huh?"

"Retired," Sarge replied with a smile.

Dennis looked him over, "You sure got a funny idea about retirement."

"This is Sheriff Morgan Carter," Sarge said.

Mark dropped the sunglasses that were resting on top of his

head over his eyes and leaned back. In a wretched attempt at Bob Marley, he sang out, "I shot the sheriff!" Dennis joined in with a chorus, "but I did not shoot the deputy!"

I shook my head, "You two are idiots." Looking at Sarge, I asked, "Relatives of yours?"

Sarge smiled, "We're all cut from the same cloth."

Stuffing a fry in my mouth, I replied, "Y'all need some new cloth. This batch is tainted."

"Next time I'll just keep my Hell Fires to myself," Mark replied.

Dennis laughed, "That was pretty cool. First time we ever shot an MRAP."

"Things like that aren't meant to be kept to yer'self," Sarge replied. "They're meant to be shared liberally with those you hate the most."

Mark grinned an evil grin, "An' I got some hate."

"A deep burning, white-hot hate," Dennis added.

"Wel,l I appreciate the help boys. We didn't have anything to hit that damn thing with. You saved our asses," Sarge said.

Dennis jabbed a fork at Sarge, "This is starting to become a habit, us saving your ass."

I snorted, "It's a full time job for some of us."

Sarge looked over at me and boomed, "What the hell are you talking about? I've saved your ass more times than I can count. If you were a cat, there'd be a litter of dead cats!" Sarge looked down at his plate grumbling under his breath. *"Saved my ass, talking out his ass."*

Dennis and Mark laughed, and I couldn't help but chuckle too. We ate our meal while we talked with the guys. They were much like Mike and Ted; didn't seem to take themselves too seriously. I thought that was odd for officers.

"What rank are you guys?" I asked.

"We're both Chief Warrant Officer Three," Mark replied.

I shook my head, "What's that? Is it like a commissioned officer?"

"It is; but it's for guys that came out of the enlisted ranks and don't have the table manners for real officers," Sarge replied.

Dennis stuck a French fry in his nose, "Hey, what are they talking about?"

Sarge looked at me, "See?"

Mark leaned back and crossed his arms. "Yeah, well, you're still supposed to salute us." He had a smug grin on his face.

Sarge jabbed his fork at him again, "You'd have a better chance of seeing the face of God than seeing me salute your ass."

Mark sat there stone-faced for a moment, then started to laugh. "Better chance of seeing the face of God! That's funny shit!"

A soldier walked up to the table, "First Sergeant Mitchell, General Fawcett requests you return to his office."

"Alright," Sarge replied with a nod. We stood to leave, and Dennis and Mark rose as well.

"First Sergeant?" Dennis said, he and Mark sharing a look of mock respect.

"Retired," Sarge replied. Smiling, he added, "So I don't have to salute no damn body."

Dennis leaned across the table, "Retarded?" He suddenly let out a yelp. Sarge, with uncanny accuracy had kicked the shit out of his knee.

With a sickly sweet smile, he emphasized, "*Retired.*"

Dennis was rubbing his knee, "Retired; ok, ok, retired."

I reached across the table and shook their hands, "Thanks for the support guys." Looking at Sarge, I said, "I appreciate it."

After shaking my hand, Dennis held his hands out like

two pistols. "Call us any time you need a precision application of whupass."

I laughed and shook my head. Sarge shook their hands and said, "Try and keep them contraptions in the air boys. I'm sure we'll be seeing one another again."

Dennis and Mark both took on a serious tone, "You guys be safe out there. Keep your powder dry," Mark said.

"Yeah, keep an eye out for them Feds. Let us know if you find them all bunched up in one place. We'll be more than happy to come in and prosecute the target," Dennis said.

"With extreme prejudice," Mark added.

We headed back to Fawcett's office. As we walked across the base, Sarge patted his belly, "Damn that was good!"

"I know, just having something different was great." I patted the cookies in my pocket, "The girls are going to love these." Holding the box of tea out in front of me, I added, "And I *love you.*" I leaned in and kissed the box.

Sarge smiled, "Yeah, we're going to be real popular when we get back." Then looking me up and down, he said, "And you need help."

"More tea for me," I quipped.

Sarge snorted, "Yeah, you just try and deny me a glass of tea and you'll need the help of a proctologist to get my boot out of yer ass."

"Well, since you asked so nice an all…" I said with a smile.

We found Fawcett in his office. He was standing with another officer.

"Linus, I got you some party favors that should take care of the armor issue if it comes up again. They're loading a M3 aboard your return ride now, along with the ammo and some of the other stuff you've requested."

"A Goose! Well General, I love you long time," Sarge said with a smile.

"You're getting a dozen and a half of assorted rounds. It's all I can spare right now," Fawcett said.

"What about the mortar rounds?"

Fawcett nodded, "You're getting more."

"Tomorrow at 1100 hours, we'll be bringing in the field hospital. You need to have an LZ cleared where we can set it down. Call us with the location later today. I'm also sending a squad to provide security for it; that way we don't draw down the available force."

"Wow; that's awesome, General. Thank you," I said.

"We're trying to get things back together, but it's going to take a long time."

"What about fuel? Could you guys help us out with that?" I asked.

"Right now the fuel situation is pretty good. We could airlift in a bladder tank to you."

"That would be great. I have another question," I said. Fawcett looked up, "You've got power back up here. We have a small turbine station in town that we've thought about trying to get online. Is there any way you could get some engineers to come down and take a look at it?"

"I'll have to see where they are on their current projects, but I think we can work it out soon." He looked at Sarge, "I'll be in touch and let you know when we can do it."

"That would be appreciated," Sarge nodded.

Fawcett held his arm out towards the door, "Gentlemen, your chariot awaits."

Sarge snapped to attention and saluted smartly. Fawcett looked at him and came to attention and returned the salute. Sarge smiled. "Thank you, *General.*" I couldn't tell if it was sarcasm or not in his voice, but Fawcett smiled, and we headed out to the Hummer for our ride back to the airfield.

As we rode back, I asked Sarge how long he'd known Fawcett. "We've crossed paths a few times. Never knew him really well, but he was always a good man. Took care of his soldiers, the real measure of an officer."

At the helicopter, the aircrew was hanging around the ship. Seeing us pull up, they immediately started prepping the aircraft for takeoff. These guys were all business. As the pilots got into their seats, the crew chief and gunner did their preflight. Sarge and I got aboard and took our seats. The back was considerably more crowded this time. Several large green cases were stacked inside, along with a bunch of ammo cans.

The pilots applied power and the giant beast began to shake and seemingly scream out as it finally produced enough lift and rose into the air. Riding in one of these was an experience. The sound, vibration and air rushing in through open doors was an assault to all senses. In wasn't long before we were climbing into the sky, the base falling away beneath us.

I settled in this time for the flight. I felt good; we'd secured a lot of valuable resources for our community. Hopefully it would save lives. Watching the world pass by outside, my mind drifted back to what awaited me at home. A sudden sadness filled me as I thought about having to bury Jeff. There was nothing I could have done to prevent it. And I know Thad surely did all he could, but it didn't make it any easier. Jeff was a friend, more than that. He was part of my family, and now he was gone.

It was an emotional roller coaster of sorts. First was Jeff's death, then flying away to a totally different world where a number of our needs would be met. The food was a high too. Having so much to eat at one time was a high of sorts. I could feel it pulsing through my body. Then the returning realization of Jeff's death. Even with all the food, I was suddenly very tired. Closing my eyes, I rested my head against the firewall.

I woke with a start. One of those flailing moments when you feel as though you're falling. Sarge looked at me like I was nuts. I waved him off and looked out the door. We were in a hard bank, the obvious reason for my waking. I quickly recognized the ground below and knew we were home. I must have dozed off and slept for better than an hour.

The helicopter circled and I could see the burned remains of the vehicles from the earlier fight. Then I saw Sarge's Hummer sitting in the field as well; the guys were sitting on the hood. The pilot brought the Blackhawk around and set it down near the Hummer. The guys quickly ran out to us as the crew chief and gunner started throwing the cases and ammo cans out. Sarge and I each grabbed some and headed for the truck. As soon as the supplies were off, the pitch of the helicopter increased and the pilot pulled it into the air. I looked up to see the gunner giving me a thumbs up. I returned it as they climbed higher. Soon, the sound of the machine faded and it was just us.

"How'd it go?" Ted asked.

"Good, we got some trash from 'em." Sarge looked at Doc, "Tomorrow they're bringing in a field hospital with a four-man staff."

Doc's eyebrows went up, "No shit? I'll be damned, didn't see that coming."

"They're sending a squad to provide security for it as well," Sarge added.

Suddenly Mike yelled out, "Holy shit! You got us a Goose!" We looked back to see Mike open the case with the Gustav M3 recoilless rifle. Taking it out, he shouldered it. "Hot damn, I'm gonna blow some shit up now!"

"Put it away dickhead; let's get this shit loaded. I need

to call Captain America and let him know he's got a delivery coming in the morning," Sarge barked.

Mike laid the weapon back in the case and caressed its tube before closing the lid. We loaded all the stuff up and got in the truck for the ride home. As Ted pointed the truck at the road, I saw the barricade was empty. Looking at Ted, I asked if they'd moved back to the bunker.

Nodding, he replied. "Yeah, we pulled back to it. Been quiet today though."

"Good, I like quiet," I replied.

Ted pulled up to the bunker and stopped. I was surprised when Taylor came out with Danny and Jamie. Looking at her as I got out, I asked, "What are you doing down here?"

She shrugged, "Just trying to help."

While I didn't like the idea of my little girl doing security work, I knew it needed to be done. Besides, she was a woman now, no longer a little girl; and I knew she was fully capable of doing it. I smiled at her, "Good deal," and put my arm around her. We walked down into the bunker, I wanted to see what it was like with people actually manning it.

"What's it like down in here?" I asked as we stepped in.

"It's ok, kinda creepy."

One of the SAWs was sitting in the front opening. A couple cans of ammo sat on the ground beneath it. Someone had brought in some chairs and a small table like a sturdy TV tray and put the water jug on it. It looked like everyone was getting into the swing of using it. Coming out, Danny was talking to Sarge.

"Where's Jeff?" I asked.

"We buried him. Thought about waiting for you guys to get back, but we didn't know how long you'd be, so we went ahead and did it."

"It was the right thing to do," Sarge added.

I nodded, "Yeah, it was."

"Thad is over there now cleaning up the area," Danny said.

"Where'd you do it?" I asked.

"We put him out by the pond. Mel and Bobbie thought it would be a good place. You know, keep him close."

Sarge had the guys move some of the ammo from the Hummer to the bunker. He kept the Gustav though; that would stay with him. There were enough folks around here for now, and I didn't need to be here, so I told everyone I was heading home. I wanted to go see Mel and check on what was done with Jeff. I walked home and found the house empty. Going over to Danny's, I found Thad at Danny's shop. He was brushing varnish onto a cross.

"Hey man, how's it going?" I asked.

Thad shrugged, "It's going."

"That looks really nice," I said looking at the cross.

Thad stopped for a moment to look at his work. "After carving his name in it I burned it with a torch then sanded it some." He brushed more varnish on, "This will protect it. I wanted him to have something that would last."

I put my hand on his shoulder, "This will do it. Looks good."

Thad set the brush into a small container of paint thinner, "When this dries, we'll go put it up."

"I'll help."

Thad nodded, there was no smile this time. I could tell he was disturbed. He was always such a happy guy, but not today. I told him I was going to check on Mel and left him to wrap up his work. Mel was in the house with Bobbie. Little Bit was sitting on the couch playing on the iPad. Seeing it made me think of Jeff again. I doubt she made the connection, that it was his. She looked up, "Hey Dad."

"Hey kiddo," I replied.

Mel came up and gave me a hug, "I'm glad you're back. Where'd you go?"

"Camp Riley; it's up in the panhandle."

"What for?"

I walked over to the bar and sat down. "Some General wanted to meet with the old man. But it was good. Tomorrow they're bringing us a lot of stuff. Oh, that reminds me, hey Little Bit, I have something for you."

She quickly jumped up, "What is it?"

I reached into my pocket to find most of the cookies were now crumbs. But there were some large pieces. I raked all of it out and piled it on the counter. Her face lit up, "Cookies!"

"Yeah, have some. Go get Lee Ann, and tell her to come get some too."

With a handful of cookie crumbs, she took off. Mel took a few pieces and ate them.

"Oh, that is so good," Mel said. "Where'd you get them?"

"Well, we went to the mess hall on the base. They had them there."

"What'd they have for food?" Bobbie asked. "I mean, if they had cookies they must have had other stuff."

I smiled, feeling a little guilty. "Yeah, they did. I had a hamburger and fries. Some coleslaw and baked beans. There was all sorts of stuff."

"Oh man, a hamburger. With a bun?" Mel asked.

"Yeah, it had a bun too. And pickles and mustard, all the fixin's."

Bobbie looked sideways at me, "Must be nice."

I nodded, "It was. Good news is they're bringing us some food tomorrow as well."

"Really? What are they bringing?" Mel asked.

I shrugged, "I don't know."

Lee Ann and Little Bit appeared. The two of them sat down at the bar and shared the cookie crumbs. There was no bickering, no arguing. They sat together and actually laughed as they went through the pile. It was nice to see. In the Before there would have been all manner of back and forth.

"These are really good," Lee Ann said as she funneled crumbs into her mouth.

I smiled, "Thought you guys would like them."

Bobbie was standing at the stove. She took the lid off a large stock pot and raised a ladle out of it. As she poured the contents back into the pot, she said, "Well I guess you won't be having any of this delicious stew."

"It actually looks pretty good," I replied.

"Pffft, It ain't a hamburger," Mel shot back.

Lee Ann and Little Bit both looked up, "Hamburgers?"

Mel leaned against the counter and crossed her arms, "Yeah, someone had hamburgers today."

The girls' heads swiveled in unison with a look of deep longing on their faces. It was funny and I laughed, "Sorry girls; I had it with the Army guys. No takeout."

Lee Ann scrunched her face up, "I want a burger."

"We'll have to see what we can do," I replied. It gave me an idea; I needed to go look at what was left of our storage.

As we were talking, Jess, Fred and Aric came in. They were quiet as they came through the door. I asked what they were up to and Aric answered they were coming for dinner before taking over at the barricade. We cleared the bar so they could sit down, and Bobbie quickly served them up. She slid a steaming bowl in front of each before making herself one as well. As she leaned on the counter blowing on the steaming hash, Jess sampled it and commented how good it was.

Bobbie cut her eyes at me, "It ain't hamburgers, but it's not bad."

Leaning over his own bowl, Aric added, "Man, I'd love a hamburger."

I narrowed my eyebrows at Bobbie and she laughed. Sarge and the guys came through the door like a gaggle of raucous geese. It sounded like they were arguing over something. Once in the house Sarge spun around and performed a Three Stooges routine that would make Moe Howard smile in his grave. Mike was saying something when Sarge slapped his chin shut real hard. Ted started to laugh and Sarge went to poke him in the eye in classic Three Stooges style when Ted put his hand up between his eyes stopping the forked fingers. He slapped Sarge's hand down and Sarge brought it all the way around and banged Ted on the head.

Everyone in the house started to crack up; it was hilarious to see them go at one another. Sarge turned around with a big smile on his face and started towards the kitchen. Mike kicked the back of his boot, sending his foot flying forward in a giant step. Ted cracked up and sent the rest of us into another laughing fit. The old man spun around and pointed at Mike, "Keep it up!"

"Hey! You started it!" Mike replied.

"You guys take that mess out back, I'll bring you something to eat," Bobbie shouted, pointing at the backdoor.

The guys filed out the door with Doc bringing up the rear. He was shaking his head as he passed, "You can't take these idiots anywhere."

Mel and Bobbie filled bowls and carried them out to the guys. I went out and sat down with them. When Mel set a bowl in front of Mike, Sarge reached across the table and stuck his finger in it, "You gonna eat that?" He asked.

Mike jerked the bowl away, "Yes!"

Sarge jerked his finger from the bowl, "Shit that's hot!"

Mike smiled, "Serves you right."

"You guys done?" I asked.

Ted was blowing on a spoon of steaming stew, and with his eyes darting around the table he replied, "For now."

"Doc are you going to want to stay up there with the clinic?" I asked.

He was stirring the contents of his bowl around and replied, "Maybe for a bit. But only if they need me. I don't really want to hang out up there."

"At least go up there and get resupplied."

"And get them antibiotics," Sarge added.

"Yeah, I checked on Tyler's family today. He's in pretty rough shape. The kids are actually doing better than he is. We'll see what they send; maybe it will help," Doc replied.

Mary came downstairs to join the rest of us. When Doc saw her, he waved her over. "Hey Mary, got a question for you."

She sat down beside him. Like Thad, she seemed to have a perpetual smile. "Sure, what is it?"

"The Army is bringing in a field hospital tomorrow; would you be willing to work as a nurse there? You know we have a bunch of people hurt really bad and could use the help."

Mary nodded, "Of course. I'd like that."

Doc smiled and patted her hand, "Great. You'll work with me. I'll come get you tomorrow."

"Okay, I'll be ready."

Thad came in and told me the cross was dry. All of us went outside following Thad, who carried the cross in one hand and a large mallet in the other. Jeff was buried on the east side of the pond in a small clearing surrounded by cypress trees that Danny planted years ago. Thad walked to the head of the grave as the rest of us gathered at the foot. We stood in silence as Thad hammered the cross into the disturbed earth.

As he performed his task, I thought of the number of burials I'd seen since things changed. More than I'd seen my entire life leading up to it. I looked down at Little Bit who'd made her way to my side. Already in her short years she'd seen more than any child should. Death had become a constant companion, always ready to take the unsuspecting or unlucky.

With his job done, Thad joined the rest of us at the foot of the grave. We all stood in silence for some time before Thad asked, "Anyone want to offer any words?"

We were not a religious bunch. I'm sure some among us had some deep belief, but that was always kept internal. It just wasn't something we spoke about. It was Ted that broke the silence.

"Greater love has no one than this, that he lay down his life for his friends."

Giving Little Bit's hand a squeeze, I said, "The difficulty is not so great to die for a friend, as to find a friend worth dying for. Sorry to see you go my friend."

"Bravely and gladly a man shall go, till the day of his death is come," Sarge said, then bent over and scooped a handful of earth. Holding it over the grave, he sprinkled it out.

I don't know why we did it, but we all repeated the deed. Each in their turn scraping a handful of dirt and slowly, silently sprinkling it out over the grave. When the last of us had our turn, we stood in silence for another moment before heading back to the house. Checking the board, I saw I was to be on security later in the night. Sarge came up beside me and looked the board over. It was just the two of us and I used it to satisfy my curiosity.

"Why do you carry on with those guys like that?"

Sarge looked over, "Huh?"

"That little Three Stooges routine earlier. You are always playing grab ass with 'em."

Sarge smiled, "I've known them boys for a long time. Hell, they were only boys when they first showed up." Sarge smiled again and shook his head. "I used to smoke Mikey's ass, grind him until he couldn't stand. He was such a smartass; shit, still is. But he'd take it and come back for more. He didn't know how to keep his mouth shut.

"But he was so damn good. You hear people say they were born to do this or that. He's a born killer, a true professional. He grew on me like a damn mold I couldn't scrub off. Teddy was the same way, though not nearly as bad. Ted always knew when it was time to work and when you could fuck around. Mikey never did figure that out. But I watched those two boys become men, and over the years I came to love them." He paused for a moment and looked at me with a deep furrow in his brow. "And I don't mean in a queer way either, so don't get any ideas peckerwood. But I trust them with my life, anytime, anywhere. If someone would open the gate to hell, I'd wade into the seven circles with them and the fires would be out by dinner time."

I looked at him, and in a deep gravelly voice said, "You're funny, not funny ha ha—" He cut me.

He quickly snatched his hat from his head and started to swat the shit out of me. "See dammit! You're just like 'em! Bunch of damn smart asses!"

I tried to fend off the flurry of slaps from the hat. "Alright, alright! I give up!"

He stopped and laughed, "Smart ass. But that's exactly what I'm talking about. You get it, I know you do."

Nodding, I replied, "I do." I knew why. When I worked

heavy industrial work we horsed around a lot too. At least with the guys we were friends with.

"And that's why I'm always fuckin' with 'em. If I didn't, they'd think I was pissed off. It's just what we do. We always goof around with one another. Just be glad Mikey hasn't walked up to talk to you with his nuts hanging out of his zipper."

I started laughing just thinking about it, "Now that's messed up."

Sarge got that evil grin again and chuckled, "Yeah, but I don't think he'll try that one again."

"On that note, it looks like I'm in the bunker later, so I'm headed home for some sleep."

Sarge slapped me on the back, "Get some rest."

I went inside, telling everyone good night; and then I left the house. Mel and the girls wanted to stay a while as everyone was in a somber mood and no one really wanted to be alone.

Heading over to the house, I decided there was no way I could sleep just yet, so I went in and turned on the Ham radio. I'd strung the antenna in the backyard between some trees in a north-south orientation. It allowed me to pick up transmissions from out west, something I was interested in lately. Turning on the radio, I started to scroll through the bands. It was a clear night and propagation should be good. It didn't take long to start finding conversations.

I'd stop and listen to the chatter for a moment as I came across them. Most were mundane comparisons of the hardships of the respective operators. All were familiar, no matter the locations. I picked up a few locations, Kansas, Texas and one in Arizona. I listened to the latter for some time as it appeared to be tactical conversation of some sort. From what I could gather, there was a rather large operation ongoing in the area. The operators were using codes so it was hard to discern what they were talking about exactly; but it didn't take much of an imagination to deduce they were in a protracted struggle with Mexicans looking to reclaim some ancestral lands.

Not interested at the moment to try and decipher the cryptic conversations, I continued on through the spectrum. Slowly turning the dial, I caught the end of a transmission, *coming out of Gillette.* I paused on the frequency for a moment. Fawcett's revelation earlier of an operating refinery in Wyoming immediately popped into my head.

"*The road's blocke;, they'll never make it out here.*"

"*Just wanted to let you know they were headed your way.*"

"*Thanks for the info, pardner. I appreciate it. Reid out.*" The voice was heavy with a western accent, not quite Texan in nature, but close.

Listening for a few seconds, it appeared the conversation was over. Picking up my mic, I keyed it and asked, "How are things out there in Wyoming?"

After a long pause, there came a reply, "*We're getting' by. Where are you?*"

"Florida, north of Orlando," I replied.

"*Sheeit, better you than me. How the hell have you managed to stay alive in a place like that?*"

I chuckled, "It ain't been easy. But at least we won't freeze to death."

"*We've had our share of that. Lost a lot of folks to the weather. But there's too many people down there; and I imagine most of them lost their friggin minds.*"

"There's not as many now."

The voice on the other end laughed, "*By God I guess not! I bet millions are dead down there by now.*"

"Probably, there have been a lot of people on the move

and all. We're kind of out in the boonies, so we missed a lot of the trouble."

*"I'm out in the boonies friend. You're in the heart of the shit in my opinion."*

"I hear you've got a refinery running up that way."

There was a long pause before a reply finally came, *"I wouldn't know anything about that. There aren't any refineries around me."* There was no doubt in my mind he knew about the refinery. But I didn't blame him for not broadcasting it. For the same reason I wouldn't say where it was.

"Just a rumor I heard."

*"You're hearing rumors in Florida about shit that's supposedly going on out here?"*

Now I had his attention, "I talked with the folks using the products coming out of there today. They're good people."

*"Well, I wouldn't know. Lord knows I could use some fuel. It'd be nice to give my horses a break."*

I laughed into the mic, "I wish I had horses! I think the last ones around here were eaten long ago."

*"Horse is good meat. We only eat 'em if they ain't fit for work. Which reminds me, I've got cows to bring in. Good talkin' with you; by the way what's your name? I'm Reid Mcculloch."*

"Name's Morgan Carter, stay safe out there." I laid the mic down and thought about his last statement, cows to bring in. I could just imagine herds of cattle wandering the plains. All that beef and people starving to death. But there was no way to move it, not efficiently now. It would require an old-fashioned cattle drive. Now that would be a sight to see. But now those with the cattle were the only ones eating beef. What a problem that would be, more beef than you could eat. With that thought, I headed for bed where I'd dream about herds of cattle as far as the eye could see.

# CHAPTER 10

CHARLES TABOR JUMPED FROM HIS chair and
swept his arm across the top of the desk in front of
him, scattering stuff all over the room.

"How in the hell did those fucking rednecks take out a
fucking MRAP?" He screamed.

The man before him stammered, "They, they had
an Apache."

Tabor's fury paused. "They had a what?" he shouted.

"An Apache came in and took out the trucks. Then a
Blackhawk landed and a couple of them got on it and it left."

Tabor kicked his chair over, "Shit!"

Mooreland stood the chair up, and looking at the trooper
he said, "You can go." The man quickly left the room. "If they're
working with the Army that closely, we're going to have to come
up with a different plan."

Tabor stared at the ceiling with his hands on his hips, "If we
only had air support, I'd crush those bastards."

"At least we're not in that damn prison in Frostproof. Look
on the bright side."

Tabor fell into his chair as a slight smile creased his face.
"That was sweet." He looked at Mooreland. "They didn't see
that shit coming, did they?"

Mooreland shook his head. "No, no they didn't. We're just

lucky our people got wind of it. I still say you shouldn't have executed all of them."

Tabor waved him off, "Whatever; fuck them. They deserved it." He leaned over the desk and looked Mooreland in the eyes, "The penalty for treason is death."

"Yeah, well just remember, they're probably thinking the same way now."

Tabor spat back at the remark, "Let 'em. We've got more men, and more equipment than we had the last time. It'll be different this time; you can bet your ass on that."

Mooreland picked some papers up off the floor. "Maybe so," he replied, holding the sheets up in front of Tabor. "But don't forget what our primary mission is. Your little revenge scheme comes second to that."

For the first time in a long time, Tabor smiled. "No, don't you see? That's the best part! We get to use those idiots to get the job done." He moved closer to Mooreland and put his arm around Ed's shoulder. "You see, when we're done with those fuckers, everyone's going to hate them. Everyone's going to want to kill them."

"We'll see," Mooreland nodded.

Tabor jumped up, "What else have you got for me?"

"One of our patrols found a group that wants to talk to you."

"About what?"

"I think you'll want to talk to them," Mooreland said as he turned for the door.

Opening the door, a tall dark-haired man stepped in. Tabor looked at him and instantly recognized the arrogance in the man just from the way he stood. Tabor slowly sat down behind his desk.

"What can I do for you?"

"I hear you're the man in charge. That you guys are the law around here now."

Tabor nodded, "I am. And who are you?"

The man straightened, "Name's Billy, and I've got a pretty good-sized group. A lot of strong well trained men. We're looking to maybe join with you, join forces as it were."

Tabor leaned back in his chair with his hands behind his head. "Well Billy, we saw you coming in here; I've got a lot of men myself." He stood up and walked to a window and looked out. "Lots of equipment too. I've even got a resupply chain." He spun to face Billy, "What have you got?"

Billy crossed his arms over his chest. "Talking to one of your people, he said the federal government was in charge."

Tabor nodded but didn't speak.

"Well I have a problem with some ass clown calling himself a Sheriff. He's killed a few of my people and claims to be law of the land around here." Now Billy walked to the window. "You've picked a good spot here. Who would've thought an Elks Camp would be turned into a military base."

"Tactical outpost. We are not the military. Most of those knuckle draggers forgot who they worked for," Tabor spat back.

Billy turned back from the window. "I've heard that. The thing is, this Sheriff's got some Army types hanging out with him."

Tabor sat up, "Some Army types?"

"Yeah, one's an older guy, gray-headed and talks a lot of shit."

"Wears a hundred and first hat?" Tabor asked.

Billy nodded, "So you know him too?"

Tabor slowly stood up. "Oh yeah; I know him, and I've got a plan for his ass too."

"Then we have something in common."

Tabor sat back and looked at Billy for a moment. "This isn't going to be easy. You've got to have the stomach for this kind of thing."

Billy stared back, "We can stomach anything you throw at us."

Tabor thought for a moment, then nodded. "Alright Billy; we'll see if you're up to the challenge." Tabor stood up. "Just remember, you asked for this."

"I'm good. I assure you that."

"Mooreland will show you guys where to bunk up. I'll be in touch later."

Billy smiled, "I think you'll be happy with us."

Tabor waved him off and Billy followed Mooreland out. Now he had some expendable bodies; and if he had read the man right, they wouldn't be as squeamish about what he had in mind.

———※——※——※——※——※———

About midnight, I got up. It was kind of strange that I could wake myself when I needed to without aid of an alarm. Mel was sound asleep, so I quietly got out of bed, trying not to wake her. The house was cool. Stepping out the front door, it felt like rain, so I grabbed my raincoat from beside the door on my way out. Since it was so nice out, I decided to walk. I found Fred, Jess and Aric in the bunker; they were tired and ready to go.

"Glad to see you, I'm about to fall asleep standing here," Fred said.

"Soon as the guys get here, you can leave," I replied with a smile.

"What happened on your trip today?" Jess asked.

I shrugged, "We met with some General. They're going to get us some help, food and whatnot."

"What'd they say about the DHS?" Aric asked.

"They told Sarge the gloves were off." I laughed and said, "I'd hate to see what that was like if he'd been wearing them all this time."

"Yeah; no shit," Aric replied with a chuckle.

"They're bringing in a field hospital tomorrow too. I told them we needed some help with all the wounded from the incident at the store the other day."

"Wow, that's nice. I didn't know they had those kinds of resources," Jess said.

"Apparently they've got a lot of stuff. It's just that the need is so great that it's hard to make a difference."

"At least we're getting some help," Fred added.

Looking out the front port, I saw two guys coming down the road. I grabbed the NVGs that were hanging on a nail and took a look. "Here come Ian and Perez. Looks like you can head home for some sleep."

Aric stuck his head out and looked up into the dark sky. "Good; let's get out of here before it rains."

"You better hurry; I got a feeling it's fixing to pour!" Ian shouted as he jumped off the top of the bunker.

"We'll see you guys tomorrow," Jess said as she went outside.

Perez stepped down into the bunker carrying a folding chair. He set it up in a corner and immediately sat down. I laughed. Shaking my head, I said, "We're not interrupting anything are we?"

"He hates the nights; old man needs his sleep," Ian replied.

Perez was smoking a cigarette and took a long hard drag on it, bringing the tip to a bright cherry red. He flicked it at Ian and it bounced off him with a shower of red embers in the dark bunker. "Shut up peckerhead. I'm not awake yet."

"This is going to be a long night," I said as I took another look through the NVG.

It was so dark I had to adjust the gain on the device to the extreme to be able to see. It caused the image to be very grainy and pixilated. "I can't see shit."

"Yeah, wish we had thermal," Ian said.

The rain started about an hour later. What started as a slow drizzle turned into a downpour, making it nearly impossible to see anything, even with the NVGs. Ian stood at the front port looking out, "This is bullshit. There could be a hundred people out there and I wouldn't see them."

Perez walked over and looked out, "There ain't anyone out there. No one's going to be out in this shit."

"Shit, this is exactly the kind of crap that crazy old fucker would want to go out in."

"I doubt even Sarge is out in this crap," I replied.

"Maybe; but this is exactly the kind of night you'd want to hit someone on. Can't see or hear anything," Ian said as he scanned the murk with the NVG.

"Well, let's hope there's no one out there that's motivated to come after us," I said. I had a feeling it would be a tense night.

But the night would prove to be uneventful, as after what felt like an eternity, the sky began to lighten. The rain had slacked off to a dull drizzle that showed no signs of letting up. We had spent considerable time trying to keep water out of the bunker, but the bottom was now full of water. It was obvious we were going to have to put some sort of floor in the thing. Putting on my raincoat, I went outside and looked around. With the sun coming up out there somewhere, I could actually see; though everything was gray and murky with a very depressing feel.

I was standing beside the bunker when a voice behind me said, "Good thing I'm not out to get your ass. You'd be deader n' shit."

I spun to see Sarge standing in the rain. He was wearing a poncho, and rain dripped from the bill of his Boonie hat. "You scared the crap out of me."

"Let it be a lesson. You need to turn the hell around from time to time. You didn't even see me coming, dumbass."

"I saw you the whole time," Ian said from the bunker entrance.

"You didn't see shit, ya sea-goin' mutt," Sarge shot back.

"Maybe; but I knew you'd be pokin' around at some point."

Sarge laughed, "You don't know nuthin' and you suspect even less, dumbass."

"What's got you in such a chipper mood this morning?" I asked.

"Choppers won't fly in this soup. If this crap doesn't blow over soon, we won't be getting any delivery today."

I looked up, "I didn't think about that, damn."

"This is bullshit!" Perez shouted from the bunker.

"What the hell's eatin' that Mexican?" Sarge asked, looking at the bunker entrance.

Perez came out of the bunker, "I ain't no fuckin' Mexican. I'm Puerto Rican!"

Sarge waved him off, "It's all the same; dry up Maria. What's rubbin' yer ass this morning?"

"This damn hole in the ground is full of water! This is BS!" Perez shouted, pointing into the bunker.

"Huh, who'd a thought a hole in the ground would fill with water?" Sarge said in a snarky tone.

"We're going to have to do something. It's a fucking mess," Perez replied.

Sarge bent over and twisted his face up, "Maybe your madre will bring you a warm cup of horchata and tell you it's going to be alright."

"Horchata is for kids," Perez spat back.

"Eres tan hombre!" Sarge shouted back and smiled, "Sí, hablo español cabrón."

Perez leaned against the side of the bunker, "Chupas mis huevos culero."

"I'd fall asleep and you'd fall in love mamón," Sarge replied with a smile.

Perez let out a loud belly laugh, "You gonna look at this shit or not?"

Sarge walked around to the entrance and looked in. "I knew I'd get you to smile one way or another. Yeah, I see what you mean. We're going to have to do something about this."

"I'll find some pallets," I said.

Sarge nodded, "That would work."

"Anything would be an improvement," Perez grunted.

Looking up, I asked, "Well, are we going to town today or not?"

Sarge shook his head, "Not till I call Fawcett and see if they're even going to try and make a lift today."

"Alright, just let me know. I'll be heading home soon, whenever the relief shows up."

"Keep your radio handy today," Sarge replied, looking up. "This sort of weather begs for a probing attack today. I've got the boys and Jamie out on patrol right now. If they make contac,t they'll call it in."

"You really think anyone would be out in this shit?" I asked.

"Hell yes. If I was out to get someone's ass this, is exactly the weather I'd do it in."

I looked at Ian, who was laughing, "Told you so."

"Think about it. No one *wants* to be out in this soup. Most everyone's inside trying to stay dry." Sarge held his hands up, letting rain collect in his palms, "Anyone out in this shit is a bad hombre. Days like this and late at night after two AM are the times you want to shwhack someone."

"Yeah, I've heard people sleep hardest after two." I looked up, "And the weather makes sense. I guess if you were going to do it, this would be the perfect day."

"I'm going to make a call. Keep your eyes and ears open," Sarge said as he started to walk off.

I chose to stand in the rain instead of the nearly ankle-deep water in the bunker. It wasn't long before I saw three figures coming up the road. I'd heeded Sarge's advice and looked back from time to time. I knew one of them was Danny, but I was confused about the other two. As they got closer, I realized it was Lee Ann and Taylor. I was at the same time proud and worried. My little girls were growing up way faster than I wanted. Here they came, in the rain with slung weapons to stand guard for our community.

I wished they could stay little girls forever. A smile came over my face as I thought of them greeting me in their footy PJs when I'd come home from work. God, it seemed like ages ago. And now I saw two women approaching. It was only a matter of time before there would be some man in their lives. My hand inadvertently moved to the grip of my carbine at the thought. This too caused me to smile; I pity the poor bastards.

"You guys going to hang out here today?" I asked as they got closer.

Taylor nodded, "Yeah, Danny said we could."

"It's about time they started doing their part," Danny said with a smile.

"That's what I was thinking."

"Hey! We do our part!" Lee Ann shouted.

I reached out and took her hand, "You bet you do kiddo."

Thad announced his arrival by asking, "Is this is a private party, or can anyone come?"

I was happy to see that on such a dreary morning he had that signature smile. "You're always welcome brother," I said as I gripped his hand.

Perez came stomping out of the bunker. "I'm outta here; you guys can have this shit."

Thad slapped him on the back. "You got it, buddy. Go dry out."

"I'm out too," Ian said as he fell in behind Perez.

"Thanks guys; appreciate it," I said as they headed off.

"Eww, this thing is full of water!" Taylor shouted.

"Yeah, I'm going to get some pallets. Thad, you want to come give me a hand really quick?" I asked.

"You know it," he quickly replied.

"Let me go get the truck. There are some pallets out behind my old place. I used them for the bee hives I had back there."

"We'll be here," he replied.

I quickly headed for the house and got the truck and drove back up the road. Thad was standing in the rain waiting, and hopped in. At the house, I pulled around back to where the pallets were stacked up.

"Think it's going to rain all day?" Thad asked as he got out of the truck.

"I hope not. We were supposed to get some stuff airlifted in today. Sarge said they won't fly in this kind of weather."

I opened the back of the Suburban and Thad tossed in one of the pallets. As I turned to walk to the stack, I thought I saw something. Actually, I was certain I saw a person over at the burned-out remains of Don's old place. Thad was bent over grabbing another pallet, and I moved up beside him.

"I just saw someone at the place next door."

Thad didn't react; he hefted a pallet and started to move towards the truck. "Where at?" He asked in a quiet voice.

"To the left of that big downed tree. The one he was cutting when the chainsaw got him."

Thad nodded and tossed the pallet into the truck. I was behind him with another, and threw it in as well. As he passed me heading back to the stack, he said, "I don't see anything."

Picking up another pallet, I said, "I'm certain I did."

"I believe you; you need to call Sarge on the way back and let him know," Thad said as he grabbed the last pallet.

Once the last one was in the truck, we got back in and headed out the way we had come in, which took us a little closer to the spot we were talking about. As we passed by, I casually looked at the tree but didn't see anything, and told Thad. He told me to call the old man as soon as we got to the road. As I pulled out onto the paved road, I did just that. Sarge responded quickly to the radio call, and I informed him of the situation.

"*You sure?*"

"Positive."

Before he replied, Ted's voice came over the radio in a hard whisper, "*We'll move that way and take a look.*"

"*Morgan, let the folks at the bunker know, and tell them to keep a sharp eye out. Ted, you check in every ten minutes and watch your ass.*"

We both replied in the affirmative. At the bunker, I helped Thad and Danny get the pallets in place. They made a huge difference keeping everyone out of the water.

"This is real nice, a lot better," Lee Ann said.

"Yeah, it's not so bad now," Taylor added.

Thad and I told them about the person we had seen, and that the guys were moving in to take a look. I stressed that they needed to keep a sharp eye out, and that meant behind them too. Thad and Danny said they'd be extra cautious and for me to go get some rest and dry off. I was tired and wet and didn't argue. Besides, I had the radio and would know if anything happened. I told Danny I'd leave the truck though, just in case they needed it; and I walked home.

Slogging through the mud on the way home, Dalton came out of the trees on the side of the road. I was surprised to see him because I never knew where the guy was.

"What the hell are you doing out here in the rain?" I asked.

"Just out poking around. It's the perfect day for someone to start some shit, so I'm just wandering around, kinda keeping an eye out."

"I appreciate it. You really stepped up the other day at the barricade. Having someone else around to help with security is a big plus." Any concerns I had about this vanished at the barricade. He was all in when the chips were down. Everyone here now knew where he stood, with us.

"Thanks. It's nice to be some place I can close my eyes and actually sleep. I don't mind pitching in."

I looked around. "Well, be careful. Some of the guys are out on patrols. I'd hate to see a friendly fire incident."

"Murphy's Law, friendly fire isn't." Dalton replied with a grunt.

"I'm headed home, need some sleep."

Dalton wiped some rain from the brim of his Boonie hat, "I'll be around."

"For how long?" I asked. He cocked his head to the side and looked at me. "You know, how long are you going to hang around? As you've seen, everyone here pitches in, and you kinda fell right into it as it seems. I'd like to think you're now part of our team and that you're going to be around."

Dalton sniffed and looked out into the woods. After a short pause, he said, "I've never been much of one for the whole group dynamic. There's always some asshole that wants to be King Turd on shit island." He looked me directly in the eye, "But it does seem a little different here. Hell, I can't tell who the chief of this band of Indians is, and I like that. There's obvious order; and like you said, everyone pitches in without being told what to do. If you'll have me, I'd be happy to stay on."

I offered my hand. Dalton surprised me by grabbing my forearm in the manner of the Romans. I gripped his as well. "We'd be honored to have you," I said.

Dalton gave my arm a firm shake. "I'd be honored to be a part."

"I'm going to get some sleep. You need to start coming around for meals too. We eat together, I think you know when," I said.

Dalton nodded, "I'll be around." He turned and walked back into the trees on the side of the road. He was certainly a man of few words.

I stopped on the porch to take off the coat and my boots. Hanging the coat on a nail, I sat down and pulled my boots off. I was soaked from the waist down and didn't want to go in the house sloshing water all over. The dogs were all on the porch, and in their usual manner, paid no attention to me. I reached down and rubbed Meathead's ears. He lifted his eyes and thumped the floor with his tail a couple of times but made no other effort.

"You are positively worthless," I said with a smile.

Hearing me speak, Drake lifted his head and looked at me. Not finding whatever it was he was expecting, he laid his head back down. Again, I smiled. Maybe they weren't worthless; they did bring a smile to my face. Opening the door, I was met with a wave of warmth. While the temps outside weren't cold by any stretch, the rain had cooled things off noticeably. Looking across the living room, I saw a small fire burning in the fireplace. Mel and Little Bit were all piled on the couch. They'd pulled the coffee table up and had their legs sprawled out on it.

Little Bit looked up, "Hi Daddy. I made a fire." She pointed at the fireplace and beamed with pride.

I smiled and stepped in. "You did a good job too."

Mel, who had been dozing, looked up, "Hey babe. It was chilly in here, kind of clammy feeling; so we made a fire."

"Good idea. It will keep the house dried out. I'm soaked, so I'm going to go change and join you guys. Looks pretty comfy."

I went in the bedroom and stripped out of the wet clothes, tossing them into the bathtub. After changing into dry clothes, I went back out to the kitchen. I wanted a glass of tea. The box of tea was sitting on the counter. I smiled and ran my hand across it as I passed. We'd separated a lot of it out, with most of it at Danny's. Since everyone was eating meals at his place, it only made sense. But I made sure to have plenty here.

With a glass in hand, I headed for the living room. Stopping by the fireplace, I prodded the fire with the iron and added a small log to it. I fell into my recliner and rocked back. We spent the afternoon like that. No talking, just relaxing to the sound of the rain on the roof and the crackling of the fire. It was so nice.

Our relaxation was interrupted by the dogs barking. I got up and looked out the window to see Sarge coming down the drive in the Hummer. Mel sat up and looked over, asking, "What's going on?"

"Sarge is here. Let me go see what's up."

I slipped on a pair of Crocs and went out on the porch.

---

Sarge pulled up and shut the wagon down. "Come on; we're going to town."

I looked up into the drizzle. "Why?"

"We're going in to talk to Sheffield and get things ready for tomorrow. Fawcett said the weather will be cleared up this evening and they'll be able to get in."

I stretched, "Alright, give me a minute." Going inside, everyone was up now. The fire in the fireplace was just a smoking pile of ash. "I've got to go into town."

Little Bit jumped up, "Can I go?" She shouted.

I looked at Mel, but this time she didn't object. Smiling at Little Bit, I replied, "Sure. Get dressed."

She jumped up and ran off to her room. Mel waited till she was out of sight to tell me to be careful. I smiled and told her I would.

"We shouldn't be too long; just going in to set up for the delivery tomorrow."

"Ok, I'll be next door when you get back."

Little Bit came out of her room, dressed and ready to go. She had the small pack she carried everywhere with her. It was her *kit* as she called it, and was actually a pretty good one. I'd put it together for her a couple years ago when she started to get interested in what I was doing. She carried it every time we went into the field on hikes or kayaking. Now though, she got to use it for real, not just sit in the living room floor and play with it.

"I'm ready," she announced.

"Come on then, let's go."

She ran over to Mel and gave her a hug, "See you later, Mom."

I gave Mel a kiss, "Love you. See ya later."

We went out and saw Doc sitting in the turret. I waved at him, "Didn't see you up there earlier."

"I just got here. Coming along to figure out where to set up the clinic."

Little Bit waved at him, "Hi mister Doc."

Doc smiled, his teeth shining through his beard, "Hey princess, you coming too?"

She patted her pack, "Yep, I've got my pack."

Doc gave her the thumbs up, "Good; we're prepared then."

We hopped in, and Little Bit shared my seat. Sarge patted her head.

"I see you brought the boss," he said with a smile.

She smiled at him and leaned over and gave him a hug, "Hi mister Sarge."

It was heartwarming to see how he acted with her. He was definitely a grandpa at heart. Sarge started the truck and announced, "Let's get this freak show on the road!" Getting a giggle out of Little Bit.

We stopped at the bunker on our way out. Lee Ann and Taylor came out to the truck. We asked if they'd seen anything, and they replied that it had been quiet. Danny and Thad were there, and told us they had it under control. Giving them a wave, we pulled off. Approaching the old barricade, Mike stepped out into the road. Sarge slowed to a stop and asked, "What's up?"

"We found a hide someone was using over there. Looks like someone's been poking around and keeping an eye on us."

"Was it in that old tree?" I asked.

Mike nodded, "Yeah, right where you said it was."

"Any idea how they were coming in and out?" Sarge asked.

Dalton walked out to the Hummer. "They were pretty careful, but I picked up a track."

"Don't go too far. Be a damn good way to get ambushed," Sarge said.

"We're not going to follow it far. I just want to see what direction they're coming in from," Mike said.

Sarge tapped his radio, "Call me if you see anything."

Mike slapped the roof of the truck. "Will do, boss."

When Sarge pulled out onto Hwy-19, I told him to swing by Gena's place so we could check on her and Dylan. He thought that was a great idea; and in no time we were pulling onto their small road. Pulling up, Sarge honked the horn. Dylan cracked the door and looked out, the muzzle of an AK poking out as well. Seeing the Hummer, he smiled and the door swung open. He stepped out onto the porch and waved.

"Come up to the porch and get out of the rain!" He called as Gena came out of the house.

Sarge and I got out, and Little Bit ran past me up to Gena and gave her a hug. Gena bent over and took her by the hand, and with a smile said, "I bet you've got a sweet tooth."

Little Bit jumped up and down, "You have honeycomb?"

"Of course aunt Gena has honeycomb. You come with me," Gena replied, and led her into the house.

On the porch, Sarge and I shook Dylan's hand. Dylan asked Doc to come in out of the rain, but Doc insisted on staying in the turret. We chatted for a few minutes, asking if Dylan had seen anyone or anything out of the ordinary.

"Nope, been quiet around here." He held his hand out and let the rain running off the roof fill his palm. "Just the rain; we needed it."

"Yeah we did," I agreed.

Dylan pointed to a couple of blue drums sitting off the end of the porch, "Filling up my rain barrels."

"Nice, nothing better than rainwater," Sarge said.

"Keep your eyes open Dylan. Someone's been poking around over near us. Don't know what they're up to, or even who they are. We just wanted to let you know and make sure you guys were alright," I said.

Nodding, Dylan replied, "Thanks for the heads up. We'll stay on our toes."

Gena and Little Bit came out of the house. Little Bit was licking her fingers and I could see the sticky shine around her mouth. Smiling, I asked, "Was it good?"

Wide-eyed and sucking honey off her thumb, she nodded, "Mmhmm."

"Thanks Gena," I said, rubbing Little Bit's head. "She sure likes coming to visit."

Gena smiled, "She's welcome here any time. Do you need any more veggies? We've got plenty."

"No, thank you though. I think we're alright for now."

"I sure do like your squash though," Sarge said. "Miss Kay fried some up in pig fat, and it was terrific."

"We've got plenty. Just come by when you need it," Dylan offered.

"We'll take you up on it another time. We've got to get to town," I said.

A slight frown appeared on Gena's face, "How are those poor people?"

"We're on our way to see. The Army is bringing in a field hospital tomorrow and medical personnel to help out for a while."

"That's really nice. Everyone thinks it was the Army that did the shooting." Dylan said. "We were up at the market yesterday, and they're still talking about it."

"Makes me scared to go up there," Gena added.

"We're trying to fix it so you don't have to be," Sarge replied.

"That'd be great. It was nice to go up there and talk to someone other than Batman."

"Hey! I'm not good company?" Dylan asked with a smile.

Gena patted his arm, "You know I love you. But it's comforting to talk to a woman sometimes."

I laughed and made a mental note to bring Mel by. Maybe she and Bobbie could come pay a visit. We said our goodbyes and got back on the road. As we passed through Altoona, I saw that the market was up and running again. Though as we passed, everyone stopped and watched us. I hoped Doc didn't have that SAW pointed in their direction. I saw one guy give us the finger; but thankfully no one did anything more offensive.

The road was getting more and more cluttered. In places where trees were near the road, it was usually matted with fallen debris, limbs and leaves. The collected dirt and dust carried on the breeze and created small mounds. I knew over time these would grow and the road would begin to break down. Hopefully things would turn around before that happened. But it was an interesting study to see how nature reclaimed what we'd taken from her.

Weeds, trees and vines were growing in cracks in the roads, parking lots and around the edges of buildings. Vines were climbing utility poles, signs and the sides of buildings as well. The vines broke through the paint, allowing water to get under it. The wood swelled, windows shifted, and more water got in, speeding up the process. If things didn't change, the buildings would eventually collapse. It reminded me of a show I once saw on the History Channel, *Life After People*. But we were still here and it was happening.

We were passing the old tavern in Umatilla when we saw the crowd. A large group of people was in the intersection of Central Ave and Bulldog Lane. As we got closer, it was obvious something was going on.

"Keep a sharp eye out up there Ronnie," Sarge said as he slowed.

As people moved around, I was able to see through the crowd, and could see it was a fight. "Let's stop," I said.

Sarge stopped the truck and I told Little Bit to stay inside. She protested, but I made it clear she was not to get out, and to stay with Doc.

"I got her," Doc said as I got out.

Sarge and I walked up to the crowd. Seeing us coming, people moved out of the way and we were able to get to the front and see what was going on. Two men were fighting, and a couple of women were trying to stop them. When one of the women saw us, she ran up.

"Do something! Stop them!" She shouted at me.

Hearing the woman shout, the two men took notice of us and stopped. They looked around uncertainly. "What do you want me to do?" I asked the woman.

"You're the Sheriff, aren't you? Stop them!"

I looked at the two men. One of them wore a stained white t-shirt that was soaked from the rain. The other had no shirt. "What's this about?"

The shirtless man pointed to the other, "That son of a bitch can't keep his mouth shut!"

The other man scoffed, "Me? You're just a lying bastard!"

I looked at Sarge, he smiled and shrugged. Looking back at the two men, I pointed to the shirtless one and asked the guy in the white t-shirt, "You want to fight him?"

"Damn right I do!" I then asked the other man the same question.

He pointed at his adversary, "I'm gonna whoop his ass!"

I held my hands up, "Don't let me stop you."

The woman that approached me, spun around. "What do you mean? You're the Sheriff; you can't let them fight!"

I laughed and looked around the crowd. "It ain't no business of mine if these two want to beat the shit out of one another. They both want it. It's obviously something that's been brewing for a while. The old days of having someone else solve your problems are over."

"Then what good are you if you're not going to help?" The woman shrieked.

"Ma'am, if this were a one-sided ass whoopin', I'd step in. If one was stealin' from the other, I'd step in. If one of them had bushwhacked the other and killed him, I'd step in. But two grown men that want to go at one another? They can deal with that themselves." Looking the crowd over again, I added, "The nanny state is over. You're responsible for your own actions. You cuss a man, and you're likely to get a boot in your ass. Likewise, if someone does something wrong to someone, against another person, they will pay the price. Don't think for a minute we won't get involved. But this, this ain't nobody's business but theirs."

The two men eyed one another while I spoke, but it seemed the break took the fight out of them. They exchanged more words, hollow threats. But their respective women were able to push them away and get them headed home. As the crowd began to disperse, Sarge grunted.

"Damn, I was hoping to see a fight."

I shook my head, "You're not helping."

We were walking back to the truck when a shot rang out. Sarge and I both instinctively ducked and turned to find the source of the shot. A thunderous boom quickly followed the first shot. It was over behind the old ice cream stand that sits across the road from the Kangaroo. The people that had been moving towards home were sprinting in the direction of the shots. Sarge let out a loud breath, "I guess they're shooting at one another now."

We started walking in the direction of the shots, following those who were running. As we came up to the small ice cream stand, a man burst around the corner with a wild look on his face. He carried an old single shot shotgun; and upon seeing us, ran towards us.

Pointing over his shoulder, he shouted. "They're trying to kill me!"

A number of people poured around the corner he'd just rounded. The man in the lead had fire in his eyes. The one with the shotgun skidded to a stop in front of us. Sarge reached out and snatched the smoke pole from his hands, and he didn't resist. Instead, pointing at the crowd, he reaffirmed his fears.

"Help me, they're trying to kill me!"

The man with the fire in his eyes was at a dead run for the other. Sarge stepped out and raised his carbine at the man, who skidded to a stop. Breathing hard, he wiped the rain from his face and raised an accusatory finger at the man in front of us.

"That son of a bitch just shot my brother!"

Yet another man came running up, cradling his bleeding left arm. He stopped short and looked at his brother, then at us.

"That asshole just shot me!"

The one in front of us looked at me, "He shot at me first! It was self-defense!"

The bleeding man shouted, "You were stealing my chickens! You're a damn thief, Nathan!"

Nathan looked at me, "I gotta eat too! He's got so many of 'em. It ain't gonna hurt him none!"

"So you were stealing chickens from this man, and when he caught you, you shot him?" I asked.

Unbelievably, he replied, "He shot at me first. I didn't just shoot him."

"You steal from everyone around here!" Someone from the crowd shouted.

Nathan became enraged. "I got as much right to eat as the rest of you do! You're all a bunch of selfish assholes! You won't share, there's lots of people around here in need!"

The crowd was becoming agitated. The bleeding man began shouting, "I'm going to kill your ass for this! If I ever see you again, you're a dead man!"

"I just want to make sure I understand this. Since you feel you have nothing and these other folks have something, you feel it's alright for you to take it?"

"I've got as much right as they do!"

"To their property?" I asked.

"Well, it's not really their property. They're just chickens."

"You stole canned goods from me!" Another person in the crowd shouted.

The rain was still falling and everyone was getting soaked. Nathan looked like a drowned rat, pitiful really. But he was a thief, and he'd just shot a man. I turned to face the crowd, "Is this man a thief?"

My question was met with a chorus of *Hell yeah* and *Thief!* Still looking at the crowd, I said, "I told you earlier what was and wasn't my business. This is my business." Turning to Nathan, I said, "You're a thief, and you just shot a man while stealing from him. You've admitted it, there is no question about your guilt."

I quickly drew the Springfield from its holster. As fast as I was moving, Nathan saw it coming and his eyes went wide and he began to shout. He raised his hands to cover his head and the bullet I fired went through his hand and into his forehead. He collapsed like a marionette whose strings were cut. The crowd that moments ago was shouting for his head, was suddenly silent. I looked around at them, then at the body on the ground. Blood was still spilling out onto the wet pavement.

"I told you I would get involved when it was required." Pointing to the body, I added, "Let this be a lesson. Stealing, shooting and killing will not be tolerated. There is no jail, no probation, and no court. Court will be held in the street."

Maybe it was the rain. Maybe it was the death they'd just witnessed. But the crowd started to drift away. I stood with Sarge for a few minutes. He said nothing, just rocked back and forth on his heels. Looking over, I asked, "What?"

Sarge shook his head, "Nothin'."

"Bullshit, spit it out? You think I shouldn't have done it?"

Sarge laughed. "Hell yes, you should have. I was just wondering what was taking so damn long. I thought for a minute you was going to talk him to death! Good thing you did it when you did, I was about to."

I shook my head, "You're a whole lot of help."

Sarge smiled that toothy grin he used when he was laying the smartass on extra thick, "I'm here to help Sheriff."

"Let's get the hell out of here."

At the Hummer, Doc was still in the turret, looking down and shaking his head. Walking up, I asked, "What?"

He shrugged in reply, "Nothin'."

Little Bit came boiling out of the truck, "What's going on? I couldn't see anything; Mr. Doc wouldn't let me get out."

I looked up at Doc; he gave me a wink, and I looked back at Little Bit. "Nothing kiddo; just some men fighting."

We got back in the truck and headed towards Eustis. As we passed through the intersection, Little Bit saw the body lying in the road. As yet no one had bothered to move it. Looking out the window, she asked, "Did he lose the fight?"

I reached back and grabbed her, pulling her towards me and away from the window. "Yeah, he lost. Come up here and sit with me."

As she climbed into my lap, she asked, "Is he going to wake up?"

Sarge looked over, "He's just taking a dirt nap, Princess."

She cocked her head, "What's a dirt nap?"

I rubbed her head, "Ole Sarge is just messin' with you." I gave him a look that screamed *shut the hell up!*

We made it into Eustis with no further issues. With the rain set in like it was, it was keeping people indoors. The guys manning the roadblock waved us through without delay. We rode past the lake where Cecil had been hard at work planting crops along the narrow strip of usable ground between it and the road. The furrows were full of water now and there was no sign of anything poking above the soil. But it was an impressive amount of work he'd managed to get done.

Out on the dock, a couple of hardy souls, probably more hungry than hardy, were fishing from the little gazebos. A hand-to-mouth existence meant a constant effort to provide food for oneself and family. They didn't even bother looking up as we passed, and I felt for them. It made me thankful for what we had. What my family had.

We parked outside the gate of the armory and walked in. Little Bit was excited to see all the trucks and soldiers, and they seemed equally happy to see her. Everyone she passed, stopped to say hi. Many of them knelt down to talk to her. Sheffield was leaning in the doorway of the building when we came up. He waved us inside and gave Little Bit a curious look as she went in before me. He stopped me and asked why I brought her along. Doc said he was going to wander around for a while.

"Shoot, every kid likes to go for a ride," I replied.

"Yeah, but aren't you worried about bringing her out? You never know what could happen."

I slapped his shoulder, "You worry too much. She's fine. We're fine."

He shook his head and followed me inside. We went to the small conference room and took a seat. Naturally, Little Bit was enamored with the swivel chairs, and spent her time spinning in circles. Livingston sat at the foot of the table with a smile on his face, shaking his head.

"Fawcett says there's going to be a break in the weather sometime tonight, and the rain will stop. It will still be overcast, but he says they can fly in it," Sarge said.

"Good. We've already lost one of the wounded. We need that field hospital," Livingston replied.

"We need a place they can get a Shit Hook into," Sarge said.

Livingston looked up at Sheffield, "I think we should have them set down on the road out in front of the police department." Sheffield nodded, "I think a *Chinook*," he emphasized the word looking at Sarge, "could land there. Nothing around to obstruct it."

Sarge stood up, "Well let's walk over there and take a look to make sure there's nothing to get in the way. Last thing I want is for them to show up and us not have a place for them to land."

"Let's do it." Livingston said as he got up.

We walked over to the police department as it was just next door. Little Bit made a point to splash in every puddle she passed, and there were many. Standing in the parking lot of a defunct business just south of the PD, we looked down South Bay Street. There were no real obstructions, and it was decided the best place would be the intersection of West Stevens Ave. The wide intersection would provide plenty of room to get the large helicopter into.

With that settled, we started back towards the armory. As we came into the parking lot of the PD, we were met by a group. There were men and women, and all of them were armed. I was taken aback at the sight of them. We were so close to the armory it didn't make sense that they would try anything. They stood strung out in a line facing us without saying a word.

Sarge, being the diplomat he is, spoke first. He took a step forward and eyed them up for a minute, then said, "I hope this ain't gonna take long. I'm already soaked to my nuts."

A couple of the group exchanged glances. I don't know what they were expecting, but whatever it was, this damn sure wasn't it. After a brief silence, a short stocky man with blond hair and matching beard spoke up.

"We've been watching you guys for some time. We were unsure what your intentions here were."

Sarge looked back at us. Perplexed he asked, "And?"

"We're what's left of the Eustis PD."

I looked at Sheffield. He appeared just as confused as I was. Stepping up to Sarge, I asked, "Where the hell have you guys been?"

"We've been here. We stayed on the job for a long time. But when we realized this wasn't a short term deal and things went to hell, we decided to take care of our own."

"Can't say I blame you none for that," Sarge replied.

The man pointed at me, "You're the Sheriff now?"

"I'm a Sheriff. Name's Morgan Carter."

"I'm Sean Meador. A Lieutenant with the Eustis PD."

"What do you guys want?" I asked.

"We want to help." He held his hand up to display a set of keys hanging from his finger. "I have the keys to the PD, and it's full of stuff."

I certainly wasn't expecting that.

"This is Shane Shackleford and Steve Donnelly," Sean said.

I shook the other men's hands. Sarge was eyeing them up and down, and in his typical fashion, had an interesting greeting.

"Three S's huh? Shit, shower an shave."

They didn't know what to say, and looked at one another. "Ignore him I said. He's not a people person. His name's First Sergeant Mitchell."

Sarge stepped up and shook their hands. When shaking Sean's, he asked, "What took so damn long?"

"Like I said, we stayed as long as we could. But once we realized this wasn't a short term deal, we had to go take care of our families. We've been here the whole time."

"And we've been dealing with some things too. Just doing it quietly," Shane added.

"I'm glad to have the help, thanks," I said.

"You should have come to us sooner," Livingston said.

"You wanna check out the PD?" Sean asked.

Nodding, I said, "Sure; let's see what you got in there." Sean unlocked the roll-down shutter protecting the front door and opened it. And we followed him in.

# CHAPTER 11

J ESS LOOKED AROUND THE TABLE and asked, "What do you guys think?"

Lee Ann nodded, "I'm in."

"Me too," Taylor said with a smile.

Fred leaned back and crossed her arms, "You know where I stand."

Jamie rubbed her hands together, "I love the idea."

Aric raised his hand, "I only have one question. Can I be part of the group?"

Fred leaned back and looked at him, "You can be our token man," she said with a smile.

"Yeah, we could use a beast of burden. You know, strong back and weak mind," Jamie added.

Aric started to protest, "Hey—" But Fred cut him off.

"Hush man."

Aric leaned back. Shaking his head as he ran his fingers through his hair, he said, "This is just weird." Getting a round of laughter out of the women.

"What about Mary?" Taylor asked.

Jess quieted and a looked off in the distance. After a moment, she said, "I don't think Mary would want to be part of this."

"She's been through enough," Fred agreed.

"Let's go find the guys then. I want to get better," Fred said. She smiled and looked around the table, "I really like the training."

"But it's raining," Lee Ann said.

Jess stiffened up, and in a gruff voice trying to imitate Sarge, she replied, "You can't pick the weather yer gonna fight in."

The girls started laughing. Aric shook his head, "That was horrible."

They collected their gear and headed out. The two previous training sessions were conducted out behind the cemetery across the road from Danny's house. But they had to go get their trainers first. At the house the guys shared with Sarge, Fred knocked on the door. It swung open to reveal Sarge standing there with a cup of some hot brew in his hands. He looked at the five of them for a moment before bellowing, "I already found Jesus!" and slamming the door.

Fred looked back; she was met with shrugs. The door suddenly swung open again. Unsure what to say, they stared at the old man who stared back. "I already know who I'm voting for!" Sarge shouted and slammed the door again.

Taylor started to laugh, and her sister quickly joined in. From inside the house, they heard Kay's voice. "Linus, you quit teasing those girls and let them in!"

The door opened again and Sarge eyed them up and down. Over his shoulder he called out, "You sure you want to let this band of refugees in? Look like a bunch of damned drowned rats."

Kay came up behind Sarge, "You girls come in. Don't mind him."

The girls smiled and filed in. When Aric got to the door, he smiled at Kay, "Can I come in too?"

Sarge was still standing in the door. "No," he replied, and slammed the door shut.

Aric stood there staring at the door. He never was sure how to take the old man. After all, he'd shot him once and wasn't certain Sarge was over it yet. After a moment, the door opened and Kay took his hand, "You can come in too."

Aric shook his head, "I was starting to wonder."

"Never mind him. You're always welcome."

As Aric stepped past Kay, he put his arm around her and gave her a kiss on the cheek. Kay patted his back and directed him to the kitchen. The kitchen was full of people; all the guys were there along with Kay and Sarge. A Coleman stove sat on top of the useless range, its blue flame licking the bottom of a teapot. Jamie looked around sniffing, "What's that smell?"

Sarge grinned and held his cup up, "Coffee," he said before taking a drink.

Jamie's eyes went wide. "Where'd you get that?"

"Morgan got some tea; I got the important stuff. Coffee," Sarge replied.

"I want some!" Taylor shouted. The rest of the gang chimed in as well.

"Pshh; you don't drink coffee," Sarge said to Taylor.

"Yes I do!"

Kay went to the cupboard and took down cups and started to pour. She handed them out until everyone had a cup of the steaming brew. The pot was empty, and she dumped what was left in the sink. Turning around, she asked, "Should I start another pot?"

"You'd be an angel if you would," Sarge replied.

Kay smiled and turned back to the counter. From a large blue container, she put more water in and swirled it around before dumping it into the sink. She then refilled the kettle and added several heaping spoons of coffee before setting it back on the flame.

"Wow; this is strong!" Taylor said with her eyes half crossed.

"He likes his coffee like he likes his men, strong and black," Mike said with a smile.

The girls laughed and Mike looked over at Sarge. He was taking a sip from his cup and looking over the rim at Mike. His eyes were two narrow slits with what looked like two thick caterpillars resting over them. Sarge didn't say a word, but Mike couldn't hold the gaze. He knew at some point he'd pay for it. But it was funny.

"What're you all doing out in the rain?" Sarge asked.

"We were hoping to get some training in this afternoon. You guys got back from town early, and there's still time," Jess said.

Mike pointed at the window. "Maybe you didn't notice, but it's raining out there."

"Yes Mike; we're aware," Fred said as she rang some water from her hair.

"The rain will stop tonight. You guys can wait until tomorrow. I'm not going out in it unless I have to," Ted said.

Sarge looked at Lee Ann, "Your daddy know you're out in this crap?"

"We told him we were going to their house," she replied, nodding at Jess.

Sarge nodded, "You can wait until tomorrow." He sat back in his chair and crossed his arms over his chest. "What's got you all stirred up anyway? Why are you guys wanting this training all of a sudden?"

The room was quiet; all eyes were on the girls. They shared glances around at one another. Of course they'd talked about this a lot, hours; but only among themselves. All of them were nervous and waiting for the other to speak.

Jess stared into her cup as she swirled the coffee around. "We want to do our part. We want to be able to defend ourselves and our community. Morgan made us deputies." Looking up, she added, "We're not weak little girls. We're just as capable as anyone else."

Sarge smiled and winked at her, "You're damn right you are."

A wave of relief washed over Jess, and smiles spread across the faces of the other girls. Taylor leaned over and shouldered her sister. They were proud of themselves; they were becoming part of the group and not just *kids* anymore.

Sarge looked at Aric, "What's your position in all this?"

Fred looked at him, and his chin dropped. "I'm the token man."

Mike and Ted started to laugh, loud hard belly laughs. Aric shook his head and Sarge looked at the two guys.

"What the hell are you idiots laughing at? He's the only man in a group of four women; probably the smartest man here." The guys stopped laughing as they thought about it.

A smile spread across Aric's face for a moment, until Sarge spoke again. "Kinda." He pointed at Lee Ann and Taylor, "But I know their daddy. Watched him shoot a man today." Sarge took another sip of coffee, "Imagine what he'd do to you."

The smile was completely gone now. Aric looked at Sarge, "It's not like that. It's nothing like that."

"Yeah," Lee Ann started, looking at Aric and shaking her head. "It's not like that at all!"

Kay slapped Sarge's shoulder, "Stop teasing these kids."

Sarge smiled, "I'm jus' sayin'."

"Did Dad really shoot someone today?" Taylor asked.

"He did."

"Why?" Lee Ann asked.

"Up in town some dipshit was stealing his neighbor's chickens. The neighbor caught him and they started shooting at one another. The man with the chickens was hit, and the thieving bastard ran to town where we were." Sarge laughed, "Thought we was going to help him."

"And Dad just shot him?" Taylor asked.

"It's like this. The man was a thief. When he got caught, he shot the man he was stealing from. What are you to do with a man like that?"

In a voice totally devoid of emotion, Ted replied, "You put him down."

"Hard," Mike added.

"He didn't say anything about it when he came home," Taylor said.

"Yeah, he was normal. Like always," Lee Ann added.

"It isn't the sort of thing you brag about. No normal man does anyway. Your daddy just does what needs to be done when the time comes," Sarge replied.

Always one to try and lighten the mood, Kay rose from her chair, "Coffee's done. Who needs a fresher?"

Lee Ann looked down into her cup, "There's coffee grounds in my cup."

"Where do you think it comes from?" Mike asked.

"Don't worry, I'll drink yours," Sarge said as he passed his cup to Kay.

"No, no; I'll take some," Lee Ann replied, getting a laugh out of Sarge.

As they were talking and enjoying the spoils of Sarge's scrounging abilities, there was a knock at the door. Sarge looked up, "Who the hell is it now?" He asked as Mike headed for the door.

Dalton was standing there when Mike opened the door. Mike looked at him, he was soaked. Water dripped from the brim of his boonie hat. "What's up, man?" Mike asked as Ted came up behind him.

"Found another hide."

"No shit, where?" Ted asked.

"Out behind that house where those folks are quarantined."

"That ain't good. Let's get our shit Mikey and go take a look," Ted said as he headed back into the house.

"Come on in and get a cup of coffee," Mike said, waving Dalton in.

"Coffee? Where the hell'd you get that?" Dalton replied as he followed Mike.

"The old man's a first rate thief."

Dalton came into the kitchen and all eyes were on him. Sarge looked down at his boots. "You track that mud all through my house?"

Dalton looked down at his feet, "Oh, sorry about that. I'm not used to being inside anymore." He looked back the way he'd come, and the muddy tracks he'd left.

Sarge laughed, "I know what ya mean; don't worry about it. Coffee?"

Dalton looked at the pot on the stove, "I'd almost do unnatural things for a cup."

"You're lucky I'm here then," Miss Kay said as she handed him a cup. "I'll just give it to you."

Dalton took the cup, "Thank you." He held it up to his nose and sniffed deeply. Closing his eyes, he moaned, "My God that smells good." He took a long sip, holding the hot liquid in his mouth for a long moment before swallowing it. "Damn that's good."

"Few things in life are as good," Sarge replied.

Dalton nodded, "I'd have to agree."

"What's up this morning?" Sarge asked.

"I found another hide; we're going to go take a look at it."

"Where is it?" Sarge asked.

"Out behind Tyler's place," Ted replied as he came in.

"You going to take a look?" Sarge asked.

"Yeah, we'll check it out. You coming?" Ted asked.

Sarge looked around the table, "Nah, you guys can handle that. I'll stay here and keep the women folks safe."

Ted laughed, "Yeah, they look like they need your protection alright."

"Hey!" Jess shouted.

Sarge smiled, "I'm just playin'."

"He's looking for an excuse is all Jess," Ted added.

Dalton finished the coffee and unslung his pack, setting it on the table. He fished around in it and pulled out a Titanium cup. Looking at Kay, he asked, "Can I have one for the road?"

Kay took the cup with a smile. "Of course; but you could have taken that cup with you."

Dalton smiled, "I like this one. Plus, when I'm done, I can drop it back into my pack."

Kay handed the filled cup back to him, "Here you go."

He took the cup and thanked her. Mike was standing in the hall and called out, "You guys coming, or are we going to make this tea party an all-day thing?"

Dalton spun on his heels, "Let's go lads!"

Taylor quickly spoke up, "Can we come?"

Ted looked at her, then at Sarge. He made no indication either way. Ted looked around the table at the group. He could see the pleas in their eyes. "Alright. You guys can come. This will be treated as a combat patrol, and you will be treated accordingly."

The girls were quickly on their feet amid the sound of chairs sliding on the floor and banging into the wall. It looked a lot like a Chinese fire drill, and caused Sarge to laugh.

"You guys be safe," Kay said as everyone headed for the door.

Once outside Ted called everyone's attention. "Alright guys;

like I said, this is a combat patrol. Order of march will be as follows: Dalton on point, then Jess, Taylor and Lee Ann. I'm next with Fred, then Aric and Mike; and tail end will be Charlie."

Dalton cleared his throat. "Don't bunch up; keep your intervals and pay attention. I'll pause often to look and listen. If you see something, be sure to call it out. When we stop, your focus is outward, not what everyone else is doing. Pay attention."

His comments seemed to add a little apprehension to the group. They looked around nervously.

"Don't worry about it guys, this is just practice. We're probably not going to come across anyone, but treat it as though we will. You never know," Mike added.

"Alright Dalton, lead off. Everyone fall in as we move out," Ted instructed.

Dalton shook the last of the coffee from his cup and stuffed it in his pack. Shouldering it, he checked his weapon and started out towards Tyler's house. Ordinarily, Dalton would simply have walked straight to the spot he'd discovered. But since this was being used as a training exercise, he treated it as a real patrol. Every so often he would stop to look and listen. The three experienced men would make corrections to the rest of the group; but for the most part they did well.

Approaching the bunker, Dalton stopped and took a knee. Everyone followed suit; they were doing well. Dalton looked back and waved Ted forward.

"What's up?" Ted whispered.

"Is there any sort of challenge/reply set up?"

"No. But we should do that. Good idea; let's move out to the bunker and we'll talk about it with the guys there."

Dalton nodded and moved out. Ted waited as the group passed him and fell back in at his position. Dalton could see Thad looking at him through the front port of the bunker. He had a curious look on his face. Dalton waved, and Thad waved back. Soon he and Danny appeared from behind the bunker.

"What's with all the sneaking around like a bunch of ninjas?" Thad asked.

"Patrol training," Dalton answered.

The group made it to the bunker and grouped up, talking, chatting and generally not paying attention to what was going on. Ted looked around, "Hey!" He called in a harsh whisper. "Form a security perimeter! You're still on a patrol."

Unsure of exactly what he meant, the group started to shift around. Mike, Ted and Dalton helped direct them. Taking the time to explain where they needed to be and what they needed to be looking for.

"The threat is out there, not here where we are. When we stop, you form a perimeter, facing out so we have 360 degrees of coverage, and no one can sneak up on us," Dalton said as he moved around the circle the girls started forming.

Thad watched in amusement as the guys worked with the girls to get them in place. Even Aric got some pointers. Lee Ann looked at Thad, "What are you smiling at?" She asked in a friendly jabbing manner.

"Just watching you all carry on."

Lee Ann looked out at her area of observation, then back at Thad. "We've got to learn at some point."

Thad nodded and the smile disappeared, "Yes you do. Take it seriously too. This kind of thing ain't no game."

She nodded before turning her attention to the area in front of her. They maintained the security perimeter for a little longer before Ted gave the order to move out. Dalton nodded and headed off towards Tyler's house as everyone fell in behind him. Dalton worked his way off the road and into the woods.

He moved slowly and paused frequently to listen and eyeball the area.

As they moved, if he heard a stick break, he'd pause and look back. Whichever of the three guys was closest to the offender would admonish them and offer some advice on stealthy movement, but this was never done in a mean or belittling way. The guys would try to encourage the girls to pay attention and reinforce just how important these skills were.

When they were close to the place they were headed to, Dalton dropped to his knee. Everyone followed suit almost immediately. Dalton waved to Ted and pointed out the spot.

"It's that oak right there."

Ted looked at the old tree. "Good hide location." The old oak had probably been struck by lightning, causing nearly half of it to collapse.

"Yeah, they can see the road from here and tell who's moving around."

"Is it empty?"

"It was when I found it. But the ground was dry under that big limb."

"Alright, I'm going to get Mike to take a couple with him and move over there behind it. He can be our cover as we approach it," Ted said, and quickly turned and headed off.

He told Mike what he wanted done, and in no time Mike, Fred and Aric were moving off. Ted told the rest of the group how to spread out. Jamie directed Lee Ann and Taylor where to go, then pointed out a place for Jess. Once they were all in position, Mike called and said they were ready. Ted looked at Dalton and nodded, and the two started moving towards the old tree. It didn't take long to get to it and see it was unoccupied. Dalton pointed out the hide, and Ted knelt down to inspect it.

"There have been at least two different people here," Ted whispered.

Dalton knelt down beside him. Pointing out through the field behind him, he replied, "And they come and go through there."

Ted looked out across the field. "That's a long way to get in here."

Dalton nodded, "Let's get out of here and talk about it. I have an idea."

Ted nodded, and they moved out and regrouped at the bunker. Much to the guys' delight, the girls immediately formed a security perimeter.

"What's your plan?" Ted asked Dalton.

"I figured we should set up an ambush for whoever is coming back. See if we can bag him," Dalton replied.

Ted looked around and nodded, "I agree. I'd like to know who's poking around. We'll sort out who's going and get it ready soon."

"I'm thinking just the three of us, you, me and Mike. I don't think we'll need more than that, and these guys aren't ready for that sort of thing yet," Dalton replied, nodding towards Jess.

Ted smiled, "Don't let Jamie hear you say that."

Dalton looked at her, "Wasn't talking about her. I think she can hold her own."

"You have no idea my friend. She's a bad ass chick."

The two got with Mike and told them what they were going to do. The girls and Aric agreed to take over at the bunker and let Thad and Danny take a break.

"You guys be careful out there," Thad said as he slung his AK.

"We will, but if you hear any shooting come a runnin'," Mike replied.

Thad smiled and winked, "You know I will."

"I'm headed home to dry out," Danny said.

The girls and Aric moved into the bunker. Ted took time to explain to Jamie what he wanted her to do if any shooting started. She, Aric and Jess were to be a quick reaction force and come to the ambush. Lee Ann, Taylor and Fred were to remain at the bunker to cover them. With the details sorted, everyone moved out.

The guys moved into the woods and took up positions on the trail that was being used to access the hide. It was across a small pasture, and whoever would be coming would surely stop inside the tree line before moving across it. They would take them here when they paused for a look. They took some time setting up their hides, camouflage would be paramount. Once their hides were ready, the guys settled in for the hard part, the wait.

———— * * * * * ————

About dinner time, we got ready to go over to Danny's. Little Bit was in the floor of the living room playing with a bunch of small plastic animals. I asked if she were hungry, and she immediately jumped up, "I'm starvin'!" She shouted.

She was holding a plastic snake, its tail draped on the floor. Seeing that, I smiled. "Let me see that." She handed me the snake and I observed that it was nearly three feet long and almost as big as a paper towel tube. I looked at her, "You wanna have some fun?"

Her eyes lit up, "Yeah! What are you going to do?"

I knelt down. "Mr. Thad is scared of snakes. Let's take this out and put it in the garden. He goes out there every day after supper; it'll scare him good."

She jumped up and down clapping her hands, "Oh yeah, let's do it! It'll scare him good."

"You shouldn't do that. If he's afraid of snakes, why would you do that?" Mel asked.

I looked at the snake, then at her, "Cause it's funny."

"I bet he won't be laughing about it."

"Oh sure he will. Eventually," I replied with a chuckle.

As she rounded the corner into the kitchen, Mel replied, "You still shouldn't do it."

I followed her around the corner. She was wiping down the counter and I came up behind her. Wrapping my arms around her from behind, I said, "I love you."

Without pausing from her cleaning, she asked in a very sarcastic tone, "What do you want?"

I spun her around. "It's not what I want. It's what you want." I reached into my pocket and took the Tiffany's box out and held it behind my back.

She tried to look behind me, "What do you have? What are you doing?"

Obviously she wasn't over the little incident on the porch. "Nothing," I said.

She tried to look again and I swiveled. Narrowing her eyes, she said, "You better not be up to anything."

I brought the box around where she could see it and held it up. "I just thought you might want this."

Seeing the blue box, her eyes lit up. Then the excitement faded, "Where'd you get it? You didn't take it off a dead body did you?"

I stepped back, "No! That's really messed up. Here I am trying to give you a present and this is how you act?" I went to put the box back in my pocket, "If you don't want"…….

She cut me off and grabbed the box from my hand, "I didn't say that!" She opened the box and took the cuff out. Smiling, she said, "It's really nice. I always wanted one."

I smiled at her, "I know you did. When I saw it, I knew you'd like it."

Slipping it on her wrist, she replied, "Where did you get it? It's so nice."

"A lady at the Altoona store. She had a bunch of jewelry."

She held her wrist out to look at the cuff. Smiling, she gave me a hug and a kiss, "It's very nice. Thank you, I love it."

I squeezed her tight, "Love you too. Let's go get some dinner."

We went over to Danny's where those not otherwise occupied were gathering. Ian, Perez and Mary were there along with Danny and Bobbie. Shortly after we arrived, Kay, Sarge and Doc rolled in as well. Everyone was sitting on the back porch chatting when I made my escape and headed for the garden. While I would still be in view, I hoped to be able to get the rubber anguis out of my pocket.

Once in the garden, I wandered around looking at the plants. Thad was doing an incredible job with them. They were growing strong and vibrant. The tomato plants had golf ball-sized green fruits on them. The peppers were already fruiting as well. The squashes had large bright flowers; it wouldn't be long before they had fruits as well. Hearing laughter from the porch, I looked up. Everyone was wrapped up in some BS Sarge was telling, so I quickly knelt down and whipped the snake from my pocket.

I couldn't help but smile as I thought about a line from Blazing Saddles, *excuse me while I whip this out.* I rolled the snake into a coil under the broad leaf of a yellow squash. I was chuckling to myself as I did it. Remembering Thad on the side of that lake, I couldn't help myself. Now, if he responds the same this time I'll probably shit myself. With my dastardly deed done, I headed up to the house.

We sat around and had dinner. Ian and Sarge kept taking

shots at one another, which added some levity to the evening. Thad's shotgun was lying on the table in front of him tucked inside of a leather scabbard. I pointed to it, "What's that?"

Thad picked it up, "I made it from an old saddle I found in one of the sheds. The saddle was pretty torn up, but the base of it was nice leather. I've oiled the hell out of it, so it's really nice now."

He handed it to me and I inspected the work. Thad was a patient man and had obviously spent a lot of time on it.

"Now I can sling it over my back and always have it with me," Thad added.

I handed it back over, "Man that's really nice. Can't believe it was an old saddle."

"I know. He should go into the leather business," Danny added.

"Only one problem with that," Thad replied. "You need leather!"

"Yeah, might be hard to get new material," Danny said.

"Not if we were in Wyoming," I replied. Both of them looked at me for an explanation. "I talked to a guy on the radio out there. They're covered up with beef, more than they can eat."

"That'd be a hell of a problem to have," Sarge boomed.

"Wouldn't be a problem for me; I can eat my own weight in beef," Thad said with a smile.

Perez looked sideways at him and asked, "In one sitting?"

Thad started to laugh, "I'll take a break in the middle and get a nap in."

"Man I wish we had some beef," Ian said.

"Florida was one of the largest beef producers in the country. There still has to be some out there somewhere," I added.

"Thank you for dinner, Miss Bobbie and Mary. I'm headed

out to the garden for a bit," Thad said as he rose from the table and slung the scabbard over his shoulder.

Bobbie pushed her bowl away. "It wasn't much, but you're welcome."

"I'm coming too, Thad," Mary said as she quickly got up from the table.

As they left the porch and headed towards the garden, the women started talking about Thad and Mary spending so much time together. I waved at Sarge, and when he looked over, I pointed at the garden and mouthed the word, *watch*. Sarge's brow furrowed, but he leaned over to be able to see. Ian caught on that something was up, and asked me as much.

Smiling, I replied, "Just watch. You'll see."

"Oh, you didn't really do that did you?" Mel asked.

"What'd he do?" Kay asked.

I turned back to her and Mel, "Don't say anything, you'll see."

Thad and Mary made their way to the garden. Normally Thad would kneel down in the garden to pull the stray weeds and talk to his plants. But with the recent rain, the ground was saturated; so he squatted instead. A smile spread over my face as I watched him work from the far end of the garden towards the squash plants. The tomatoes delayed him for a bit as he and Mary picked worms from them. They painstakingly checked each and every leaf, removing the parasites as they were found. Thad carried a small cup with him, and he'd drop the worms in for feeding to the chickens later. The chickens loved the worm treats.

I leaned forward in anticipation as he got to the squash, any second now. But Mary got to it first. I saw her jump back and point. Thad looked down and back-peddled a couple of steps while reaching for the shotgun on his back. He quickly shouldered the old side by side as he pulled Mary out of the way. The shotgun went off with a roar, and Thad stood there for a moment. Then I saw his head turn to the side, and he stared intently for a moment. Then he reached down with the barrel of the gun and lifted the rubber snake up and inspected it.

Realizing it was a rubber snake, his attention turned to the porch. It was still draped over the barrel when he shouted out, "You ain't funny, Morgan!" He looked back down into the garden than back up, "You're lucky there weren't any flowers on this side of that plant!" He tossed the snake into the yard before calling out, "I'll get you back!"

"It didn't scare him," Little Bit said as she sat back down at the table.

"Smooth move Ex Lax," Sarge barked. "You didn't even scare him."

"Ahh, Mary saw it first. If he'd seen it first, he would have pooped himself." Choosing my words carefully because of Little Bit. "I've seen it before, and it's funny as hell."

"I suggest you start looking over your shoulder. That big man is going to break your ass in half," Perez offered.

Looking to change the subject, I glanced at Doc, "How are Tyler and family?"

Doc jerked his head, "Not good. He's sick, bad sick. Brandy is sick too, and will probably get worse."

"How about the babies?" Kay asked.

Doc rested his elbows on the table, "That's the funny thing. They appear to be fine. I would have expected them to get ill too, but they're OK. They want to go outside really bad; and Brandy and Tyler are having trouble taking care of them. Other than that, the kids are good."

"Maybe we should get the kids out of there," Kay replied.

"I'm still nervous about that. They could be infected and not yet symptomatic. I think we need to give it a little longer."

"If they can't take care of them, then we're going to have to do something," Bobbie said.

Mel stood up from the table, "We can't let the kids suffer. They're in there watching their parents suffer. We should get them out."

"We're getting some help tomorrow. Let's see what this clinic is capable of when it gets here. I know it's hard, but we can't risk exposing everyone here," Sarge replied.

"Speaking of that, is it on for tomorrow?" I asked.

Sarge nodded, "Yep. Talked to them right before we came over. The rain's moved out and we're good to go tomorrow."

"Good. We'll get some help then. Hopefully it comes in time for some of those folks in town," Mel said.

"Are they bringing any ammo?" Ian asked.

Sarge nodded, "Oh yeah. I gave 'em a shopping list. We'll have to see what they bring; I doubt they will give us everything I asked for. Plus, with what we brought back from Riley, we should be in pretty good shape."

"I'll take anything they give us," Perez added.

"They're bringing some food out too," I said.

"That's good. We're getting low, really low," Bobbie said as she collected bowls from the table.

"Don't hold your breath; we don't know what they're going to send out," I replied.

Ian stood up and stretched, "Alright Perez; time to go to work."

"You guys on watch?" I asked.

Perez moaned, "Yes. You relieve us at midnight."

"Yeah; you and me," Danny added.

"We'll be there," I replied with a smile. "Have a good night."

"I want to wait here for the girls," Mel said.

"We'll go relieve them. I'm sure they're hungry," Ian said as he collected his gear.

Ian and Perez left to change the watch, and Thad and Mary came back up on the porch. Thad had a look in his eye that was less than comfortable. He was pointing at me as he came through the door.

"You think you're a funny man." He smiled and added, "That's alright. I'll get even."

"Ahh, come on. It didn't even scare you," I replied.

"It scared me," Mary said with a light giggle.

"I wasn't trying to scare you. I'm sorry," I replied with a smile.

A sudden racket at the front announced the arrival of the girls. They were very loud, as if they were really pumped up about something. When questioned, they all said it was nothing, and they were starving. While they ate, we all chatted around the table. Doc soon announced he was tired and headed home. He reminded Mary about their trip to town in the morning. She said she'd be packed and ready to go on time. Sarge and Kay joined Doc, and everyone said their good nights. As soon as our girls were done with their dinner, we also headed home.

"I'll see you about midnight," I said to Danny as I headed out the door.

He waved, "See you then."

The girls were still pretty wound up, and carried on all the way home, though it wasn't far.

"What's got you guys all spun up?" I asked.

"Nuthin'," Taylor said. "We're just glad to be able to help out. You know, do our part."

We walked for a minute before I replied. "You girls just be careful. This isn't a game."

"We know. That's why we've been training with Ted. He's really good," Lee Ann replied.

"Dalton scares me," Taylor said with a shiver.

"He is kind of scary. He yells a lot," Lee Ann agreed.

"He yells at you?" Mel asked.

Taylor snorted, "He yells at everyone!"

"I'd pay attention to him. From what I've seen, he's pretty good at what he does," I replied.

We got into the house and everyone headed for their rooms. Mel went and tucked Little Bit in; and soon we were in our room. I was tired, even though we had spent the afternoon snoozing. As the girls quieted down, I climbed into bed.

"It's going to be hot tomorrow," I said as I flipped the sheet back on the bed.

"Why? It's been nice with the rain. Cooled things off."

"The rain is why. It's going be like being in a steamer."

"Oh great. Just what I need."

With a chuckle, I noted, "Well babe, like I said; it only gets worse."

Mel jerked the sheet, "Well aren't you just a little black rain cloud."

# CHAPTER 12

I woke up about a quarter till midnight. Moving quietly, I got dressed and collected my kit before slipping out of our room. After getting my boots on, I grabbed a quick cup of tea and chugged it; the caffeine would help. Heading out the door, I woke the dogs up. They all got up, staggering around and began yawning. I rubbed their heads and was rewarded with tail wags all around. When I headed out for the bunker, they fell in behind me and followed me silently down the road.

With the rain now spent, the sky was clear, and I could see the stars shining brightly overhead. There were even more stars visible now, or so it seemed. But it only made sense. With nearly all man-made pollution gone, the sky was clearing up. It was like stepping back in time, to a time before the Industrial Age. Approaching the bunker, I could hear voices, certainly more than just Perez and Ian.

Someone turned on a light as I approached. "Hey Morgan. Look what we found," Mike said.

Turning his head, the light fell onto a man on the ground. "Who the hell is that?"

"He's one of the people that's been watching us," Dalton said.

"Where'd you guys find him?"

"Dalton found a hide over behind Tyler's place. We laid up an ambush and managed to bag this turd," Ted replied.

I looked down at the man. He was wearing mismatched camo and worn sneakers. He had a camo ball cap on his head with the logo of some concrete company on it.

"He doesn't look like DHS to me," I said.

"He's not. I think he's part of Billy's group," Ted said.

"He looks a little rough even for that bunch."

"We'll find out soon enough. When the old man gets ahold of him, he'll talk," Mike said.

"He is persuasive," I replied.

The man never looked up, choosing instead to keep his eyes on the ground in front of him. I kicked his foot, but he still wouldn't look up. Looking at Ted, I said, "You guys taking him home with you?" Ted nodded, and I looked back at the man and kicked his foot again. "Take my advice, make it easy on yourself and just answer the questions. We're not going to kill you, but that old bastard will make you wish you were dead."

Mike grabbed the man by his arm and jerked him up, "On your feet, shithead." They led the man away towards their house, leaving me and Dalton in the darkness.

"You can take off. Danny will be here in a minute," I said to Dalton.

Dalton rolled his shoulders, "I'm good. We laid in our hides for hours. I need to stand up."

I went down into the bunker and grabbed the NVGs from where they hung. Coming back outside, I fired them up and took a look around. With the clear sky, I could see quite well. Hearing footsteps, I looked back to see Danny coming down the road.

"Yo!" I called out. He responded in kind.

When he got to the bunker, we filled him in on the night's

events. He listened to Dalton then asked, "How did you get him?"

"Oh that was easy. He didn't come in until after dark, and we had night vision. We watched him walk up, and I just stood behind a big tree. He came ditty bopping down the trail with his rifle slung over his shoulder. When he passed me, I just stepped out and quickly put him in a sleeper hold. Wasn't even a fight."

Danny laughed, "You guys are nuts. I don't know if I could do that. Just reach out and grab someone."

"It gets easier the more you do it."

Now it was my turn to laugh, "*The more you do it.* Just how many people have you, *put to sleep?*"

Dalton shrugged, "How many grains of sand on the beach?" Danny and I both laughed at the reply.

"I can count how many I have, three. Only people I ever put to sleep were my daughters when they were babies," I said.

Dalton cocked his head to the side and said, "You put babies in a sleeper hold?" he laughed after making his little joke.

I shook my head, "You're not right."

"You going to hang out or go get some sleep?" Danny asked.

"I'll hang out. Might go in and take a nap in the bunker."

"Go on inside and we'll hang out here," Danny replied.

"Wake me up if something happens," Dalton said as he ducked down into the bunker. He came back out almost immediately with a bucket. "What the hell is this? Smells like piss." I looked back. Dalton swirled the liquid around for a moment and sniffed it, "It is piss! Who the hell keeps a bucket of piss?"

I laughed, "I guess the girls used it for a latrine."

Dalton walked over to the side of the road and dumped it. "We need to do something about this. That's just nasty."

"I'll sort something out today. We need a way for the girls to go when they're up here," Danny said.

"I'll help," Dalton said as he tossed the bucket to the side of the road and went back inside.

Danny and I went to the front of the bunker and sat down on it. With the top rising above the ground it was about the perfect height. We talked in soft whispers to kill the time. As always, we'd scan the area with the NVGs from time to time, but the night would thankfully prove to be uneventful. When the sky started to lighten in the east, I saw headlights swing out onto the road from one of the small side streets. I figured Sarge would be here early, but he was even earlier than I had anticipated.

He pulled up beside us and stopped, "We're going to get Mary. Be right back." I nodded and he pulled off.

"You guys going into town?" Danny asked.

"Yeah, I guess they're bringing in some stuff. The clinic is the most important. We'll see what they bring."

"Thankfully, we haven't really needed the clinic until that shooting. I hope it goes back to the way it was."

I looked over at him, "We may not have needed it, but those folks in town sure do."

"You keep messing with Thad, and you're going to need the clinic," Danny said with a laugh.

I laughed, "You should have seen him when we were walking home." Thinking about it got me to really laughing. "It was hilarious. When I asked what kind of snake it was, he replied, *it was a snake kind of snake!*"

Sarge pulled back up in the Hummer. "Saddle up, buttercup. Time to make like a baby and head out."

I shook my head and couldn't help but smile, "They're

getting worse by the day." As I got in, I asked, "You learn anything from that guy?"

Sarge waved me off, "I ain't even talked to him. He's stewin' in his juices right now." Sarge looked out at Danny, "Thad will be up here shortly."

Danny nodded, "That's cool. Dalton's in the bunker asleep."

Just as he said that, Dalton emerged from the entrance. Rubbing his head, he said, "I was. You're a noisy ass bunch."

Sarge looked over at me, then back at Dalton. "Damn, I should have become a psychiatrist." Dalton looked at him and leaned back against the bunker, waiting for what was surely to come. Sarge didn't disappoint. "That way, I could get paid to pretend I give a shit."

Dalton chuckled. "Don't you have a leg to hump somewhere?"

Sarge smiled, "That I do, and it ain't going to hump itself!" he shouted as he stomped on the gas and we pulled out.

I spun around and smiled at Mary, "Good morning. How are you doing out this early?"

She smiled in return, "I'm good. I'm always up early."

I reached back and slapped Doc's leg. He ducked down through the turret, "Sup?"

I smiled a broad cheesy grin, "Mornin' Sunshine."

Doc shook his head saying, "You ain't right," and disappeared back up top.

We headed out to nineteen and towards Eustis. It was still very early, the sun just barely peeking above the horizon. The road was littered with debris from trees. The rain had pulled all manner of crap down. Other than the debris though, the road was empty. We quickly passed the Kangaroo and I saw one person there setting up for the day's trading. Seeing the market made me think of Mario and Shelly. It had been a little while since I had seen them; maybe we'd go look them up on the way back.

We made it to Eustis without issue. After pulling through the barricade, I wanted to see the progress of Cecil's crops. As we moved through town, it was obvious he'd been very busy. Every possible space in town that could be planted, was. But studying the progress, it just didn't look like it would be enough. Even the green space where the old hospital once stood was planted. The corn was now poking out of the soil. But we needed more land, and I had an idea.

Sheffield and Livingston met us as soon as we got out of the truck. They looked amped up and ready to go.

"Plan's changed a bit," Livingston said.

"How so?" Sarge asked.

"We're going to use the front parking lot as an LZ. The first Chinook will land there and unload. Once we move everything, the second one will sling in a bladder of fuel."

Sarge shrugged, "Whatever floats your boat. Have you talked to them this morning?"

"Yeah, they're in the air already."

"Then all we've got to do is wait," Sarge replied as he climbed up onto the hood of the Hummer.

"Have you seen Cecil this morning?" I asked.

"Not yet; he'll be around later," Livingston replied. Shaking his head, he added, "That guy is something else. All he does is work; he doesn't stop."

"I could see that coming in, but I don't think it's going to be enough."

Livingston looked surprised, "What do you mean? We've got crops planted everywhere."

"Yeah, but there isn't more than an acre or two in any one place. We need more, a lot more. I've got a place in mind not far from here where there's probably sixty acres of open ground we could plant."

"How far from here?" Livingston asked.

"Couple of miles up nineteen, not far."

"How would we secure that? It would just get picked clean at night."

I laughed, "That's why you'd have to position people over there. Set up a camp and cycle some of your people through it."

Livingston swept his arm out, "We're already providing security for all the crops here."

"True; but now that the Eustis PD is back in the picture, we can use them to keep an eye on things here. That will free up your people, and you can move some of them out to the other farm. Because it would be a farm."

Livingston thought about it for a minute. "I guess you're right. If the police step up, we could do that." He looked at me, "But they have to stick around. No disappearing."

"I think they will. Seeing you guys here gave them the confidence to come back. I can't blame them for leaving. Hell, I would have done the same thing."

The thumping of an approaching Chinook ended our conversation. We moved around the armory to the north parking lot to watch as they came in. These machines always amazed me. The two huge rotors beating the air to carry the massive machine aloft was a sight to witness, from the ground anyway. I had no desire to ride in one. The thing looked to me like it defied the laws of physics; and I didn't want to be around if the law won.

The two choppers came in and circled once before the leader began his descent to the parking lot. The pilot made it look so easy as he drifted down, sliding in sideways for the last bit as the tires connected with the asphalt. Sheffield and

Livingston had their people ready and they were at the back of the big machine as the load master lowered the ramp. Several people ran down the ramp; and with the help of the crew and the Guardsmen, the supplies inside were unloaded. The pilots stayed in the cockpit with the engines roaring, ready to take off in an instant.

Some of the material was on pallets, and thankfully Sheffield had come up with a couple of pallet jacks from somewhere. This really expedited the off load. Faster than I would have believed, the machine was empty. The crew chiefs were leaning out of their positions to make sure no obstructions created a hazard as the pilots applied power and the behemoth began to lift off. It wasn't long before it was climbing high into the sky and falling in behind the other with its sling load of fuel.

Once the first machine was at altitude, the second began its approach. This one was a little different, as they didn't have to actually touch down. The pilot demonstrated exceptional skill as he brought the load slung beneath him in and seemed to make the load arrest its forward momentum right over the parking lot. As soon as the bladder was steady he began to slowly drop it down while his two crew chiefs leaned out, calling distance to him. Once the bag was on the ground, someone inside released the cable holding it, and the machine began to climb up to join his wingman.

The whole operation went fast and smoothly. I was surprised at how quickly it all happened. But in short order, we were standing in silence among the piles of material just delivered. Doc immediately found the medical personnel, and they were quickly sorting out where to put the clinic. Sheffield and Livingston joined the discussion, having their own ideas about where it needed to be. I stayed by the Hummer. None of this was up to me; and I thought it better if I just stayed out of the way. Sarge was still sitting on the hood, paying little attention to the activity.

"Why aren't you helping them figure out where to set up?" I asked.

Sarge leaned back, resting on his hands. "For the same reason you're not. It ain't my business."

"I'm going to see if I can find Cecil," I said as I looked around.

Sarge hopped off the truck, "I'm going to go through some of this shit and find what's ours before these booger eaters steal it all."

I left Sarge and headed off towards the gate. Quite a crowd had formed to watch the show this morning, and I had to make my way through them. As I did, I was peppered with questions.

"What's on those helicopters?" A man asked as I passed him.

I shrugged, "Army shit I guess."

"When are they going to bring in some food? We're starving!" A woman shouted.

"I don't know," I lied about that one.

"If they've got helicopters and stuff, they should be able to help us!" Another voice shouted.

I finally made my way through the crowd. I didn't see Cecil, but didn't really expect to. I had an idea where I could find him. I made my way towards the lake and the crops planted along its edge. I wandered along for a while, looking at the plants in their various stages of growth. It did look like a lot; and it would be for a family or two, but not for a whole community. In that context, it was woefully inadequate.

I eventually found Cecil. Like me, he was wandering around the lakeshore, checking on his crops. The sun was finally up, and the price the rain brought from the heat would now come due. As I walked towards him, steam rose from the saturated ground as the sun climbed higher into the sky.

"Morning Cecil, looks like it's going to be a blister of a day."

Cecil looked up and smiled. In the way of some old men, he stood with his hands on the back of his hips and looked up. "I think you're right. Sun's gonna boil all that water off and it will be like a damn jungle."

"The rain was nice; but it comes with a price," I replied with a chuckle.

Cecil turned and looked back towards the armory, "You boys get a delivery this morning?"

"They brought in a field hospital and some other stuff."

Cecil nodded, "That's good. Them poor people are sufferin' something terrible up there. When I saw those birds coming in, it reminded me of a little mountaintop firebase I was on in Vietnam. We called them things shit hooks," he laughed. "I hated riding in them. Just seemed unnatural that the thing could or should fly."

I laughed, "I know what you mean. They say the bumblebee shouldn't be able to fly. Guess no one ever told them."

Cecil gave out a laugh. I liked him; he was an easy person to be around. "You just out inspecting the crops this morning?" He asked me.

"No; actually, I was looking for you." I looked around at the small patches of planted ground. "I really don't think this is going to be enough for everyone here."

Cecil snorted, "Hell no it ain't! I tried to tell that snot-nosed Captain up there; but like all brass, he won't listen. You hang some color on an asshole's collar, and he thinks he knows it all. Sad part is they usually don't learn until people are dead."

"How much land do you think you could plant?" I asked.

Cecil shrugged, "No limit really. The deciding factor is fuel, manpower and seed. We've still got quite a bit of seed." Cecil winked and leaned in close, as if he were about to offer up a secret. "I've found more seed, by the way."

Surprised, I asked him, "Where?"

He smiled broadly, exposing large white, straight teeth, "That's a need to know-only basis. And you don't need to know, Sheriff."

I chuckled at him. "As long as you know, I don't give a shit."

"And that's how it should be!" He barked in reply.

"I've got an idea about a place we could plant. It's a lot of beautiful open land."

"Where you thinking?"

I pointed north, "You know where that big piece of property is on forty-four just east of nineteen?"

Cecil nodded. "Yeah; on the north side of the road there across the road from the Trout Lake Center." He paused and shook his head, "You ever hear of a dumber name for a lake in Florida? Trout Lake. There ain't no trout in that damn lake!"

He cracked me up, "You're right about that. Always thought the same thing. But that is the place I'm talking about."

Cecil rubbed his chin as he thought about it. "That's awful far from here. It'd probably get picked clean before we ever got the first bean from it."

"I've already talked to old Snot Nose. They've agreed to station some soldiers there to provide security. We could also move some folks in there to tend to everything."

Cecil's eyes went wide, "I've spent my time sleeping in a damn Army tent. I ain't doing it!"

He really was funny, "I didn't mean you. You go up there and get it going. Use some folks from town here. Once the seeds are in the ground, you can just go up and check on it from time to time to make sure everything is going smoothly."

Cecil calmed down a bit, "That sounds alright. For a minute there I thought you were losing your fool mind."

Laughing, I replied. "Can't say that isn't happening, but I'm not trying to get you to sleep under canvas either."

"We need to go take a look at the land. I've seen it a hundred times, but never actually looked at it."

"Come on; let's get a ride."

We walked back to the armory. I found Sarge at the Hummer piling ammo cans into the back. When he saw us, he bellowed, "Where the hell have you been?"

I laughed, "You ain't my daddy. I don't have to tell your old ass what I'm doing."

"Thank God! If I knew I was responsible for bringing something as ugly as you into this world, I'd cut my pecker off!"

"You done?" I asked with a smile.

"We need to get this shit loaded up. That damn Sheffield is trying to keep all my shit, and I ain't having it!"

Cecil smiled, "Morning Top."

"Morning Cecil," Sarge replied curtly.

"He knows some of this is ours," I said.

"Yeah; well he's suddenly got a fat fucking head about things," Sarge spat back.

Doc walked up with a couple of boxes under each arm, "Here are some med kits to take back to the ranch." He tossed the boxes into the back of the truck.

"They giving you any trouble?" I asked.

Doc looked up and shook his head. "No; they're great folks over there. There are a couple of engineers here too. They're helping set up the clinic tent now, and said they need to get with you after that."

"Alright; tell them I'll find them later."

"Come on Morgan; we need to get the rest of what's ours," Sarge barked.

"Calm down. It isn't us versus them. We're all in this together," I replied as I followed him.

At the edge of the parking lot, the pallets that came off the chopper were being sorted. Sheffield and Livingston were there directing the action. Sarge moved in like a bull in a china shop and grabbed a large green case.

"Hey! That stays here," Sheffield shouted.

"Like hell is does!" Sarge shouted back. He tilted the case to expose the label, "You don't even have a damn Goose to fire these with!"

"Like you do?" Sheffield shouted back.

"Of course I do! What the hell do you think I requested the ammo for?"

Sheffield shook his head, "What? Where the hell did you get it?"

"None of your damn business. These are mine and I'm taking them."

This was going downhill fast. Like Christmas morning at an orphanage; get it while the gettin's good. I stepped between them.

"Come on Captain; you know we went to Camp Riley and requested all this stuff. We made sure to get you guys some supplies; but we need ours as well. We've already had one run-in with a DHS MRAP. If the Apaches hadn't arrived, we'd have been toast. This is to make sure that doesn't happen again."

Sheffield threw his hands up, "Fine! You two sort this shit out!"

Sarge stiffened and looked at Sheffield. "Awe, poor fucking baby! You going to take your ball and go home now?"

That did it. I watched as Sheffield's head turned red. The blood boiled up out of his collar and over his ears.

"What'd you say to me? You seem to forget First Sergeant that I'm a Captain in the United States Army; and you will address me accordingly!"

All work had stopped as everyone within earshot was now watching the show. Sarge guffawed, "And you seem to forget *Captain* that I'm retired and don't give a fuck!"

Sheffield lunged for the old man and crashed into me. Sarge likewise went for Sheffield. I pushed Sheffield back and turned to face Sarge. He was looking right through me with a crazed expression in his eyes. He tried to go around me and I grabbed his rifle and used it as a handle to swing him back around. With the two separated, I started shouting.

"You two, knock it the hell off! What's wrong with you guys? We're on the same team here; we've got to work together or we're all screwed! I don't care which one of you has the bigger pecker, and neither do the people here! You fuckers made me Sheriff; so knock it the hell off, or I'll lock both your asses up!"

Both men stopped and stared at one another. Sheffield looked around at the supplies scattered around, food, ammo, medical equipment and other gear. He rubbed his temples for a minute then looked at Sarge.

"I'm sorry for being a dick. There's just so many people to take care of; it's stressing me out."

"Hell, I know that. That's why I requested all this. We didn't get everything; but we got more than I thought we would. I know you don't like me Captain; but I really am trying to help you," Sarge replied.

"It's not that I don't like you. You're just a little cavalier in your attitude. I pity the COs you worked for."

"Some people talk; some people do. If the machine gets in

the way, go around it or through it. I don't care which. I take care of my people, by any and all means at my disposal."

"I know," Sheffield replied.

He stepped towards Sarge and stuck his hand out. Sarge spun his heels to face away from him. I rolled my eyes and thought, *aw shit, here we go again.* Sarge looked at the soldiers still gawking, and shouted, "Company! Form up!" The soldiers shared looks around, but no one moved. Sarge gritted his teeth, "What the hell's wrong with your booger eaters? I said form up!" As a Chinese fire drill erupted before me, Sarge continued to shout, "Move! Move! Move!" Once the troops were formed up, Sarge called the assembly to attention.

"Contrary to my actions here this morning, I have nothing but respect for Captain Sheffield. He is the CO of this post and will be addressed and treated accordingly." Sarge spun on his heels again to face Sheffield. "Captain Sheffield, I apologize for my actions this morning." With that, Sarge snapped in a crisp salute.

Sheffield looked at him for a moment, and I prayed he'd return the salute quickly. After a moment, Sheffield came to attention, "Your apology is accepted First Sergeant." Sheffield dropped the salute, and Sarge did likewise. He then spun on his heels to face those assembled, "Diiiiissmissed!"

The assembly broke up and everyone got back to work; though the display obviously confused some of them. Sheffield walked up to Sarge and offered his hand again, "Thank you for that show of support."

Sarge grabbed his hand and pulled him in close. With a wink, he said, "Don't get used to it."

Sheffield chuckled, "Believe me, I won't."

"Are you two done with the pecker-measuring contest now? I've got things to do," I said.

Sarge smiled a sickly sweet smile at me that I knew to be complete bullshit. "Of course, Sheriff; what can we do for you?"

"I want to take Cecil to look at some new dirt for planting."

Sarge clapped his hands, "Let's go then!" Then his expression changed. An unnerving look I couldn't quite place. "Lock my ass up, huh?"

"In a heartbeat. I'll knock you in the head and throw your old ass in the hoosegow."

Sarge's eyes narrowed. "You'd have a better chance at getting a job as a break-in man at a whore house!" Then he smiled and slapped my shoulder. "Come on; let's go look at your patch of dirt."

Mike was rummaging around in the garage. Bucket in hand, he went through the tools on the tidy workbench. Finding something that caught his eye, he'd hold it up and inspect it. Then he'd steal a glance at the figure hanging from a rope in the center of the garage, and drop the tool in the bucket. In true Sarge fashion, he'd had the guys truss the man up. They had to open the scuttle hold to the attic in order to hang the rope from a truss; but it worked out, and he was now slowly swiveling back and forth.

The man watched Mike, but tried to remain calm, at least outwardly. He knew the kinds of things he'd done to people. Mostly just for fun. These guys were going to want answers; and it certainly appeared they intended to get them. But he wouldn't make it easy on them. Sure, they'll get what they want; but they damn sure were going to have to work for it.

Mike picked up a medium-sized pair of Channel Locks. Opening his mouth, he tested to see if they would grab a tooth.

Of course he knew they would; and he also knew there was very little chance of that actually occurring......... but it looked good. Seeing they could clamp on, Mike smiled at his prisoner before dropping them into the bucket with a clank. It had the desired effect; and the man spoke for the first time.

"Why don't you just get on with it already?"

Mike held a finger to his lips and shook his head.

"What the hell are you waiting for?" The man asked.

Mike tapped his finger to his lips again, then waved it at the man.

The man struggled for a moment, though it wasn't much of an effort. With his feet a full foot off the ground, all he could really do was gyrate his body a little. "Come on! What the hell!"

Mike carried the bucket over and set it down so his prisoner could see into it; though far enough back that he couldn't get to it with his feet. He looked the man in the eyes, smiled broadly, and walked into the house. His actions had the desired effect as the man stared down into the bucket. His mind raced with the possibilities of the instruments displayed before him. But one in particular put real fear in him. Lying on the top of the pile was a drywall saw. Its jagged shark-like teeth glared at him; and he could already feel it tearing its way inside him.

———

Thad and Danny took turns in the hole. They'd decided to dig a conventional latrine. Dalton had suggested a basic slit trench to make things easier. Luckily for the girls though, they disagreed. Dalton stood watch for them as they worked on the side of the road not far from the bunker. Thad had suggested putting the latrine in the woods a short distance from the bunker, but

Dalton overruled that idea, pointing out it had to be within eye and earshot.

It would be a primitive affair consisting of a small wooden box with a hole cut in the top resting over the pit. They thought of using a bucket, but it would be tricky to mount it so as to prevent the bucket from falling into the hole. Danny had already made the box out of scrap plywood. Only the front of it was covered for obvious reasons, and there was the top with the hole to serve as a seat.

"Once we get this deep enough, we can work on an enclosure for it," Thad said as he tossed a spade of dirt onto the pile.

"I was thinking of just planting some posts and wrapping it in black plastic. I've got a roll," Danny replied.

Thad stopped working and looked up, "Why don't we just thatch it with palmettos? Save the plastic for times we really need a waterproof barrier."

Danny nodded, "That's a good idea. We may end up really needing the plastic at some point. Probably should save it."

Thad smiled, "It'll be a tiki shithouse."

"I'd avoid the coconuts in there if I were you lads!" Dalton shouted.

Danny and Thad both laughed. "Yeah; avoid all the nuts you find in there," Danny added.

He and Thad traded places in the hole that was now about waist deep. Thad went off to cut palmetto fronds while Danny finished off the hole.

"Do you ever take a break?" Danny asked Dalton as he worked the shovel.

Dalton shrugged, "I'm on a break now. You're the one in the hole with a shovel in your hands. This isn't work just standing here."

"You always seem to be switched on. I don't think I could live that way. Seems like it would wear you down after a while."

"It's not like you think. Or maybe it is, actually. I've always been this way, even before things went to shit. I worked in prisons for years; and in that environment you have to be switched on, all the time." Dalton waved his arm. "So this, this is just normal to me."

Danny shook his head. "I'm getting used to it; but it's far from normal."

Dalton laughed, "Imagine what it was like when I was around people all the time. This, this is easy!"

Thad returned with a massive bail of fronds over one shoulder. Danny laughed at him. He looked for all the world like some poor bastard from India toting the load, ike something out of a National Geographic.

"Damn Thad, you know we can make more than one trip right?"

Thad dropped the load. "Sure; but I want to get this done today."

"We need something for the frame. You stay here, and I'll go see what I can find." Danny said.

Thad nodded and went to the water keg. Danny wandered off to see what he could find to frame up the new shitter. He found a thick stand of Sumac and started cutting. He checked each piece before doing so to make sure there were no flower heads on them. There were several large red clusters of the small flowers that would make a refreshing drink later in the summer. Even with the extra caution, he ended up with a large stack of fairly straight stalks.

Pulling a piece of paracord from his pocket, Danny tied a loop in one end and ran it under the stack. Once they were tied up, he hoisted them onto his back and carried them back to the latrine. When he arrived, the girls were there with Aric. They seemed to move in a pack now, always together. Taylor was looking at the hole, and asked, "What's this?"

"It's your new toilet," Dalton replied.

Jamie looked around, "Where's our bucket?"

"No more piss buckets in the bunker. You'll have to use the latrine now."

"Oh yeah; we should have emptied that," Jess said with a smile.

"This will be better than a bucket. You'll have some privacy; and it's sanitary," Thad said.

"Yeah; why don't you girls come over and help," Danny said.

They rolled their eyes, but did help. The Sumac stalks were laid out and formed into a lattice. Four of these were created; three of them were used for sides, and the last for the top. The open side faced the woods, maintaining a little privacy. Once the frame was up, Thad showed the girls how to weave the stem of the fronds into the lattice. With so many hands working on the weaving, Thad kept them supplied with fronds, and they quickly had the exterior covered.

The roof was thatched on the ground and placed on top. Danny grabbed a couple of long palmetto stems, cutting the fronds off. Pulling his knife, he ran the blade down the edge, cutting all the thorns off. He then made a slit in the end and pulled the edge piece off. The process was repeated a couple of times until he had a handful of them.

"What are you going to do with that?" Thad asked.

Danny held one up, "Tie the roof on."

Thad took the thin strip, "Really?"

"It's really strong," Danny replied. Thad gripped the piece in his hands and tugged on it. Raising his eyebrows, he pulled harder. Seeing it hold, he wrapped it around his hands and really pulled; it still didn't give.

"Dang! That's stuff's tough!" Thad said with a nod.

"Told you. It's also really flexible. You can tie up just about anything with it."

The two picked the roof up and set it on top of the walls. Using the strips, they tied the roof on. Once they were done, they stepped back and looked at their work. Danny asked the girls, "What do you think?"

Jess went around to the opening on the back side and looked in. Looking back at Danny, she smiled, "Nice toilet seat."

"Better than a bucket," Danny replied.

The rest of the girls gathered around to inspect it. As they were talking, Dalton waded into the group shouting.

"Make way! Make Way! I shall christen this throne!" Assuming a spread-legged stance he reached for his belt buckle and shouted, "I shall purge the temple!"

"Eww!" Lee Ann shouted as she ran off.

Jess pushed him, "Oh no you don't!"

Dalton started laughing uproariously. Catching his balance, he said, "I'm just kidding."

"You better be. That's for us ladies," Fred said. "You guys can pee on the ground."

Squinting one eye, Dalton said, "I wasn't goin' to pee."

When Fred realized what he was saying, she looked almost like she was shocked, "Eww!"

With a surprised look, Dalton replied, "What? Like you don't?"

She flipped her hair. "No; as a matter of fact, I don't."

Aric started to laugh. "Uh; yeah she does."

Fred spun on her heels and pointed at him, "Shut it mister!"

Still laughing, he replied, "I'm outnumbered right now."

Everyone inspected the new latrine and voiced their approval. The thatching was done in a shingle method, tightly enough that it should shed all water. Close enough to the bunker for security reasons, yet far enough away to allow for some privacy. The girls volunteered to take over the watch so the guys could get some rest.

"Where's Jamie?" Danny asked.

"She's with Ian somewhere. They said they were going to creep around," Jess replied.

"I'm going to check on our new guest," Dalton said as he shouldered his rifle.

"I'm going to muck out the pig pen; need some fertilizer for the garden," Thad said.

"Need a hand?" Danny asked.

Thad nodded, "Can always use a hand shoveling shit."

"You're going to spread pig poop on the garden?" Taylor asked.

Thad smiled, "Make's the plants grow big."

Taylor grabbed her stomach, "I don't think I can eat stuff from the garden now."

"You get hungry enough, you'll be surprised what you can eat," Thad replied.

"You guys keep your eyes open," Danny said as he collected the shovels.

"We will, don't worry," Fred replied as she ducked into the bunker.

Danny and Thad headed for the barn. As they walked, Thad said he an idea he wanted to run past Danny.

"What is it?"

"I want to try and get water hooked up over here," Thad replied.

"That would be nice, but we don't have enough solar panels and batteries."

"We don't need power."

Danny looked over, "How are you going to pump the water?"

Thad smiled, "Gravity."

Skeptically, Danny replied, "Okay."

"I found another one of those big tanks like we have on the fire trailer. I also found some large poles, like telephone poles. I figured we could use them to make a platform about ten feet high to set the tank on. Fill the fire tank from the well and use the pump to push it into the tank on the platform. Running water."

"How would we get the tank up there? They're not super heavy, but we couldn't lift it that high by hand."

Thad winked, "That's the easy part. We'll use the tractor to pick the tank up. Chain it to the bucket and I can set it right up there."

Danny thought about it for a moment. "All we'd have to do is run some pipe to each house and tie it in. That much water would have some good pressure."

"Exactly; we could flush the toilets, use the showers."

Danny smiled, "Be some cold showers."

Thad looked up. "You kidding me? I'll take a cold shower. I already sweat like a crooked politician on election-day. Besides; sitting out in the sun, it will heat up some."

As they walked, they talked about the project some more. Thad said there were enough poles for the four corners; they'd just need some cross-bracing. Danny suggested pulling some of the treated fence posts from around the neighborhood. A couple places there had almost new posts. They agreed the platform would need to be made from posts as well to support the weight.

"After we're done with this little task, let's go look at the poles and tank," Danny said.

# CHAPTER 13

WE STOOD IN THE MIDDLE of a beautiful grassy field. Cecil climbed up onto the hood of the Hummer and looked around.

"What do you think?" I asked.

He hopped down off the truck. Kneeling down, he pulled up a clump of grass and dug out a handful of soil. He sifted it through his fingers as he studied it. "It looks good. Real good." Cecil stood up and looked around the field again. "We'll have to bush-hog this grass first. Then we can disc it and get some hands out here with rakes to pull as much of this damn Bahia out as possible. But I think it'd be a good spot."

"There's plenty of acreage. We could probably plant every seed we have right here," I replied.

"We could use another tractor up here for a day or two," Cecil said.

"Thad's got one. He could bring it up here and help out getting the ground broken up."

Cecil nodded, "That would be great. It'd really help."

"Let's get you back to town Cecil. We'll get Thad up here in a day or two so you guys can get started," Sarge said.

"Roger that Top. Let's ride," Cecil replied with a smile.

We rode back to the armory and dropped Cecil off. I went to look for Doc and check out the field hospital that would serve as our clinic. Word of which was already spreading as a line was starting to form in front of it. It wasn't ready for patients yet, but would be soon. I found Doc inside with the other medical staff setting up equipment. Mary was stocking a shelving unit with bandages and other items. She waved and smiled when she saw me. I waved back as I walked up to Doc.

"You good here for a few days?" I asked.

"Yeah, we've got our work cut out for us for a couple of days at least."

"Alright, let me know when you need a ride home."

He grabbed a couple of large bottles and handed them to me. "Here, take these with you. Give them to Tyler and tell him and Brandy to take two pills, three times a day." He then handed me a handful of filter masks, "And wear these when you're over there. As soon as I get back I'll check on them."

I looked at the bottles, "Are these going to help them?"

Doc shrugged, "It all depends really. But it's something. Don't make contact with them. Set the bottles on the porch and let them pick them up, got it?"

I nodded, "Got it Doc, thanks. I'll see you in a couple of days."

Outside the tent I found the engineers that were setting up a generator to power the clinic.

"When you guys are done, tell Sheffield to call me and I'll come up so we can talk," I said.

One of the guys nodded, "Sure thing. We'll be busy for a day or two." He stabbed a thumb at the generator, "These things always have issues the first day or two."

"No worries, thanks."

I found Sarge at the Hummer. He was loading some large sacks into the back.

"What the hell is that?" I asked.

"Flour," Sarge said as he dropped a sack into the truck.

Looking at the bag, I replied, "No shit? Where the hell did that come from?"

Sarge turned, "They brought it in on the choppers this morning. Look at the label."

I checked out the bag and was surprised to see it read *Product of Russia.* "Holy shit, the Russians are helping us?"

Sarge shrugged, "It's their flour; don't know how we ended up with it. But there's a lot of it, so I'm taking some with us. We can give it out at the market."

"That's good, it'll make people happy for sure. I want to go by Mario's place on the way in and check on him. We can leave them some and drop some off at Gena's too."

Sarge nodded and got in the truck, "Get your ass in the turret; let's ride."

Sarge headed out of Eustis and I directed him to Mario's. It seemed as though things were calming down some. People were out everywhere tending to their daily tasks. The search for food was constant and unending. I had a good view from the turret of the truck as the hot noontime air rushed around me. With the end of the rain came the steam bath that always followed as the sun burned the moisture off.

As we passed through Umatilla I was happy to see the body had been moved. The rain had washed most of the blood away, and there was nearly no evidence of what had happened. On the other side of town I directed Sarge to turn onto Keene Road. We rode past the old Lakeview Terrace retirement community. From where I sat it looked pretty bad. The once-manicured lawns were now overgrown and weed-choked. It made me think of all those people and how they were doing now. Though the logical conclusion wasn't very pleasant.

I was saved from playing the thought out any farther when

Sarge pulled into the drive of D&J Apiary. The place looked deserted, so I told Sarge to lay on the horn. The gate was shut and we couldn't get in. Hopefully they'd hear it and come up. The horn sounded in long blasts and we waited. Sarge would give it a couple of honks and wait, then give it a couple more. After about fifteen minutes I saw a side by side coming towards the gate. As it approached I waved.

Mario built a very successful apiary with a lot of sweat equity. He got his start from his grandfather who also worked bees. Mario took those lessons and poured himself into the work. With the help of his wife Shelly, they'd developed a bit of an empire in the bee business. Not the biggest, but certainly a large and profitable concern.

Being smart with the success they'd achieved, Mario and Shelly updated their infrastructure. New warehouses and processing equipment. Heavy equipment was also on the list, loaders and skid steers as well as tractors and trucks. They had a lot of resources. But the smartest and arguably the most impactful upgrade was the solar system. The entire facility was powered via a large distributed solar system. Installed so that the loss of power in one section would not affect other areas, it was an expensive and hugely beneficial addition to their operation. More so now than ever because they had power all over their compound.

Mario rolled to a stop on the other side of the gate and leaned back in the seat. "I'm surprised to see you here. What can I do for you fellas?"

I climbed out of the turret and Sarge got out as well. "Just came to check on you, haven't seen you in a few days."

"We're processing some hives and haven't been out," Mario replied. He took a small controller from the dash of the ATV and hit a button. The gate swung open and he walked out to meet us.

Shaking hands, I replied, "That's good to hear. I was worried about you after the shooting at the market in Altoona."

"Yeah, we weren't there for that, thankfully."

"I was hoping so, and when we didn't see you guys I was relieved," I replied.

A radio on Mario's hip crackled, *"Who is it, Mario?"*

He picked up the radio and replied, "It's Morgan."

The tone on the reply changed, more cheerful. *Oh, bring him up to the house. Lunch is ready.*

Mario looked at me, "You guys hungry?"

"I'm always hungry and never turn down a meal," Sarge replied with a grin.

Looking at him, I replied, "Especially a free one."

Sarge jerked his head and smiled, "That's the best kind!"

Mario laughed, "Follow me up to the house. Shelly's got a nice lunch ready."

"That's good; we've got something she'll like," Sarge replied as he climbed back in the truck.

We followed Mario through the gate that closed automatically behind us. A nice paved road led us past the honey house where the delicious golden substance was extracted from the heavily loaded frames. Continuing, we passed the equipment storage area and then the property opened up into a large grassy pasture. A tractor sat in the center of the field with numerous round bales of hay scattered throughout.

Pulling up to the house, we got out and were greeted by Shelly from the porch.

"Hey guys. Hope you're hungry!"

Sarge patted his belly, "Yes ma'am. I'm always hungry!"

As we walked up on the porch I looked at Mario's garage and asked, "You still have that deuce-and-a-half in there?"

"Oh yeah, it's still in there. Don't have much fuel now for it, but I've still got it," Mario replied.

His comment surprised me. As part of his preparations Mario had some rather large fuel tanks filled and ready to go. "Really? You've used that much fuel?"

"We've used quite a bit, but someone also got in here weeks ago and stole a couple hundred gallons."

"Damn; did you catch 'em?"

Mario shook his head, "Not yet. But if they come back I will."

As I followed him into the house, I replied, "Let me know if you need any help."

Inside, Shelly had food set out on the kitchen bar. She pointed us to seats and we sat down.

"I'm sorry all I have to drink is water," Shelly said, "but I do have ice for it!" She said as she set a glass of ice water in front of Sarge.

Sarge picked the glass up and admired the ice cubes, "That's great!" He took a long drink, closing his eyes as he did. Pausing for a moment, he drained the glass before setting it back on the counter. "Wow that's good. A cold drink on a hot day; I'd do unnatural things for a glass of ice water most days!"

I looked at my glass and commented, "How are you getting ice?"

Mario jabbed a thumb in the direction of the warehouse, "There's an ice maker in the warehouse, so we've always got ice. One of the perks of the solar power."

"Your system's big enough to run stuff like that?" I asked.

"I only run the ice maker during the day and shut it off at

night so we can use the battery power for other stuff. It'll fill the chest in a couple of hours, so it doesn't need to run long."

Shelly set out plates of barbequed pork, shredded and covered in sauce. It came with a side of large round fried disks. I picked one up and looked at it asking, "Are these tomatoes?"

Shelly nodded, "Mmhmm, fried green tomatoes. You like them?"

A smile spreading across my face, I replied, "Oh yeah!"

We ate lunch and chatted about the general state of things, small talk really. It was nice to be eating with friends as if it were just an ordinary afternoon in another time. When we finished, Sarge rose to his feet and began collecting plates. Shelly protested, "Just leave those, I'll get them."

"No ma'am," Sarge replied. "You fed us a good lunch; the least I can do it clear the dishes." She smiled and didn't protest any further.

Looking at her, I asked, "You don't have any tea?"

Shelly shook her head, "No; we put a lot back, but it went faster than I thought it would."

"I think we can help you out with that," I replied.

"Really?"

"Yeah, we got some from the base. I'll bring some by."

Mario smiled, "That would be great. I'd love some tea."

"I also have an idea on your fuel situation. I can't offer you any of that but there is another way we may be able to stretch your fuel out," I said.

Mario rested his elbows on the counter, "Well, I'm all ears. Do tell."

"You still have some fuel, right?" I asked.

"Yeah," Mario replied.

"There are transformers sitting around all over the place. They're full of mineral oil. We could double your diesel supply by adding the same amount of mineral oil to it. Your truck would run fine on it," I said.

"Really? I knew you could do that with vegetable oil, but mineral oil?" Mario asked.

"Sure. You could pour paraffin into the fuel and it would burn that."

"We used to filter old motor oil and pour that right into the tanks of the old trucks. Lubes the injectors real nice," Sarge added with a smile.

"This is different. Mineral oil isn't a lubricant, it's a coolant. So you couldn't pour it into the crankcase and lube the internals. But it does burn, and will extend your fuel supply," I replied.

Shelly looked at Mario, "That would be great. The Mule runs on diesel too. That would give us a lot of fuel."

"How do we get it?" Mario asked.

I laughed, "That's the tricky part. Most of the big pad-mount transformers have a drain on them. Pull the plug, and out it comes. But it's mounted low and as soon as the plug comes out, so does the oil."

Mario thought about that for a minute. "I'll come up with something. There's got to be a way to get it out."

"I'm sure we can come up with something. The stuff burns in oil lamps too, and would give you something else to sell," I added with a smile.

"I'll think on it for a while and figure something out," Mario said. "We really could use it if it works."

Sarge stood, "Mario, Shelly, thanks for the lunch, but we've got to get on the road."

We all headed out to the porch where I told them we had something for them.

"Grab a big container of some kind," I said to Mario.

He looked at Shelly with a typical husband's look of *where is it,* and she disappeared into the house. Mario followed us out to the Hummer.

"What'cha got?" He asked.

Sarge pulled one of the bags of flour out and dropped it at his feet. "We got you some commie flour!"

"Some what?" Mario asked.

I laughed, "It's just flour. We thought you guys would like some."

Mario brightened up, "Sure we would. Where'd it come from?"

"We got it from the Army. The sack says it came from Russia," I replied.

"With love," Sarge added with a smile.

Shelly came out and looked at the bag, "Oooh, flour. That's awesome."

Sarge opened the bag and poured several pounds into the large plastic container she'd brought out. Once it was full, Shelly capped it and thought about the potential of this gift.

"This is great. I'll make us some bread."

"Yeah, thanks a lot," Mario added.

"We've only got a little to give out; just wanted to make sure you folks got some," Sarge said.

"Hang on a second," Mario said as he disappeared into the house.

I smiled, "I know what he's going after."

Shelly smiled, "Ya think?"

Mario came out with a quart jar of honey and handed it over. "How's that for a trade?"

Looking at the gold liquid, I replied, "Hell of a trade!"

"Let's get together in a couple of days and talk about this transformer thing," Mario said as we were getting into the truck.

Giving him a thumbs up, I replied, "Will do."

We headed out with full bellies. As we drove out, I looked out over Mario's place and thought about what a tremendous resource he was. We definitely needed to work with him more to make sure he had what he needed to keep his operation going. If we helped him, he would be able to help us; and that was the only way any of us would make it. As we passed the market in Altoona, I saw it was back to business. People were manning their stalls, and quite a crowd was there trying to make a deal one way or another.

Sarge stopped in front of Gena's house and tooted the horn. I extracted myself from the turret and climbed out as Dylan came around the side of the house. He smiled when he saw us and waved.

Sarge waved, "Hey Dylan."

"Hey fellas, didn't expect to see you guys today."

I pulled one of the sacks out, "We brought you something."

Dylan looked over, "Oh yeah?"

"Go get something to put some flour in," Sarge said.

"Flour, really?"

"Yep, courtesy of the United States Army," Sarge said proudly.

Dylan quickly headed into the house. He returned with Gena and a large tin with a Christmas theme printed on it.

"We thought you guys could use some flour," Sarge said when he saw Gena.

She was looking at the sack, "That's what Dylan said, that you got it from the Army."

Dylan set the tin down and I started to pour flour into it. "We've got a little, just wanted to make sure you got some."

"That's awful nice of you to think of us," Gena said.

I looked up, "We've got to look out for our own."

"We sure appreciate it," Dylan replied.

Gena wandered off while we were talking. Once the tin was full, I tapped the lid down on it and set it on the hood of the truck. Sarge asked if they'd seen anyone around, and Dylan said no, that it had been quiet. He asked about the helicopters he had seen a couple of days ago, and we filled him in on the story.

Shaking his head, Dylan replied, "I'm so sorry to hear. I don't think I ever met him, but I'm sorry to hear you lost a friend."

"Thanks. It was a bad day," I replied.

Dylan shook his head, "We could hear it, all the shooting. It sounded like D-Day or something."

"It was for us at the time," Sarge replied.

Gena returned with a sack full of fresh yellow squash. Setting it on the hood, she said, "Since you have some flour, you need some squash for frying up."

"Aww, you didn't have to do that Gena. The flour is yours, no trade this time."

She smiled, "I know. But you take this. We've got plenty."

Sarge smiled, "If you insist. I love fried squash." He picked up the bag and set it in the passenger seat of the Hummer.

Gena grabbed the tin of flour, "This is a lot of flour. I'll make some biscuits."

"Biscuits would nice!" Dylan nearly shouted.

Sarge nodded, "Yeah they would." He looked at me, "Have to see if Kay can whip us a batch up."

We said our goodbyes and loaded up into the truck. Dylan and Gena stayed in the yard waving as we drove off. I had to smile because she was holding that big tin. Being as small as she was, it made the tin look all the bigger. It's a short drive from Gena's to our place, and we were approaching the bunker in no time. Something was going on, some kind of project from the looks of it. I could see the tractor out and drag marks in the dirt road near the bunker. *What the hell are they up to?*

Sarge rolled to a stop by the bunker where quite the crowd was gathered. Getting out of the truck, I looked at Thad and asked what was going on.

With his usual smile, he replied, "Public works."

Staring back, I replied, "Huh?"

He pointed down the little dirt road where one of the large IBC totes was sitting. "We're building a water tower."

As soon as he said it I understood what they were doing; it made a lot of sense. Nodding, I replied, "Going to pipe water into the houses?"

"Yeah. Thad had a good idea. We should be able to get water to all the houses over there. Everyone will have running water," Danny added.

"About damn time!" Sarge barked. "I was beginning to wonder what kind of operation you guys were running around here."

I looked at him, "What? You never suggested it."

"Just because I didn't say it doesn't mean I wasn't thinking it!"

I waved him off, "Oh whatever."

I looked around the bunker, then at Danny. "Where are the girls?"

"I think they're out checking snares. They made some squirrel snares a couple days ago and are out checking them."

I smiled, "Do they ever get tired of hunting them?"

"I showed them how to make that pole snare you created out at the river. Let it hunt for them," Danny replied.

"It's a good idea," I replied, then looked at Thad. "What's next on this project?"

He grabbed a set of posthole diggers, "Time to dig."

"Holes for the tower legs?" I asked. He nodded. "You going to dig them by hand?"

"You got a better idea?" Danny asked.

I looked at them like they were crazy, "Uh, yeah. Why don't we get a posthole auger and mount it to the PTO on the tractor?"

Thad and Danny looked at one another and started to laugh, "I don't know why we didn't think of that," Thad said.

"I'm sure we can find one around here someplace," I said.

Thad shook his head, "I know where one is! That's the worst part!"

"While you idiots sort this out I'm going to get this stuff unloaded and visit with my house guest," Sarge said.

Looking at him, I said, "You scared of a little hard work?"

Sarge bristled, "I ain't scared of shit! Least of all, hard work. I can lie down right beside it and go sound to sleep."

Thad started laughing. I shook my head, "Somehow I'm not surprised."

I laughed, "I'm sure your *guest* is looking forward to it."

"I am the host with the most!" Sarge shouted as he got back in the truck.

Danny was shaking his head, "I pity the poor guy."

Thad looked at him, "You have no idea."

"You want to go get that auger?" I asked.

Thad nodded, and Danny said he'd go help. While they went off to round it up, I headed over to Tyler's to drop off the antibiotics. I put the mask on as I approached the house. Things like this scared me. You can't see a damn virus. The bugs float on the air and I felt like I was entering some kind of contaminated zone. I set the bottles down in front of the door before knocking and stepped back. Brandy came to the door and I was shocked; she looked like hell.

"Hi Morgan," she croaked.

Trying not to let the shock show, I replied, "Hi Brandy. How are you guys doing?"

Tears welled up in her eyes, "Tyler's not well and I don't feel too good either." She turned her head and hacked.

Pointing to the bottles on the porch I said, "Take those in with you. You guys need to take two pills three times a day. Start right away and make sure you don't miss any. They should help, and hopefully turn this around."

With much effort, she bent over and picked the bottles up. The act of leaning over as she did, sent her into a coughing fit that sounded harsh. Her lungs seemed almost to rattle and produced a lot of sputum. She covered her mouth and excused herself. After a moment she returned to the door.

"Thank you Morgan." She looked back over her shoulder, "The kids aren't sick. Can we get them out of here? I'm afraid they're going to get ill if they stay here with us."

"I'll have to talk to Doc and see. We've got more doctors in town now, I'll see if they can come out here and take a look at everyone. If they say the kids are okay, then we'll move them out and take care of them."

She nodded, "Thank you."

"Go in and get those pills into Tyler. Do you need anything?"

"The kids are hungry."

"I'll get you some food over soon. We've got some flour now, maybe I can get you some bread."

She attempted to smile, "That would be nice."

I said goodbye and headed for the house. It was horrible to see her like that. Doc had been tending to them, and this was the first time I'd seen them since sending them home. I felt bad, like I was sending them off to die out of sight. But I also knew if it hadn't been done, many of us would probably be sick. We were just lucky it was only them at the moment.

My house was empty so I went to Danny's. Sarge was there unloading the sacks of flour. We carried the open bag into the house where everyone was hanging out. Seeing the sack, Kay asked, "What's that?"

"Flour!" Sarge announced as he dropped the bag onto the floor with a dusty thud.

Kay jumped to her feet, "Really!" She came over and unrolled the top of the sack and looked in. "This is wonderful!" The she paused and said, "If I had an oven I could bake bread."

"We have one," I replied. She looked at me for more. "I have an oven we can set on top of the kerosene stove. You can bake in that."

Her eyes brightened, "Oh that would be wonderful! I love to bake."

"Can you imagine the smell of fresh baked bread?" Mel asked.

Smiling, Bobbie replied, "I can already taste it!"

While everyone was going on about the possibility of the bread I went back out to the truck and got the squash Gena gave us and the honey from Mario and Shelly. Taking it inside, I set it on the counter.

"Maybe we can have some fried squash tonight too."

Key picked up the jar of honey, "Oh, I can make honey-crusted bread. It's so good."

That got everyone going even more. Sarge excused himself, saying he had things to attend to. Thankfully, he didn't elaborate on what exactly those things were. I followed him out to the truck.

"Let me know what he has to say," I said as he got behind the wheel.

Sarge nodded, "I will." Jabbing his thumb over his shoulder he asked, "What do you want to do with the rest of this flour?"

"We'll take it up to the market tomorrow and distribute it. I think they're going to use it in town to make bread, and give that out there. We'll just give folks the flour and let them use it as they will. Maybe take one bag up to Umatilla and give it away there."

Sarge nodded, "Sounds like a plan to me. I'll holler at you in a bit."

I slapped the door of the truck, "See you in a bit."

Going back inside, Mel, Kay and Bobbie were in the kitchen. They were already washing the squash and getting it ready for tonight's dinner. Looking out the kitchen window, I saw Little Bit circling a tree and looking up with her rifle in her hands.

"She out hunting?" I asked Mel.

"Yeah, she really likes it. I told her to stay in Danny's yard."

The reply was funny to me. Back in the day, Mel was decidedly against squirrel hunting. She'd raised many of them from babies, bottle feeding them. In those days, there was no way in hell she would have allowed such hunting around the house. Now it was just part of life.

"She's pretty good too," I replied. Looking at Kay, I asked, "You really think you can make bread?"

Looking shocked, she replied, "Of course I can! We have some yeast; and now that I have flour, we certainly can."

"We need a loaf made for Tyler and Brandy. I want to take them one and some of the honey as well."

"How are they?" Mel asked.

I gave a little shrug, "Honestly, she didn't look too good. But Doc sent some antibiotics home with me, and I gave them to her. We'll just have to wait and see."

"I feel so bad for those poor children," Kay said. "All cooped up in that house with their sick parents."

I nodded, "I know how you feel. I'm going to get the docs from town down here in a day or two and have them check them out. If the kids are okay, we're going to take them out of there."

"That would be good. Where would they stay?" Mel asked.

"I don't know; we'll figure it out."

"They can stay with us. We've got plenty of room," Bobbie said.

I was surprised by her comment. She and Danny never had kids, and it was by her decision. So her volunteering to take them in, came as a bit of a shock. I told everyone I had to go, gave Mel a kiss and headed for the door. As I went through Danny's gate, I saw the girls in the field across the road with Mike and Dalton going through some drills. They were really serious about being trained, and worked hard at it. It was both exciting and scary to think about, that they would be able to defend themselves and be an asset to the community. Scary, because they would want to be part of things, not content to sit around if something kicked off. I just hoped for all of them that nothing did.

Ian and Perez were at the bunker when I passed it. Perez was sitting on the top of the bunker smoking a cigarette. I laughed inside at him and asked, "How many more of those things do you have?"

Perez shrugged and blew a smoke ring, "I don't know. Couple more cartons."

"You know you could probably trade those for anything you want, don't you?"

He held the butt up and looked at it, "This is what I want."

I laughed and shook my head as I walked off to find Danny

and Thad. They were at the site of the water tower construction. Thad was sitting on the tractor, and the auger was already buried in the ground. A pile of dirt was growing around the top of the hole, and Danny was raking it back with a shovel.

Examining the hole, I said, "We're going to need to widen it by hand."

Danny nodded, "Yeah; but it's still easier than digging the whole thing by hand."

Once the auger was buried to its top, Thad raised it out of the hole. Danny grabbed a set of diggers and set to work cutting the side of the hole out and removing the dirt. Thad pulled the tractor up and started on the next hole. The process was repeated until all four holes were complete. It went rather quickly, and in an hour we were standing around talking about raising the poles.

We discussed several options on how to get the job done. We settled on lifting them by hand and using a small pole to apply pressure to the top and assist. We rolled the first pole towards the hole and positioned the butt over it.

"You get on the end, Thad," I said with a laugh.

"It's always the big end for me, ain't it?" Thad said as he straddled the pole. Looking over his shoulder at Danny, he asked, "You ready?"

Danny had the push pole, and he nodded that he was ready. Thad hefted the pole, I knelt down and helped lift, straining as it was so damn heavy. Once it was off the ground, I got under it and put my shoulder to it. Thad and I grunted and heaved, and the pole slowly rose. Danny got the push pole against the top and added some leverage to our efforts. Once the butt was in the hole, it got a lot easier, and practically fell in the hole. Danny leaned against the push pole, and it fell the rest of the way to the bottom. We all stepped back while catching our breath. It was crooked, but it was in there.

"Only three more to go," Thad said with a smile.

"Wasn't as bad as I thought," Danny added.

"For you!" I shouted. "I thought that damn thing was going to squash me!"

Thad laughed, "I wouldn't let it squash you......... all the way."

I chuckled, "Gee, thanks."

"They aren't going to stick themselves; let's get it over with," Danny said.

We got back to work, repeating the process. While it was hard and heavy work, it didn't take all that long, and we had all the poles up in a little more than an hour. We leaned on the hood of the tractor looking at the caddywhompus poles. They'd get straightened out later. For now, we were just glad to have them in the ground.

"I don't know about you boys, but I think that's enough for the day," Thad said.

"Yeah, I need a break anyway. I think Morgan and I are on watch tonight," Danny said.

"Probably," I said. "I think the ladies are making some bread for tonight."

Thad's eyebrows went up, "Bread?"

"Yeah, the Army sent some flour in with the delivery today," I replied.

Thad rubbed his chin, "Miss Kay gonna make some bread?"

I nodded, "That's what she said. Was pretty excited about it too."

"I wish we had some peanut butter," Danny said.

Thad's hands moved towards his mouth as he closed his

eyes, "Oh man. A big ole PBJ with strawberry jam oozing out the sides."

"Yeah, and a glass of cold milk," I added.

Thad jerked his head, "Alright! That's enough. Man that sounds so good!"

"I'm going to head home and get cleaned up," Danny said.

We all agreed we'd had enough for the day, and headed home. I walked with Danny as we walked. We chatted about the water tower project and how it would really help everyone, and take some pressure off his place. Everyone has been taking showers there because it is the only house with sufficient power and water to accommodate them.

"We'll still be eating dinner there though," I said with a chuckle.

"I don't mind everyone around at all. It's kinda nice actually. It'll just be easier for everyone to be able to shower at their house when they want."

"Not to mention using an indoor shitter," I added.

"Yeah, you know the girls are going to be happy about that."

Kicking at the dirt as I walked, I said, "Wonder how Sarge's inquisition is going."

Danny shook his head, "I really don't want to know."

Sarge stepped into the garage with a broom. His house guest didn't move at first. He was obviously exhausted and passed out from the strain. He went to the garage door and pulled the bypass handle on the door motor and raised the door. Smiling, he looked at the man and said, "I didn't wake you did I?" Sarge went to the workbench and took a hand saw down from the peg board. Bracing the broom on the bench, he cut a piece about a foot and a half long off it.

The man didn't reply. Sarge eyeballed him for a moment, noting just how beat the poor bastard looked. Turning back to the workbench, he poked around in the a little cabinet full of small pull-out trays. It was the sort of thing you'd store a few nails or screws in. The old man pulled out tray after tray until pulling one out that contained a couple of the old hook and eye style latches. Finding what he wanted, he removed the tray and took one of the small eyes out. Picking up the old bar stool that sat in front of the bench, he walked over and placed it in front of the suspended man.

Taking a seat, Sarge used a pair of pliers from his pocket to work the eye into the end of the broomstick. He didn't speak to the man while he worked, but would glance up from time to time to gauge his response. The man's eyes remained transfixed on the handle. Once the eye was screwed all the way in, Sarge stood and went back to the bench. Picking up a piece of rope and a Phillips screwdriver, he walked back to the stool and sat down. This he looked the man in the eye and asked his name, he got no reply.

"Come on now; what can telling me your name hurt?" Sarge pressed.

The man eyed him for a moment, looking at the rope Sarge held. He'd pulled it through the eye and was unwinding the end. After a moment the man spoke, "What are you going to do with that?"

Without looking up from his work, Sarge replied, "Tell me your name, and I'll tell you what I'm going to do with this here rope."

There was a long silence. Sarge had unwound the appropriate amount and now shoved the screwdriver through the rope on one side of the eye. He then pulled one of the three weaves of the rope through the hole, drawing it tight back against itself. Turning the rope slightly, he repeated the process. As he passed the next weave of the rope through, he looked up and asked, "Well, what's it going to be?"

The man licked his lips. His eyes darted around the garage. Then he said, "If you give me a drink of water, I'll tell you my name."

Sarge laughed, "That wasn't the deal. You tell me your name and I'll tell you what this is." He held the rope up. "Then we can talk about a drink of water."

"Aaron, Aaron Altman."

Sarge looked up, "Good to meet you Aaron, Aaron Altman." He continued working on the loop. When it was done, he held it up. "This here is going to be a whip of sorts." He held it out so it dangled on the floor. "I'll soak it in water and use it to beat you with." He looked at Aaron when he finished the statement, like he expected some sort of affirmation of his work; but Aaron didn't reply. Instead he stared at the rope.

Sarge let him stew for a while as he finished his work. When he was done braiding the tag end back into the rope and it was affixed to the handle, he cut the strands off and pulled his lighter out and cauterized the ends of the nylon. Leaving the whip on the stool, Sarge disappeared into the house. He returned almost immediately with a large jug. Ted followed him and hopped up on the bench. Sarge grabbed a bucket and poured water from the jug into it. He then dipped the rope into it and removed it. Giving it a quick snap of his wrist, it let out a surprisingly loud crack that caused Aaron to flinch.

Satisfied with his work, he stepped outside the open door and looked back at Aaron, "Now for the good part." He laid the rope in the sand at the edge of the driveway and ground it with his boot, all the while keeping his eyes locked on Aaron's. Happy that it was sufficiently covered in sand, he walked back in and laid the whip on the stool.

"Now, about that drink of water," Sarge said. Aaron's eyes were still fixed on the whip. Sarge snapped his fingers and Aaron's eyes drifted back to him. Sarge crossed his arms over his chest, "You one of Billy's boys?" Aaron didn't answer right away, so Sarge encouraged him. "Answer the question and I'll give you a drink. I promise, no games. I'm sure you're thirsty."

Aaron licked his lips and looked around. After a moment, he nodded his head. Sarge asked the question again, and again Aaron nodded. Faster than Aaron could react, Sarge slapped him on the left side of his face. So hard that Aaron saw small white orbs dancing before his eyes and his ears were ringing as well.

"When I ask a question, you answer. Like momma used to say when you were a little snot-nosed shit, *to use your words.* So I'll ask the question again; you one of Billy's boys?"

Aaron nodded, quickly saying, "Yes."

Sarge smiled and held his arms out wide, "See! That wasn't hard now was it?"

Ted jumped off the bench and walked up to Aaron. He held a bottle to Aaron's mouth allowing him to drink. He gulped greedily at the water, much of it spilling and running down his chest. When the bottle was empty Ted returned to his seat. Sarge went over to the bench and took down a large pair of scissors. He walked behind Aaron who struggled to spin himself. Sarge used them to cut away Aaron's shirt. He howled in fright at first, but a quick blow to his kidneys silenced him.

"Shut up, I ain't even hurting you yet!" Sarge barked.

With the shirt removed, Sarge stepped up in front of Aaron and grabbed his belt buckle to undo. Aaron wasn't having any of that, and he kicked Sarge, knocking him off balance. Ted was immediately on his feet and closing quickly. Aaron saw him coming but there was nothing he could do. Ted stepped in and delivered several fast sharp blows to his liver. Aaron howled in pain as Sarge regained his composure. Breathing heavily, Aaron looked at the old man, who was holding the whip.

"You just fucked up, son." Sarge held the whip out, "See, this was just to scare you. I wasn't going to actually hit you with it." Aaron's eyes went to the whip, then back to Sarge. "But I am now." Sarge looked at Ted, "Grab his legs and pull 'em out Teddy."

Aaron tried to kick, but he was so weak from hanging there for so long, there was little he could do. Ted grabbed his legs, tucking one under each arm and pulled them out as far as he could. Aaron was now belly up and in no position to resist. He watched as Sarge stepped back, flipping the rope; then it began.

# CHAPTER 14

FTER CHANGING CLOTHES, I WENT back over to Danny's. The house was full of incredible aromas. There was the smell of rising bread, a doughy yeasty smell that was like heaven. Then there was the smell of the squash frying in pig fat. It was more intense, a more incredible aroma than I had encountered in a long time.

"Damn, it smells good in here!" I shouted.

"Just wait until I get these loaves in the oven," Kay replied.

Mel was at the stove frying the squash. I went into the kitchen and looked at a very large platter full of golden brown rounds. Picking one up, I shook a little salt on it. Mel looked at me, "Get out of it. Wait till dinner."

Smiling, I stuffed the whole piece in my mouth, "I just wanted to sample it."

Little Bit busted through the back door. She was holding a dead squirrel by the tail. "Dad, there's something wrong with this squirrel."

"Get that thing out of my house!" Bobbie shouted.

Little Bit stepped out onto the porch and I followed her. She laid the limb rat on the deck and squatted down as she examined it.

"There's something inside it," she said as she poked at it with her knife.

I reached down and picked it up to take a closer look. "Ah yes," I said. Opening my folding knife, I said, "It's called a Warble. It's a little grub that lives under their skin." I stuck the tip of the blade into the air hole the grub had cut through the skin, and split it open to expose the fat larva.

"Eww! That's gross!" Little Bit shouted. "What is it?"

"It's the larva of the Botfly. They get into the squirrel and grow up under their skin. When it's big enough, it comes out," I said.

"Does it kill the squirrel?"

"No, when it comes out, the squirrel heals and lives on."

She looked at me, her face twisted, "Can we still eat it?"

Bobbie had come out on the porch and was looking over our shoulder. "I'm not eating that!" She shouted.

I laughed. "We could eat it, but it is kind of gross. Take it and toss it into the woods."

Little Bit nodded, "Yeah, I don't want to eat it either."

"Looks like squirrel hunting is over until the weather turns cold," I said.

Little Bit looked at me, "The Botflies go away in the winter?"

"Yep. We'll just have to wait a while."

I walked with her out to the tree line behind Danny's and tossed the rat into the woods.

"I feel bad I killed it and we're throwing it away," she said.

I put my arm around her, "That's good. I'm glad it bothers you. You should be bothered, but in this case there's a reason."

She looked up, her lip pulled into a sneer, "It was kinda gross."

Chuckling, I patted her shoulder, "Yeah it was. Come on."

Back in the kitchen, I took a seat at the bar again. It was getting late and we needed to get to the bunker for our shift. The good news was that meant we could eat now!

"Hey, we have to go on watch soon, so we need to eat now," I said.

Mel dismissed the comment, "Whatever; you're just looking for a reason to eat."

Danny came downstairs and wandered into the kitchen. He did the same thing I did, grabbing a piece of squash. Looking at me, he said, "We better eat now so we can take our watch."

Pointing at him, I shouted, "See! He says the same thing!"

Mel took a couple of plates and piled the squash on. Shaking her head, she replied, "Here, go ahead."

Danny and I sat down to enjoy the fresh veggies. They were so damn good. As we ate, Thad came in, announcing his presence by saying, "Something smells good!"

"Dinner's not ready yet," Bobbie replied.

He looked at me and Danny, and I smiled. "We have to go on watch."

"Guess I'll just have to wait then," he replied as he sat down at the bar beside me. I picked up a piece of squash and held it up. Looking at him I shoved it into my mouth and rolled my eyes back. He smiled and shook his head.

"You may have to wait Thad, but you'll get some fresh bread too," Kay noted.

I looked up with a piece of squash half in my mouth, "I like bwead," I mumbled.

Mel smiled at me, "You have to go on watch."

"That's just wrong," Danny added.

"Don't worry boys; we'll save you some," Kay replied with a smile. She was always so nice, and I smiled in reply. That is, until Thad spoke up.

"Yeah, we'll save you the crusts," he said as he started to laugh at his own sad joke.

Looking at him, I said, "And I thought we were friends."

Still laughing, he said, "We are; but we're talking about fresh baked bread here."

Looking at Danny, I said, "Add that to the list of how to tell your true friends. Roofing, moving, plumbing and fresh baked bread." The comment got Thad to really laughing.

We finished our meal and grabbed our gear. I gave Mel a kiss and told her I'd be home later. As we were heading out, I remembered the job Thad had waiting on him.

"Oh Thad. We've got a job for you to do."

He looked up, "What is it?"

"Cecil's going to plant a large field up towards Eustis. It's huge, and he needs you and your tractor for a couple of days. It needs to be mowed and to have a disc run over it to get it ready to plant."

"Sounds good to me. When do you want me to go?"

I shrugged, "Soon. Tomorrow maybe."

Danny interrupted, "We need to get the water tower done first. We need the tractor to set the tank with."

Thad nodded, "Yeah, we better get that done first."

Agreeing, I said, "Let's try and set it tomorrow. Once it's up, you can take off. We can do the rest of the work without the tractor."

"Sounds like a plan," Thad replied.

Danny and I left and walked towards the bunker. Once we were out on the road, we saw the girls and Aric walking towards us.

"They're always together now," Danny commented.

"Yeah but I think it's good for them."

He glanced over at me, "You aren't worried about them and all this training they're doing?"

"I am, but they aren't little girls anymore. They're growing up. Sadly, they're growing up in a world where they need to learn how to handle a weapon and use it to defend themselves. It makes me feel a little better knowing they're being taught how to do so."

"I guess you're right."

Taylor saw me and shouted, jumping up and down, "Hey Dad!"

I waved as we got to them, "Hey kiddo, what are you guys up to?"

"We're going to eat."

"I'm starving!" Jess added.

"The guys working you to death?" I asked.

They all laughed, "Yeah they are. Dalton scares the crap out of us."

"He is slightly intimidating," Aric added.

"Where in the hell did he come from?" Jess asked.

"He wandered in one night," I replied.

"And you let him stay? Just like that?" Jess shot back.

"I think we had this discussion once about trusting your gut, remember?"

She crossed her arms and cocked her hip to the side, "So now we're just taking in every stray that comes along?"

I laughed, "You're one to talk! You were the first stray!" The comment got laughs out of everyone.

She flipped her hair, "I am not a stray."

Smiling, I said, "You have come a long way since that day at the rest stop."

She rolled her eyes. "I cannot imagine what would have happened if you hadn't let me come with you."

"Pfft, whatever. I didn't *let* you. You just wouldn't take no for an answer."

With a comically indignant look, she replied, "And look

how much better off you are as a result." She walked on, not giving me the chance to reply.

Lee Ann gave me a hug as she passed, then Danny as well. We watched them walk away and Danny said, "You're right. They're not little girls anymore."

We went to the bunker and found Ian, Perez and Jamie hanging around outside. Ian looked at his wrist, although there was no watch, and said, "It's about damn time!"

"I'm ready to get out of here, it's hotter'n shit," Perez said.

"Dry up you whiney babies," I replied with a smile.

"I think dinner is ready at the house," Danny said.

"Good, I'm hungry," Jamie said.

"Why aren't you hanging out with the cool kids?" I asked.

She laughed, "I had to be here. The cool kids, whatever."

"Just do me a favor and let me know if those girls get any crazy ideas."

Cocking her head to the side, she said, "Their ideas are no crazier than anybody else's."

"That really doesn't make me feel any better," I replied.

Jamie winked at me and looked at Ian, "Let's go eat."

They left us there to face the coming onslaught. The early evening shift of the watch had become the most dreaded. As the sun dropped towards the horizon, thousands of spike-beaked Kamikazes would materialize from everywhere. Knowing what was coming, I slipped into my raincoat. As the sun kissed the horizon, the mind-numbing buzzing started quickly, and would persist for several hours.

Hearing Danny slap, I looked over to see him rubbing his neck, "Damn these things are horrible!"

Pulling my hood up, I grunted, "Tell me about it. Look on the bright side, it's only going to get worse before it gets better."

Slapping again, he replied, "Thanks for that."

We settled into the same old routine of looking through the NVGs, listening and slapping the incessant mosquitoes. A flash of light broke up the monotony. Danny slapped me on the shoulder, "Someone's coming."

I brought my rifle up and rested it on the lip of the bunker, "Where is he?"

"He's walking down the middle of the road. Here, take a look." He handed me the device and I took a look.

Just as my eye was focusing, whoever was coming shined a flashlight at me. A really friggin bright one, that caused the NVG to shut down. It was quickly followed by a voice.

"Hey Morg, you in there?" It was Mike.

"Yeah I'm in here. You trying to get your ass shot tonight or what?" I shouted back as I walked out of the bunker.

"Someone wants to talk to you," Mike said as he came up.

"Who?" I asked.

"It's Livingston," Mike replied as he handed me a radio.

"What the hell does he want?" I asked.

Mike smirked, "How the hell should I know. He just said he needed to talk to you."

Keying the radio, I asked the obvious, "What's up?"

"*Hey Morgan. We've got an issue we need you to come take care of.*"

"Now?"

"*Yes now.*"

"What the hell is so important you need me to come to town in the damn dark?"

"*We've had a murder.*"

I looked at Danny, "So fucking what. I'm not going up there tonight."

Danny shrugged, "Don't tell me; tell him."

"Have you got the guy?"

*"Yes, we've got the offender."*

"Then lock his ass up. Give him to the PD for the night, and I'll come to town tomorrow."

*"This can't wait. There's a crowd of people wanting to lynch this guy."*

"Then let them. If he killed someone and there's no question, let them have him. Either way I'm not coming up there tonight. The PD is there, they'll deal with it till tomorrow. Out," I said the last word with a tone of finality and handed the radio back to Mike.

"He's out of his fucking mind if he thinks I'm going to drag my ass up there tonight," I said.

Mike shrugged, "Whatever dude."

"Where's the old man?" I asked.

Mike leaned back against the bunker, "Oh, he's still on his play date. Ted's supervising."

"Still?" Danny asked.

Mike shivered, "Yeah. I don't know what the hell he's doing in there but it sounds medieval." He paused for a moment, then added. "Or maybe some sick S and M sex game."

Danny's head came around. He had the look of someone that just smelled something offensive. "Why'd you have to add that?"

Mike bounced off the bunker and smiled, "Cause now you've got that image burned into your mind. You're welcome." He stretched and took a deep breath, "My work here is done."

"Yeah, go home," I said.

---

Aaron hung limply from the rope. His throat was nearly as painful from the screaming as his body was from the lashes.

The old man had been sadistic with the delivery of the lashes. One moment they would land on his back, then his stomach or his sides. But before that began, the old man had ripped the shirt from his back to ensure he'd receive the full effect. And the effect had been profound.

Sarge pulled the whip from the bucket of now pink water. He looked at Aaron for a moment before laying the handle on the stool and picking up the bucket. He unceremoniously poured it over his head. Aaron's head jerked and he inhaled sharply.

Sarge pulled the stool a little closer and sat down. Dangling the whip in front of him, he shouted, "Wake up numbnuts!"

Aaron jumped again and looked up, bleary-eyed. He tried to focus on the man in front of him. His head spun as the memory of where he was slowly faded back into his mind. Blinking, he managed to almost focus his eyes.

Sarge smiled at him. "That sack of shit you call a head starting to clear up?"

"What do you want to know?" Aaron croaked.

Sarge smiled, "That's more like it. You one of Billy's boys?"

Aaron nodded, "I needed to eat, and he let me in his group. I just did what I had to do to survive."

Sarge nodded, "And just what have you been doing?"

With pain raking his body, he replied, "I'm not some kind of monster." He started to cry, "I'm not a bad guy. I was going to starve to death."

"Why are you watching us Aaron? What's Billy got up his sleeve?"

Aaron didn't answer right away. Sarge waited a moment before standing. Aaron looked at him, but still didn't reply. Sarge let out a breath and took a quick step towards him. In one quick motion he grabbed Aaron's pants and jerked them down.

Aaron jumped, "What are you doing?" He howled.

Sarge sat back down on the stool without saying anything. Leaning over, he slid the bucket of tools Mike had set out over in front of him. Reaching down, he pawed through it and removed a pair of tin snips. Looking back up at Aaron, he repeated his question. Aaron simply stared back.

"Look, we were doing so well. You and I are just talking. I can assure you that whatever sort of threat Billy's laid on you pales in comparison to what I *will* do to you." Aaron still didn't reply. Sarge looked at the snips, working them a couple of times as he looked into Aaron's eyes. "I see you're not circumcised."

Aaron's head was suddenly clear. The haze in his head vanished as the fog retreats from the rising sun. He looked at the tin snips, then at himself. *Surely he isn't serious?*

"I'm only going to take a little off the top," Sarge said. Then Sarge raised his hands and made a show of trembling them. "But at my age, they shake just a bit." When Sarge started to reach for his manhood, Aaron screamed.

"Alright, alright!"

Sarge stopped and leaned back on the stool, "I'm listening."

Aaron looked at the snips again. "Billy hooked up with some DHS guys." He looked up at Sarge, "They have a real hard-on for you guys."

Sarge smiled, "I wonder why?"

"I, I don't know. They just told me to come over here and watch you guys. I was supposed to count how many of you there are. Get a feel for your security routines, patrols, that sort of thing." He paused for a moment and winced, "Can you please cut me down. Please, my shoulders hurt so bad."

Before Sarge could answer, Ted leapt from the workbench. Sarge quickly stood up and spun around. From outside the garage, a voice said, "Too late, you're already dead."

Dalton stepped through the open garage door. Ted shook

his head and mumbled, "You creep around like a damn cat or some shit."

"That's a good way to get your ass ventilated," Sarge added.

"Nah, you knew it was me," Dalton replied as he leaned against the workbench beside Ted. Looking at Aaron, he raised his eyebrows, "Oh, I didn't know it was that kind of party."

Sarge laughed, "We were just talking about his upcoming circumcision."

Dalton jerked his head to the side, "I wouldn't take too much from the poor boy."

Sarge laughed, "That's what I said."

"He tell you anything?"

Sarge looked back at Aaron. "Oh he's been pretty chatty up to this point. But he says his shoulders hurt and he wants down. Tell you what Aaron, I've got one more question for you. Answer it and I'll cut you down. How's that sound?" Aaron hesitated for a minute then nodded slightly. "Where's Billy Boy and his merry band of fucktards holed up?"

Aaron's eyes closed as he replied, "We're at the Elks Camp."

"Good man, Aaron. I'm a man of my word and I'm going to cut you down." Sarge pulled his knife from its sheath. Aaron saw the large piece of steel made by Busse Knives. Pointing the knife at Aaron, Sarge said, "But you know I'm going to have to tie you up."

Aaron nodded and Sarge swept the blade through the rope and Aaron crashed to the concrete floor.

"I'll tie him up," Ted said as he hopped off the bench.

Dalton quickly stepped forward, "Let me do it."

Dalton went up to Aaron and knelt down. He untied the piece of rope from Aaron's hands. Aaron didn't resist, he was spent. Dalton rolled Aaron onto his stomach and grabbed his left hand. He brought the arm up over Aaron's head and folded it down behind his back. Aaron moaned in pain as it was certainly uncomfortable. Grabbing the right hand he swept it behind Aaron's back and brought the hand up to meet the left hand. With the hands now together Dalton used the piece of rope and bound them. Aaron cried out in pain once again.

Sarge was shaking his head, "Damn Dalton. I've seen some twisted shit, but that takes the cake."

Dalton stood up and examined his work, "Just a little something I learned over the years."

"What kind of fucking work did you do?" Ted asked.

Dalton glanced over and said, "Corrections," bouncing his eyebrows.

"I didn't think that kind of shit was legal."

"If the cameras didn't see it, it didn't happen."

Sarge knelt down beside Aaron, "How many peckerwoods does the DHS have?"

"I don't know," Aaron moaned.

Sarge rapped his knuckles on the back of Aaron's head. "Come on now. You've got to have an idea."

"There's a bunch of them, I don't know how many. We're kept away from them. They put us in some cabins on the east side of the camp. We weren't allowed in the rest of the camp," Aaron replied. He was talking into the concrete so the words came out slightly muffled.

"Why were you guys hooked up with the DHS?" Sarge asked.

Aaron groaned, "Billy said we were going to have some fun."

Sarge tapped Aaron's head again, "And just what do you and Billy consider fun?"

"It wasn't my idea."

Tapping his head again, Sarge replied, "But you said we."

"That's not what I meant," Aaron croaked.

"Back to my question, how many?"

Mumbling into the concrete, Aaron replied, "I heard Billy say once that there must be close to a hundred of them."

Ted let out a low whistle. Sarge looked back at him and nodded. Looking back at Aaron, he said, "Aaron, we'll be back later to talk some more. Don't mess around in here."

Sarge rose to his feet and motioned for the others to follow him, and headed into the house. Once in the kitchen, Sarge poured himself a cup of coffee and sat down at the table. Dalton poured himself a cup as well before taking a seat. Ted spun a chair around and sat down, resting his elbows on the back of the chair's back.

"How can you drink that shit cold?" Ted asked.

"Hot or cold, it's always good," Sarge replied as he took a sip.

"What are we going to do with him?" Dalton asked.

"Shwack him," Ted said.

Sarge looked at Ted for a moment, "You think that's the right call?"

"You wanna be looking over your shoulder?"

Sarge sipped the coffee again, "Fawcett did say the gloves were off."

"Should we let the Sheriff decide?" Dalton asked.

Sarge looked at Ted. Ted shrugged in reply.

"I guess it comes down to whether this is a military issue or a law enforcement issue," Sarge said.

"I don't think the Sheriff will want to execute the poor bastard. Is there any way to lock him up?" Dalton said.

Sarge laughed, "You don't know Morgan too well. He's got no issue with putting a sack of shit down. None."

Dalton thought for a moment, then said "But does he deserve it?"

"There's the rub. How do we deal with these guys when we

take them. Putting them in the dirt is the easy solution. But is it the right one?" Sarge asked.

"Fuck it, shwack 'em," Ted replied.

Sarge chuckled, "That's your answer to everything, isn't it Teddy?"

"Sometimes, it's the only answer."

"Every time it's a permanent answer," Dalton added.

Sarge nodded his head slightly, "We need to have a discussion on this."

Mike came back into the kitchen, knocking Ted's hat off as he passed him.

Catching the hat, Ted said, "Cut it out, dickhead."

"You get that radio to Morgan?" Sarge asked.

Mike nodded, "Yeah, he told Livingston to stuff it up his ass. Said he'd be there tomorrow."

Sarge shook his head, "That's what I figured he'd say."

With my plans for the day changed, I was having a quick breakfast before heading to Eustis. The chickens were really laying well now and keeping us in plenty of eggs. Each morning Little Bit would go check the laying boxes for new eggs. What she didn't tell us was there was a broody hen in the coop sitting on eggs, and she'd let her. Bobbie was scrambling eggs when Little Bit came through the door shouting.

"We've got baby chicks!"

Surprised, I looked up, "What?"

She ran up holding one in her palm, "There's seven of them! They're so cute, look at it."

She held her hand out to show me the little yellow puff ball. "Where are the rest of them?" I asked.

"They're out in the coop with their momma," she replied. Holding her hand up, she rubbed the chick's head as it peeped. "He's so cute."

Her sisters, along with Fred and Jess, came over to look at the chick. All the girls were oohing and ahhing over the hatchling.

"I thought you were getting the eggs every day," I said.

She smiled, "I was, but there was one hen sitting on eggs and I let her. She hatched them all out."

Rubbing her head, I said, "Good job kiddo; now we have even more chickens."

Mel set a plate of eggs in front of me. "Where are you going today?"

"I have to go to town. Livingston called and said there was an issue they needed me to deal with.".

Taylor's head popped up, "You're going to town? Can we come? We haven't been anywhere, please!"

"Yeah, let us go with you. You can't go alone," Jess said.

I looked at Mel. They wouldn't be able to go without her permission. She shrugged, "Don't let them get hurt."

I smiled, "Just a milk run. No big deal," I replied.

"We can go?" Taylor asked.

I nodded as I stuffed a bite of eggs in my mouth, "Sure. Get your stuff together; we're leaving soon."

The girls jumped up and ran off to get ready to go to town. I guess than once again such an event was a big deal. It was kind of funny to see them so excited about something as simple as a ride to town.

"Can I come?" Little Bit asked.

"No, not this time sweety," Mel answered before I had to.

Putting on a pout, she said, "I never get to go anywhere."

I smiled at her, "When you're bigger, baby girl."

I went out on the back porch where Danny and Thad were sitting, and flopped onto a chair.

"You guys going to work on that water tower?" I asked.

"Yeah, Dalton said he'd come help too. The three of us should be able to handle it," Thad said.

"Sorry to bail on you guys."

"Don't sweat it. I know you have an aversion to hard work," Danny replied with a snicker.

"Believe me, I wish I were going with you guys today."

"Don't worry about it. We'll get the tank up today. Be careful up there," Thad said.

I nodded and stood up, "Thanks, guys. See you later."

I went out to the old Suburban and started it up. It cranked immediately and settled into that typical Cummins rumble. I was amazed at the old truck. It was beat when I bought it, and it had only been more abused since. Walking to the house, I grabbed my pack and a bag of mags I'd put together for road trips. With recent events, I wanted plenty of ammo when leaving here.

When I got back to the truck, Sarge was there with Mike and Dalton. "We need to talk," Sarge said.

Setting the pack into the truck, I replied, "What's up?"

"What do you want to do with that guy we caught?"

"You done with him?" I asked.

Sarge nodded, "He told me what I needed."

"Where are they hiding out?"

"Billy's hooked up with around a hundred DHS, and they're at the Elks Camp. You know where that is?" Sarge asked.

I was surprised how close they were. "Yeah; and it's not far either. Just off 450 west of Umatilla."

"We'll have to get over there and take a look then. Back to the original question," Sarge replied.

It was a tough question. Sure, we'd caught the guy snooping around, but he hadn't done anything to us. He was obviously on the wrong side of the equation, but how should that be dealt with?

I shrugged, "I don't know. He didn't do anything other than sneak around."

"Teddy wants to plant him. Says if we turn him loose, we'll be looking over our shoulders. And he's right about that," Sarge said.

"What'd he say he was doing with them?" I asked.

"Same thing they all say, just doing what they had to do to survive."

I rubbed my head. I hated these kinds of decisions. But in the end, I didn't want to kill someone for no real reason. "Let's take him to town. I'll give him to the Eustis PD. Cecil's going to need labor in the fields, and he can be put to work there."

"I like it," Dalton said.

Sarge nodded, "Sounds good to me. We'll fetch him from the shed, and I'll go with you."

"I want to stop in Altoona and distribute the flour we've got. It would be good to do it from the Hummer so they know it's the Army giving it to them," I replied.

Sarge nodded, "Alright, we're going to need some security though."

"The girls are going with us. That should be enough."

"It'll be good for them. They need to get out and put their skills to use," Dalton said.

"That's what I was thinking."

"Let me go load his ass up and I'll meet you by the bunker," Sarge said as he got back in the Hummer.

Looking at Dalton, I said, "Danny and Thad are inside. Go get you some breakfast."

"Thanks, I think I will. I'm hungry."

The girls finally showed up with Aric in tow. They loaded up and I drove over to the bunker to wait for the old man. Ian and Perez were at the bunker, having relieved us earlier that morning. Perez was sitting on top of the bunker smoking as he usually did. Sitting in the truck waiting on Sarge, the girls were wound up. They talked, all of them, at the same time. It was driving me nuts, so I got out and walked over to Ian.

"Does he ever take a break from those things?" I asked, nodding at Perez.

Ian shook his head, "Only to light he next one."

"He is going to be a pain in the ass when he runs out."

Ian laughed, "No shit right? Just think about that, he's already a huge pain in the ass."

Perez had lain down on the top of the bunker and raised his hand in middle finger salute, "I can hear you assholes."

"You were supposed to," I replied, getting a laugh from Ian.

Perez rolled over and looked at us, "Trust me, I've got plenty of smokes." He pulled a lighter from his pocket and shook it next to his ear. "Lighters, on the other hand."

I laughed, "That's hilarious. What are you going to do when you run out of lighters?"

"Whatever it takes. I'll rub two sticks together if I have to."

Sarge's Hummer rounded the corner. Looking up, I said, "About damn time."

"Have fun in town," Ian said with a grin.

"You wanna go?"

Waving his hands, he replied, "Oh hell no. You can have that shit. I'm perfectly fine right here."

Going over to the truck, I asked for volunteers to ride with Sarge. Aric and Fred said they would, and quickly traded vehicles. Pulling up beside Sarge, I asked, "You ready?"

He nodded and pulled off. I followed him out of the neighborhood for the short ride to Altoona. As we rode, Lee Ann asked, "What are we doing?"

"We're going to stop up here at the market and give away some flour. Then head into Eustis."

"Where'd we get flour, and why are we giving it away?" Taylor asked.

"We got it from the Army, and we're giving it away because a lot of people are starving. You may not think so; but we've got it a lot better than a most folks out there."

She didn't say anything else, just looked out the window as I turned into the parking lot of the old Kangaroo. The place was pretty busy. I was surprised to see a couple of people offering some early vegetables. They must have gotten a jump on their gardens. We pulled up near the gas canopy and stopped. As we got out, I told the girls to form a security perimeter, which they did quickly and efficiently.

Sarge opened the back of the Hummer and pulled one of the sacks over and cut it open. We were starting to get a little attention from some of the folks there as a couple of people wandered over to see what we were doing. Sarge looked at the first woman in earshot and said, "Get a container I can put some of this flour in for you."

She looked at him uncertainly, "Flour? You giving it away?"

Sarge nodded, "Yes ma'am, just get something to put it in and I'll give it to you."

She quickly ran off to the table where she was trading small bundles of lighter wood. Grabbing a cloth grocery bag, she dumped lighter wood from it before running back. "Here, you can put it this," she said, nearly out of breath.

Sarge shook several pounds of flour into it, "There you go."

The woman looked down into the bag, "I haven't seen flour

in a long time." Looking back at Sarge, she asked, "Can I get just a little more?"

Shaking his head he replied, "I'm sorry but we want to give everyone some if we can."

She smiled, "Oh, yes, of course. Thank you so much."

"Don't thank me, thank the Army."

Word quickly spread of the giveaway, and soon people were pouring in to get their share. It started out orderly enough, but when you have so many desperate people and a very limited resource, things get ugly. The girls were holding people back and only letting them through in a single file. But as more people arrived, they began pushing and shoving to get a turn. I stayed with Sarge to try and control the people there.

One man came up with a five gallon bucket and set it down. While the measurements were strictly by eyeball, Sarge was being as fair as possible. Sarge dumped flour into the man's bucket as he stared on. When Sarge turned the bag up to stop the man grabbed the bag and shouted, "Give me more!" Sarge jerked the bag and it split open, spilling the rest of the flour onto the ground. People in the line fell to their knees to scoop it up. The man tried to rip the bag from Sarge's hands as chaos ensued around us.

I cracked the guy in the head with the butt of my rifle, knocking him down. Someone in the crowd grabbed his bucket and made off with it. The people waiting to get in the line started pushing past the girls. I could hear them shouting and the people screaming at one another. Then, just as things were about to get completely out of hand, there was a sudden burst of automatic weapons fire. It was joined by another, and everyone dove to the ground, including me.

I looked up to see Lee Ann and Taylor holding their H&Ks

over their heads. Taylor was looking around wide-eyed. Sarge was still on his feet and his voice boomed.

"What the hell is the matter with you people? I know you're hungry, that's why we're here! But you're acting like damned animals! This is done for today. We'll try again another time; but if you people behave this way next time, we will not give food out here!"

The people slowly got to their feet and looked at one another. You could see a little shame on their faces, but it was nearly masked by desperation. They were hungry, their kids were hungry, and this was free food. What else would they do?

We pushed everyone back from the truck and I had the girls move in closer to keep everyone away. Lee Ann and Taylor both changed the mags in their weapons.

"Good job girls. This was getting out of hand," I said.

"It was getting scary. I was afraid someone was going to knock us down," Taylor said.

Looking at the crowd as they moved off, I said, "They're desperate. You can't really blame them."

Sarge closed the back of the Hummer, "We need to come up with a better plan next time. It would be better if we could portion it out ahead of time and hand it out that way."

"It would. But what the hell are we going to put it in?" I asked.

He shook his head, "I don't know, but we need to find something. This sure as shit isn't going to work."

"I agree. I wanted to stop in Umatilla and give some away, but that isn't going to happen now. It would just be a repeat of this."

"Your guy is awake in the truck," Aric said.

Sarge glanced inside, "He still tied up?"

"Yeah, he is. Who the hell tied him up like that? Looks painful as shit," Aric replied.

Sarge laughed, "That would be Dalton."

I went over and looked in the truck. Aric was right, it sure as hell looked painful. "Damn that's all kinds of fucked up."

"True. But it's effective," Sarge replied.

"Alright, let's head to Eustis," I said as I headed for the truck.

As I followed Sarge down nineteen, Taylor asked, "What was wrong with those people?"

"Remember the other day I was telling you how good we had it compared to most people?" I was looking at her in the rearview mirror. She nodded, "Now you see it."

"It's sad," Lee Ann commented.

"We do have it good compared to everyone else," Jess added.

"You girls remember that," I added.

# CHAPTER 15

S ARGE AND I WALKED AROUND the side of the table to get a look at the snake oil salesman. We found an older man standing behind the table with two younger men. The old guy was a big man with gray hair, what was left of it. Sweat beaded up on his bald head in the heat of the day. All three men were armed; and the younger two stood back, keeping an eye on everyone. The old man noticed us standing there and smiled. He stepped away from the table, and one of the younger men immediately took his place.

"So you come to run me outta town?"

Shaking my head, I replied, "Hell no. You can sell what you want."

The old man smiled. "Well, that's a first. We're usually not welcome too long in most places."

"People still trying to control what other folks are doing?" Sarge asked.

Nodding, the man replied, "Yep. It's crazy, really. They think if they can't get a drink, then they are somehow cured."

"I say, let folks make their own decisions and live with the consequences," Sarge replied.

The man stuck his hand out, "Name's Bob Maples. Everyone calls me Big Bob."

Sarge shook his hand, "Linus Mitchell; call me Sarge."

I shook his hand as well. "Morgan; good to meet you, Big Bob."

"You going to be around for a while?" Sarge asked.

Bob shrugged, "Until the market dries up. We don't really have a plan. Just kind of go with the flow."

"Well, good luck," I said. "Let me know if you need anything."

Bob smiled, "Will do."

Sarge and I headed across the park on our way to the armory. We found the girls checking out the offerings laid out on tables and blankets. They acquired quite the following of young men as well. As we approached, I heard Taylor nearly shout, "No! It's not for sale!"

Seeing me, she gave a look of desperation. Walking up, I asked, "What's up kiddo?"

She pointed to an emaciated figure, "He keeps asking if our guns are for sale. I told him no; but he keeps asking."

Looking at him, I said, "She said no. What don't you understand?"

He looked at the H&K, "Just a whole lot of gun for a little girl."

I laughed. "She ain't a little gir;l and she handles it just fine."

Taylor smiled. "Thanks, Dad."

The man looked at me, "You're her Dad?"

I nodded. He took another look at the weapon before wandering off. Taylor let out a sigh of relief.

"Glad he's gone. Everyone wants our guns; and they keep asking."

"Don't let them bother you. Just keep your eyes open," I said.

"Dad; do you have any silver? We want to get something, but don't have any money," Lee Ann said.

Reaching into my pocket, I pulled out some silver dimes.

I remember when I started collecting junk silver with this very scenario in mind. It was fun to collect, kind of like a treasure hunt. I'd go to the bank and get rolls of coins sometimes, and go through them looking for occasional silver. Dimes minted prior to 1965 contained 90% silver. The Coinage Act of 1965 resulted in dimes from that point forward consisting of 75% copper and 25% nickel; no silver at all. That wasn't terribly effective though; and I ended up buying most of it. Handing the dimes to Lee Ann, I said, "Don't spend it all in one place."

She shook the coins in her hand and smiled, "We won't."

"Don't be too long; we have to get back home shortly."

"Okay; love you," Taylor said as they walked away.

Sarge chuckled. "They're growing up fast, aren't they?"

"They sure are."

---

The girls wandered through the market looking at everything. A smell drifted on the air that caught Jess's attention.

"That smells good; what is it?" She asked, looking around.

"Smells like pancakes to me," Taylor added.

"It's over there," Lee Ann said, pointing.

They walked over to table with a small hibachi grill set up. Sitting on it was a small cast iron pan. Arranged on the table, were jars of colorful jelly. A woman stood in front of the table eating a thin rolled pastry. Bright red jelly oozed from the other end and fell into the hand she held out.

"Is it good?" Taylor asked.

The woman didn't take the sweet treat from her mouth. She replied by nodding her head and half smiling. Lee Ann looked at the old man and held out a dime. The old man took it and examined it, then held up two fingers. Lee Ann nodded, and he pocketed the coin. Taking a plastic container out, he poured a thin batter onto the skillet that covered the bottom. It cooked quickly, and he flipped it with a couple of sticks, chopsticks style. When the other side was done, he removed it from the heat and laid it on a piece of cloth.

Lifting the pan, he examined the coals glowing under it, and fed in a small piece of wood before setting the pan back down and starting the process again. Once the batter was in the skillet, he picked up the first one and motioned to the jars. Lee Ann pointed to a jar of purple jelly; and the old man spooned in a generous helping and rolled it up. Lee Ann anxiously took a generous bite.

"Oh, that is so good!"

Jess reached for it, "Let me have a bite."

Lee Ann swiveled away from her, "Get your own. This is so good."

The old man never spoke as he worked. No words were ever exchanged. A couple more coins were handed over, and soon everyone was eating their own crepe. They walked through the market enjoying the amazingly sweet treat and talking about how good they were.

"We need to get another one of those. They are so delicious," Fred said.

"They are terrific. Hey, look at all the people over there," Jess said, pointing to Big Bob's booth.

"That's the guy selling the booze," Aric said.

"We got enough dimes to buy a bottle?" Fred asked.

"I doubt it. Plus Dad would kill us if he caught us drinking," Lee Ann said.

Taylor snorted, "Yeah; he would."

"Let's just go look," Fred said.

As they approached Big Bob's booth, a man walked up to

the long line of people and looked around. He was wearing a backpack, and slipped it off his shoulder as he craned his neck. Moving around the group, he set the pack down and started to walk away. Jess saw the pack and called out to him.

Pointing at the pack, she shouted, "Hey! You forgot your pack."

The guy looked back for a moment, then at the pack. He seemed to hesitate, then turned and started to quickly walk away.

"That guy just left that pack over there," Jess said, pointing at the man.

"That's weird; it's like he's running away," Fred said.

"I think we need to get him," Jess said as she turned to follow him.

"What about the bag?" Taylor asked.

Jess looked over her shoulder, "Go get it; we'll get him."

---

Dalton and Thad looked up at the tank. It was perched on the edge of the bucket of the tractor. A chain held it in place.

"So close," Danny said.

"I could climb up there and push it. It's almost there; looks like a little shove would do it," Dalton said.

"It ain't going to get up there by itself," Thad lamented.

Dalton climbed up onto the tractor and scrambled up to the bucket. Removing the chain, he shouldered the tank and heaved. It slid out of the bucket and landed on the plywood platform with a thud. Danny and Thad both let out a whoop as the hardest part of the project was now over.

"Thank God!" Danny shouted.

"Now all we gotta do it plumb it in," Thad added.

Dalton climbed off the tank and looked at the stack of pipe. "How do you plan to tie it into the houses?"

"I was thinking of just running a pipe to the nearest hose bib on a house and connecting it there. Open the valve and you've got water into the house," Danny replied.

Dalton nodded, "Sounds easy enough."

They got to work on the plumbing. A two-inch pipe was run down from the tank to the ground. There, an elbow was installed and a manifold of sorts was constructed with some T-fittings. This is where Danny's habit of collecting and keeping things really paid off. They had all the fittings they needed, and were able to get pipe run to all the houses. Every house had a hose somewhere. The hoses were run out to meet the pipe to save as much of it as they could.

"We got lucky with this glue," Thad said as he shoved the last pieces of pipe together.

Danny looked into the can. "Yeah, we did. I do have one more, but it's never been opened; and I didn't want to open it yet. Soon as you do, it starts to dry out."

"Danny; while we wrap this up, why don't you go fill the fire tank?" Thad asked.

Danny nodded and took the tractor to get the trailer. Once the trailer was in place by the well, he dragged his generator out. While the solar set-up would run the pump, it would to have to run for a while to fill the large tank; and that would be rough on the system. Connecting the generator to the house, he flipped off the breaker that the solar system was connected to, and started the generator. Once it was running smoothly, he flipped on the breaker for it, and back-fed the house.

Back at the well, he dropped a hose into the tank, and turned the water on. It would take a while for the tank to fill, so he went in the house for a cold drink. While Danny was gone, Dalton and Thad finished tying the houses in, and went through them to make sure all faucets were turned off. It would be a shame to get the tank filled and lose the water into a septic tank because a sink was left on.

Once they'd done all they could, the two men walked over to Danny's house. Maybe it would fill faster if the three of them stared at it. Danny was sitting on the trailer when the guys got there.

"That thing is going to take forever to fill up," Thad said.

"It's doing pretty good. I think it will take about an hour to fill it," Danny replied.

Thad rubbed his hands, "I can't wait to see if this works."

"Oh, it'll work. That much water that high off the ground has to work," Dalton said.

The guys sat around shooting the shit while the tank filled. Once it was full, they pulled the tank back to the tower. Thad climbed up and dropped the discharge hose into the top of the tank on the tower. Danny started the pump, and soon water was pouring into the tank. Thad had to stay on the tower to keep the hose in, as it tended to jump out from the force of the pump.

"This thing is a lot faster than the well pump," Dalton said, admiring the little gas pump.

"Yeah; it's a good pump. We found it in a Forestry Service building. Saved our ass when the fire came through," Danny replied.

"I remember that. Was keeping an eye on that, and getting ready to bug-out if it got too close."

"We went and fought it. It was hard work, but the Guard helped us a lot, and we managed to beat it back."

The gas pump had pushed the water quickly. Danny shut the pump down, and Thad dropped the hose off the tower and closed the fill port. As he climbed down, he announced, "Now's the moment of truth!"

"Let's go see what it looks like," Danny said.

They went to Thad's house and filed into the kitchen. Thad stood there a moment with his hand on the faucet, looking at the guys. "Cross your fingers." He raised the handle and there was a gurgle, followed by small blasts of air. A little water trickled out, then more air and gurgling. After a moment, a solid stream of water began to pour from the faucet. It was greeted by cheers from the guys.

"Let's go see what the shower looks like," Danny said.

Thad led the way down the hall to the bathroom. The sound of the toilet bubbling, told them the tank was filling. Pulling the shower curtain back, he opened the valve, and the gurgling and spitting started again. It didn't last as long this time, and soon water was running out of the showerhead.

"It's real low pressure, but I think it's enough to take a shower," Thad said as he ran his hand through the cascading water.

"Yeah; that's plenty strong enough to take a shower," Dalton added.

"How long do you guys think a tank will last?" Danny asked.

Thad shrugged, "We'll have to see."

Dalton chuckled, "I bet the first one goes fast, everyone wanting to try it out and all."

"I bet you're right. And to kick it off, I'm taking a shower right now." Thad said as he stripped off his shirt.

"On that note, I'm out of here!" Dalton shouted as he disappeared down the hall with Danny in tow.

# CHAPTER 16

I was talking to the engineers when we were hit by the shockwave of the explosion, followed immediately by the sound. So close together, they seemed to arrive as one. Staggering, I looked up, "What the hell was that?"

The engineers were looking around as well, rattled from the blast. Then we saw the cloud of smoke rising over the armory, and people running. I followed them around the corner and realized the blast had come from the market. Then the reality hit me; the girls were at the market. The air was filled with cries and people shouting as I started to run towards the sound of chaos. I prayed my girls were alright, and terrified at the thought of what could be.

The market was destroyed. Debris littered the ground, as well as more grisly things. There were body parts everywhere. Seeing this, increased my heart rate, if that was at all possible. The first person I found was Jess. She was on her knees in a daze. Her hair was a mess, all disheveled and full of dirt, pieces of wood and other debris. I dropped to my knees and grabbed her.

"Are you ok?" I shouted as I looked her over.

She just stared back at me. I ran my hands over her looking for blood, but found none; so I checked her head. There was blood, but thankfully it didn't appear to hers, as bad as that is. I gave her a little shake, "Jess, where are the girls? Where are my girls?" She still stared back without replying. I shook her again, "Come on, where are my girls?"

She raised her hand and pointed back towards the blast site, and my heart shrank. I jumped up and started looking at the bodies on the ground. I found Lee Ann sitting on the ground. She too was covered in dirt and debris, plus broken glass. Glass littered the ground everywhere. Like Jess, she was dazed and was trying to stand up. I grabbed her arm and helped her to her feet.

"Are you ok?" I asked as she stumbled.

She looked around, brushing her hair out of face. "I think so; my ears are ringing really loud, and my head hurts."

I was looking her over and found a bad gash on her left arm. Blood was running down and dripping from her fingers. I pulled a battle dressing from my vest and wrapped it tightly around her arm.

"Where's Taylor?" I asked as I cinched off the bandage.

"She was just here, right beside me."

I looked around, but didn't see her. There were several bodies on the ground, and anxiety grew even more. Pointing back to where Jess was, I told Lee Ann to go stay with her. More people were showing up to help. Sarge and Doc appeared with Mary.

"Where are the girls?" Sarge asked as he trotted up.

"I don't know, I've only found Lee Ann and Jess so far." As I said that, Fred and Aric walked up. They too were covered in debris from the blast, but appeared unhurt.

"Are you two ok?" Sarge asked.

Aric was holding his head and nodded. "Yeah; I think we're alright. My head hurts though."

"You're probably concussed," Doc said. "Go over there with Jess and Lee Ann while we find Taylor."

Aric nodded, and held onto Fred as they walked back to

where the girls were. Doc was already helping another injured person when I started looking for Taylor. There were a lot of wounded around, but I had to find my daughter. The cries of the wounded filled the air. Some were still screaming, while others moaned in pain.

"Morgan! Over here!" Mary called out.

I turned to see her knelt down beside a body on the ground. A body wearing a shirt I immediately recognized. There was also an H&K lying on the ground. I ran over to her and slid in on my knees, which turned out to be a huge mistake, as glass tore into both of my knees. I didn't even notice it though as I rolled Taylor over.

What I saw, shook me to my core. She was covered in blood. Her face had numerous cuts and scratches, some deep and bleeding profusely. I immediately checked her for a pulse and found one, thankfully. But she was hurt really bad.

"Doc! Doc over here!" I shouted.

He looked up from the person he was helping. Tying off a bandage, he jumped to his feet and ran over. He quickly checked for a pulse, and then started to cut her clothes off with a pair of EMT shears. Removing her clothes, revealed a number of deep wounds.

"Is she breathing?" Doc asked as he worked.

I didn't hear him. All I could do was stare at her. It looked so bad. So much blood, so much blood. Doc screamed at me. "Morgan; get your shit together. Is she breathing?"

I snapped out of it and leaned my head down to her face. I was trying to feel her breath but I couldn't. "I don't think so. Do something, please do something."

Doc handed me the shears as he shifted around to her head. "Cut her pants off; I'm going to get her an airway."

He pulled a small green tube out of a plastic wrapper.

Squirting some lube on it, he placed the tube into her right nostril and gently guided it into her nose. I was cutting her pant leg with the shears, but couldn't take my eyes off what he was doing. At one point, he gently rotated the tube back and forth, and it continued down into her nose, coming to stop at a rubber washer.

Doc reached into his pack and pulled out a plastic bag the size of a Nerf football. It had a mask on one end, which he placed over her face. He then gave the bag a squeeze. Her chest rose as he did, and the mask fogged as the breath was pushed back out. Doc looked at Mary and told her to keep squeezing the bag in a slow steady rhythm.

Now that her airway was secure, he went to work on the many wounds. I worked as well, stuffing gauze into the larger ones and wrapping them in more. She was cut to pieces. Once the more severe wounds were dressed, Doc pulled a compact Mylar-style blanket out of his pack and laid it out. It was green on one side with some sort of reinforcing material woven through it. With the blanket laid out, Doc told me to grab her feet and help get her on it.

Once we had her on the blanket, we picked her up to carry her to the clinic. Mary walked closely with us to keep operating the bag. Sarge and Livingston ran over to help carry her, and soon we were making our way to the clinic.

"Is she going to be alright?" I asked Doc as we quickly carried her.

"We need to get her to the clinic and see what's going on. I hope so."

"We'll do everything we can for her," Sarge replied.

"Who is she?" Livingston asked.

"One of my daughters," I replied. He didn't respond, but I could tell he felt it.

There was already a number of people at the clinic. Many of the lesser wounded had already made their way there. We ran past them into the clinic and set Taylor up on a gurney. Doc pushed her towards one of the two operating suites in the clinic. As we crashed through the door, one of the medical staff stopped us.

"You're going to have to wait; she hasn't been triaged yet."

"Yes she has; I did it. She needs to be seen right now," Doc replied.

"There are a lot of people that need to be seen," the man in green scrubs replied.

I stepped up and pushed him out of the way. "She's going in now."

Doc continued into the OR with her and started calling out for a surgeon. The man I'd pushed out of the way started to protest. I spun around and drew my pistol, "Get us some fucking help in here! Now!"

The man raised his hands and disappeared out the door. Doc ran over to me and grabbed the Springfield. "Put that shit away, Morgan! What the hell's wrong with you?"

As I holstered it, I said, "I'm not messing around with these people. They need to get in here."

Two people in scrubs came through the door and went straight to her. Doc started telling them what he'd found, and the doctor began calling things out. He turned to us and said, "You need to clear out, we need the room."

Sarge grabbed my shoulder. "Come on, Morgan. Let them do what they do." I resisted a bit, and he pulled on me. "Come on; there's nothing you can do here."

Looking at Doc, I said, "Save her, Doc. Please save her."

Doc looked up and nodded. I could see the determination on his face. Sarge pulled me out the door and we walked outside.

A number of the Guardsmen had gathered at the clinic to assist those needing help. The medical staff consisted of four people and they were overwhelmed.

"She's going to be alright, Morgan. Doc will do whatever it takes," Sarge said.

"I know. I just can't imagine any alternative."

"Let's go see what we can find at the blast site. I think we know who did it, but let's take a look."

"Oh we know. And they're going to fucking pay for this," I replied.

We walked back over to the park. Gone were the wounded, leaving behind only the dead. The ground was littered with broken glass, blood and body parts. As we walked, the ground crunched beneath our feet. I stepped around the larger pools of blood, and the old man didn't seem to even notice.

"Pure evil genius," Sarge said as we approached the blast area.

"What do you mean?"

He pointed to the smoking remains of Big Bob's truck. "They set the damn thing off right beside all that hooch. It increased the effect of the device by adding all that flying glass to the blast."

I looked at what was left of the truck. There was no sign of Big Bob or his two boys. Unless of course the pile of intestines hanging in a nearby tree were his.

"That's why she was so cut up," I replied. "Taylor, I mean."

Sarge nodded, "Yep." He kicked at some glass on the ground as he shook his head, "These are some sick fuckers."

Taking in the scene, I said, "Look at this place. No one will ever come here again."

Sarge snorted, "Shit. In Iraq, they'd bomb a market, and it would be up and running again an hour later. It'll take some time. All these body parts will need to be cleaned up first. but the people will be back."

We wandered around the park a little before heading back to the clinic; I really wanted to check on Taylor. We found the rest of the girls sitting on a bench on the sidewalk.

"How are you guys doing? Anyone hurt?" Sarge asked.

Jess rubbed her head, "My head hurts; but we checked each other, and Lee Ann is the only one with any injuries."

"How's your arm?" I asked.

She looked at the bandage. "It hurts, but not that bad. Someone checked it out, and told me to keep it wrapped up. He said it didn't need stitches or anything."

Trying to smile, I replied, "Good."

Lee Ann looked up at me with tears in her eyes, "How's Taylor? Is she going to be alright?"

Seeing her like that, caused me to tear up for the first time. "I'm going to check on her." It took everything I had not to break down right there. But I didn't want to do that to her. She was already shaken up; and seeing me upset would only add to it.

"I saw the guy. The guy that left the bomb," Jess said.

Her comment had Sarge's attention. "You did? Would you recognize him? If he wasn't vaporized?"

"Oh he wasn't. He set the pack down and started walking away. I called out to him that he forgot his pack, but he took off, moving quickly away. We were chasing him when it blew up."

"Taylor was going to get the bag," Lee Ann added. "That's why she was so close."

It pained me to hear that. This was one of those times when the "*what if*" game started in your head. *What if she hadn't turned to go back? What if I'd said no to them about walking around the park?* This sort of thing will eat you up if you're not careful. I felt it was my fault; I had let them come with me. I'd let them walk around the park. But in the end, it wasn't my fault, though it was hard for me to see it. There was only one person responsible; and he was still running around town somewhere.

"We're going to go check on her now," I said. Lee Ann nodded.

As Sarge and I walked back towards the clinic, a Hummer rolled up beside us. The Guardsmen in the passenger seat waved me over.

"What's up?" I asked.

Stabbing a thumb over his shoulder, he said, "I think you guys need to talk to this guy."

I looked in back to see a man in his thirties sitting between two other soldiers. "Who is he?"

"We don't know. But he was running like hell away from town. We thought it odd since everyone else was running towards town after the explosion."

Sarge looked in, eyeballing the man. Looking at me, he said, "I'm going to get Jess."

I nodded, and looked at the soldiers. "Drag him out."

They got out and stood the man against the Hummer. One of the two in the back with him handed me a pistol, "He had this on him."

I examined the Sig, but didn't think much of it; everyone carries a gun now. But, turning it over, I noticed a bar code on the frame. This caught my attention, as I know only government-issued weapons typically had these. Sure, there were some on the civilian market. Sig made the 229 Navy edition, and a ridiculous 226 with Homeland Security engraved on it. Plus the government barcode. But this was neither of those. Looking back to the man, he made eye contact with me for a second before looking back to the ground.

Sarge returned with the girls and Aric. As Jess approached, she started shouting, "That's him! That's the son-of-a-bitch that set the pack down!" She closed on him quickly and delivered a devastating knee to his nuts. He collapsed as if he'd been shot, issuing a loud, deep moan. I grabbed Jess and pulled her back as Fred and Aric both chimed in, reaffirming Jess's statement.

"It's him, definitely him," Aric said.

"What do you want us to do with him?" The Guardsmen asked.

"Take him to the PD and lock him up for now. We'll get to him later," I said.

Slowly nodding his head, Sarge added, "Oh yes; we will."

Lee Ann stared intently at the man as he was pulled to his feet. She moved in close to him and he flinched, expecting another knee. Within inches of his face, in a quiet voice she said, "If my sister dies, I'm going to kill you."

I was shocked. In the Before, the two got along okay, but they were never really tight. It wasn't until things fell apart that they seemed to become a lot closer. Maybe it was the fact that there was no internet with Facebook, Snapchat and all the other distractions that come with it. Maybe that forced them to connect to the people around them, instead of people they'd never meet.

The soldiers loaded the man up and drove off towards the PD. With the girls in tow, we continued towards the clinic to check on Taylor. It was still very crowded at the clinic. The initial chaos had subsided, but there were still many people there being treated. We walked inside and found Doc working on a young boy that had lost a leg from just above the knee.

"Where's Taylor?" I asked.

Without looking up from his work, he replied, "She's over there." He nodded towards an area closed off with a curtain.

"She's sleeping now. She regained consciousness, but we sedated her so she can rest."

"Is she going to be alright?" I asked.

"She's suffered a severe concussion, in addition to all the lacerations. It probably qualifies as a traumatic brain injury."

"What's that mean?"

Doc looked at the nurse assisting him, and said, "Go ahead and dress it up; it's the best we can do for him." Looking back at me, he said, "She's hurt bad, Morgan. But we've learned a lot about these injuries recently. She may have some lingering issues with memory and some changes to her personality. Some of these may not manifest themselves right away, and could take months to show up. But to answer your real question; for now she's ok. She'll live. She needs some rest; and we're keeping her here to watch for swelling on her brain. If she looks good in the next day or two, you'll be able to take her home."

Walking over, I pulled the curtain back. Mary was sitting with her. She was in a bedside chair, watching her sleep. Taylor was covered up, and appeared to be peacefully asleep. She still had dried blood on her face, the only part I could see. Looking at Mary, I asked, "Can you clean her up? I'm going to have to bring Mel up here, and I don't want her to see Taylor like that."

With a slight nod of her head Mary replied, "Sure." I smiled and nodded, then left to find Doc.

"Doc, we'll leave you to it. There's nothing we can do here; and we're just in the way," Sarge said.

Doc looked around. "Yeah; we kinda have our hands full at the moment."

Giving Doc a nod, I said, "Thanks," and followed Sarge out the door.

Outside, I looked at the girls. "She's sleeping right now.

Doc said she's going to be OK; but it will take her some time to get back to normal."

"Can we go see her?" Lee Ann asked.

I put my arm around her. "No baby; not now. They're very busy in there." Her shoulders dropped and she looked at the ground. "Sorry, kiddo. Later."

Sarge snorted and looked at me, "Now what?" He asked.

I looked back towards the park. The fire was nearly out now; just some smoke rising from what was left of the truck. Taking a deep breath, I said, "Now I have to go tell Mel that Taylor was nearly killed in an explosion." I looked off towards the lake before looking back at Sarge, "Then we get even."